What Others are Saying

"Visually enticing, with a very masculine, but fractured lead character trying to find his way that many young men can relate too...the story arc's strong thematic and through-line keeps you engaged all the way to the last page."
- New York Times

~

"His aim is to stimulate your mind, touch your heart, and inspire your soul." -
Authority Magazine

~

"Stunning fictional account of a young man's journey that includes a historical and cultural lesson." - Reader, ICM Partners

~

MOUNTAINS OF THE SEA

GUNTER SWOBODA

Second Edition

LCCN: 2020946410

ISBN: 978-1-947782-09-9

Books may be purchased by contacting the publisher and author at:

www.WinterwolfPress.com

Info@WinterwolfPress.com

Cover art by José Suárez

Interior design and formatting by Laura C. Cantu

Cover design © 2020 Winterwolf Press

Dedication

This book is dedicated to my wife Lorin.
E lei kau, e lei ho'oilo i ke aloha,
our love is forever,
and
to my children Alexis and Tristan.
Uahilo'iaikeahoakealoha. Enjoy the journey.
And finally to my dear friend
He ho'omana'o
(In memory)
Tom Kamaki Linker 7.7.1949-18.11.2008
Glad to have known you and glad to have shared the journey, the
stoke, and your knowledge.
Ke aloha nô me ka mahalo,
E ko'u 'aikane, a hui hou kâua, Kamaki.

Acknowledgments

A special thank you to my mother and father whose interest in the South Seas awakened my passion; to Matt Meyerson for urging me to tell Mountains of the Sea for the screen.

Special thank you to my friend Marc A. Levey for his work writing the screenplay with me; to Richard Routh for his enthusiastic support and work while I was writing the novel.

Warm thanks also to some great friends, Martin and Leanne Alfonso, Brett Dunstan and Michael Fronzek for support and friendship through some challenging times.

And finally my deepest gratitude to Lorin, my wife, whose unfailing belief in me keeps me inspired and who never grows tired of editing my work.

"Let him go abroad to a distant country; let him go to some place where he is not known. Don't let him go to the devil, where he is known."

—James Boswell, Life of Johnson

Chapter One

*I*t was a mild summer night, and only a few faint lights illuminated the tiny English village where laughter and music literally spilled from the windows of the local brothel, which was as always, crowded with raucous patrons, barmaids and whores.

Renowned for its pretty young girls, gambling, and excellent hospitality, this little house of ill-repute was the meeting place for many of the local gentry, most of whom at this very moment were in various states of undress and drunkenness and not in the least bit noble. At least that was Edward's assessment, as he let his critical eyes wander around the room.

Underscoring this earthy atmosphere, a couple of musicians accompanied some revellers singing an obscene ballad at the top of their lungs.

"As Oyster Nan stood by her tub, to shew her vicious inclination; she gave her noblest parts a scrub, and sigh'd for want of copulation."

The bawdy chorus bellowed through the room, as Edward watched one of the serving wenches attempting to squeeze by her patrons, wrestling with several massive jugs of ale. Some of the more impatient guests tried to pry them from her grasp, while others, seeing that her hands were occupied, gave her generous bottom a lusty squeeze. One even tried to slip his hand up her skirt, searching for a much more intimate encounter. She squealed loudly, feigning anger, but unable to maintain her mask of displeasure, she laughed, obviously delighted at being the centre of attention. Pushing on through the crowd, she continued to gracefully squirm away from the many groping hands to deliver the ale.

Standing to the side, Edward peered through the crowd into the darker corners of the room, confident that he would find his child-hood friend Walter, immersed in some form of lascivious activity. As his eyes adjusted to the light, his attention was caught by a familiar laugh and turning to follow the sound, Edward found his friend lust-fully engaged in undressing one of the prettier girls that frequented this slightly seedy establishment.

Strikingly handsome and expensively dressed, Walter looked utterly dishevelled, his clothes showing the signs of a man who had taken little care with his grooming over the last few days. His shirt might well be of the finest cloth, but it was dirty and stained, as were his buckskins. Anyone else looking at Master Walter Beau-mont, the youngest son of Lord Alexander Beaumont, would have immediately recognised that he was a dissolute nobleman.

Edward was all too aware that Walter had spent the last few years seducing as many young virgins as he could, deliberately causing his family an extraordinary amount of embarrassment. Not only had he hurt his own chances of securing an appropriate marriage, but he had also compromised his family's reputation significantly.

And now, despite being in desperate need of a bath and fresh clothes, his childhood friend was engaged in a flirtation with a pretty, half-naked girl whom Edward knew of as Bess. She appeared to be chatting comfortably with Walter, sitting on his lap with her arms wrapped around his neck, and she did not appear in the least bit put off by his filthy appearance, or what Edward assumed would be his pungent body odour.

He watched them, cosily engaged in an erotic banter, as Walter, almost absentmindedly, fondled her exposed pink nipple. She, in return, playfully ran her hand over Walter's thick, blond hair. Amid this exchange of what looked like real affection, Walter suddenly spun Bess around and drew her close to his face as she squealed with delight, and he buried his face in her cleavage. Then, laughing loudly, he lifted his head towards her ear and whispered something. Whatever it was that Walter confided to her, it obviously excited her even further, and she threw back her head so that her auburn hair cascaded down her back, and laughed out aloud.

Walter then reached into the inner lining of his luxurious brocaded coat, his expression conspiratorial as he extracted a small meticulously folded brown paper satchel. Edward, only too familiar with Walter's vices, sighed as he watched his friend place the packet on the table and unfold it. There, in the centre of the waxed paper, rested some small black pills.

Seeing the content of the package, Bess squealed with delight and clapping her hands in child-like fashion, she planted another kiss on Walter's lips. He, in turn, took two pills between his thumb and forefinger, and grinning broadly, he popped one into his mouth and the other into hers. Bess closed her eyes and swallowed. She then opened her mouth, poked her tongue out, and giggled.

Edward had seen enough of Walter's revelries. He walked resolutely across the room to his friend and tapped him on the shoulder. He knew that Walter thought he was stuck up, and unable to have fun, but Edward had always known that he was the more sensible one of the two. Ever since they were children, he had been the one who had extricated Walter from numerous precarious and compromising situations.

As Walter peered up at him, Edward sighed. The glazed eyes told him all he needed to know. Tonight Walter would be very challenging to manage, but despite his own father's exasperation that he continued to call this man, his friend, Edward loved Walter, and couldn't walk away. Walter's father was a cold and hard man and Edward understood that it was the the conflict between Walter and his father that fuelled this disreputable behaviour.

Pointing at the satchel on the table Edward spoke, knowing his disapproval was evident in his expression but unable to pretend that he didn't care. "Walter, you should really desist from using that infernal concoction! It leads to absolutely no good at all!"

Obviously annoyed at the interruption, Walter just leaned back and squinted up at him."On the contrary, dear Edward," Walter's voice had a discernible edge to it, as he abruptly sat forward and pierced Edward with his gaze. "It dulls my perpetual boredom, but more importantly, it helps to sharpen my senses." He paused, looking up at Edward with a calculating look, then slyly he suggested, "Join me and Bess, my friend."

Then, as if to prove a point, Walter turned away and, grinning mischievously, he reached for a jug of ale, lifted it to his mouth and downed the entire contents in one well-practised motion. Edward watched as Walter sat for a moment with his eyes closed, clearly savouring the effects of the alcohol as it permeated his body.

Edward knew that he was fighting an uphill battle, but he was determined to try.

"Well, in any case, I do think it is time we left."

Walter's response was to run his hand over Bess's shapely back, and then, lifting her thin linen chemise, he affectionately slapped her bare behind. She let out a little squeal of delight and laughed, kissing Walter on the forehead, as if to encourage him to do it again.

Walter smiled at the girl and winked, then turned back to his friend. "Edward, truthfully now, does it appear to you that I am ready to leave?"

The lustful demonstration had the desired effect, and Edward sighed with resignation. He knew he couldn't compete with Bess's charms nor Walter's determination to continue the night into the early morning. "Well, I suppose not, Walter, but I do have a life to get back to, even if it is, at least for the foreseeable future, in the colonies."

Walter's expression darkened. Edward knew that his friend felt he was abandoning him when he had decided to take up a commission in the army. But he was also worried about him. They had been over this many times. Walter believed that he was underestimating the danger he might face in the colonies.

Walter believed that, although most people saw the rebellion in the Americas as a simple nuisance, which would be quickly quelled by the British, the mission Edward was about to embark on was far more dangerous. Walter had told Edward he believed he was heading into a conflict that had been seriously underestimated by the government. Edward had not dismissed Walter's assessment. He knew his friend. Walter, despite his faults, was knowledgeable, perceptive and astute, and he paid far more attention to politics than most people realised. Edward however, needed to face the reality of his own situation. A commission won at the frontier would set him up for life, and he couldn't pass up this opportunity. Looking at his childhood friend, dissolute and intoxicated, Edward made his decision.

"In any event, Walter, I want you to take good care of yourself. And for God's sake, try to stay out of trouble."

Suddenly Walter snapped and shouted at him. "Damn it, off you go then!" He drew a breath. The next sentence was virtually spat at his friend. "At least you have a life to get back to."

Edward was not at all surprised by his friend's bitter retort. He quietly shook his head and, a little saddened, turned to leave, thinking that Walter was proving to be his own worst enemy as usual. Edward knew the source of Walter's frustration and anger. The two men had often spoken about the fact that as the second-born, Walter had been given no place in the running of the family business or affairs. All this was left to Jonathan, who would take over after their father's death. Resentful, Walter had used this to justify his pursuit of pleasure and the high life.

❧❧❧❧❧

Staring at Edward's back, Walter looked to distract himself from his friend's departure. He feared for Edward. Having no control over the decisions of the people you loved was a pain Walter knew only too well, so turning his attentions back to Bess, Walter closed his mind to his worry for his friend. Winking at his lovely lass, he deliberately schooled his expression so that it hid his true feelings. "Come, my lusty wench, a guinea to do your part for my posterity."

Obediently, Bess dropped her only piece of clothing, revealing flawless alabaster skin and sensually seductive curves. As one hand demurely covered herself, the other ran alluringly down the length of her body.

"Like this, m'Lord?" She coquettishly dropped her head to one side, her hair tumbling down her front, covering a pert breast and dark pink nipple. She waited patiently for Walter's reaction while he continued to squint at her for a time, straining to focus.

He suddenly broke into a grin. There was never any doubt that he liked what he saw. "How wonderfully salacious you are, my dear little doxy." Walter smacked his lips together, emphasising his appreciation.

On the other side of the table lay a small sketchbook and a piece of charcoal. Walter pulled them across to rest within his reach, then moved a candlestick closer to the figure of the girl to shed more light on her. Drawing and painting were his joy. The play of light on the skin of his subject, the shape and line of her form. It took his mind to another place where his life was filled with beauty and reality disappeared.

As he ran his charcoal pencil across the paper, occasionally looking up and across the room, his fear and anger receded to the background of his thoughts, and he relaxed, loving the sense of contentment that filled him with each line he drew.

Suddenly, his concentration was interrupted by a noise near the entrance. Geoffrey! What an ass! He watched as the man arrogantly planted himself in the entryway as if expecting a heroic welcome. Dressed to impress in his impeccable scarlet coat, white leather breeches and black leather belt and boots, Seymour failed miserably to make any impression other than a bad one. Army recruiters were never popular. Nonetheless, Seymour paused at the door for a moment, his hand resting casually on the pommel of his sword, which Walter thought was more for appearance than action. Looking for more cannon-fodder, Walter thought sourly.

He couldn't help himself, he turned to watch as Seymour arrogantly ignored the disdain in the expressions on the faces of the Inn's patrons, and took another step into the establishment. Seymour, a recruiter for the King's army, was looking around the room and it was obvious he was weighing up likely candidates. Walter was appalled when he realised that Seymour's eyes had landed on Hugh, a young, particularly well-built farmhand, sitting alone at one of the tables.

Now more vigilant, he watched as Seymour casually walked over to Hugh's table calling out to the Innkeeper. "Another round for my friend here, my good man! And keep them coming!"

The Innkeeper, a fat and unappealing man, had always trod a fine line in his relationship with Seymour. The recruiter generously provided the owner with cash and made no bones about their arrangement. Though this was generally not popular with the patrons, almost all turned a blind eye to the deal. Unless, of course, it happened to interfere with personal relationships, as was the case with Hugh.

The young farmhand was well-liked. He was a kind and friendly soul, always willing to help if it was required. An employee of the Beaumont's, he had recently gotten married to a local girl and was soon to be a father, and Walter watched closely as Hugh looked up and tried to focus on his newly arrived benefactor. "Why, thank ye, good Sir! A right generous man you are, Master Seymour."

Seymour smiled as the Innkeeper placed a large clay jug in front of Hugh and watched the young man greedily scull the potent ale. Having finished, Hugh put the empty vessel down on the table. One of the barmaids was obediently waiting alongside the table and with a worried frown on her face, immediately put another pitcher in front of the young man.

In the background, Walter continued sketching, but his attention was now more and more drawn to the scene at the table from where he could hear Seymour's seductive flattery above the noise of the surrounding patrons. "You know, the King could use a stout fellow such as yourself."

"He could?" Hugh looked puzzled.

"Indeed he could, my young friend." Seymour leant forward to tempt Hugh further. "Just think of the riches and glory you could gain from being in the King's service. Gold, silver, women, whatever your heart desires!" Seymour reached into his pocket and slapped a shiny coin on the table.

Hearing the King's shilling hit the wood of the table, Walter's blood finally boiled over. Trying to maintain some semblance of calm, he took a deep breath and got to his feet. That cad! Walter thought. The alcohol and opium had well and truly intermingled. The heady mixture caused Walter to sway for a moment, and the stool he had been sitting on crashed noisily to the floor. Being much less steady than he would have liked to have been, but determined nonetheless, Walter walked resolutely over to Hugh's table.

Seymour, appearing surprised by Walter's intrusion, looked up and sneered at him. There was a long-standing animosity between the two men dating back to their early years as boys, playing together on the Manor grounds. Walter had frequently endured the brunt of his brother Jonathan's bullying, and Geoffrey had always been only too happy to be a part of Jonathan's schemes to torture him. Walter subsequently learnt to despise Seymour, even more than his brother, and could think of nothing better than to best the cad at every turn. This was not difficult, as Seymour was neither courageous nor overly intelligent. But the boy had grown into a cunning man.

"Ah, Master Beaumont," Seymour observed, mockingly, "'tis unusual to see you in a vertical orientation." He didn't wait for an answer. "You know," Seymour wagged his finger at Walter, "I do believe you are at the wrong table."

Trying to ignore Seymour, and still attempting to hold his temper, Walter turned to Hugh. He shook his head momentarily, trying to rid himself of the effects of the ale and opium. Having gathered at least some of his senses, he leant unsteadily across the table. "Hugh, you have had enough! Take yourself back to your wife, before you do something you will regret."

"M'lord?" Hugh appeared more confused than before. He had enough difficulty trying to cope with Seymour's attention. Walter's sudden appearance had the young man wholly perplexed. But before Hugh could respond to Walter, Seymour tried to take control of his deteriorating prospects in finding a suitable recruit. "My dear fellow, dare I say that the man is entitled to decide for himself."

Still trying to deal with his befuddled senses and, more importantly, his growing rage, Walter turned on Seymour. "Geoffrey, for God's sake, the man is drunk! He is not fit to decide anything!"

Seymour responded with a weak attempt to deflect the exchange from the issue of Hugh. "Whatever our past familiarities, Master Beaumont, let us not forget our manners."

"As you wish, Master Seymour." However, Walter was not going to be deterred and leant menacingly closer towards the recruiter using his height to try and intimidate the man. "Now, I will insist you leave this man alone!"

Walter started to relax when Seymour nervously got to his feet. His anticipated satisfaction was short-lived, however.

"Or what?" In the silence, Seymour's question sounded a little too pointed. The man's attempted brashness made Walter suspicious.

Walter realised that the Inn was no longer the noisy, raucous place it had been moments ago. Now, in the heavy silence, the barkeep tried to reassure his guests. "Nothin' to see, gentlemen! More ale and another song, eh!"

He saw the Innkeeper anxiously motion to the musicians to play. They ignored the man, obviously more interested in what was about to unfold. As the tension rose between him and Seymour, everyone seemed to be waiting to see what would happen next as they squared off.

Geoffrey was not known to bravely face any threat unless he had backup or a quick escape. His own healthy sense of self-preservation made Walter carefully search the Inn. Across the room, he saw five men with hands-on their swords. They began to push towards him, their progress impeded by the onlookers. An immediate surge of adrenaline set Walter's heart racing, thankfully clearing his head some more.

Angrily he turned on Seymour. "You coward! Still not game to
take care of things yourself, are you!"

Before Seymour could make a move, Walter pulled the table
over and delivered a left hook knocking the man to the floor, then
with his right hand, he snatched the recruiter's sword from its scab-
bard. He heard the other patrons of the brothel erupt into a lusty
cheer as he grabbed Hugh by the scruff of his neck. Turning
towards the door to the courtyard, he was confronted by Seymour's
men, swords drawn and blocking his way.

As one of the men charged forward, Walter reacted quickly by
hitting the soldier across the head with the hilt of the sword. The
sound of steel on the man's skull reverberated loudly, followed soon
by the dull thud of his body crashing to the wooden floor. As the
other four soldiers rushed in, the interior of the brothel resounded
with more cheers, and suddenly chairs were pushed into their path,
and wine jugs started flying at their heads. Amidst the chaos and to
the sound of musicians playing, Walter began to fight his way to the
door. Dragging Hugh behind him, he used all his skill with a sword
to force his way through, while the other patrons and whores
continued to block the soldiers' path. One of the barmaids held the
large oak door open just long enough for Walter and Hugh to rush
outside before it closed behind them with a resounding thump.

Hugh, obviously having finally figured out the perilous situation
he had been in a minute ago, looked relieved to be in the open.
Sobered by the excitement and crisp night air, Walter scrambled for
his horse. Not having a mount himself, Hugh stopped, looking lost.

"Quick, Hugh, just take one of the other horses. Once you are
home, send it back to the stables. I'll make sure it gets back to its
rightful owner."

Desperate to escape, Hugh did as he was told. Safely in the
saddle, Walter and Hugh spurred the horses along the road out of
town. Once on the open road leading away from the village, the two
men took the opportunity to pause for a moment.

Walter addressed his worker, sternly, "Now, Hugh, get yourself
home before you cause any more strife!"

With a grateful expression, the farmhand tipped his forehead. "Much obliged, milord." He paused. "And God bless!"

In the dead of night, Walter rode like a man possessed, the horse's hooves pounding against the ground. The tree-lined road he was on was only dimly lit by the partially obscured full moon hanging above him. The barely visible overhanging branches kept Walter's attention fixed on what was ahead so as not to get swept out of the saddle.

Walter leant forward, stroking the neck of his mount and whispering encouraging words. The stallion eagerly rewarded him by picking up the pace. His horse, a beautiful chestnut stallion, was covering the distance in a smooth rhythm, snorting every now and then with the pleasure of the chase. Walter loved this horse, a gift from a relative when he was eighteen, the stallion had been a significant part of most of his adventures. He knew that this horse could outrun those that followed, but he remained wary. Seymour was a dullard, but he carried a grudge. That made him dangerous.

In the distance, the sound of the pursuing soldiers fused with his absorption in the thrill of his steed's power. Then a bullet suddenly whistled past Walter's head and he ducked and looked back his own fury erupting, and without thinking, he pulled up his horse and turned to face his pursuers. Walter snatched his pistol from the saddle pouch and fired off a shot in his pursuer's general direction.

It was meant to be a warning, but a faint cry of pain cut through the damp night air. Barely visible in the dark, Walter saw the shadowy figure of a man fall from a horse and instantly felt a sinking feeling in the pit of his guts. *Damn it, just my bloody luck!* Walter turned and spurred the stallion back into a gallop towards home.

Chapter Two

*I*t felt like an eternity before Walter arrived at the massive wrought-iron gate of the stately Beaumont home. The house, a beautiful Baroque mansion, loomed in front of him. It was surrounded by a spectacular garden, complete with a small lake, a labyrinth constructed of dense bush, and fountains located strategically around the property. In the early light of dawn, the place lay eerily quiet. Walter desperately hoped that his mother and father were asleep. He thought it best to break the news to them in the morning when they were rested. After all, shooting someone was a little different from his usual escapades.

Walter leant down and patted the horse's neck to reassure it and the stallion whinnied in response as Walter eased him into a trot. He felt bad for pushing the animal so hard. Its flanks heaved, and froth streamed from its mouth around the bit. The poor beast, he thought.

Straightening up in the saddle, Walter tried to stretch his weary limbs. He continued to calm the horse with soft words and pats on his flank as they got closer to the grand stairs leading up to the house.

In the distance, Walter could see Thomas, his fifteen-year-old footman, scrambling into his clothes and at the same time trying to run towards them. By the time Walter arrived at the bottom of the stairs, Thomas was already waiting to take charge of the exhausted stallion. Grabbing the drenched reigns, the boy patted the horse gently while also stroking its flanks, whispered soothing words in its ear.

Walter jumped out of the saddle and affectionately ruffled the boy's hair. "Good lad, Thomas!

The quick sprint up the stairs stretched Walter's weary legs some more, and with long strides, he arrived at the oak doorway of the manor, just in time for George to let him in.

"Ah, George, you needn't have gotten up." "Good evening, Master. His Lordship is anxiously awaiting you in the library."

Walter's heart skipped a beat. Impossible! There was no feasible way for news of the incident to have arrived before him. No, Walter thought, there must be another reason for his father to be waiting for him in the early hours of the morning. Then, he remembered. Felicity! He had forgotten entirely that he had agreed to attend dinner with her and her family. He felt a small tug of guilt at having embarrassed the girl his parents had hoped he would marry, but it was their plan. Not his.

Walter straightened up and drew a long breath in as he turned to climb up the grand marble stairway. He had no doubt that his tardiness in failing to join the family at dinner would be forgotten once he told his father he had shot someone. Arriving in front of the library doors, Walter braced himself and knocked. He stood there, his heart thumping in his chest, waiting for a reply.

His father's voice thundered through the door. "Enter!" Lord Alexander Beaumont was a genuinely formidable man. He had rebuilt the family fortune to a substantial level after it had been poorly managed by previous generations of Beaumonts, who had either gambled poorly or invested stupidly. Shrewd and ruthless, he now had considerable wealth and therefore influence, even in the highest circles of society.

Steeling himself for what was to come, Walter stepped into the library to find his father, a mature but still good-looking man glaring at him from behind his desk. But it was the presence of his brother Jonathan, standing by the fireplace, grinning maliciously that made his heart sink.

The shock on his father's face reminded Walter what he must look like. He glanced at his reflection in the mirror above the fireplace. He had dusty clothes and matted hair, a grey complexion and dark circles around his eyes. There was no hiding what he had been up to. Seething rage darkened his father's face. Furious, Lord Beaumont snapped, "Do you have any explanation for this filth and tardiness?!" He paused, again surveying Walter's filthy clothes and matted hair with a look of disbelief. "Just look at the state you are in."

There was no escaping the inevitable. Walter took a deep breath to brace himself. He set out to speak as calmly as possible. "Father, please, I am very sorry. I-"

Lord Beaumont cut his son off mid-sentence. "Apologise all you want! You have finally pushed me too far!"

"Father! I have something of urgency to tell you. There was an altercation at the Inn." Walter raised his voice interrupting Lord Beaumont's imminent tirade. "Please listen to me!" Walter paused to catch his breath.

Unable to contain his rage any longer, Lord Beaumont bellowed over the top of Walter's feeble attempt to explain his predicament. "You are constantly besieged by altercations—!"

"Father! I have shot someone!" Devoid of any attempt to remain calm, Walter's voice roared through the library. In the sudden, shocked silence, Jonathan, always quick to put the boot in, declared derisively. "So you've gone from debauchery to murder!"

Lord Beaumont immediately put his hand up to silence his older son, then looked closely at Walter. "What are you saying?"

Walter flicked his head across to Jonathan, who was smirking at him.

"Jonathan's lackey, Geoffrey, was attempting to recruit Hugh and, well, one thing led to another."

Jonathan snorted dismissively. "More than likely just another of your apparitions, Walter!"

Undaunted by his brother's barbs, Walter continued. "He and his men then decided to pursue us. Someone shot at me, and I stupidly returned fire."

"Liar!" Jonathan's voice rang out from the other side of the library. "None of them would ever have fired a shot at you!"

"Quiet, Jonathan!" Lord Beaumont cast him a steely look. He then turned to Walter. "Damn it, Walter. Do you know who it was you shot?"

"No! It was too dark!"

Shaking his head, Lord Beaumont pondered his son for a moment. "Well, I suppose it matters little whether the man is dead or alive. This debacle makes your troubles with me a minor issue. By now the authorities will surely be looking for you."

Walter watched as his father exerted his prodigious iron will to calm himself and think through the implications of the situation before he continued. "Perhaps it is best for all concerned if you left the country for a time. We know you have good fighting skills, and your friend Edward is already making moves to embark for the Americas. He could organise it so that you could join him. I would suggest serving your King in the colonies."

The sound of a metallic click distracted Walter. He turned his head towards the noise and was shocked to see his mother emerge from one of the panels in the library wall. Her gaze swept past him to his father and brother as she spoke.

"Well, the two of you must be very pleased. Finally, Walter has indeed disgraced himself." Her sarcastic tone bit hard. "I suspect you have had this in mind as a solution for some time. All you needed was a good enough reason to send Walter packing."

Lady Eleanor Beaumont was an attractive, stylish woman with a commanding poise. But more to the point, she was as formidable as her husband in temper and disposition. Furious, she stood resolutely facing her husband and eldest son. "However, let me assure you both that I will not let Walter go to war. Do I make myself clear, my Lord?"

" Absolutely, my dear." Lord Beaumont's attempt at endearment only solicited a chilling gaze from his wife.

Then, looking at Walter, she continued. "Walter, I want you to stay out of sight. One of the priest's holes will do for now until we have found a solution to this appalling situation."

Having been a Catholic residence in the past, the manor had numerous hiding places and secret passages built during the religious troubles in earlier times. A wave of exhaustion swept over Walter. Decisions would now be made for him, none of which would be appealing to him, and so he saw no point in remaining to discuss anything further. Mentally and physically drained, the situation had become unbearable for him, so without another word, he abruptly turned on his heels and stormed out of the library.

"Walter!" He heard his father shout as he slammed the door and headed down the hall.

❧❧❧❧

"Well, good riddance!" Jonathan's voice dripped with glee. Before he could respond, Lord Beaumont heard his wife snap at their eldest son.

"For pity's sake, Jonathan, be quiet!"

Alexander Beaumont suddenly felt very tired, after watching his son slam his way out of the room. Torn between his fear for Walter, and his fury at his younger son's rebelliousness, he shook his head to try and clear it. What was to be a reprimand for a failure of etiquette had turned into a significant catastrophe. He looked up at his wife. "We need to sort out some practical details right now before we make any decisions," he said as he rang a small brass bell.

A minute later, George entered the library. "My Lord?"

"George, unfortunately, we have quite a serious situation at hand, the details of which do not concern you." Lord Beaumont stopped and drew a deep breath. "However, it is imperative that the servants are told that under no circumstances are they to reveal to anyone that Master Walter was here tonight. Should anyone inquire of his whereabouts, they are to say that Master Walter is in his lodgings in London." He hesitated and looked across at Eleanor. With her nod of approval, he continued, "I'll need you to arrange for

Walter's horse to be taken to London as quickly and as discreetly as possible. Is that clear?"

George bowed and quickly scuttled out of the library.

Turning to look directly at Jonathan, Lord Beaumont pinned him with his gaze. "You are to follow my lead and do as you are told. It is a matter of family honour. Now your mother and I have much to discuss. I'll send for you later."

As Jonathan left the library he sighed deeply. He could feel his wife's eyes watching him. "What would you propose, my dear?"

Lady Beaumont looked across the room at her husband. "I think this would be a good opportunity for Walter to leave on his Grand Tour."

Lord Beaumont shook his head and snorted. This he would not agree to.

"Ha, and squander more money on a lascivious lifestyle? I will not consent to any such endeavour!"

"I am not surprised by your answer. It is, however my first choice, there is another option, and it's not the war in the colonies. As you know I have been following the latest plans of the Admiralty to expand our knowledge of sea routes. It has come to my attention that Captain Cook is about to embark on another voyage. Perhaps I could contact him. My father's connections may help convince him to accommodate Walter as a favour to me."

In what capacity? As a naval officer? Lord Beaumont recognised that this could be the compromise they needed. Walter would not be leaving on an extended and expensive frivolity but would be forced into the regimented discipline of the navy without being at risk of being in a war. More importantly, he would be away for a considerable time, allowing the scandal to be forgotten. "My Lady, I believe that it is an excellent solution."

⁊ᴀ⁊ᴀ⁊ᴀ⁊ᴀ

Eleanor Beaumont made her way down the hall towards her youngest son's room, full of misgivings. She knew that Walter had to go away, but a voyage of exploration into the Pacific Ocean was a compromise she was not completely happy with. Well, the die is cast. Over the last few hours, the servants had already left on their journeys to deliver the letters she had written to Captain Cook.

She hesitated at Walter's bedroom door to collect her thoughts, then knocked firmly. "Come in." Her hand rested lightly on the door handle as she drew a deep breath, braced herself, and stepped into the chaotic world of her son.

Walter's spacious apartment was in its usual mess, with clothes, drawings and other odds and ends littering the floor. The air was stale and the light dimmed by the heavy curtains drawn across the large windows. Across the room, a panel in one of the walls was open, revealing the priest's hole.

Lady Beaumont crossed the room towards the bed but she stopped when she was close enough to smell Walter's stale odour. Wrinkling her nose in disgust, she stepped back, puzzled as to how Walter could bear his own company. Turning her head to survey the room, she saw an open piece of brown paper on this desk. Nestled amongst the folds were several small black pills. She knew only too well what it was. Opium. The glassy look in Walter's eyes was evidence that he had helped himself to more than one of them in the last hour.

Saddened, Lady Beaumont sighed. She turned back to Walter to find him watching her in a strangely intense manner. Before she could say anything, he launched into a self-righteous defence of his behaviour, railing against the injustice of his having to be punished when he knew he had done the right thing.

She refused to be baited into an argument and replied as calmly as possible, "And what of you, Walter? You have been reckless and irresponsible. If you had been where you were supposed to be last night, none of this would have happened!"

Still committed to some form of defence, Walter snapped, "Then I wouldn't have been there to save Hugh." He turned away from his mother and somewhat unsteadily sat down amidst the turmoil of his bed.

Eleanor Beaumont once again surveyed her son's room and sighed deeply, her eyes moistening as she spoke. "We need to talk about what is to be done to keep you out of the hands of the authorities. You can't just go about shooting people. There are ramifications."

She watched him closely as his head lifted, and his glazed eyes seemed to focus. "So, am I to be sent to the Colonies with Edward? Into peril for the sake of the family honour?"

"No. I intend that you join Captain Cook on his latest expedition to the South Seas."

Walter's face told her that he was having a difficult time comprehending what she had said. He knew of the proposed expedition because she had discussed it with him. Eleanor found the whole venture fascinating, and her father had kept her abreast of the plans as they had unfolded.

"What are you saying, Mother? You do understand that I am in no way inclined to cross any body of water, let alone spend a goodly part of my youth in a floating prison with the risk of drowning."

"Walter, through your own actions, you have made sure that you have very few choices."

"Choices! What choices do I ever have?" His fury propelled him to launch himself from the bed and start pacing around the room. Agitated, he struggled for words. "I will not imperil my life to appease you or Father!"

"But you can imperil your life with stupidity?" She drew herself up, her own anger and fear strengthening her voice. "Look at yourself! Have you no shame? Whatever your feelings on the matter, Walter, you will need to pack. You have to leave the country one way or the other."

Angered by his childish refusal to take responsibility, Eleanor abruptly turned towards the door. She couldn't stay in Walter's room for another minute.

⁂

Walter's rage flared and made him stiffen. Catching sight of his reflection in the mirror, it occurred to him that he didn't recognise the person looking back at him. His eyes were hollowed out and he was ill-groomed and dirty with a snarling mouth. Disgusted with himself, he turned away. His first impulse was to reach for a glass of wine, and he let his gaze sweep the room looking for the half-empty bottle he had been drinking from earlier. But for some reason he couldn't quite fathom, the sight of the jumble of papers and books and the packet of pills on his desk made him pause, and Walter suddenly saw what his mother had seen.

Shame filled him. Anger had been with him for so long now. The loss of Emma still haunted him, but his little concoction of wine and pills no longer eased his pain. He clearly remembered being summoned to his father's library as if it was yesterday. Emma had joined them a few moments later, and standing in front of his father's desk he had been acutely aware that Jonathan was standing beside Lord Beaumont in an all-too-familiar alliance against him. The sneering look of amusement on Jonathan's face meant that he was clearly enjoying Walter's predicament.

Telling Walter that it was for his own good and that he was learning a valuable lesson, his father had berated Emma, calling her a strumpet and ordering her out of the house. He had no interest in listening to reason. He gave no thought to what would become of her, and he insisted that somehow it was all her fault for luring Walter into her bed. Emma had been dismissed, and she ran weeping from the room.

When Walter had gone to his mother for support, Lady Beaumont had informed him that he should have thought about the consequences of his actions. Especially the consequences for Emma. After she outlined what could happen to Emma now that she had been sent away, Walter's anger towards his brother and father grew into a rage that had burned in his heart ever since. His mother had promised to make sure Emma was safe and settled comfortably, but only if he promised to never see her again, and to this day, Walter had no idea what had become of her.

Wrenching himself away from the painful memory, tears streaming down his face, he thought about how for a short time, the opium had dispelled all his pain and anger, leaving him in a euphoric state where little other than pleasure mattered. Now the thought of that elusive euphoria simply deepened his sense of loss.

All Walter knew was that of late, the few times he had tried to stop his 'little indulgence', he had felt ill and deeply disturbed, only to feel better again after consuming one or two of the black pills. It seemed to him that now he took to them simply to feel normal again.

As Walter looked around his room at the clutter and mess, he came back to the present. He was the one being sent away this time. Walter had no idea what to do. He could refuse, but then he would be cut off without a penny and have no way of supporting himself. He had lost most of his friends over the last few years as they had moved on with their lives. Edward was the only real friend he had, and he was going to the American colonies.

It occurred to Walter that he could join Edward, but he quickly dismissed this idea. So, a journey across the ocean to who knows where with a ship full of strangers on a mission he knew little about was to be his future. A knock on his door interrupted his thoughts. His mother entered at his invitation and in her hand was a leather-bound journal which she held it out to Walter.

"Here, I had this made for you to have on your birthday. But . . ." her voice drifted off. "I want you to take it and use it well."

Walter reached out to take his mother's gift from her hands. The leather felt cool to the touch, and he couldn't help but admire the refined craftsmanship. He ran his hand lovingly across the embossed leather. "It's lovely, Mother."

From a young age, Walter had loved to draw, and he was aware that his mother thought he had a true gift. She had always admired his work in charcoal and had encouraged him to use his talent. Walter had been aware that she had ideas about how he could find some direction through his art, but being an artist was not his father's vision for his life. Looking up at his mother, he realised that she hated what was happening, and he felt a niggling sense of guilt that he had caused her so much pain over the years.

"Please bring it back to me safely, Walter. I am making an assumption that the arrangements for you to join Captain Cook's voyage will go ahead. You will need to find your own path on this journey. I thought that you may be able to demonstrate your usefulness by illustrating the discoveries that will be made on the other side of the world. But you must return to me. Walter, I want you to promise me!"

As she stepped closer to him and tenderly kissed him on the cheek, he embraced her, and they held each other tightly, knowing that very soon they would be parted. Walter also knew that he had no choice.

Drawing another deep breath, she straightened up, and, holding him at arm's length, and she looked at him directly.

"Now, I want you to disappear into the secret passages of the house. Under no circumstances are you to show your face in any part of the manor or to anyone other than your father or George. I will finish your packing and organise your baggage to be taken to rooms in Plymouth. George will look after you while you hide, and I will let you know when it is time to leave."

Chapter Three

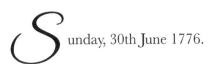

unday, 30th June 1776.

The sheer noise of the crowds of humanity, whose business it was to be on Plymouth docks on a Sunday in June, hit Walter almost like a physical blow as he stepped out of his carriage. Looking around at the almost frenetic activity, he couldn't get his bearings at all, and he felt his temper starting to rise. It took a fair amount of determination not to get back into the carriage and insist he be taken home.

But that was the last place he could go. Geoffrey Seymour's death had changed everything. Even if the constabulary accepted that he had shot that disreputable menace in self defence, the scandal would make life impossible. He had no choice but to leave, and this plan of his mother's was far more preferable than his father's idea that he should enlist in the Expeditionary forces and get shipped off to the colonies.

He was furious at his father. How dare he refuse to fund his exile. That he, Walter Beaumont would have to work for his passage on some dubious expedition to the South Seas was unconscionable. Looking around him, his gaze alighted on the refitted collier that would be his home for the foreseeable future. Surrounded by military vessels, it stood out, its inelegance another insult to his stature and position. He knew from his mother that the Captain, Lieutenant James Cook had chosen the Resolution and had complete faith in its fitness for purpose, but compared to the sleek lines of the ships that lined up around it at the docks, it was squat and ugly.

Turning back to the carriage, Walter found Thomas, his footman, struggling to unload the baggage. Looking around, he spotted a likely looking lad and called him over to help, offering him a coin for his trouble. Not noticing the calculating look, the boy gave him, he retrieved his personal items including his journal, from the interior of the carriage and turned to face his future.

Having given no thought to blending in with the crowd, Walter was elegantly dressed in a lightning-blue jacket, trimmed in gold. In contrast to the blue, his breeches were sparkling white buckskins. Oblivious to the reality that he looked distinctly out of place amidst the military, the sailors and the working class, and therefore would be easily noticed, Walter affected a confident swagger. With his journal securely tucked under his arm, and refusing to let anyone suspect the trepidation he felt, he headed down the dock.

Trailing behind Walter, Thomas struggled to drag a cart loaded with his master's numerous pieces of luggage through the mass of people. Along the way, Walter surveyed the thick of the crowd and a flash of red and a glimpse of dark curly hair that looked familiar caught his attention. "Edward!"

Decked out in full military kit, Edward looked impressive. The bright, red coat emphasised his tall figure, and with a set of very broad shoulders, his friend was the classical picture of a military officer. With a wry smile, Walter observed that quite a few of the ladies present were casting approving glances in Edward's direction. Smiling and twittering amongst each other, they made no secret of their admiration. Some of the whores who had been seeking business along the wharves tried to tempt Edward by pulling their blouses down to expose their breasts, while shouting lewd invitations to him.

Seemingly oblivious to their attention, Edward stopped to look around, obviously having heard the familiar voice of his friend. When he finally caught sight of Walter, a look of concern spread across his face and he quickly rushed over to greet his dear friend.

"Walter, what are you doing here?" Before Walter could reply, Edward continued,

"Have you heard? Geoffrey is dead."

For a second, the dire words hung between the two men. Then, Walter nodded, "Yes, Edward, dear friend, I do know, since I am the one who killed him."

Edward, clearly shocked at Walter's revelation, fell silent while Walter quickly sketched out the circumstances that led to Geoffrey's death. Another moment of silence hung between them, then Edward, his expression filled with confusion asked;

"So, Walter, what are you going to do? Why are you here?"

Keeping his voice even, giving no hint of his internal turmoil and dismay, Walter turned his gaze down the dock and pointed to the Resolution. "I am joining Captain Cook as an assistant to John Webber, his Illustrator and Archivist."

"An expedition to the South Seas?" The look of surprise on Edward's face was not unexpected. Walter was well aware that his friend not only knew how much he disliked sailing across open water, but he also knew him well enough to know that having to endure primitive conditions on-board Cook's ship would really test Walter.

But before Walter could say anything else, Edward questioned him about the choice of the voyage. "Surely a trip to the Continent would have sufficed, Walter. You could be gone for a year or two, and everything would calm down."

Not wanting to admit that his father was not prepared to pay for him to travel through Europe on a Grand Tour, Walter kept a tight reign on his emotions and evaded the suggestion, putting a cheerful grin on his face. "Edward, you're the one who has been telling me about the alluring beauty and charms of the women of the South Seas."

Edward's expression, which had been filled with concern up to this point started to relax, so Walter added; "If your stories are true, then this could be a far more interesting adventure than Europe could offer. I will know in due course, and then, the Fates willing, I will return and share with you my exploits over a decent jug of ale."

Amidst the banter, Walter felt a dark sense of foreboding creeping into his mind. He may be afraid for himself, but Edward's deployment to the Colonies to fight a rebellion was a much more dire course. The very fact that he was here at the docks meant that Edward was probably getting ready to embark on one of those sleek ships he had been so envious of.

As their discussion turned to Edwards plans Walter's outrage at his own predicament faded. As the time for them to part arrived, Walter rested his hands on Edward's shoulders, and he looked closely at his friend. "Take care of yourself, Edward. I know that I have treated you abominably at times, and yet you have always stood by me."

"Friends forever, Walter, you know that!" Edward looked at him intensely for a moment. "I must go as my Commander is waiting. Stay away from trouble my friend, I won't be there to help you this time."

The two embraced without another word, lingering, reluctant to let each other go. Edward finally pushed Walter gently away. Walter searched his friends' face, thinking Edward was about to say something, but his friend simply turned and disappeared into the crowd.

Saddened by Edward's sudden departure, Walter stared at the empty space in front of him. Then he squared his shoulders and took a breath. "Come, Thomas, destiny—or whatever there is —awaits us."

Thomas nodded. "Yes, M'Lord." The young footman obediently fell in behind his master showing no evident enthusiasm for their impending adventure.

Arriving at the gangplank of the Resolution, Walter found himself confronted by a young Marine who demanded that he identify himself and state his purpose. Initially taken aback, Walter almost uttered an automatic dismissal when he suddenly realised that everything was different. He was not known here. Reminding himself that the Marine was following the protocol of Naval vessels, he identified himself, informing the young man that he was expected.

When the Marine remained where he was, blocking his path, Walter's temper stirred. His situation may have changed but being barred from boarding the ship and left standing on the dock was unacceptable and humiliating. Raising his voice he demanded that the Marine explain his refusal to let him and Thomas embark. He could see Captain Cook on the quarterdeck surrounded by his officers and hoped that the sound of his voice would carry and attract their attention. However, not only did the young Marine inform him that he couldn't let him on board without proper authority, but not one of the officers or the Captain appeared to have heard him.

His anger getting the better of him, Walter snapped at the Marine; "Well you had better get someone with that authority down here to sort this out. Now!"

This did attract attention but of the wrong sort. Several of the sailors appeared to have stopped work to watch. Needing to take back some semblance of control in the situation, Walter turned to humour. Looking back at his footman, he loudly proclaimed, "As you can see Thomas, this is most trying! We've not even started this wretched journey, and our path is blocked."

Walter's loud and theatrical delivery had the sailors burst into laughter. It didn't take long for one of the Officer's to notice the commotion, and after a quick word with the Captain, who also glanced down towards the dock, he made his way from the quarterdeck to the head of the gangplank. Apparently ignorant of Walter's social position, he pinned Walter with a cold stare and addressed him in an imperious manner. "You there, Sir! State your business!"

Walter, was a bit shocked by the rudeness of the Officer, but he was heartedly fed up with standing around on the dock being gawked at by the riffraff. Calming himself, he bowed gracefully. "Master Walter Beaumont, Illustrator and Archivist, at your service!"

The Officer shot back a terse reply. "Lieutenant John Williamson, Third Officer, His Majesty's Ship, Resolution!" He paused for a moment, then a frown wrinkled his forehead. "I do not appear to recall your name in the manifest, Sir."

"Sir, my business is with the Captain of this vessel, and I would have you present me to him."

The Officer was looking at him speculatively, then for some reason that Walter couldn't fathom, he repeated his demand that Walter state the nature of his business.

Walter's reply was terse," Unless my memory fails me, Sir, I have just done so!"

Walter's observation elicited a burst of laughter from the crew which just made the situation worse. Williamson turned and barked orders at the men to return to work, then turned back to the young Marine. " 'Till my return, Corporal, do not let this man pass. Understood?"

The Officer quickly headed back up the gangplank. Left in limbo, Walter reminded himself that patience was a virtue he needed to exercise more regularly, so he swallowed his anger. A few minutes later Williamson was back at the gangplank in a slightly more agreeable manner. He addressed Walter civilly, though a steely edge remained in his voice. "Follow me". Was all he said as he turned back towards the ship's deck.

Walter stepped on to the plank but froze as it gave way and bent slightly under his weight. He peered anxiously down into the inky-black water. Inexplicably, Walter always experienced a tightening in his guts when confronted with the ocean. Although he had to admit that lakes precipitated an equally uncomfortable reaction. '*Let Fate be kind to me*' he thought as taking a deep breath, he braced himself and boarded the Resolution, but as Thomas started to follow him up the gangplank, he heard Williamson call out sharply. "Alone!"

Almost speechless at Williamson's insolence, Walter immediately snapped back. "Sir, how dare you address me in this manner! What's more, I cannot possibly travel without my valet!" Walter struggled to calm himself. "As you can see, he is of small stature and will not take up excessive space."

Williamson looked at him flatly. "My Lord, unaccustomed as you appear to be to the nature of seafaring, allow me to enlighten you. Captain Cook, the undisputed master of this ship, has given me the clearest of instructions. "You alone are to come aboard and with only one of your chests."

"Well, I am certain that the Captain will resolve this misunderstanding."

Walter responded through gritted teeth, not able to believe that this was the Captain's orders. Williamson remained undeterred. "Be that as it may, Master Beaumont, my orders are that you may come aboard with one chest and no valet."

Walter decided at this point to stubbornly ignore the Officer, and took another step, only to find his path firmly blocked by Williamson.

"For the last time, Sir, choose a chest, and then accompany me to the Captain!"

This time Walter surrendered. He had no option. If Walter didn't get out of England soon, he would be arrested, and he had no access to enough money to fund his own escape. He had never found it easy to back down, and as his mother had pointed out to him many times, he was his own worst enemy. Walter acquiesced, and turning back he joined Thomas who was still standing on the dock, and opened up his chests, quickly sorting through his clothes and personal effects, and re-packing what he needed into one of the chests. Then, taking his coin pouch out of his pocket he extracted several gold coins as he spoke. "I'll take the large chest, Thomas. The rest can be sent back to the estate."

Walter hesitated for a moment, his tone softening as he gave the boy far more money than he would need to return with the luggage to the Manor. "Take what you need for yourself, lad. Who knows when I'll need them again, if ever."

The lad stared at the gold for a minute before he took it, his eyes wide with incredulity. "God bless, m'Lord, and, uhm, I do hope to see you again, Sir."

Walter smiled wryly and nodded in acknowledgment before he turned sharply back to The Resolution and climbed the gangplank. He followed Williamson to the quarterdeck while behind him a cabin boy, who could have been no older than ten, struggled to take

charge of the massive trunk, pulling it out of the cart and manoeu-
vring it across the dock and up the gangplank to the deck of the
ship.

Navigating his way around the men working on the deck, Walter
felt entirely out of his depth. Nothing in his life had prepared him
for this. As he had boarded the ship, the stark reality of his situation
had hit him, and he realised he was entirely alone. He recognised
Captain Cook because he had seen him before when he had
escorted his mother to one of the Admiralties functions, but they
had never met formally. Now, keenly aware that his future depended
on this man who had agreed to aid him, Walter introduced himself
asking formally for permission to come aboard.

Captain Cook smiled politely. "Ah, Master Beaumont. Allow me
to welcome you aboard my ship." Turning to indicate the four offi-
cers who were standing close by, the Captain introduced Walter.
"These fine gentlemen, are my trusted officers, Mr James King and
Mr John Gore. This is Mr William Bligh, Master of the Ship and,"
Cook broke into a bemused smile, "you have met my third officer,
Mr Williamson."

Cook then pointed to a strikingly handsome Islander. "This is
Mr Omai, a native of Tahiti, which will be one of our ports of call."

Omai was a tall, well-muscled, young Islander dressed in elegant
European clothes. He had a pearly smile and an intelligent look in
his eyes that Walter found quite engaging. He nodded politely, and
the Islander returned the gesture.

Walter had heard about this man who had been the talk of the
King's court. Omai had been in England for a few years after
arriving on the HMS Adventure. He had made a favourable impression with Lord Sandwich who had introduced the Islander to the
King. Walter had heard the gossip about how the ladies of the court
thought Omai was handsome and exotic. Now seeing him up close,
Walter could see the attraction, especially since he had also heard
that there had been quite a lot of salacious twitter about Tahiti
having much freer attitudes in relationships between the sexes.
Walter smiled mischievously at the Islander and winked. "If what I

have heard is true, you have had quite the time of it during your stay here."

The Islander smiled back. "Perhaps. But I think I have had my fill of English hospitality. I must say, I yearn for the warmer waters of my home."

Walter had started to relax during this brief exchange, but the sound of the Captain clearing his throat brought him back to the moment. "Could you join me for a moment, Master Beaumont. " The Captain moved away from the group of officers to a quiet corner of the deck out of earshot from any of the crew. "I am very well aware that this is your first voyage on a Naval vessel, and therefore it is vital that you understand your place here. You will be one of the crew, with none of the privileges you are used to."

The Captain then proceeded to emphasise that Walter would have to obey all directions any of the Officers gave him and that he, Captain Cook, had final say over everything that happened on the ship.

Sobered, Walter bowed to the Captain. "Quite so, Sir." He added in a more sedate tone, "You will have my complete obedience."

Looking unconvinced, Captain Cook persisted. "Mr Beaumont, your reputation precedes you. I can assure you that there will be consequences to any of your actions aboard my ship that do not follow the strict rules I have established. Is that understood?"

"Of course, Sir!"

Cook nodded. "You are officially here to assist Mr Webber as an illustrator and Archivist. I expect that you will apply yourself to these duties. You will meet Mr Webber later as he has gone ashore to procure some last minute necessities."

Walter nodded his head in the affirmative but Cook had already shifted his attention. Walter watched him as he called out for Williamson to join them. "Mr Williamson would you organise a berth for Mr Beaumont and get one of the crew to show him around the the ship".

Being handed over to Williamson was somewhat alarming, but

Walter nodded politely to the Captain and simply said; "Thank you, Sir."

Stepping over the lines and tools still cluttering the deck of the ship as the men completed their inventory, Walter followed Williamson to the large hatch leading below deck. The commotion that emanated from below suggested to Walter that there was an excellent time to be had down there in the belly of the ship. I could do with a little diversion, he thought. As he followed Williamson, Walter wondered about the Officer who on the surface at least, appeared to be someone with little tolerance for frivolities.

Climbing into the dark interior of the ship, Walter saw a mass of people pursuing a variety of activities. Some were milling around two large coppers filled with a boiling broth, some were asleep in hammocks, while a small group were playing a game of cards. One of the sailors was playing a lively tune on the fiddle to which one of the midshipmen was enthusiastically tapping his feet.

On the last rung of the ladder, Walter became aware of the overpowering stench of sweat, urine and other bodily odours inter-mingled with the smell of cooking. He wrinkled his nose and unthinkingly pulled a lace handkerchief from the cuff of his left sleeve to cover his face.

Walter's delicate gesture had all the sailors, except for Williamson, burst into raucous laughter. Realising how he must look to the sailors who lived with these odours, Walter grinned and theatrically bowed to his impromptu audience. "Gentlemen!"

To the claps and cheers of the crew, Walter dramatically stuffed the handkerchief back into the cuff of his sleeve. He silently coun-selled himself to be more aware of his surroundings, after all he had to live with these men, and the last thing he needed was to alienate them.

Apparently irritated by Walter's ability to turn what could have been a disastrous introduction to his crew mates into a shared joke, and the sailors' enthusiastic response, Williamson snapped. "Silence!" The laughter stopped instantly.

With the distraction at an end, Walter was able to survey what was going to be his lodgings for at least the next two years, possibly more if the whim of the Captain decided to extend the journey.

The mess deck was where the crew slept, ate and drank together and in foul weather sought shelter if not on watch.

Walter contemplated the stark reality that faced him now. He leaned against the ship's mast and looked around. Behind the fire-hearth were cabins and assuming that he would be assigned one of these Walter asked Williamson to point out which of them was to be his. He was appalled when Williamson just smirked at him and pointed to a grey sea chest set against one of the tables and then to the beams overhead. "Mr Beaumont, this will be your locker, and you may hang your hammock here."

Not prepared to let the man see just how devastated he really felt, Walter took a breath and thanked Williamson in a stiffly polite voice. That was all he could manage. Walter felt deflated. The bravado that had enabled him to stand his ground had been stripped away by the demeaning reality of his new circumstances.

As the Officer turned away and left him to his own devices, Walter became aware of an increasing weariness and malaise. He automatically reached into his pocket to bring out a small vial from which he extricated one of his pills and popped it into his mouth.

Turning to his luggage, Walter managed to stow his trunk and bag in an empty space and then, after carefully observing the way in which the crew had organised their hammocks, he proceeded to string up the one he had found in the sea chest. The crew were berthed in a confined space, with some areas no more than four feet high, the low head room making his task extremely difficult. After bumping his head quite painfully several times, he could easily understand why most of the men were either sitting or lying down, lacking the space to do much more.

He also noted that although his hammock was a simple canvas affair, some of the others had proper sides with a sort of frame that to Walter's melancholic perception, appeared almost coffin-like. He thought ruefully that at least he had been spared sleeping in one of them.

Once more, Walter surveyed the mess deck." Sir, do you need a hand with anything?" The cabin boy had suddenly appeared and startled Walter. "No, lad, that will be all for now."

The boy turned and ran up the ladder, and as Walter watched him disappear into the light like an agile monkey he ruefully appreciated that the boy's size was more fitting for the accommodations. How was he ever going to adjust to this? Walter thought to himself.

The interior of the mess deck was suddenly even more oppressive, and Walter felt an urgent need to go topside and get some air. Making his way to the ladder, Walter looked up to see a face appear in the hatch. Obscured by the backlight, he could barely distinguish the man's features.

"Mr Beaumont, I presume?" The voice was warm and resonant, even in the midst of the noise that surrounded them.

"Yes. To whom do I have the pleasure of speaking?" Walter still couldn't make a face out. "Please, allow me to step on deck and we can get properly acquainted."

"Splendid!" The face abruptly disappeared from Walter's sight.

As he reached the foredeck, Walter faced a sober-looking young man in his early twenties, impeccably dressed in the Calvinist fashion of a dark buttoned-up suit. What was most noticeable was the man's light-filled grey eyes that shone with a sharp intellect, however he seemed to be a little distracted as he extended his hand to Walter and introduced himself. "Mr John Webber, at your service, Sir!"

Walter detected a slight accent but was unable to place it. "I am pleased to make your acquaintance, Sir." Walter paused. "Hopefully we shall enjoy working together on what appears will be quite an arduous journey."

Webber smiled. "You'll get used to it soon enough, Mr Beaumont. I can assure you of that." He looked around for a moment. "You have your accommodation?" He looked about again. "Unfortunately, space is limited, and there are no cabins available."

Walter watched as the man in front of him kept looking towards the dock, his eyes sweeping the area around the ship. "Yes thank you, Mr Webber, I have been given a berth. I do not mean to be rude, but are you looking for someone or something?" Walter stopped, aware that he did not wish to offend the man he would be working with.

John Webber cleared his throat. He looked conspiratorially at Walter. "Uhh, I had a misunderstanding with someone's husband. Une affaire du Coeur, you do understand?"

Walter laughed. "Then you and I have more in common than you think!"

Webber spoke, his eyes scanning the docks one more time. "I have to unpack my supplies before we depart so I will come and find you later and we can speak more then." He had apparently found nothing to be alarmed about, as he again turned back and smiled at Walter. And with that, the Archivist quickly disappeared back down below deck.

Walter, suddenly alone and aware of the increased activity around him, found himself in the way. Several times he was politely asked to move from where the sailors were trying to work. He knew that the ship was due to leave port. That had been the whole point of his surreptitious flight from his home the previous night. It wouldn't take the authorities very long to figure out that he wasn't in London.

Now watching the preparations for departure, his predicament reminded him of something that Samuel Johnson, the noted writer and intellectual had said: "For being in a ship is being in a jail, with the chance of being drowned." He wondered if he wouldn't have been better off facing up to the courts or the colonies.

Chapter Four

*S*ailing out of Plymouth Harbour, the atmosphere onboard the Resolution was buzzing with excitement. All over the ship, small groups of men pursued their part in making the ship run out to sea and Walter was intrigued by the way the crew worked in the most disciplined manner. It seemed at odds with the mayhem of the port where there appeared to have been little cooperation between the men. In fact, discipline appeared to be the last thing these men were concerned about while in port, yet here at sea, under the guidance of Bligh and Williamson, the ship and crew functioned like a well-oiled machine.

Walter had deliberately placed himself at the bow of the ship with its high gunwale's, determined to rid himself of his fear of the sea. Despite the heaving of the ship as it ploughed through the waves having an unsettling effect on his stomach, Walter focused his attention on his surroundings looking for the beauty and majesty that others found in the vast expanse of endless water that now surrounded him.

The artist in him noted the colours of the sky and the sea. He thought about what shades of paint would do the sight justice, and how he could use his brush to wash the canvas in such a way as to mirror the translucence of the light. Walter was envisioning the painting he would like to craft when he felt a wave of dizziness overcome him, and he almost fell. Grabbing at the rails, he felt a sense of dread as the growing queasiness seemed to be spreading from his gut to his head.

Unthinkingly, out of habit, he pulled a small hip flask from his pocket. He took a long swig but no sooner had the warming liquid made its way to his stomach, it forcefully returned to the light of day, projecting across the railings of the ship into the sea below. For a tiny moment, Walter felt relieved. He sucked in a deep breath, thinking that the worst was over.

Keenly aware of the foul taste in his mouth, he decided he needed water and looking around searched the deck for a water bucket. He found one and began to make his way toward it, all too aware of the rocking movement of the deck, but as he reached for the ladle and took a sip to clean his mouth, another wave of nausea washed over him. In its wake he was assailed by gut-wrenching convulsions, emptying the contents of his stomach all over the deck in front of him. This time, there was no reprieve. In the wake of the waves of biliousness, Walter found himself gripped by successive cramps that shook his whole body and that drove him to his knees.

Staring piteously at the deck, it slowly dawned on Walter that no one was particularly perturbed by his condition. He could hear the sniggers of those that thought it amusing to see him succumb to this wretched state, but no one offered him a hand. As Walter folded himself into a sitting position with his back propped against the side of the ship, he did see a few glances of sympathy in the expression of some of the sailors. He didn't feel any antipathy towards them for not helping him, after all, he was a stranger to them, but he wondered at the lack of interest in his welfare from the quarterdeck.

As another wave of nausea swamped him and new convulsions wracked his body, Walter slipped prone onto the deck where he found himself heaving bile that slowly oozed from his mouth. What an ignominious end, he thought, to be covered in his own bodily fluids while expiring right here on the deck of the ship. While still convulsing, his gaze fixated on a crack between the planks, he became aware of a shadow falling over him, and he awkwardly tried to twist his neck to identify the source of the shadow, but his body refused to cooperate, and his head collapsed with a thud onto the wood.

"Walter, come, let me help you up." Omai's words could not have been more welcome.

The Islander was strong, and having got a good grip on him, he had hoisted him to his feet. Walter clung to Omai's arms, comforted by the powerful muscles rippling beneath his desperate hands. Step by step, Omai shepherded him to the nearest ladder leading below. Navigating the creaking wooden stairs was almost the end of him, but with the Tahitian's persistence and support, Walter finally settled into his hammock.

⋦⋗⋦⋗⋦⋗⋦⋗⋦⋗

The harsh clanging of the morning bell cut through the stale stench of the cabin and Walter woke with a start. As he struggled to get out of his bedding, the ship's motion rudely rolled him out onto the floor, where he fell harshly onto his hands and knees. Paralysed for a moment, his tortured body twisted, the now frequent convulsions began anew. Overcome by seasickness and incapable of getting up, Walter collapsed into the mess on the floorboards, breathing heavily.

A young midshipman, Mr Charlton, who was about to walk past Walter, stopped and offered his hand to help Walter back to his feet. Embarrassed by his condition, but grateful, Walter reached out, thankful for the mercy.

Walter leaned heavily against the young man. "Thank you, Mr Charlton," his voice a whisper, "I fear, I'll never feel myself again."

The young midshipman nodded knowingly. And, as he aided Walter to reach the table and take a seat, he told him about his own battle with seasickness and how long it had taken him to get his sea legs. He assured Walter that he would, sooner or later, adapt to the ship's motion. Walter found this difficult to believe given that he had now spent several weeks in this state, but he tried to find comfort in Charlton's words.

Having sat quietly for a time, Walter felt a little stronger and he decided to take the risk of unsettling his stomach again by moving, so he carefully made his way over to the pale of water closest to the table and proceeded to dip his head into the bucket as far as he could. The sudden cold was a welcome, although temporary, relief from on-going nausea. He pulled his head out of the water and dried himself off with a cloth he found beside the bucket. A little steadier, he sat down on a crate close enough to reach his locker.

Walter was aware that the crew had been speculating and placing bets on how long it would take before he was acclimatised to the rolling motion of the ship and life aboard. Pinned to the cross beam above the table was the evidence that if he was taking a lot longer than most of them had expected. Walter felt a stirring of anger at himself for being an invalid, but he was determined not to succumb to his emotions.

Opening his trunk, he caught sight of his leather-bound journal, untouched since boarding the ship. He should have made more of an effort to draw and write, after all that was his role on this venture, to aid in the illustrative record of the Resolution's journey. Assessing his level of discomfort, Walter decided that it was time to pull himself together and start work.

It seemed apparent to Walter that he needed to put some sort of routine into his day, and he decided that the first step should be writing daily updates of the journey for his Mother. It didn't matter that she would not receive the correspondence until he returned, if he did return that was, it would help to distract him from never-ending nausea.

Walter spread some of the paper out in front of him and laid the quill beside the ink well, and amidst the ship's rolling and heaving he had just begun his first brave attempt to write, when Erik the cabin boy passed by him, and stopping looked over his shoulder.

"What're you doin', Sir?" the boy asked inquisitively.

"It's time to do some work, my boy. In fact, right now, I am preparing to write a letter to my Mother."

The boy was quiet for a moment and then matter of factly announced. "My mother's dead, no point writin' to her even if I could write, which I can't."

Walter was taken aback by Erik's casual observation said without a hint of any emotion and he watched thoughtfully as the boy went to one of the kettles to get a bowl of soup. Then, shaking his head a little, he returned back to the task at hand. Walter had managed to glean some information about the vessel and its crew despite his illness, so this is where he would begin.

"Dear Mother,

For my sanity, I've decided to keep my journal in the form of letters to you so that upon my return, I can amuse you with my various exploits and adventures.

We are now a few weeks into our journey, and the monotony of the weather and ocean is stifling. The only wretched diversion is my propensity to seasickness from which I hope to be spared at the earliest. I have been told that I will eventually get my 'sea legs', but to my dismay, no one could say to me when that may be. So for the moment, suffer I must.

Believe me, from what I have seen so far, I can assure you that this will be a long and arduous voyage indeed.

The ship's company are plain men and strong in character, consisting of officers, sailors and Marines, totalling one hundred and ninety-two men.

Captain Cook is an excellent officer and is knowledgeable enough about all things maritime, but I sense he can be prone to a temper if displeased. In fact, some of the men who have sailed with the Captain on previous occasions say that his disposition has deteriorated considerably. Some even suspect that he may be suffering from an illness, so different has his mood been from earlier voyages.

Mr King, although a serious man, has shown himself to be balanced in his moods and very reasonable to deal with.

The more interesting of the officers is Mr William Bligh, who is the Master of the ship. He has a sharp mind and unpretentious tongue, which may be taken as rude at times, but I find him a likeable fellow. Everyone speaks highly of his skills as a seaman and navigator, and all expect him to go far in his career.

The third officer is Mr Williamson. An unfortunate fellow I have found to be prone to aggression and possibly violence. I certainly do not care for him much, but, alas, I have to contend with him. Most of the ship's company cannot bear him and see him as a tyrant, lacking any compassion or kindness.

In the same vein, the food is similarly abominable and only marginally better for the officers. However, I am thankful for the daily ration of rum that does lighten my mood. You would, my dear Mother, be quite shocked at the lack of privacy for my lavatory and the complete absence of any other comforts. Although I have little choice in the quality of my surroundings, I am choosing to challenge myself in regards to my fortitude and courage. I have every intention of making you proud."

Walter stopped writing. He was suddenly struck by the absence of nausea. As he looked through the porthole at the vast expanse of ocean and sky, it occurred to him that today was not such a bad day after all and that there indeed was a certain beauty to the vast expanse of blue water. He smiled, thinking that Mr Charlton may prove to be right after all.

Chapter Five

A few more weeks passed, and the Resolution was bearing down on the Azores, an archipelago in the North Atlantic. Despite the heavy seas, they had made good headway. The climate had been pleasant enough, and Walter had made the most of his newfound sea legs. He felt that he had done well acclimatising to life aboard ship and had even adapted to precariously perching himself on the 'seat of ease' on the bow of the ship, a humorous reference one of the sailor's used to describe their lavatory.

Walter smiled, remembering his first encounter with the convenience. His rear, exposed to the elements was occasionally splashed by a bow wave and he had found himself without the accustomed paper to clean himself with. As he sat there, he further felt his dignity challenged when Midshipman John Watts handed him the end of a rope.

"Here, Sir, use this. Paper won't do the job where you're sitting." Gathering whatever dignity Walter could muster under the circumstance, he replied as formally as he could," Thank you, Midshipman Watts."

The midshipman nodded and continued to stand there, watching

Walter, a good-natured grin on his face. A little irritated, Walter asked him to turn around. Abandoning his look of amusement, Watts nodded and apologised. He was about to turn around, when, as if he had a sudden thought, he turned back to warn Walter.

"One hand for the ship and one for yourself, Sir."

At Walter's puzzled look, Watts earnestly advised him that it could get slippery. Seeing no reason not to heed Watts' advice, Walter became aware of the potentially dire consequences to his nether regions from exposure, resulting in his quickly figuring out how to use the end of the rope.

Amidst it all, Walter took great care not to soil his clothes. He was fully aware that Captain Cook had strict rules on hygiene, and even in such primitive and crowded conditions as The Resolution, he expected his men to wash both themselves and their clothes. Walter had managed to keep the bathing routine that he had observed on land, and together with the weekly change of shirt, was able to maintain a reasonable appearance on board.

There was just one problem. It left Walter few articles of clothing. Despite having studied up on The Resolution before embarking, Walter had not taken into account the need to pack appropriate attire for a long journey that would take him across many climates and conditions. Once he had packed away clothes that he had brought that were more useful for the London Theatre season, he had very little left. Fortunately, with the generosity of Cook, King and some of the senior crew, Walter had been able to assemble some items that were better suited to seafaring. But for now, he needed little as the current temperatures ranged from mild to hot. Cook turned a blind eye to Walter stripping down to his waistcoat, dispensing with his heavy brocade coat, which was a welcome concession he did not give his officers

Now below deck and looking through a porthole, Walter watched the Islands the ship had been heading towards, become clearly visible. They were so close that he could see the rocks and he was captivated by the sight of the breaking surf on the reef. As the ship pounded through the rough waves, Walter became aware of a rising commotion on deck. Suddenly a heated exchange erupted between the crew.

Walter could hear one of the sailors shouting angrily, "You're running us, aground!"

Walter raced topside just in time to see Captain Cook and Lieutenant King rush to the quarterdeck. He looked towards the bow. Shocked, he realised that The Resolution was heading straight for disaster. Cook shouted at the helm, "In God's name, hard to starboard, man!"

Walter watched as the hapless sailor, William Harold, instantly obeyed the command, only to be rudely shoved aside by King, who immediately took charge of the wheel.

The ship groaned and heaved as her rudder forced a change of course. Ever so slowly, she swung away from the dangerous rocks. As the waves smashed into her, the deck erupted in utter chaos as crew and gear were flung from one side of the ship to the other. The ship barely avoided running aground.

Cook was utterly enraged by their close call with the reef. Barely able to restrain himself, he screamed at Harold. "Consider yourself under arrest, man, for you will not neglect your duties again, mark my words!"

As the Marines secured the sailor, Cook continued to stomp and rave on the deck, as if performing some odd dance. Walter had heard some of the crew referring to it as Cook' having a heiva,' a reference to Polynesian dances that apparently have similar attributes. At the peak of his fury, Cook suddenly turned to the Marines. "Tie this man to the gangway and give him six of the best!"

King and the other officers looked shocked. Although Walter was not privy to the nuances of the relationships amongst them, he had been aware that they were finding Cook's outbursts a little alarming. It was King who asked quietly. "Sir, surely we should hold an inquiry?"

It wasn't just that the action was not in keeping with the articles of war that had been recently instituted on board all British Naval Ships, it was not in keeping with Cook's reputation. He had always been known as a more reasonable man in regards to discipline. The fact was, Cook usually had the fewest number of floggings aboard his ship compared to many of the other Captains. This was one of the reasons that Walter's mother had been interested in his career, but sadly those days appeared to be gone.

The Captain turned his fury onto his Officer." I'll not be questioned like this, Mr King," Cook shouted, "Do you understand? I have given my orders, and I expect them to be carried out."

Chastened, King quickly saluted, "Aye, aye, Sir!"

Standing beside the mast, Walter watched the drama unfold with a sickening realisation that he was about to see an aspect of life at sea he had not previously considered.

The Marines dragged the unfortunate man across the deck to the gangway where some of the crew had erected a grate into an almost vertical position. Face first, Harold was pushed against it and, by extending his arms to the top corners of the frame, he was securely tied to it. In defiance and to maintain a sense of dignity, the sailor put on a stoic face, devoid of emotion.

Walter wondered whether this was in keeping with some tradition or merely the man's reaction to the inevitability of his circumstance. It was possible that being able to choose whether he would react or not allowed the man a small, but essential sense of dignity.

"Fall in, men!" Williamson was going about assembling the men, roughly ordering them to line up into position on one side of the rigging while the officers took their posts opposite them.

The boatswain's mate, Mr Evans, had gotten hold of the cat, a cruel adaptation of a whip, studded with pieces of lead, and he casually took his position beside the grate awaiting the Captain's order to execute the punishment. As Cook stood beside his officers, he sternly declared this a warning to anyone derelict in their duties and that they should consider what was about to follow a light punishment. "Let the punishment commence, Mr Evans!"

The boatswain's mate drew his arm back. He suddenly brought the whip hissing through the air. The cat's tails landed on the man's back with a sickening squelch. Repeatedly, the sound of the whip cut through the air, and each time it struck the bare flesh of the sailor's back, only to peel more skin back, exposing raw flesh.

Watching the blood ooze through the criss-cross of wounds, Walter was suddenly overcome by a sense of disgust and a wave of nausea. Not being able to hold back the vomit, he lurched forward towards the side of the ship, the taste of bile thick in his mouth, stinging his throat.

Leaning far over the railing, he threw up overboard. Time and again, he heaved, emptying his stomach. Finally, exhausted, Walter slumped to the deck-boards, where he lay moaning.

In the background, the punished sailor was finally cut loose from the grate, from where he was taken below, bleeding and groaning.

Erik, the cabin boy, had rushed over to assist Walter. "Sir, are you alright?" Walter looked up at the lad and nodded, acknowledging his concern. "Just give me a moment."

Walter's constitution had strengthened over the last few weeks, and this allowed him to recover a little more quickly than when the journey began, but he was still fragile. He hated his weakness and found it especially galling to have to lean on the shoulder of the young cabin boy, but it was the only way he could get to the gunwale and catch the wind in his face.

Sitting there, he could hear some of the crew quietly talking about the day's events and it occurred to him that they were less guarded around him, and that he was frequently privy to information and gripes amongst the men that was kept from the officers. In this instance, some of the crew felt the punishment entirely unjust as the helmsman had directly followed Cook's orders, and that the error lay with Cook and King who had charted the course that nearly cost them their ship.

Chapter Six

_M_r Webber had warned Walter that the humidity and damp of the ship's interior was the natural enemy of any art materials. So he had decided to sort through his possessions and take stock. It had been another awful week of seasickness brought on by their return to the open ocean. He hated being so enfeebled, and he felt irritable and edgy.

He had also found that the sight of that poor sailor being flogged had coloured his dreams, turning the nights into frightening visions of violence and darkening his mood even further. He found trying to work in the cramped space allotted to him frustrating, and as he dropped yet another sheaf of papers and watched them scatter over the floor and slide away with the motion of the ship, his fury erupted.

Slamming down the lid of his chest and without taking the time to think his situation through he decided then and there, that he deserved more respect and proper accommodations. He impulsively threw on a heavy woollen coat and storming up the ladder headed to Cook's cabin, where he brushed past a surprised marine. Walter burst unceremoniously into the large cabin where the Captain sat behind his desk, working. Clearly irritated by Walter's sudden appearance, he nevertheless motioned the soldier to leave.

As Walter began his litany of complaints, he was too engrossed in his own self-righteousness, to notice that Cook looked more and more irritated as he listened to Walter's grievances. When he had finished, he looked at Cook expectantly and was a little surprised by the cutting edge in the Captain's voice when he responded. "So, as I understand your dilemma, Mr Beaumont, you require more space than is currently available to you."

"Yes, Sir. My accommodation is simply inadequate for my needs and the work you wish me to carry out." Walter responded, starting to relax as he thought that the Captain having understood his concern would now resolve the problem. Cook leaned back in his chair and frowned. "So what might you suggest?"

Walter had not really thought his demand through, but in his mind, the simple answer was that he should be provided with a cabin. The fact that there were no spare cabins led to an inevitable conclusion, but before he could fully answer Cook, there was a knock on the door. Having been invited in by the Captain, the door opened to reveal Williamson. "Ah, Mr Williamson, how fortuitous. You are just in time to hear Mr Beaumont put forward a proposition."

Williamson looked at Walter suspiciously. "Sir?"

Walter, hesitated and looked to Cook only to find himself being impatiently ordered to continue. "As I was saying, Sir, my needs are simply not being adequately accommodated in the crew's quarters. I need more space and a cabin would provide that for me." Then ploughing on without too much consideration, Walter came up with what he thought was an acceptable solution. "Mr Williamson is more accustomed to the crowded confines of a ship. To serve more effectively, I could take his berth and allocated space, and he could join the crew in their quarters." Walter paused, "It is my papers, you see."

Williamson, stunned by Walter's audacity, interjected." Sir, I must protest!"

Cook calmly silenced his officer and looked Walter squarely in the eye. "Mr Beaumont, whatever makes you think that I would contemplate removing one of my officers from his accommodation? You need to appreciate that all of us have our duties and responsibilities, some to a greater degree than others. And some of us are more expendable than others. Do you follow my point?"

Walter, understanding Cook's insinuation was shocked. "Sir, are you suggesting...?"

"Mr Beaumont, I am simply saying that given the expectations and demands of your duties, I believe that you are more than adequately accommodated. Your challenge is to become accustomed to your unfamiliar surroundings, which I am sure you will do in due course."

Frustrated, Walter realised that to pursue this issue further was pointless. All this time he had thought of Cook as an ally, someone who appreciated his station and circumstances, someone he could turn to, but such was apparently not the case. He suddenly felt bitterly disappointed and very alone.

Williamson turned to Cook and tipped his forehead. "Thank you, Sir."

"Very well, then." The Captain leant forward to look back down to the pile of papers on his desk. He was about to continue his work, when he suddenly looked up at Walter, his eyebrows drawn together. "Sir, I consider this matter closed." With that said, he resumed perusing the papers, his signal to the two men that they had been dismissed.

As both men turned to leave the Captain's cabin, Williamson smirked at Walter who declined to take the bait. As they opened the door to step into the narrow space in front of Cook's cabin, they saw one of the sailors and Erik snap abruptly to attention. The two looked sheepishly at each other and then at the emerging men. They had a conspiratorial look about them, suggesting that they had been caught out in some misdemeanour.

The sailor grinned and quipped at Walter. "I guess you'll just have to put up with us riff-raff then, eh, Sir?"

Walter, irritated by the lack of success in procuring better accommodation on board, simply shrugged his shoulders and pushed roughly past the crew members. It would be much later that he would review what had happened and realise that he had been insensitive and arrogant and that he may well have damaged the fledgling alliance he had built with the crew.

As he made his way topside, the crew's cackling followed him to the deck. Angry at how he had been treated, but also spurred on, Walter decided that he was going to be more determined than ever to persevere as best as he could. Just as he had with Jonathan, he would show them that he was made of sterner stuff.

Walking forward across the deck, he went below to the small corner of what was going to be his only private space for a long time. Back with his chest and hammock, he accessed his little pouch of pills, and for the first time in several weeks, he dealt with his anger medicinally. He then went back to trying to organise his belongings.

Sometime later, satisfied with his morning's efforts, Walter sat at a table, looking over a page of his journal. The opium had lifted his mood, and he had not felt any nausea at all despite the heavy seas. Of course, Walter had not attempted to eat anything. That would be the test, but overall Walter felt like he had his sea legs back, and his usual optimism returned.

Over the next hour or so he put the finishing touches on a sketch showing a stormy sea and the Resolution short-rigged for lousy weather, and pleased with his work, he slid the page back into the folder and selected a blank page. After inspecting the tip of a quill, he took out a knife to sharpen the end of it and then taking a few minutes to gather his thoughts he started to write.

"Dear Mother,

As we are reaching the Cape of Good Hope at the bottom of the African coast, and in spite of the appalling weather, I am simply reborn! After endless weeks of this wretched seasickness, I do indeed appear to have found my sea legs. In the meantime, I have not just resigned myself to make the most of these sordid circumstances, I have decided to immerse myself into this experience to the utmost.

One of my newly found highlights on this journey has been the Islander, Omai. A native of Raiatea, one of the many islands in the South Seas, his real name is apparently Mai. Still, for some inexplicable reason, it appears that we English added the O, which, in his language, means 'it is', and he has decided to keep this peculiar version of his name. I have no doubt that you have heard all about him through your connections to the court.

You would find him a delight, Mother, for he is not only pleasing to the eyes but a man most intelligent, with a keen sense and wit. In fact, he has quite the talent for cards and chess, beating numerous opponents many times. He has also mastered the English language very well. At times, he pretends not to be as eloquent in our tongue, but this is more often merely a ruse and not to be taken on face value.

It appears that he is the eldest son of a manahune, a landowning class in their society. Although not a noble, he may as well be, for all the graces and diplomacy he musters. Dispossessed in a bitter war, he vowed to go to England to secure the means to avenge his family. Such are our circumstances that we share to one degree or another.

As the two of us are essentially passengers with little to do, for the most part, I have asked him to teach me the language of his home, a melodious tongue, beautiful and simple in its form.

Fascinated by my drawings and sketches, he frequently sits patiently for hours as I draw, never saying a word, but at times merely observing and some-times nodding with approval.

Insensitive to his situation and history, some of the crew simply see him as an oddity, amusing but generally irrelevant. Even the Captain, who places great store in his opinion on matters relating to the islands and their people, has from time to time expressed prejudices against him. Of course, Mr Williamson harbours great animosities and mistrust towards Omai, who in turn chooses to ignore the man. For my part, I believe that there is some bond between us, although its nature, I am unable to determine."

Walter decided to put the letter away. Well aware that he was still regaining his strength, and that the best way to tackle his work was to break it into small tasks, he had managed to avoid being so focused that he tired himself too much. He had found that it tended to bring the seasickness on more. He had also learnt that if he started to feel ill, then the best place was on the deck of the ship, exposed to the fresh air blowing across his face. Walter could not fathom why that helped, but it did.

A little apprehensive that the nausea may return, Walter decided to head topside to get some fresh air. As he stood by the railing, and looked out across the ocean watching the rolling waves coming towards them from the horizon, he noticed that the weather seemed to be taking a turn for the worst. The colours had changed from blues to greys, while the remaining daylight had dimmed quickly, giving the heaving ocean an ominous appearance. The gusts of wind flicked the tops of the waves into white tips, while up around the top of the mast, it screeched through the sheets and sails.

Bligh was on watch, and Walter heard him call over to Williamson that it was time to prepare for the weather. "Have the men see to it immediately."

Making sure he was not in the way, Walter observed as the crew responded to the order and the changing conditions. As the light dimmed further and the wind tore at the rigging, the deck became extremely slippery, leaving both men and gear in danger of washing overboard. Wisely, Walter took this as an invitation to retire below. He had a selection of books for just such times as this, and it seemed that now was as good a time as any to pull one out.

Below deck, Walter quickly and adeptly secured himself into his hammock having become very proficient at all sorts of ways of keeping himself safe from the often-unpredictable movements of the ship. He must have fallen asleep, for the next thing Walter knew, was that the distinctive clanging of the ship's bell suddenly woke him. 'Eight bells, supper time.' He could hear the fury of the wind and the water smashing against the hull and across the deck above.

Despite the infernal racket of the storm, some of the crew were fast asleep in their hammocks while others calmly ate a meal. Walter closed the book that had fallen across his chest and skilfully rolled out of the hammock, landing steadily on the floor. He was hungry, and despite the risk, Walter knew he needed to eat. Reaching for his heavy woollen coat and securing his hat to his head with a scarf, he headed over to the ladder. Walter usually ate at the officers' table, and this meant he would have to brave the weather.

As the ship lurched through the heavy seas, Walter walked carefully to keep his balance as he navigated the perils of the deck. It
had only been a little while ago, that Mr Gore had laughingly
suggested that now he had developed a good set of sea legs, he was
no longer suitable for riding a thoroughbred. Walter smiled at
Gore's comment, but as he got closer to the ladder leading to Cook's
cabin, he reflected on his earlier attempt at negotiating his accommodation with Cook and Williamson. Walter hoped that the discussion was now well in the past as it would not do to make dinner
uncomfortable.

The ship suddenly dropped away from under him, and Walter
braced himself for a moment, preparing for the imminent crash as
the ship landed in the trough of the wave where it groaned and
shuddered as if in pain. He took several quick steps across the deck
just in time for a sheet of water to crash over him, almost forcing
him off his feet, while the screaming wind in the rigging was ringing
painfully in his ears.

'One hand for the ship, the other for yourself.' Walter remembered the advice given to him by one of the old salts when he had
slipped and fallen hard against the capstan during some heavy seas
earlier in the voyage. Luckily he had only sustained bruises, but they
were bad enough and had taken a week or more to heal, during
which time every move he made was a new experience in pain.

Walter took a firm grip on the lifeline running the length of the
ship and began to carefully make his way to the Captain's cabin.
Every now and then he paused, accommodating his weight to regain
his balance but finally, in what seemed to be an age, he finally
reached the ladder leading below.

In the great cabin, the evening meal was well underway.
Compared to the crew's quarters, Cook's cabin seemed large and
luxurious. Sitting at the table were Cook, his three officers, King,
Gore and Williamson, along with the ship's surgeon, William Anderson, and Omai and John Webber.

Walter climbed out of the drenched coat and pulled off the hat,
draping it across a chair before pushing past those already seated, so
that he could sit down beside the Islander.

Captain Cook tapped his knife on the side of his glass, and the conversation died down. "Gentlemen, your attention, please. As we get further into our journey, we will face significant challenges. However, none are as important as maintaining solid discipline amongst the crew and keeping the men healthy." Cook paused and frowned. "Now, as you well know, the natives of the South Seas are generally friendly and willing to trade. The women, especially, are very open with their sexual favours. As I do not agree with the men availing themselves of these opportunities, I ask you to discourage sexual intercourse between the crew and the natives. Accordingly, I also expect you to see to your own conduct as officers and gentlemen."

Walter, watched the faces of the men around the table when he noticed a glint in Bligh's eyes. Obviously straining to keep a straight face, the young officer cleared his throat. "Sir, surely if the women are open to this, then why not allow the men the pleasure of their company?"

The officers chuckled at Bligh's pun. He was not known to make jokes and, on the odd occasion when he did, they sometimes fell flat, but this one had hit the mark. Cook, apparently not amused, chose to ignore Bligh's attempt to make light of his concerns and pressed his point. "Mr Bligh, I do not think it prudent to introduce the clap to these people. Do you?"

Before Bligh could attempt to redeem himself, King interjected. "They may stop being so hospitable, Sir?"

Cook frowned. "Gentlemen, this is a serious matter of concern. These people have none of the experience with venereal distemper that we have, and I think it most intolerable to change that." He paused. "And, yes, I agree, let's not make enemies of them. Come to think of it, I dare say that they would be quite formidable in a fight."

Williamson, who up to this point had been quiet and reserved, now looked directly at Cook. Walter sensed that Williamson was irritated. The man's complexion had a tendency to change to a rusty colour when annoyed. "Sir, respectfully, these savages are no match for a pistol or musket. A good volley will have them running for the hills."

Cook was visibly taken aback by Williamson's forthright opinion. He had recently become less tolerant of any dissent amongst officers and crew, and this issue was apparently important to him. "Mr Williamson, in my experience, these natives have shown considerable fortitude and courage under all sorts of circumstances."

Lieutenant King similarly felt the need to put Williamson straight. "I agree with the Captain, Mr Williamson. I certainly would not like to test your theory on my watch."

Williamson frowned, but wisely said nothing and simply continued to eat in silence. Walter looked across at the third officer. From the time they had met on the gangplank, the man had been an aggravation to him. He had found Williamson to be ill-tempered, consistently critical of the crew's efforts and Walter was convinced that the man's temper made him unreliable, and would, therefore, make him a danger to everyone on the expedition. Furthermore, Walter had rarely seen the man smile or make light with someone unless it was at their expense. Stiff and formal, Williamson kept himself aloof.

Having already imbibed his rum ration, it worked with the opium to put Walter into a pleasant state of intoxication. Unfortunately, this led Walter to believe that the current situation was an irresistible opportunity to draw Williamson further into the verbal fray. "Mr Williamson, I suspect this conversation has taken a turn, not to your liking?"

Looking surprised, the officer answered curtly that he was simply stating a fact and with that resumed eating. Unwilling to let Williamson off the hook, Walter doggedly pursued him. "A fact, Mr Williamson?"

Walter felt a slight tingle of excitement. *'The game was afoot.'* Casually he sat back in his chair and dramatically placed the tips of his fingers together. As he scrutinised Williamson for a reaction, it did cross his mind that perhaps it would be wiser to give Williamson an honourable way out. But Walter dismissed this idea immediately. Where was the fun in that, he thought?

Williamson stared at Walter, possibly unsure of how to respond. It was evident from previous interactions that he was unaccustomed to the subtler points of verbal sparring. The steely glint in his eyes told Walter that he was aware of the situation that Walter had now foisted upon him.

Williamson's lips thinned, and he pulled himself up in the chair as he firmly framed his reply. "The suggestion, Mr Beaumont, that these savages are a match for us implies that they are as civilised as we are. As far as I am concerned, Mr Beaumont, it is evident that they are not. In God's scheme, there is an order, as opposed to chaos. If he had meant these creatures to be civilised, then, in my view, they would present a threat to us. Since they are not, then I see no reason to disturb God's plan by attributing abilities to them that they do not possess."

With a wry smile, Walter closed the trap. "Does this mean, Sir, that you presume to know God's plan?"

A sudden, hushed silence gripped the table, which was abruptly interrupted by the boatswain William Erwin, who burst into the cabin drenched to the bone and looking agitated.

"Sir, the ship is leaking badly! I have ordered extra crews to the pumps, but we may need to find a safe harbour!"

Cook turned to Bligh. "Mr Bligh, see to it."

Without question, the young officer reached for his coat. "Yes, Sir!" Putting his hat on, he quickly headed out the door.

Without any prompting, the other officers also jumped to their feet.

"Let's all step lively, Gentlemen!"

As the men positioned themselves to file through the door of the cabin, Williamson shot Walter a hostile glance and hissed, "You and I will finish this later, Beaumont."

"That will be Master Beaumont to you, Sir!"

Walter's terse reply appeared to irritate the third officer further, but there was no time for either of them to continue to pursue this dialogue. As Walter watched Williamson leave the cabin, a small ember of regret flickered into being. Sport was one thing, but here he was, confined to a small space for months to come, and he had just goaded a man who actively disliked him. Sometimes Walter had to wonder how intelligent he actually was. When would he learn?

Left behind with Omai and John, Walter thought ruefully that he persisted in making life much more difficult for himself than it needed to be. Sitting back down to finish his meal, he was aware that Omai was looking at him with a quizzical expression. Walter squirmed under that gaze. Being forced to see himself from another's perspective was confronting, and he knew he had shown himself to be petty and vindictive. Walter was grateful that neither of the other men mentioned the previous conversation.

Chapter Seven

The poor state of repair of the ship became only too apparent as the inspection progressed. There were leaks everywhere, with water not just seeping through, but at times, as the ship heaved in the swell, it appeared to flood in between the timbers and corking. Privately, Cook was furious with himself. Unlike his previous expeditions, where he had involved himself with every aspect of the preparations and overseeing most things personally, this time he had left most of the preparations to others, and now he and his men were paying the price.

The ship had been sloppily refurbished using inferior materials and shoddy workmanship. This no doubt reaped the contractors a tidy profit and without any concerns about the consequences of such actions. But right now, he needed to focus on the present. Propped cup beside a bulkhead, Cook watched as most of his crew was feverishly working to cork the leaks as best they could. " Mr Erwin, can we keep her afloat?" He asked looking over at the boatswain, who's already weather-worn face looked even more worn.

"I will do my best, Sir." He glanced at Cook. "A prayer wouldn't go astray."

"So noted, Mr Erwin."

After the boatswain had disappeared up a ladder and into the weather, Mr King reported to the Captain. "Well, Mr King, what have you discovered in other parts of the ship?"

"Sir, the worst appears to be the corking on the seams of the deck. The heat during the day has opened them up, and the water now simply pours in. Someone made a handsome profit at our expense, Sir."

"So it appears." Cook paused, still looking concerned. "Do we still need to find a harbour, Mr King?"

King shook his wet head. "I don't think so, Sir. I believe that the worst has been contained and that with a little more work and attention to the corking, we should be sound."

"Good. Please keep me informed of any problems arising, Mr King."

❧❧❧❧❧

Thankfully, it didn't take long for the weather to clear, and by daybreak, it was evident that they were in for calm seas and a clear sky. By mid-morning the sun was blazing onto the deck of the ship whereby now every available space was being used to dry linen, clothes and bedding. A combination of the heat and the exhaustion felt by everyone was having a particularly unfavourable effect on the crew's temper. Every now and then a short burst of anger would erupt between some of the men, but it usually settled down quickly, and everyone just got on with what needed to be done.

Walter, along with John Webber and Omai, had set themselves up on a quiet part of the ship's deck and were carefully examining papers and charts spread out on a makeshift table. Carefully reviewing their work for water damage, they found that the majority of the documents had survived unscathed. A few showed some marking around the edges but nothing more. Pleased with what they were seeing, Walter now began examining some of Cook's charts and was amazed by the detail Cook had included in his work.

He couldn't help but admire the man's craftsmanship and

artistic skill, and pointing out some of the more exciting areas of Africa's coastline to the other two men, they all became thoroughly engrossed. Suddenly distracted by an altercation on the mid-deck, Walter looked up to see Williamson standing above the cabin boy Erik, who was looking terrified and clutching a piece of bread.

"So you have turned to thieving, you miserable wretch!" Williamson's bellow carried across the deck.

"No, Sir!" Before the boy could say any more, Williamson viciously slapped him across the face "Liar!"

The blow threw the child clear across the deck and even from this distance, Walter could see a trickle of blood at the corner of Erik's mouth. The boy was clearly hurt and without thinking Walter acted.

He was all too familiar with situations like this from his own childhood when he had been victimised by his brother Jonathan. Walter was only vaguely aware of John cautioning him as he jumped down amidships. 'That insufferable wretch!' With a few quick steps, he was in front of Williamson, placing himself between the officer and the boy.

Williamson, surprised by Walter's sudden appearance, asked caustically, "Can I help you, Mr Beaumont?"

Furious, Walter struggled with his temper, but he was beyond considering the consequences of his current actions. The man was a despicable bully who needed to be taught a lesson and ignoring the sarcasm in Williamson's tone, Walter called the man out for attacking a boy who had no way of defending himself. But Williamson showed no shame and just sneered at Walter. He looked Walter up and down, his expression filled with contempt. "I take the view, that a fop such as yourself presents little if any, challenge!"

The dare was clear, and Walter stepped closer to the third officer and snarled back that he would be happy to show Williamson just how wrong he was. To Walter's surprise, Williamson stepped back and casually drew his sword and flicked it provocatively through the air, inches away from Walter's face. "I fancy we should put that to the test, Mr Beaumont."

This was an unexpected turn of events that had Walter reconsider the circumstances he was confronted with. Unarmed, he hesitated and stepped back realising that it was a little too late to remember his promise to Captain Cook that he would not interfere with the running of the ship. And yet here he was with the crew watching, their duties forgotten while he confronted Williamson.

From somewhere amongst them, a sword slid noisily across the deck and came to rest at Walter's feet. Looking around, he caught sight of Omai amongst the crew and with a smile and a quick nod of his head, the Islander let Walter know where the weapon had come from.

Looking back at Williamson, Walter crouched and picked the weapon up and weighed it expertly in his hand, feeling its balance, hoping that his obvious familiarity with a blade might deter Williamson. Walter had not expected his defence of Erik to include a sword fight but standing here now, both of them with a blade in their hands he didn't know how to avoid it, or indeed if he wanted to. The thought of soundly beating the third officer was seriously inviting.

"As you wish, Mr Williamson."

Walter had only just started to ready himself when Williamson, without warning or any regard to protocol, suddenly lunged forward. Walter instinctively parried the officer's blade. "You persist in demonstrating such a deplorable lack of manners, Mr Williamson."

A snicker ran through the onlookers, but Williamson ignored the taunt and pushed toward Walter trying to crowd him into the mast. The blades clashed as the men engaged in a lighting fast thrust and parry. As the advantage shifted back and forth between them, Walter was forced to acknowledge that Williamson was an excellent swordsman. Still, as the fight made its way across the deck, Williamson, despite his skill, gradually lost ground against Walter who took charge of the duel.

Then a flash of Walter's steel and Williamson clutched his arm. Blood trickled through his fingers staining his white shirt, and breathing heavily, Williamson stepped back, shocked. Walter, expecting this to be an end to the fight, elegantly skipped out of

Williamson's reach and bowing, he smiled with exaggerated polite-
ness and claimed an advantage.

Walter waited for Williamson to acknowledge that he had won
the fight, expecting that the etiquette he was used to would apply
here. Deciding to prompt the officer, Walter spoke again. "I wager a
simple apology will suffice." However, the only response he received
was for Williamson to scream back at him. "Damn you, Beaumont!"

The third officer was about to renew his attack when Lieutenant
King appeared with several Marines. He pushed his way between
the two men and ordered the Marines to arrest Walter.

Walter was stunned to find himself seized. The Marines pushed
him roughly to his knees while the sword forcefully removed from
his grip. There were muttered sounds of disapproval from the crew,
but King quickly silenced them, making it very plain that he would
tolerate no further disruption of duties and discipline.

As Walter struggled against his captors, King turned back to
face him and reiterated that he was under arrest. "I had thought
that we had established that whatever your concerns, Sir," King
reprimanded Walter, "you are to refrain from interfering with an
officer's duty."

At that point, Captain Cook pushed his way through the crew
and took charge of the situation. After a brief word with King, the
Captain ordered the Marines to take Walter to the Captain's cabin.
Walter found himself being lifted to his feet and unceremoniously
frog marched across the deck.

Below, in Cook's cabin, King, Gore and Williamson flanked the
still outraged Walter. Two Marines were holding him firmly by the
arms, and although Walter had stopped struggling, he was absolutely indignant about this shocking turn of events. Williamson was
the guilty party in this; yet here he was, completely untouched,
escaping, again, any consequences for his actions. No matter how
abominable Williamson's behaviour appeared to be, he always
seemed to get away with it. Puzzled, Walter tried to simmer down.

In contrast to Walter's seething sense of injustice, Captain Cook
appeared to be the epitome of calm. He sat behind his desk, his
back to the small group of men while casually looking out to sea.

Without turning around, Cook's voice cut through the tension. "Leave me with Mr Beaumont."

The officers protested loudly. Cook turned around, quietly reached into his desk drawer and pulled out a pistol. Without saying a word, he placed the weapon on his desk. The room fell silent again as the Captain leant casually back in his chair.

Walter couldn't quite work out what this gesture meant, but he was aware that King was apparently uncomfortable with the order he had just been given. He seemed to hesitate, looking at Gore who looked just as confused. The officer started to speak. "But Sir..."

The rest of Gore's objection was drowned out as the Captain, bellowed. "You heard me! Everyone out!"

The volume of the order left no doubt about what would happen if they did not comply. The sharp sound of the men snapping to attention echoed through the cabin. It took less than a minute for the men to shuffle out of the confined space, leaving Walter behind.

Walter heard the door close and watched puzzled as the Captain's expression softened a little. Still agitated and enraged, Walter tried furiously to understand why he had been singled out,. Then, just as Walter felt his emotions start to calm, Cook reached for the pistol. Instinctively, Walter tensed, his mind in a state of chaos, his automatic reaction to danger had put him instantly on alert, but his instinctive thought to fight was quickly overruled by common sense. This was a British ship. Things were done according to strict regulations, he reminded himself as he watched the Captain.

A wave of profound relief washed over Walter as Cook simply placed the weapon back in the drawer. The squeaky, rasping noise of wood against wood echoed through the quiet of the cabin.

Walter stood there, fixed in Cook's gaze for several minutes. He knew that he was in trouble. His own sense of what was right had already asserted itself and duelling on board a vessel was definitely outside of regulation behaviour. But after all, he didn't start it. He felt a rush of words begin to form when Cook signalled for him to sit.

" You know, we are not that different, Mr Beaumont."

Whatever was Cook talking about? The Captain's curious observation puzzled Walter. He shook his head. How could this man claim that the two were similar? Back in England, they came from entirely separate worlds. The Captain continued, obviously aware of Walter's confusion. "We are both here at the discretion of our friend Twitcher, Lord of the Admiralty."

Cook drew a long breath and then let out a sigh. "Damn it! God knows I will have to name something 'Sandwich'."

The exasperation in Cook's voice surprised Walter whose own reaction to that name was very different. Lord Sandwich was part of a circle of friends and associates of his father's. He sensed the opening up of memories long-held deliberately in the back of his mind, and he fought to keep them there. This was not the time to revisit that part of his childhood, but an image came back so forcibly that he had no way of stopping it. Startled, Walter almost jumped out of the chair.

"It was you... at the Manor."

Cook, a gentle smile on his lips, just nodded. "There, you see, I do know what haunts you in the dark of night." Cook paused. "And all I ask of you, Mr Beaumont, is to keep the fight that is in you, away from my men."

Walter looked across the desk to the man who had intervened to protect him at one of the most horrifying moments of his childhood. 'You crossed both my father and Sandwich to save me."

Cook sat back in his chair, apparently reflecting on the incident that Walter realised could have cost the man everything. He waited, wondering if the Captain regretted the risk he had taken, but when Cook spoke, he showed his true mettle and an honest understanding of his own worth.

"Well, Mr Beaumont, thankfully the Admiralty has a great need for my services as a navigator and cartographer. And despite our differences, Lord Sandwich and I have been in accord when it comes to the importance of the work of the Admiralty."

"And now you have helped me again, Sir. I am in your debt

more than I realised when I first boarded the ship." Walter observed thoughtfully.

The Captain slowly got to his feet. For a second, Walter thought the man looked in pain, but Cook quickly regained his composure. He stepped away from his desk and came towards Walter, close enough to rest his hand on the younger man's shoulder. "I trust you will volunteer yourself for the brig long enough to appease my officers, yet brief enough to satisfy the crew."

Walter rose slowly to his feet and without saying a word, he nodded in assent. Cook smiled ruefully at him once more, then called for the Marine who was standing guard outside the Cabin door. "Please escort Mr Beaumont to the brig."

As Walter was marched down into the hold, he pondered on the strange ironies that had put him in this position. If the Captain had not been at the Manor that night, he wouldn't have become acquainted with Walter's mother, and she would not have known who to look to when he needed help again.

Walter was settled into the brig by the Marines and left to his own devices. It was a cramped and uncomfortable space, so reminiscent of the small nooks and crannies of the secret passages in the Manor that there was no stopping the images that flooded back into his mind. Already emotional and overwrought from his encounter with Williamson, the vivid images that assailed him now left Walter gasping for breath and nauseated.

The lights, movement and colours all felt as if he was back there at the Manor as a seven-year-old. The house, brilliantly lit up for a ball, and he a small boy, hiding in an alcove watching it all. This was the night he had been caught spying on his father. Walter felt like he was in two places at once. Here now, sitting in the corner of the brig, an adult remembering that night, but at the same time, his heart racing and his rising terror swept him back to his childhood.

Watching through the lens of these strange distorted memories, Walter was again in the alcove near the entrance to the Manor. A host of butlers welcomed the stream of guests arriving for the evening. To the swelling sounds of chamber music played by a small orchestra, elegant men and women filed into the grand foyer, while those that had arrived earlier were dancing in the ballroom.

Walter's heartbeat increased again with the memory of Lord Sandwich as he walked through the door into the entrance hall. He was exquisitely dressed with a look of aristocratic disdain on his lips, while his eyes, Walter had noted, were hard and arrogant. He had caught Walter's attention, and overhearing His Grace being told that he was to follow the servant to the chapel, Walter had made a decision that he would come to regret. Thinking that whatever was going on in the chapel would be more exciting than watching people dancing, he had quickly scurried out of his hiding place to duck around the back of the staircase to enter into one of the house's secret passages.

Looking through a peephole, Walter was mesmerised by the scene in front of him. The room was dimly lit, but he could still see a large table covered in a cornucopia of food, wine and fruit. But what caught his attention more than the gastronomic delights, were the naked women lying along the middle of the table. The adult Walter, sitting in the brig watching his memories recognised that the women were posed like classical Greek or Roman statues. But at the time, the boy Walter was only aware that the shadowy figures that were milling around the room were involved in something secret and illicit.

Remembering the events of that night as a man, Walter could have appreciated the deliciousness of this illicit bacchanalia, but the repercussions of his spying proved to be horrific. As a seven-year-old, the sight of his father pouring red wine over the body of a semi-naked woman was shocking, and at the same time so fascinating that Walter's whole attention was absorbed by the scene. It was that fixation with what was in front of him that caused him to neglect what may be behind. It was why he failed to hear the fall of steps that signalled he was not alone in the passage.

A hand clamped over his mouth, and he found himself roughly dragged along the dark corridor. Walter desperately tried to identify his assailant, but the dark made it impossible. Whoever it was, thrust him through a door into a small room and onto the cold stone floor in front of several men. Breathless from fear, Walter looked up to find his father staring down at him, then Lord Beaumont had raised his eyes to look behind him and demanded that Jonathan explain himself. Twisting his neck around, Walter was confronted by Jonathan's gleeful grimace.

His brother smirked at him as he told their father that Walter had been spying on the gathering in the chapel, and that had been the start of one of the most humiliating and frightening experiences of Walter's life. He knew that he was about to be severely punished, and he couldn't stop himself from bursting into tears and begging his father not to hurt him. It only made it worse, as Lord Beaumont despised weakness, and just like Jonathan, he had sneered at him, disgust written all over his face.

The other men laughed along with his father as Lord Beaumont pronounced Walter's punishment. Lord Sandwich was one of those who had encouraged Walter's father to allow Jonathan and his friends to meet out the penalty. Forced to bend over the back of a chair in front of every one of these men he didn't know, and amidst cheers and laughter, his breaches were pulled down. Then each of those boys, including Jonathan, took turns to wield a leather paddle and viciously slap his bare behind.

There had been only one voice amongst the group of men that had protested. Walter had not known who he was, but the man was wearing the uniform of a naval officer. It was strange to think about this now. He had suppressed these memories for so long, mainly because once his beating had ended, his father had terrorised him with threats of repercussions if he ever told anyone about the events of that night. Even now, Walter realised he remained terrified of his father.

But that had not been the end of it. His mother had burst into the room and demanded to know what was going on. This caused another confrontation between his father and the naval officer. Walter had been vaguely aware that his mother was being treated disrespectfully, but at the time all he had wanted to do was escape, and he had used the commotion amongst the adults to do so.

Unfortunately, Jonathan and his friends pursued him into the grounds. Jonathan and Geoffrey Seymour had managed to catch him, and having dragged him to the fountain they forced him underwater, pinning him there until he was almost out of breath and then releasing him, only to push him under again.

Walter had been fast losing strength to hold on to his breath. He struggled against his attackers when suddenly he had been hauled out of the water to find himself rescued by the same naval officer who had spoken up for him before. Walter remembered feeling a mix of gratitude that the torture had ended, and embarrassment that his humiliation had been witnessed.

Jonathan and Geoffrey disappeared and were nowhere to be seen. So after checking with Walter that he was able to look after himself, the officer had kindly told him to get home and get dry. Thinking back now, Walter realised that from that time on, his mother had ensured that George was always nearby whenever both Walter and his brother were at the Manor at the same time.

Feeling exhausted and emotionally bruised, Walter sat in a crumpled heap in the corner of the brig and tried to puzzle out why, out of dozens of cruel and violent attacks from his brother, this was the one that had such an impact. As he turned the memories over in his mind, he kept coming back to the way his own father had humiliated him in front of his friends and associates. A deep sadness rolled over Walter as he realised that this was the incident that proved to him as a young boy that his father didn't love him.

Over the next couple of days Walter spent a lot of his time sleeping and thinking, with the only indication of the passing time being a pale beam of sunlight streaming through a porthole opposite an opening in the door of the brig. It's direction changing as the day passed until it would leave him entirely in the dark. However, in the last few hours Walter had become aware that his health was deteriorating with alarming speed. A fever set in, and he was burning up one minute, and shivering pitifully the next. Trembling, his mind no longer clear, he was suddenly shaken by a coughing fit. As it passed, Walter collapsed back against the wall and weakly pulling out a handkerchief he wiped the spittle from around his mouth. The red stain on the linen shocked him.

Unsteadily, he reached over to a crate on which a plate and cup rested. Utterly disinterested in anything edible, if indeed the hardtack on the plate could be called edible, he left the food untouched, he was only interested in the water. He had his pouch with his store of pills in his breeches pocket, and to his feverish mind this seemed to be an answer. It always made him feel better. So poping one of the pills into his mouth, he took a long swig of water and had barely swallowed it before he was racked by another fit of coughing. When it finally ended, Walter grabbed the blanket and pulling it around his shivering shoulders collapsed back onto the floor, curling up in a tight ball.

Robert Morris, the Cook who brought Walter his food and water, and Omai who had visited Walter a couple of times both expressed their concern to Walter about his health, but he assured them that he merely had a chill and would recover quickly. And so he stayed where he was, his strength fading, and his mind wandering. Walter was determined that he would stay the course of his punishment.

Chapter Eight

*O*mai had been worried about Walter for days, but the Englishman was stubborn and had refused to leave the brig before the allotted time had passed. Now looking at him in the gloom huddled under the thin covering of a blanket, Omai was relieved that he could, at last, get him out into the fresh air up on deck.

He respected Walter's determination and pride, so he allowed him to get to his own feet with minimal help, but looking into his haggard face, Omai became even more concerned that he had been. Walter was ashen grey, his eyes sunken and his skin flaky and dry. Making their way up the ladder was difficult. With Walter ahead of him so that Omai could ensure he didn't fall backwards, they eventually got up into the sunlight. But that must have been the limit of Walter's endurance because the moment he stood on the deck and raised his head, his knees buckled, and he collapsed at Omai's feet.

Erik rushed to his side, and not needing to be told, had already called out to Mr Anderson, the surgeon, who had been on the quarterdeck but was now hastily climbing down to where Walter lay prostrate on the deck.

As they got him onto his feet, the two of them managed to lower him down to the mess deck, where a couple of sailors took charge of Walter's limp body and deposited him into his hammock. In the dark, damp and hazy cabin, surrounded by the thick linen of the coffin-like bedding, it didn't take long for Walter to drift into a feverish sleep. Omai sat down beside him, wiping his face with a wet cloth, and in hushed tones, chanted an invocation to the gods.

Mr Anderson examined Walter and noted in a solemn voice that the young man was feverish. He cast a worried look at Omai, and he pointed to the blood on Walter's shirt. "This is troubling. Unfortunately, we are dealing with a severe illness." He continued to scrutinise Walter and then motioned the sailors standing by that he needed them to roll Walter over. Moving him led to Walter starting to cough, and bright red blood oozed from the corner of Walter's mouth.

It hadn't taken long for the surgeon to finish his examination. As Omai helped him reposition Walter so that he was lying in a slightly upright position, Mr Anderson looked at him thoughtfully. "Mr Omai, are you prepared to nurse your friend until his fever breaks?"

Omai had no hesitation in agreeing to care for Walter. "What do I need to do?" He asked, wondering just how sick his friend really was. "He will need to be kept cool and forced to drink whenever able. I will look in on him this evening unless you require my assistance sooner." And with that, the Surgeon turned to the cook and instructed him to prepare a thin gruel for Walter. Just as he was about to leave, Mr Anderson again cautioned him to call for help if Walter's condition worsened.

Over the next few hours, soaked with perspiration, Walter's body trembled with such force that Omai had to steady the shaking hammock to stop him from rolling out onto the deck. Walter was raving, and Omai knew that his friend was hallucinating and that this was dangerous. His friend could be taken by the fever, so he fed him sips of water and mopped his brow with cool water from a bucket that Erik kept topped up.

Since meeting Walter, Omai had been curious about this Englishman. The two had begun to share stories and experiences about things, and unlike the others, Walter treated him as an equal, not like some odd curiosity or someone inferior. It was strange being a curiosity, Omai thought. There had been, however, some benefits to it. He had been introduced to the great King George and his court, where they wanted to know as much as he could tell them of his home and the people there. And the women too were curious about him, especially in regards to sex. He and Walter had shared this interest as well, and he had found Walter's ideas about the contradictions of English society quite enlightening. He hoped he would not lose this new friend before they had been given a chance to get to know each other better.

Omai had been dozing on the floor next to Walter when he was woken by the alarm in Erik's voice. Obviously frightened into a vague consciousness by the cataclysmic nature of his hallucination, Walter had suddenly sat bolt upright in the hammock.

Omai jumped up and gently pushed Walter back onto the bedding. "Quiet, my friend, the gods are speaking to you." As Walter settled back into the hammock and quietened for a time, he smiled reassuringly at the frightened boy.

These brief moments when he was awake between bouts of dreaming and having visions lasted for only a short time. Using these moments when Walter was more settled and could be persuaded to drink, Omai managed to feed him the gruel that the cook supplied. Over the next week with Mr Anderson monitoring him closely, and Erik and Omai taking turns to tend to him, Walter began to recover.

Early one afternoon, hearing steps, Omai looked up to find the Captain and Mr Anderson making their way around the other hammocks and lockers to Walter's sickbed. As Anderson gently patted Walter's sunken cheek, his eyes fluttered open. Omai was standing on the other side of the bed, so he was able to watch the Captain's expression. There was a look of deep concern in his eyes as he surveyed Walter's physical state.

Anderson quietly pointed out the change in Walter's condition and his hope that he had now turned a corner, and the Captain nodded. "Good. I promised this boys' mother that I would look after him, and I don't want to break my word."

As if the sound of their voices had penetrated the fog of Walter's mind, he spoke in a hesitant voice. "Father?"

"No, lad." The Captain said gently. "You're on The Resolution, remember?"

Walter closed his eyes and nodded feebly, and the Surgeon placed the back of his hand on his patient's forehead. "Well, it's about time, Mr Beaumont. You've had all of us most concerned." The surgeon paused for a moment, focusing on feeling for the fever. "It does appear that the worst is over."

Captain Cook sighed with relief and looked at Omai. "I am grateful for your help and the care you have given Mr Beaumont. I will continue to leave him in your capable hands, Gentlemen."

Walter tried to speak but choked and coughed. Once he had settled back against his pillow, he turned to the Surgeon an unspoken question in the expression on his tired, thin face.

"Steady man, just rest. You have been in and out of consciousness for some time. Besides a bout of consumption, you appear to have also been a little too indulgent in God's own medicine. We found your opium, Mr Beaumont. It never does to overindulge, Sir. Please remember that for the future. You'll need rest, good food and a temperate climate." Anderson paused. "Of course, none of which you'll get aboard this ship."

Walter's sigh rasped in his throat, and another violent cough racked his body. Looking exhausted, he fell back against the pillows and looked at both of them with worry etched in the lines of his face. "Shall I recover completely, Sir?" Walter said in a wistful-sounding voice. This seemed, to Omai to still be an unanswerable question. From what the Surgeon had told him, the conditions of this ship were not favourable for Walter's recovery.

"Rest, Mr Beaumont. I will do the best I can with what I have available to me." Anderson paused and turned to the Tahitian. "Mr Omai, I'll leave you to tend to our patient's convalescence. Good Day to you both."

Over the next twenty-four hours, Walter's condition steadily improved, and he was able to leave his hammock and spend small amounts of time up on deck. Part of the quarterdeck was converted to assist his recovery, and although he wondered how much convalescence he could achieve while lying amidst the noisy and smelly animal pens, it was as good a place as any. At least he had a superb view of the ship below him. Languidly reclining in a makeshift litter, he had his journal resting on his lap while his pens and ink were on a small table beside him.

Pointing at a partially completed drawing of a canoe, Walter repeated the Tahitian word 'Va'a', struggling with the unaccustomed pronunciation. He and Omai had been engaged in an English-Tahitian conversation, and they were alone except for the livestock penned beside them. Walter decided to take this opportunity to talk about his fever dreams. They would sound quite mad to most of the other men, but somehow he felt confident that Omai would not judge him. "Omai? When I was ill... I had these strange dreams...." His voice trailed off.

"I know, Walter, I was there with you, and whatever it was I will not think you foolish."

"I saw waves and people playing in the waves, most peculiar really... There was laughter, and then there was this face... a terrible face, a man's face. No, it was more than a man, more like a god, and it emanated such power."

Walter shook his head as if to clear the disturbing vision from his mind. Suddenly he became more resolute, bracing himself against whatever threat, imagined or real, there could be. "No, it's all nonsense, just some feverish imaginings." He shrugged his shoulders as if shaking the images off. Omai shook his head firmly. "No, Walter. I do not believe that is so."

"The gods came to you when you were ill. You have seen something with great mana, great power. Like the ancestors in Kahiki, you must listen to the dreams and visions because they are trying to tell you something." Omai paused for a moment. "Perhaps you are destined to become a great ta'huna, a man of vision and visions."

On previous occasions, Omai had spoken to Walter about the priests of Tahiti and the knowledge they possessed about their world and that of the gods. He had also shared some of his own knowledge and experience gained from travelling across the Pacific Islands in voyaging canoes where he had become aware of the mystical nature of the sea.

Walter had found some of the stories so fantastic that he thought them Omai's inventions, used mainly to amuse the ladies of the court and to make him a more heroic figure in their eyes. Overcome with melancholy, Walter sighed weakly at his friend. "You appear to have a lot of faith in me, Omai, my friend. More perhaps than I have."

Walter turned back to his sketchbook and started to work on the drawing in front of him, distracting himself from any ideas and dreams that made no sense, and was just dusting off some excess charcoal from the page when John Webber joined them. Walter had come to like this man immensely. They shared an interest in the natural sciences, and although they came from different backgrounds, they shared a curiosity about Omai's home islands. In fact, Webber was obviously becoming increasingly fascinated by botany and science, and the stories that Omai had told them of the plants and animals of his native islands seemed to have caught the illustrator's imagination.

Looking at the drawing on Walter's lap, Webber, excitement in his voice invited Walter to his cabin. "I want to show you what I have been doing while you were indisposed. If you are well enough, I would value your help."

"With pleasure, Mr Webber." Looking over at his friend, Walter cocked his head, and with Omai's grinning assent, he carefully got to his feet and slowly, with deliberately cautious steps, followed Mr Webber below to his cabin.

Opening the large chest that seemed to take up most of the floor space in the snug little cabin, Webber exposed a vast variety of drawings and notes. Walter, impressed by the man's dedication as much as his skill, was able to trace much of their journey so far through this man's work. "This is truly marvellous, John!" Responding to Walter's approval with a very pleased look on his face, Webber enthused by his work spread his hands out to encompass it all as he replied.

"Yes, I have been quite busy, and to continue to be as prolific as I have been, I need your assistance, Walter. Now that you are recovered, I would be very grateful if you could start to catalogue my work and to start to select those drawings of yours that you think should be added to the overall collection."

Walter, enthused by the idea, responded that he would be only too happy to start work on it immediately. As the two men put their heads together to plan how they would begin, Walter wondered out aloud how his work would meet the excellent standard set by Webber. "I have seen enough of your work, Walter, I have no doubt that with some more training, you could easily equal my best."

A feeling of pride welled up in Walter. Until this voyage, the only other person who had ever thought his talent for drawing had some value had been his mother. Now, for the first time in his life, Walter felt like he had some purpose that extended beyond the trivial.

꒰ᆞ꒰ᆞ꒰ᆞ꒰ᆞ

A few days later, in the cluttered interior of Cook's cabin, the Captain and Bligh were working at the large table littered with charts and instruments, taking measurements, plotting waypoints and making entries in several small notebooks.

Without taking his eyes off what he was doing, Captain Cook cleared his throat. "After our stay in Tahiti, Mr Bligh, we will sail to America's north-west coast to seek a passage there."

Bligh, already aware of the Admiralties orders, wondered where Cook was going with this line of conversation. "Yes, Sir. But after the fair weather of the South Seas, I believe the men will find this a most disagreeable leg of the journey."

Cook nodded. "True enough, Mr Bligh, and they will need to be of sound mind and body."

Cook hesitated for an instant. Bligh drew breath. 'Here it is.' "Unfortunately, for those of lesser constitution, we will need to consider alternatives."

"You are thinking of Mr Beaumont, Sir?"

Captain Cook sighed heavily. "I am indeed, Mr Bligh."

He continued to work on the map, tracing the fine lines along the edge of the ruler. "It would be best if Mr Beaumont stayed in the Society Islands until such times as we can return to retrieve him."

Bligh, seeing the tension in Cook's face, was very conscious of how difficult a decision this must have been for a man who prided himself on the care he took of his crew. It was indeed not in Cook's nature to give up on anything or anyone. Yet here he was, contemplating what must be a most unpalatable, but inevitable, solution.

As Cook's decision hung in the air, the two men continued working on the charts. After a few moments, Bligh looked at the Captain.

"Would you like me to break the news to Mr Beaumont?"

Without taking his eyes off the chart, Cook shook his head. "No, Mr Bligh, I will tell him in due course."

Chapter Nine

*W*atching the island of Tongatapu looming up out of the ocean, Walter breathed deeply hoping to catch the scent of the land. He felt an excitement building in him as they neared another of these beautiful lush tropical islands and he realised that much had changed in him since he had fled England less than a year before. He had just completed a letter to his mother, and he was still mulling over its contents in his mind.

"Dear Mother, I have been struck by the similarities and differences between Omai's culture and ours. This is something both he and I have become quite fascinated with. I must confess that his people intrigue me. They are both gentle and yet capable of extreme harshness in certain circumstances. Omai informs me that they are highly political, constantly forming and changing alliances to suit their ambitions. According to Omai, politics and religion are closely intertwined. Breaking the law appears to solicit only one punishment, death. However, at the present moment, Omai is much more fascinated by my dreams than politics."

As the deck heaved with the movement of the water, Walter relished being able to lift his head into the wind and watch the scene before him. The Discovery to the starboard of them, and the white caps of the waves around the fast-approaching reef, were all part of such an incredible adventure. That he had survived great ocean storms, where waves the size of mountains could bury a ship in an instant, was a testament to the skills and courage of the men sailing this ship and once again they had brought their vessel safely to land.

Wanting to finish his letter, Walter moved to a corner of the deck where he was able to tuck himself out of the way and work on his journal. He had finally disclosed his illness to his mother but hoped that the details of what he had seen would catch her interest and distract her from worry.

Walter had seen sights on lands he could never have dreamt of, for example, the kangaroos of Van Diemen's land. A most curious creature that would propel itself forward by hopping on its sturdy hind legs. He had met different peoples, some frightened of the English, while others, like the inhabitants of New Zealand, were proud and war-like and easily matched the English in courage and ferocity when the occasion necessitated.

The natural beauty of New Zealand had struck both him and John Webber, and while Walter sketched as much as he could, John had been madly collecting and cataloguing whatever new plant or animal species he would stumble upon.

The Queen Charlotte Sounds, as Captain Cook had named them, were apparently reminiscent of the Norse lands where green mountain walls rose steeply from the deep blue of the sea, and a million bays offered anchorage to the ships. All onboard had agreed that it was indeed an explorer's paradise.

No longer the only guests on board, Walter and Omai had been joined by two native boys, Te Weherua and Te Toa of the local Tangata Whenua, the people inhabiting the Sound. Initially, the boys must have thought it a great idea to accompany the English on their voyage, but after a few weeks, they had felt great pangs of homesickness and had needed care and attention to settle into life onboard the ship.

The older boy, more of a young man really, Te Weherua, was of a mature and sober disposition, and spent most of his time around the officers, taking care to learn as much as he could. Te Toa, on the other hand, was a child with a joyful nature and a wicked sense of humour.

Knowledgeable in their many chants and dances, the boys often entertained the sailors and officers during the many long hours of the monotony of sailing across the oceans. One dance, in particular, had the sailors well amused, but Omai had reminded them that the Haka was a war dance, a challenge to the enemy, and that these boys may be amusing to watch, but when performed by large numbers of full-grown warriors bearing weapons, the dance would send chills down your spine with the knowledge that, when it ended, your life hung on a fragile thread indeed.

Williamson had been entirely wrong. These warriors would not back away from a simple musket volley. They would fight to the death, their honour and position in the tribe at stake.

Hearing the reminder, the sailors would quieten down, recalling what had happened to some of the men of the HMS Adventure. Ten had been killed by a small group of warriors, dismembered and then ritually eaten.

On their recent visit to Queen Charlotte Sound, Omai had gotten very angry with Cook for not taking revenge on the murderers when he had ample opportunity to do so. He had been at great pains to point out that the Tangata Whenua would lose respect for them, as they did not act like warriors, but more like what the natives called taurekareka, slaves who have no mana, or power. This had made the situation most precarious and would put all English at risk.

Cook had largely ignored Omai and apparently had no intention of taking his advice, which not only angered the Tahitian but also infuriated a significant number of the sailors who felt that Cook favoured the natives, while they would be severely punished for even the smallest offence.

Walter had hesitated to relay all of what he experienced in his journal, aware that it would be read, not just by his mother, but others who could use its contents for their own purposes. Over the last few months, as he had become more familiar with the crew,

Walter had been privy to their thoughts and most recently to the dissent amongst them.

Cook had been furious with what he felt were mutinous sentiments and warned all and sundry this was a most severe breach of discipline. To avoid any further deterioration in morale, Cook and his two senior officers, King and Gore, decided that the best thing to do was to leave New Zealand immediately.

Walter had been very detailed in his recording of the stories and legends that Omai had told him about this part of the world, and as he read through them on their approach to yet another island, he now had some familiarity with the traditions and religions of a vast number of the islands, but most especially about Tongatapu and Tahiti.

Now, with the problems that had caused such concern while they were in New Zealand behind them, he was once again standing by the rail watching excitedly as they came to another of these verdant islands. Walter relished the sights of the harbour of Tongatapu, the main island in the chain, and all that it implied. The many weeks at sea had been tedious, and a drag on everyone's morale and, like most, Walter was keen to stretch his legs and mind. But most importantly he was looking forward to some decent fresh meat, vegetables and fruit.

The Tongans too seemed to be excited by another visit from the English, and they had lined the beaches quite literally by the thousands. One of the things that had the most substantial impact on Walter was just how populated these islands were. The other was the physical beauty and proportions of the natives.

They were by no means small people. The average height of most of the men was six-foot, with large frames that were heavily-muscled, giving them a Herculean appearance while the women, Omai explained, were considered beautiful and much sought after as wives when they were large and corpulent. From their size alone, Walter could understand why Captain Cook was not keen to alienate these people.

Looking across the bay's crystal clear water, Walter was astounded by the sheer number of canoes of all sizes, including a sizeable number of double-hulled voyaging canoes with sixty or so crew, that were crisscrossing the bay. His attention was caught by one of these massive canoes which was more elaborately decorated than the others. *'That must be a chief's canoe.'* Walter wondered what such a man would be like. If he went by what Omai had said, then the Tu'i Tonga was powerful and very politically astute, something that was apparently essential in keeping abreast of all the various alliances and conflicts that would erupt amongst the lesser chiefs.

The two English ships had to proceed slowly as the Resolution and Discovery were less manoeuvrable than even the largest of the canoes. Walter turned to watch the officers on the quarterdeck as they navigated through the crowd of canoes and sailed across the bay. He was impressed by the way that Cook, King and Bligh worked together. Over the time that he had been on board, he had come to appreciate the level of skill it took to determine the best approach towards shore and an anchorage.

As the ship neared an appropriate spot, Cook turned to his officers with a relieved smile. "Well, Gentleman, welcome to Tonga! I want extra watches and no one, and I mean no one is to leave the ship, nor offer a trade with the natives until I say so."

The two officers snapped a salute. "Aye, aye, Sir!"

"In the meantime, let's be well prepared for the presence of the chiefs. These people stand on protocol."

As if to emphasise Cook's point, a large, well-decorated canoe pulled up beside the Resolution with all the pomp and pageantry of European royalty. Omai had joined Walter, and he explained that it was Paulaho, the Tu'i Tonga or principal Tongan chief, and his large retinue who were preparing to board the Resolution.

The chief's retainers climbed up the nets cast alongside the ship, and once on the deck they quickly brought the Tu'i's recliner on board and set it against the quarterdeck. Omai pointed out to Walter that one of the large warriors now on the Resolution had signalled those still on the Canoe, and Walter watched as a contingent of armed men climbed swiftly onto the Resolution.

Apparently, all was now ready and the chief himself, who showed astonishing agility for a man his age, climbed up to the deck and walked gracefully to his recliner. Seated and flanked by his guards and retinue Paulaho signalled for a host of gifts and goods to be brought onto the deck of the ship.

Omai leant over to Walter and quietly explained that this was the thirty-sixth Tu'i Tonga, but he was considered by many as not the true successor because he was unable to verify his lineage, an essential issue regarding the right to rule. This, according to Omai, caused considerable disharmony amongst the chiefs and the risk of civil war was always present.

Much to Walter's surprise, Paulaho was almost fluent in English. As they watched the ritual of greeting and gift exchange from the bow, there was some discussion amongst the men about where the chief could have learnt English given the reasonably limited contact he would have had with English speakers. One of the more interesting ideas offered by the men was that a deserter may have sought refuge here and taught the Tui the language.

As to his welcome of Cook, it seemed to Walter from the fulsome extravagance of his speech that he might be seeking a strong alliance with the English. It was evident from what they could overhear that Paulaho had a keen mind, and to Walter's thinking, an alliance with English would be a right way for the Principle Chief to enhance his power with the lesser chiefs. However, Omai was a little more sceptical. He thought that the Tu'i was mainly interested in the iron and guns on board the ships, and not so much an alliance with the English. He explained that it was more likely than his wanting an alliance with people who would come and go and have no continuous presence on the island.

Having completed some of the welcoming ceremonies, the ship's longboats were being prepared to take Cook, his officers and some of the crew ashore. The English would set up their own encampment so that they could be available for the inevitable ceremonial festivities and to facilitate trade, so Omai and Walter made their way to the rails to await orders as the officers organised the Marines.

The cumbersome longboats and the difficulties of launching them obviously amused Paulaho, as he turned to Cook and insisted that the Captain accompany him on his own double-hulled Canoe.

His voice was a deep rumble as he pointed out to the Captain that it would be faster and more comfortable for him to join him than to wait for the longboats.

Walter watched as Cook thanked the Principle Chief gravely and signalled Bligh to attend him. Then, turning to where Walter and the Tahitian stood observing the disembarkation, Cook ordered them to join his retinue. Walter was thrilled to be involved, and as he and Omai clambered down to the chief's Canoe, he saw that John Webber was already ensconced in one of the longboats, clutching his large satchel and easel. Webber nodded to Walter, a quick dip of the head and smiled. "See you on land, Mr Beaumont."

The trip to the beach took little time, and as the boats slid up onto the sand, the English found themselves greeted with enthusiasm by the gathered crowd of natives. But despite the obvious welcome that was being extended to them, Walter could feel tension amongst some of the Marines, especially Williamson who looked extremely uncomfortable. As they disembarked, Williamson approached the Captain and asked if he should have the Marines stand at the ready, but Cook dismissed his concern and told him it was unnecessary.

From Walter's perspective, there was no sign of any hostility amongst the Islander's who dispersed reasonably quickly. Omai told him that they were going to prepare for the welcome feast planned for that evening, and so there was no sensible reason for Williamson to be so anxious, but despite the lack of any sign of threat the officer was tightly strung and alert. So taking his friend Omai at his word Walter, like the rest of the crew, bent his efforts to setting up their temporary camp.

Over the next few days, the crew had settled into a routine of watches and shore leave while Walter, along with John Webber, had found himself busy collecting specimens of the local flora, and the chronicling of their visit to the island with drawings and notes. He was aware that the Islander's light-fingered disposition had led the officers to organise a very tight schedule of surveillance. Thefts had become more frequent as the islanders became more emboldened, and Walter remembered what Omai had said about Paulaho's interests being more to do with metal than alliances. It seemed that the lesser chiefs were no different.

Captain Cook had become increasingly frustrated by the failure of his orders to prevent the crew from trading metal with the Islander's, and his punishments for any infringement of his rules were severe. Therefore the Officers were kept busy keeping order amongst an increasingly angry crew.

It did have the positive effect of making the Islander's wary of Cook, and this appeared to make them hesitant to take advantage of the English, but ultimately something needed to be done to alleviate the deepening rifts between some of the lesser chiefs and the English.

Apparently, Paulaho had decided that a spectacular feast would sooth and settle frayed tempers, and Walter was amazed at how quickly it was organised. Scheduled for the early evening at sunset, a distant storm provided a spectacular backdrop of light and sound, as one by one, and in groups of varying sizes, the islanders filled the vast square. Walter estimated that at least several thousand natives had assembled in the extensive arena in an incredibly orderly fashion, each seeming to know precisely where they should be.

The feast began with a traditional ceremony of drinking kava that was chewed and then mixed into the water by young girls. Walter had initially decided that despite its alleged euphoric effects it was most definitely an acquired taste. It had the flavour and texture of gritty, muddy water that bit his tongue, a little like pepper. However, after a few minutes his mouth had become numb, and a calm warm feeling had spread through his body. Suddenly, Walter decided that most of the conflicts that were causing so much anger amongst the islanders and the English were really quite humorous, and any concerns he may have had now seemed less burdensome. No wonder Paulaho thought this a good idea, he mused, as he slid into a wonderfully relaxed and familiar emotional state.

Meanwhile, sitting on an elevated platform in a prominent place in the arena, Paulaho and Cook were engaged in a lighthearted conversation, facilitated by the occasional assistance of Omai. Walter could hear what was going on from where he was, and almost giggled when he heard Paulaho's request that the Marines put on a display. Walter had watched them before, and he had no illusions that they were up to the task of impressing anyone.

He noted that King was also somewhat alarmed by the idea when Cook assented to the request. Walter watched at the officer had a private word with the Captain, after which King left Cook's side and disappeared into the dark. Within minutes the faint Sound of a military corps could be heard, and everyone's attention was drawn to the edge of the arena, where the Marines were preparing their display. In the vast space, the sounds of fife and drums were virtually lost.

Just as Walter had suspected, from the moment the Marines started, it was evident that they were not going to demonstrate any superiority in either their military, or musical skills. Led by their commanding officer, Molesworth Phillips, the troops lacked any of the discipline and precision that was expected by Cook and the other officers. In a matter of minutes, the soldiers demonstrated that they could drop rifles, trip on the grass, and fall completely out of step with one another. What was worse was the total lack of rhythm by the young drummer who desperately tried to keep time with the fife player. When neither knew where the other was in the military composition, they just chose to play as soloists, ignoring any attempt at a duet.

Listening in on Bligh's conversation with Cook, Walter was interested that despite Cooks acknowledgment of what Bligh had called their appalling display, he did not end it immediately. In fact, Cook told Bligh that they shouldn't act rashly. "Let them think it's all in fun." The Captain said in a bemused tone.

As the troop finally finished their sparse routine, they scampered back to the edges of the square to be immediately replaced by a large number of Tongan warriors. Dressed in tapa, a cloth made from the bark of the mulberry, and wielding paddle-shaped clubs, their carefully choreographed and precise military display was performed to an amazed European audience. Walter thought that it was more than fair to say that neither the officers nor the sailors could have seen a better performance anywhere in the so-called civilised world.

As the warriors withdrew from the centre of the square to the applause and delight of the other islanders, pairs of other warriors now took their place and began to compete in numerous boxing matches. Much to Walter's amazement, Williamson, who was severely intoxicated by the kava and some of the ship's rum, leapt unsteadily to his feet and challenged one of the unusually large Tongans. "Come, man, let's get to it."

The Tongan, unable to understand Williamson's slurred challenge, shot a puzzled look to the Tu'i, who in turn lent towards Cook. "What is your wish, Tuté?"

Cook looked down at Williamson and with a neutral expression responded;" With your permission, Tu'i, let them begin."

Paulaho seemed puzzled and hesitated, looking closely at Cook, but the English Captain nodded affirmatively, and so the Principle Chief turned to the warrior and signalled him to begin.

Walter was surprised that Cook would place one of his officers in such jeopardy. The outcome of this bout was only too predictable, and he wondered at Cook's motive. Was this was some indirect form of punishment? The Tongan stood at least six and a half feet tall and probably weighed over three hundred and fifty pounds. That compared to Williamson's five and a half feet, and maybe one hundred and seventy-five pounds gave the Tongan enough of an advantage, but the third officer's inebriation basically ensured that he was in for a terrible thrashing. He knew he should be feeling some sort of sympathy for the man, but Walter couldn't help experiencing some vicarious pleasure from the knowledge that Williamson was going to get the beating he so richly deserved.

To begin with, Williamson landed a few solid blows on the Tongan, who appeared impervious to the Englishman's punches. In turn, however, it only took one clean punch to Williamson's chest, and the officer fell to the ground. Winded and in pain, Williamson rolled around on the ground, trying to catch his breath. The bout was over, and as he continued to roll around, some of the Marines rushed over to assist him back to his matt where he could recover.

Even as he felt the warm glow of revenge, Walter could see that this demonstration of weakness, added to the abysmal performance of the marines was a dangerous turn of events. The crowd was overjoyed at the clear demonstration of their collective physical superiority, and they cheered their champion loudly.

Paulaho, too, despite trying to maintain a more regal reserve, could not hold back a broad smile. Letting the cheering continue for a few moments, he signalled the crowd to settle down. Then leaning over to Cook, he proved himself to be a true diplomat. "Tuté," referring to Cook with the local adaptation of his name. "Isn't it a pleasure to see our people enjoy themselves with such a spirit and there be no harm in it?"

Walter couldn't hear Cook's reply, but a sense of uneasiness forced him to pull himself together and gather his thoughts. It occurred to him that they were very vulnerable here on this island.

It was as he was thinking this through that he was caught by Omai's gaze. He appeared to be trying to surreptitiously signal Walter to join him, so Walter casually got to his feet keeping his expression neutral, and wandered over to find out what the Tahitian wanted.

Quietly greeting each other, Walter followed Omai to a less crowded part of the square. Having found a quiet spot where they would not be overheard, Omai turned to look at him and spoke, the expression on his face clearly showing the Islander's misgivings. "Walter, you need to know that there is danger here. Not everyone is happy to have us as guests."

Walter's forebodings appeared confirmed. "I, too, have sensed a tension."

"This is not just a suspicion I have, Walter. I overheard talk that there are some here, who would like us killed so they can take the ships and everything on them. . The question is not whether they intend to do this, they just can not agree when this should be done."

Walter was startled to have his fears so definitively confirmed, but wanting to appear as if he and Omai were just having a normal conversation, he simply nodded agreeably as he responded. , "We must warn the Captain and the others now before it's too late."

Omai, his eyes scanning the area around where they were standing, quietly muttered. "Let's do this quietly so as not to raise any suspicions. Walter, can you let Mr King know immediately, while I try and find out more about this plot?"

The two friends parted each with their own task. Walter, trying to maintain as casual a demeanour as possible under the circumstances, strolled over to the first officer and standing beside him as if he was merely interested in watching the festivities he whispered. "Mr King, I have just had words with Omai who has overheard talk that suggests that we are in certain danger. Some of the Tongans talk of killing us and taking the ships."

King was silent for a minute and then, shook his head. His expression remained impassive as he responded that the Tu'i was a friend to the English and would protect them.

"That may be quite true, Mr King, but he may not be in a position to assist us. It seems that we are still safe because the chiefs, thankfully, can not agree on a time to execute their plan."

"I'm not sure the Captain will act on this unsubstantiated allegation. He is fond of Paulaho, and you know his views on the Islanders. Unless we have proof..."

"Mr King, I beg you, if nothing else we must let Captain Clerke on the Discovery know of the potential peril to the ships. I do not believe that Omai would have said anything about this if he did not believe it to be a real threat. I feel that we must persuade our Captain in the strongest terms." He hesitated before continuing. "Please, ask yourself why they would want to see our soldiers in action, if not to assess our strengths and weaknesses. We have already given them enough reason to think us weak."

Walter's argument had the desired effect. King's expression hardened, and he appeared to be taking Walter more seriously. He certainly could not argue with the facts of what had happened at the festival in front of everyone." Damn it, Mr Beaumont, you are right. It was a dreadful showing, both the Marines and Mr Williamson's performance could only demonstrate to them that we are anything but a threat. Even if that were not the case, they could just overwhelm us through sheer numbers." King took a deep breath and then obviously having made a decision he continued. "Stay here so that we do not attract any attention. I will speak with the Captain and hopefully persuade him that we need to take precautions. All going well, be ready to make your way to the boats."

Walter watched as King managed to get Cook's attention and then quietly motion to the Captain to join him away from the Tu'i. The conversation was brief, and Walter watched as the Captain returned to the dais and spoke to the Principle Chief. He then appeared to take his leave of Paulaho before sauntering casually towards the tent that he had used as his office, which was in the semi-dark, apart from the torches and fires.

He looked across at Walter and called him over to his side, which reassured Walter that King had filled Cook in on what had transpired before he had hurried off into the dark. As Walter joined the Captain, he was impressed by his calm demeanour. Cook did not mince his words. "We will take our leave of Paulaho and make our way to the ships. Mr King has some entertainment organised, and so if you would kindly accompany me, we will try to ensure that this looks completely within keeping of our own protocols, and give no indication that we are aware of the danger that besets us."

As they made their way to the beach, Cook told Walter that he had informed Paulaho that he and his officers were needed on board. Cook hoped that he had managed to thank the man for his hospitality and at the same time allay any suspicions that any problems he needed to deal with involved the Islanders. He was able to frame their departure from the festivities as being purely a matter of shipboard demands.

As they departed the rostrum of matts, having made their farewells, Cook raised his hand, and within a couple of minutes, fireworks exploded over the beach. Walter having been aware that Cook had planned to give the chief and his people a gift of fireworks before their departure so he was not surprised that this was the entertainment that King had been sent to organise.

Despite their circumstances, Walter was still awed at the different colours that exploded in the sky, and the beautiful patterns of the explosions as they lit up the beach. He felt his own heart swell at the beauty of the display even though in reality, they were fleeing for their lives.

The next morning, Walter watched from the Resolution as the sailors efficiently broke camp and loaded the ships with the supplies they had already collected. Cook, accompanied by what Walter thought was quite a small retinue given the situation, took his leave from Paulaho, their departure explained as merely being a part of their overall plan for the journey north.

With the Resolution and the Discovery safely back out on the high seas, Captain Cook called his officers to his stateroom. Walter had been surprised to be invited to join them, but Mr Bligh had informed him that the Captain had insisted that he had proved himself to be part of the crew.

As the ships made their way across the Pacific Ocean, Cook convened the meeting of his officers to discuss the previous nights' events and to talk about how they could avoid being captured by the political realities of the cultures they were bound to come across in their journey.

In the midst of the discussion, it became clear that Williamson was angry that they had withdrawn hastily back to the ship and had left the island. King tried to reason with him.

"Mr Williamson, there was no reason to assume that we could have successfully defended ourselves."

"Sir, with respect, now there is absolutely no doubt in the mind of the savage that we are weak and incapable of defending ourselves. We'll suffer the consequences of this, mark my words. We should have shown them how we deal with heathens who wish us harm. The only thing they understand is a firm hand and the sound of the musket."

Walter couldn't restrain himself. "Just like children, eh, Mr Williamson? We've spoilt them, now we must discipline them?"

"Damn you, Mr Beaumont. What right have you to speak in this assembly? You are nothing but a passenger..."

Captain Cook cut Williamson off. "Mr Williamson, mind yourself. Mr Beaumont has every right to his opinion as was clearly demonstrated last night."

Walter, appreciating Cook's support, nodded. "Thank you, Sir."

He leant back in the chair, perhaps a little pompously, and said. "I think it is a mistake to regard the natives as savages. In my convalescence, I have had the opportunity to learn much from Omai about the customs and politics of these people. It is my view, that to underestimate them, is to put ourselves gravely at risk."

Williamson looked like he was going to have some sort of seizure as he spluttered that it was utter nonsense to claim that illiterate savages were political. This seemed to irritate the Captain who reminded Williamson that illiterate or not they were no fools and would gain a great deal from a prize such as the European ships.

Walter watched as the officers discussed the issue with Williamson, who demanded that they agree with him that they should be more forceful. That this would have gained the Islander's respect. At this point, Mr King turned to the Williamson and in a thoughtful voice offered his opinion.

"You do have a tendency to be too aggressive, Mr Williamson. I think we need to be careful with the use of force in these situations. We don't want to set things in motion that will be clearly to our detriment."

There were some nods of agreement around the table and Walter felt that he was vindicated, but the Captain appeared to choose to be conciliatory and suggested that they not dismiss Williamson's ideas entirely. Walter, undaunted, continued with his argument. "With respect gentlemen, it is we who are the intruders and should be thankful for their hospitality. We must rely on them, whether we like it or not."

Williamson's reaction was predictable. "So when one of ours steals, he receives the cat-o'-nine tails, but we reward the savages with more gifts?"

Cook reacted sharply. "Mr Williamson, are you suggesting that I am not proceeding in our best interest?"

Walter, sensing that the discussion had changed tack and was now fraught with problems that could lead nowhere other than more conflict, wanted to find a way out. He realised that Williamson was never going to be persuaded to take a reasonable position on the issue of the natives, but he also knew that there was some truth to his concerns about the crew.

"Gentlemen, these are important matters that need more thought and discussion. I am simply expressing my personal point of view and am grateful for your attention, however, I must beg to be excused as I am still convalescing and feel the need of some rest."

Cook, obviously pleased with the distraction, turned to Walter. "By all means Mr Beaumont, at your leisure."

Walter got up and left the table. On the way out of the cabin, it occurred to him that he still faced further altercations with Williamson. Like a volcano, their relationship was destined to erupt at some point.

During the following weeks at sea, the men returned to the monotony of their respective duties. Walter, too, had fallen into a pattern of sorts, sketching from time to time, writing letters, helping Webber with his work and then devoting himself to learning Tahitian with Omai, who was only too happy to continue to teach him.

Amongst it all, he had enough time to frequently reflect on what a strange turn his life had taken and how, despite the differences between this small community at sea and the community at home, he still had that persistent feeling that he did not quite fit in. A fact that Williamson relished in doggedly pointing out to him. It was odd, Walter thought, that even in this remotest corner he had not escaped an adversary like his brother, and he wondered if he was always going to be subjected to the Jonathan's of the world.

As he let his mind drift from Jonathan to the Captain, he was puzzled by the contradictions in Cook's behaviour. On the one hand, at times with the crew and while on Tonga with the Islanders, the Captain had displayed a cruel streak that was, in one officer's words, 'quite unbecoming of a European'. Yet, on the other hand, Cook was frequently in discussion with Anderson regarding his inability to stem the crews' sexual behaviour, thus leaving the terrible legacy of venereal disease wherever they went in the Pacific. This showed a humanitarian concern that confused Walter.

As always with him, these moments of reflection created a sense of loss and homesickness for the people he loved. To be able to speak with his mother or Edward would have been most comforting. And what would his father make of him now, sitting on the quarter-deck of a Whitby collier, converted to sail the seven seas? Master Walter Beaumont, mariner. It had a nice ring to it he felt, even if the reality was that he was here under duress and not by choice.

Chapter Ten

'*Dear Mother,*
It is the 23rd of August 1777, and we have finally arrived in the Society Islands. If there is a paradise on earth, then it must be here. The natives in these Islands are prosperous and many. I am always surprised by the size of the communities. Beauty is evident and in abundance everywhere. The people are well proportioned and fine-featured, and the flora and fauna are prolific and exquisite.

Yet even here, we face some uncertainties. The Captain is becoming more and more concerned about the pilfering and stealing that the Islanders indulge in. It puts us in an awkward position as the Islanders themselves do not have the same belief in the wrongness of what they are doing. And after our experience in Tongatapu, Captain Cook seems to be undecided about how to approach the problem if we encounter it here.

Another problem that may be of even more significant concern is that the Captain himself appears to be ill. Of late he is prone to spending more and more time alone in his cabin, and when he is amongst the men, he seems to be less involved than he was with the details of running the ship.

This has allowed ill-temper to develop amongst some of the crew. Indeed, matters deteriorated to the point where tempers flared and Mr Molesworth Phillips and the horrid third officer, Mr Williamson, went on shore to fight a duel with Pistols. When after one or two rounds, neither of the men were wounded, the Seconds were able to interfere and end the affair. I genuinely believe that the crew would have rejoiced if Mr Williamson had perished."

Walter stopped writing and looked about him. They were established in a camp at Point Venus near a place called Matavai Bay, a short distance from the nearest village and they had eaten their evening meal under a spectacular sunset. Enticing sounds of exotic rhythms and chants from a nearby village had everyone finish their dinner quickly, and the camp had emptied of all those not on duty.

Walter was now alone with his thoughts. He felt a little weary and somewhat melancholic as he sat in what most of the sailors described as a paradise that simply lacked immortality. Thinking about the Captain, and the possibility that he was ill, reminded Walter of his own close brush with death from Consumption. Over the last few weeks, it became known that Captain Clerke had also developed the disease and was becoming increasingly unwell.

Walter, having spoken at length with Dr Anderson, knew that he was not free of the illness. Consumption could slowly drain him of his life over an unspecified period and the idea that his life could be brief, had been on his mind a great deal. Walter knew death was inevitable, and when he reflected on the manner of his death, he couldn't help but hope it would be quick, but his illness had led him to a contemplation of the meaning of life, and more to the point, the meaning of his life.

Shaking his head to clear it, Walter deliberately turned away from his brooding mood to focus on more pleasant memories that he could record in his journal. Thinking back to when the two ships had arrived in Matavai Bay, Walter decided that he would try to recreate the sight in a drawing in the morning when he had some light, but for now, he was happy just to sit here in the warm evening air and reflect on the last few days.

The Resolution and Discovery had been greeted by a fleet of canoes of all sizes, some of them so large they could accommodate at least one hundred paddlers. He remembered clearly that there was no randomness to the pattern of the positioning of the canoes, they were clearly defined naval formations. He, along with the officers and the Captain had been able to observe the bay from the vantage point of the quarterdeck, and he had not been the only one that had been impressed.

In fact, it wasn't only Williamson who had noted that there was a certain war-like posturing in the formation and numbers of craft in the water. Bligh had counted three hundred and thirty double canoes fully manned and equipped. But the Captain, who had been to Tahiti before, assured them that they were friendly and that this was not a display of threat, but of welcome.

Bligh had been particularly interested in the large canoes, the double-hulled canoes that carried sixty to a hundred warriors. These vessels could be seen cutting across the water at high speed and demonstrated manoeuvrability that astounded the English. Cook had informed them that the Islanders made them with asymmetrical hulls, something that had them all puzzled. Bligh had argued that there must be some advantage or other in such an odd design, and watching the canoes cut through the water, Walter had thought that if nothing else, it could be for speed.

The spectacle in the bay had taken Walter's breath away. It had been a splendid sight. The Captain however, had been more concerned with the upcoming protocols than the beauty of the anchorage, and had repeatedly insisted on reminding them that the Islanders were their friends, and were to be treated with care and respect.

Then suddenly, a collective shout had reverberated across the water, interspersed with the drone of numerous conch shells. One of the largest canoes had broken rank and come flying towards the Resolution at high speed. Walter had been shocked to see that any vessel too slow to get out of the large canoes way, was just run over. Omai, who had joined them, was unconcerned, and had told them that everyone could swim, and that they had been in the way of the High Chief who was now coming to welcome the English.

Omai had then pointed out the man sitting on a massive chair on the canoe's platform, and identified him as Tu, the Ari'i Nui, the high chief of Tahiti, surrounded by a number of his retainers and warriors. He was a tall, robust man with a bright face. The top of his body was bare, and large tattoos around his waist and thighs were clearly visible. A huge feathered crown sat on his head, while around his neck was a beautifully crafted collar of shells and feathers. Across his shoulders, a long white cape had been slung, defining his regal appearance even more.

Omai had explained to Walter that Tu would see the arrival of the English as very fortuitous. Apparently, several political factions had been vying for power before he had left for England, and Omai saw no reason why this would have changed. Tu's friendship with Cook and the opportunities it offered the Tahitian's would give him an advantage and Omai was sure that Tu was very well aware of this.

It had turned out that this was precisely as Omai speculated. After speaking with Tu, Omai had told Walter that Tu was hoping that his relationship with Cook would shift the balance of power in his favour, and these issues could, therefore, be resolved without bloodshed.

Despite prospering in some ways in the last few years, the Islands had suffered significantly from the various outbreaks of civil wars. This was further complicated by the recurrence of small epidemics that had plagued Tu's people since their contact with the English. Some of the priests had suggested that there may be a relationship between the two, but apparently, Tu had been at great pains to quell any suspicion of a connection. He felt strongly that trade and relationships with the Popa'a, the foreigners, would, in the long-term prove invaluable to his people.

To demonstrate their relationship publicly, Tu and Cook had exchanged names, a Tahitian ritual cementing a vital friendship. The two had become Tai'o, and when they had greeted each other onboard the Resolution, Cook and Tu had greeted each other with the traditional touching of foreheads and noses and breathing in.

They had presented each other with gifts, Cook presenting Tu with a beautiful linen suit, a gold-laced hat, and a Tongan red feather headdress, highly prized gifts amongst the Islanders. In response, Tu signalled for his gifts to be brought aboard and much to the delight of the crew, he presented the Captain with fresh food, pigs, vegetables, coconuts and fresh water.

With the immediate formalities out of the way, and leaving Mr King in charge of the ship, Cook had joined Tu on board his canoe and headed to the beach where thousands of Tahitians had sung and chanted the traditional welcomes. There had been so many voices chanting that Walter could clearly make out the words as they carried across the water, and even the sudden rain squall coming in from the deep green mountains, shrouded in clouds, could not muffle the sound.

As he had stood there on the deck, looking out over the lagoon, watching the seemingly endless procession of canoes, Walter was especially struck by the vision of the girls and women. All the accounts he had heard from the sailors had been accurate, and not merely a reaction to being at sea too long. The women were as beautiful as they had described. Fine-featured with long, black hair, often reaching their waists and below, and with the most pleasing physiques, they wore adornments of ferns on the top of their heads and around their wrists and ankles, and their oiled dark skin shone in the light. Since most of them wore little, if any clothing, Walter could see that the oil was applied to their whole bodies. Even if, as some did, they wore some tapa wrap-around, most had discarded their garments as they came close to the ship, welcoming the men in a most alluring and uninhibited manner.

Even now, as Walter thought about that sight, lust fired his groin. He and Omai had watched those beautiful girls, both very aware that they had been at sea for a very long time. They had had an animated discussion about the Captain's orders for the men to resist this particular temptation, and how Omai thought they could circumvent those orders.

Still laughing as they had started to disembark, Omai became utterly distracted by a particularly beautiful girl paddling her canoe close to the ship. Omai called out and waved excitedly. Naked, except for ferns on her head, a necklace of shells and a string of beads around her waist, Walter watched as she waved back vigorously enough for her ample breasts to shake from side to side.

Omai turned and grinned at Walter. "Come, my friend, I want you to meet my sister, Vaitea!" He rapidly disrobed and then, near-naked himself, leapt off the ship into the glassy green water of the bay, and surfacing, he had quickly swum to his sister's canoe and they had greeted each other with obvious joy, before he took the paddle from her and brought the canoe to the side of the ship.

It took all of Walter's courage to climb down the ship's netting. When he got close to the waterline, he knew he had to make himself step into that canoe. His fear must have been written all over his face because Omai laughingly informed Vaitea that Walter was afraid of water.

The tiny craft rocked, as Walter barely managed to seat himself. He smiled as politely as he could, given the way the two of them were joking at his expense. Walter had learnt enough of the Tahitian language from Omai to understand some of what they had said, however, he was far more interested in getting onto dry land than chatting, even to such a gorgeous creature as Vaitea.

Omai finally stopped laughing, and the brother and sister took up their paddles and started for the shore. Walter only breathed easily again when Omai beached the canoe, and he could rather inelegantly clamber out of it onto the sand.

By the time they arrived, the welcoming feast was in full swing. To the side of the vast square, Walter saw a group of men and boys beating a variety of different types of drums, creating an intoxicating rhythm. As the three of them pushed their way through the crowd of villagers, Walter saw another group of young girls and boys dancing sensually to the music of those drums.

Speechless from the sight of so many naked and near-naked bodies, Walter merely followed his friend, while Vaitea hooked her arm into his. The sweet scent of frangipani and a hint of coconut oil drew Walter's attention to the slightly built girl on his arm. Looking down at her, he couldn't resist running his hand along the length of her back and across her shapely backside.

But instead of affront, Walter was met by her pretty face looking up at him, her dark eyes full of mischief as she winked at him. Walter's hand spoke a universal language that needed no words to interpret. Vaitea knew that he found her alluring, and she responded with an immediacy that lacked any guile or coquettishness.

Standing on her toes, Vaitea kissed Walter, her tongue eagerly exploring his mouth, while her hands sought his crutch. Finding their target, she squeezed gently and then pulled him into the group of dancers. She quickly joined in with the other girls to gyrate her naked hips to the clacking rhythm of the wooden drums in a way that promptly left Walter breathless. So absorbed was he by all the sensuousness around him, that he was barely aware of the people clapping and cheering them on.

The boys, Walter quickly discerned, were expected to shake their knees, while the girls gyrated their hips in a way that made the grass skirts some of them wore, cascade in waves around their legs. His own initial attempts at the dance proved to be more amusing than sensual, but despite being slightly embarrassed, Walter persisted, mainly to stay close to Vaitea.

Omai, standing slightly to the side of the enthusiastic audience, had laughingly waved Walter on, telling him to enjoy himself before disappearing into the crowd. Walter heard later that Omai had reacquainted himself with some of the girls he had left behind when he had sailed to England.

Now, thinking about Vaitea, Walter chided himself for his earlier melancholy. After all, his welcome to the island had been truly spectacular. But on reflection, he decided that he would leave specific details out of his journal.

Chapter Eleven

*A*lthough the Tahitians initially made Omai most welcome, within a short period, it became apparent to Walter, that while he was away, Omai had lost considerable respect and support in the local community. Walter was able, with time, to determine that this support from the community was essential because he was not of the Ari'i, the ruling class, many of whom were jealous of his friendship with Cook and the officers of the Resolution.

Some were contemptuous of Omai's lack of influence on Cook. He had failed to secure support from the English for the ruling faction in their attempts to secure power. In their opinion, this only reinforced Omai's and his family's position as political refugees of no influence.

Walter watched as Omai try to compensate for this lack of acceptance with extravagant generosity. His strategy worked, but only to a point, and he eventually spent most of his time with the English. And so, on a lovely warm day, Omai and Walter joined Cook and Bligh on an exploratory journey around some of the coastline. Cook was, of course, focused on mapping the contours of the bay, while Walter was there to sketch the land formations.

Having found a land spit that was sheltered from the light wind, they had taken a break, and while the Captain and the crew rested, Walter set himself up on a tree stump to sketch the lush scenery that surrounded them.

Looking out to sea, he noticed that the men were watching several Tahitians in outrigger canoes rounding the point. They rapidly approached the reef where the waves were breaking towards the shore, then ceased paddling, and it seemed to Walter that they were looking for something. After a minute or so, one of the men started to strike out vigorously and paddled quickly into the rising swell.

"What are they doing?" Walter enquired of Omai. The Islander had been talking to Bligh but now, like all of the others he was watching the Tahitian's out at the reef. Before Omai could answer Walter, the Islander had propelled the canoe with sufficient speed into the swell for it to begin to glide on the wave of its own accord.

"Did you see that?" Walter exclaimed excitedly. The Englishmen were utterly engrossed by the unusual activity on the water, which Bligh likened the manoeuvre of a longboat coming into shore, but instead of ploughing through the waves, they rode their canoes on top of them. They were all fascinated as they watched another native launch into the swell.

Walter looked back to Omai, wanting to understand why the Islanders were behaving in a way that seemed to have no practical purpose. Omai's answer to his question that they were just catching waves made no sense to Walter, or the other men for that matter. The Captain wondered out loud if there was some sort of ritual involved. This made Omai laugh heartily. "No my friends we like to ride waves. It's our way to enjoy the ocean."

The idea of enjoying the ocean as a playground had been raised by Omai before, but Walter never quite understood what he meant, and Omai had never really alluded to anything other than swimming and canoeing. What they had just seen, added an entirely new dimension for Walter.

"Living so close to the sea, we have learnt to harness its energy. Knowing the sea, she allows you to ride her current, as well as her waves, and there are many different ways to ride them. For me, it is

how I feel the true joy of living." Omai continued as he looked long-
ingly out to sea. "This is what I missed in your land."

Walter wasn't the only one who was intrigued by the Islanders
behaviour. Some of them had now beached their canoes further up
the spit, and taken flat wooden boards out to the reef where the
waves were breaking, in an orderly pattern one after the other. Lying
prone on the boards, and much to their obvious delight, they repeatedly caught any wave that they could to ride to shore.

The English watched this fantastic sight until eventually, after
several trips out to the reef, the Islanders retrieved their canoes and
paddled back around the point and out of sight. Turning to the rest
of them, the Captain broke the silence. "Well, Gentlemen, I think
witnessing such an intriguing spectacle was ample reward for our
exploration of this part of the island. Now I believe it is time to
return to camp." And with that observation, Cook got up and
brushed the sand from his trousers. As they headed back to camp
Cook, obviously having been thinking about the way the Islanders
had enjoyed themselves, made another announcement.

"Gentleman, personally I am of the view that tomorrow shall be
a day of leisure. What say you to that?"

The men were delighted and with Bligh's encouragement
cheered the Captain, their voices filled with pleasure as they
chatted to each other about how they would spend their free time.
Since the men rarely had any time away from their duties, this
gesture of the Captains would be much appreciated by all of the
crew. Walter knew from the Officers that Cook was keenly aware of
the poor morale that had developed on Tonga, and that he had
been looking for an opportunity to improve the men's flagging spirits. It seemed to Walter that he had found an excellent way to do
this.

Back in the camp, Walter, Omai and the officers settled down
for the evening meal and chatted amiably about the day. Unlike
shipboard fare, the meal consisted of an abundant amount of fresh
produce and Walter thoroughly enjoyed the variety of vegetables
and the fish. He had found it increasingly difficult to make himself
eat the rations on board, but now that he had an illness hanging

over his head, and aware of the healthful benefits of good food, he ate heartily.

The next morning, having slept well, Walter was just stirring in the early dawn when Omai quietly crawled into his tent. "Psst, Walter, come, I want to show you something."

Walter, fully awake now looked through the dim light at his friend. "Omai, what are you doing here? And show me what?"

Omai grinned. "Enough questions! Come and see."

Knowing Omai's fondness for intrigue, Walter knew he was not going to get any more information out of his friend, so he heaved himself out of his cot and quickly started to dress. Automatically going to pull on his jacket and boots, he was stopped by Omai taking them off him and throwing them on the cot. "You won't need those." He said cryptically. Walter, his curiosity heightened even further, followed Omai as they quietly made their way through the sleeping camp.

Walter was relieved that he didn't have to wear the heavy coat and the heavy boots that Cook insisted they all wear while onboard the ship, as befitting their social position as officers and gentlemen. He felt a lot more comfortable in his breeches and shirt as he followed Omai down to the beach, however as Omai commandeered a canoe and gestured for Walter to get into it, his apprehension about the water took hold. "You didn't tell me we'd be travelling in this pint-sized piece of wood."

"Oh come, Walter! You have been in canoes just like this one before. Just get in." Omai said with a trace of laughter in his voice.

Knowing he was being foolish, given that the lagoon was not deep and Omai was with him, Walter climbed into the canoe and gripped the rails as his friend pushed them out from the beach. With both of them settled in, Omai started to paddle towards the edge of the reef. As they got closer, Walter could see the waves breaking on the coral of the reef, wash over it and continue into the lagoon. He was apprehensive and could feel the movement of the water under the wooden hull. It was an odd sensation even after having been on a ship at sea for as long as he had.

The sound of the surf breaking on the reef thundered towards them. Uneasy and silently questioning Omai's sanity, Walter shouted, "Omai, take care! You'll swamp the boat!" But there was no reply from the Tahitian.

During the long, dull legs of the voyage, Walter and Omai had gotten to know each other's strengths and weakness and Walter had confided in his Tahitian friend that his fear of water stemmed from a particular incident when he was eight years old. Omai had been understanding to a degree but had always maintained that Walter should challenge his fear and not give in to it.

As the canoe rocked in the choppy water created by the waves, Walter was inundated with disturbing memories. Jonathan and his friends pretending that they wanted him in their secret society, enticing him to the lake on the estate. He could almost feel the cold of that bleak day, when standing in freezing knee deep water he had been taunted to launch himself out into the terrifying black depths, pitted by raindrops and swirling mist.

They had known he was frightened and that just made them push him all the more, egging him on. He could still hear them. "Come on, Walter! We haven't got all day! We are all getting wet!" Except for Edward, the boys had all laughed and chimed in, goading him.

His brother knew that Walter couldn't swim and he had done nothing to stop Geoffrey Seymour from pushing him in. He had slid beneath the surface, unable to breathe and desperate to find his footing on the slippery mud. Now, despite it being a memory, Walter could still feel the cold black water suck him down to the bottom.

Terror mounted, and he struggled to pull himself back into the present. He managed to calm himself enough to look across the glistening water of the lagoon. It was an island paradise, and he knew intuitively that Omai was right. The threats and taunts that he endured throughout his childhood at the hands of his brother were in the past. Walter did need to challenge his fear, and to do that he needed to remember the entire horrible day at that lake.

Up until now, Walter had always shied away from remembering the details, but now he willed himself to remember Jonathan calling him a dismal rat and a coward. He watched himself as a child being trapped by his tormentors as he stood in that cold water, trying not to cry, and knowing that he had no choice. Even if he refused, he would have been forced into the water, and so he had been, by Geoffrey.

Looking back now as a grown man, Walter was appalled at the cruelty of Jonathan and his friends. Turning it over in his mind, he remembered what Edward had told him about what was happening on the shore while he was basically drowning in that lake. The complete lack of concern by any of the boys that he might die had probably been the hardest thing for him to accept. Only Edward had cared, and Walter had tied his hands by making him promise not to help him when Jonathan had first proposed the challenge. But finally, seeing that Walter's own brother would let him die, Edward had rescued him.

They had both been threatened by Jonathan that if they ever told Lady Beaumont, they would regret it, and given the callous disregard for his safety that Jonathan had just shown to all of them, they had both believed his threats were real. It now occurred to Walter that it was inevitable that he was fearful of water after having almost drowned.

As the sound of the ocean pulled Walter back to the present, he realised that Omai had paddled out behind the breaking waves and around the point to another cove. As the Islander swung the outrigger around to point towards land, fear threatened to over-whelm him. It struck Walter that he was at the mercy of a crazy Islander, who was telling him to relax, while he aimed this pile of wood at the beach through the breakwater.

They were going to glide over the waves, and Walter was terri-fied. Yet at the same time, he knew that it was time for him to take back his life. He had been running away from fear and failure and the judgment of his father and brother for so long, that he had lost himself. Well, so be it. Walter decided that if he died today, he would do so as bravely as he could. So when Omai told him to either paddle as hard as he could or just lie back and let it happen, Walter decided to take control.

He grasped the paddle tightly in his hands and started to push it through the water as hard as he could. As the stern of the canoe jacked up and the boat surged into the wave, Walter's panic almost took over, but he brutally pushed it back and yelled at his friend. "You lunatic, you are going to get us killed!"

Walter let out a shout, challenging the Sea to do its worst. Then looking across the bay, he saw that they were not alone. Another canoe was racing alongside them, and Walter was astonished to see the Tahitian in the other boat get to his feet and ride the canoe to the shore.

By the time the two boats hit the beach, Walter's fear had transformed into excitement. He jumped out of the boat, grabbed hold of Omai and hugged him. His passionate embrace was partly out of relief that he had survived, but mostly in gratitude that Omai had given him such a wondrous experience. Omai seemed to understand, as he said nothing and just held Walter. In that brief moment of intimacy, their friendship deepened, and Walter felt an immense amount of appreciation for having been able to experience such a thrill.

After Walter and Omai had pulled the canoe up the beach away from the waves, Walter looked around and noticed several wooden boards lying on the sand. They had apparently been crafted for some purpose as they were rounded at both ends and smoothly polished. Walter wandered over to look at them more closely and asked Omai about their use. He was intrigued when Omai told him that they were for men who were not afraid to challenge the ocean. They were for riding waves. "You've just done something similar, Walter. You are now, whether you like it or not, living on the ocean."

Walter had to admit it was true. He experienced both fear and joy. There was no more need to always feel afraid. He had managed to survive life on the ocean, but until today he had not really ventured into the water itself. He had dealt with storms at sea that could have swept him overboard, and just now he had sat in a canoe that was propelled by the waves, but he had no water skills. On his travels over this vast ocean, he had seen many of the Islanders enjoying the sea in a manner he had never before imagined. There was not one Islander who was not a good swimmer and who did not know how to handle a canoe.

From his current vantage point, the surface of the ocean was smooth, and aside from the very orderly sets of waves approaching the reef at regular intervals, there was nothing that came anywhere near the wild power of the storms at sea. And the water was clear and beautiful, unlike the dark black lake at the estate. Perhaps, he thought, now is the time to begin a new chapter and to really take advantage of his current circumstances. Having made the decision, he looked at Omai. "You are right, Omai. It is time to lose my fear of water."

Omai smiled, "Very well, then. Let me show you." And with that the Islander pointed to one of the shorter boards, telling Walter to pick one of them and take it to the edge of the water. Doing what he was asked, Walter was surprised by the weight of the thing and found himself almost dragging it across the sand, much to his friends' amusement. Omai, of course, lifted his board onto his shoulders and casually strode into the water.

Walter watched Omai wade out until he was waist-deep, dropping the board onto the surface, while elegantly submerging himself, and getting thoroughly wet. Surfacing, Omai shook the water from his glistening, black hair.

"Walter, come out! It's only chest-deep! You can walk. See?"

Walter immediately felt the automatic tension in his gut, but this time he decided to ignore it. Still holding the board at the front end, he cautiously stepped into the warm, turquoise water, anxiously peering about, wondering what was lurking in the sand below his feet.

Ever so slowly Walter continued to wade out while continuing to meticulously scrutinise the bottom of the lagoon. He also made sure that he stayed as close to Omai as he possibly could, finding some comfort in being next to his friend in this alien environment.

"Well done, Walter."

Omai's praise sounded suspiciously patronising to him in his vulnerable state, but he decided not to say anything and merely pay attention to any impending instructions on how to ride the plank of wood he had grasped onto. He suddenly realised that his hands were so firmly gripped onto the board that his knuckles had turned white and had begun to hurt. Although he was only in waist-deep water, Walter was conscious of just letting one hand go at a time, stretching his fingers out and then changing it with the other.

"Come, you'll be fine. Let me show you how to lie on the board and paddle it through the water."

Step by step, Omai demonstrated how to get on the board, how to lie on it and finally how to paddle it to move it across the water.

Walter, preoccupied with the persistent movement of the small waves coming into the shallows, could only remember some of Omai's directions, just paying full attention when Omai announced that he was now going to demonstrate to Walter how to catch one of the waves. Before he could say anything, Omai had thrown himself prone on the board and paddled out to the edge of the reef, which in this part of the lagoon, was not too far from where Walter was standing.

"Where are you going?!" Walter shouted anxiously. Omai did not reply, waving to him instead.

Sitting now on the edge of the reef, Omai was ready to launch himself into one of the unbroken swells. As it approached, he expertly turned the board to face towards the shore and quickly paddled into the wave. In an instant, he had gotten to his feet and made his way across its small face. Walter watched in total amazement as the Islander headed towards him and then, quite casually pulled the board off the wave.

Omai now encouraged Walter to try and get on the board, reminding him of the steps he needed to take to do so. Walter, caught up in the fervour to challenge himself, threw himself on the board and instantly fell off the other side. He surfaced, spitting and spluttering, but he had remembered not to breath in when his head went under. Looking at his friend, he quipped. "Ah, it appears to be more complicated than it appears, eh?"

Omai gave him an encouraging smile and helped him to position himself on the board so that he had a measure of balance, and this time he stayed put and didn't slide off. Very slowly, fearful that any movement would topple him into the water, he started to follow Omai's instructions on how to use his arms to propel the board forward. Lying there, making the board glide over the surface of the lagoon, Walter's confidence slowly built as he learnt to manoeuvre the craft to his left and right.

After he had spent some time following Omai around their small patch of the lagoon he realised that they were paddling out towards the break line, where he had seen the other Islanders catching waves. Then, just as Walter was getting anxious, Omai slid off his board into the chest-deep water, reminding him that no matter what happened he could just stand up. Wading towards him, Omai instructed him to turn his board, so he was facing the shore. "Just lay there and hold on Walter, and I will push you into the wave," Omai said reassuringly. A second later he launched Walter into the wave.

With the sudden acceleration, Walter let out a surprised shout. Here he was, lying prone on the board clinging to its edges as tightly as he could as he sped towards the beach. Just short of land, the board nose-dived, turning tail over end it unceremoniously dumping Walter into the water. An instant later he surfaced, spitting out water, his pulse racing. But this time it wasn't fear that he was experiencing, it was exhilaration.

"My God, what a fantastic experience!" Turning to face Omai, Walter was just in time to see the Tahitian turn his own board, paddle, and then stand up and ride the wave towards the beach, where he elegantly stepped off onto the sand. He shouted across to Walter. "Now, I want you to do the same."

Walter grinned and replied sarcastically, "Of course, naturally I will do exactly the same!"

As the morning progressed, Walter became more and more comfortable with being in the water. He kept reminding himself that he could always find a footing if he needed to. Nevertheless, the idea of standing on the board seemed extraordinarily ambitious.

And so it was, that the two of them laughed with pure light-hearted joy as Walter, clumsy but determined, paddled back out where he repeatedly attempted to get up on the board, and where he repeatedly fell off that board. Omai, always nearby, encouraged Walter to keep going. And then, as Omai helped him position his board into a wave and gave him a shove, Walter managed to get up on his feet. Standing gingerly on the fast-moving board he managed to stay upright all the way to the beach.

In sheer amazement and excitement at having actually ridden the small wave to the beach, Walter fell onto the warm sand and lay there, exhausted, savouring the thrill of his success. Omai, having ridden his own board to the beach, joined him. "You have done it, my friend! You have ridden a wave like a true Islander." Walter's friend paused for a minute then winked at him. "Well not quite like a Ma'ohi, an Islander, but you have potential."

Walter smiled. He was sure that the English said the same of Omai when he learnt his first game of cards or how to play chess. He wondered whether he would ever show the same expertise in surfing that Omai had developed in the parlour games of the English court. Sitting down next to him, Omai looked at him thoughtfully. "I am surprised at how quickly you found your balance."

Thinking about it, Walter was confident that the many hours training with the blade and fencing, had given him an edge. The idea that he had, in fact, brought some of his own skills to the task excited Walter and energised, he jumped up and ceremoniously bowed before Omai. "Sir, I am forever indebted to you," he paused, creating a theatrical beat, "for your persistence in teaching me to almost drown."

Omai burst out in a hearty laugh while Walter continued in a more serious tone. "Omai, I mean it. I would be certainly honoured if you would teach me more about your oceanic skills! I am hopeful that while we are here we will have ample opportunity to ride more waves and I would be very grateful if you could teach me how to swim."

As Walter finished speaking, he became aware that Omai's mood had shifted and his friend was more contemplative. In a quiet tone, Omai responded. "We have done enough for today, and we have had an excellent time. We will see what happens and speak again later."

And with that Omai rose to his feet and started to load the canoe with the boards, signalling to Walter that it was time to go. Walter did not press Omai any further as he knew it would not achieve anything, so he just followed his friend's lead as they paddled the canoe back around the point.

Back in the camp at Point Venus, Walter was eager to document his adventure and immediately set out to write down his account of the days' events.

'Dear Mother,

Today I have experienced the most exhilarating sport. The natives here in these islands are expert with all sorts of craft in the water and have invented a way of sliding on waves by taking a long narrow board, rounded at the ends, and then paddling it into the waves.

As soon as they have progressed to the smooth water beyond the surf, they lay at length on their board, waiting for the next swell to arrive. The moment the wave is upon them, they paddle with all their might, and when the board glides on its own accord, they get to their feet and travel at a rapid velocity across the crystal face of the swell.

Omai, my Tahitian friend, taught me the most basic rudimentary skills and after many trials, and errors, I was able to ride one wave to shore.

In all honesty, I found it to be more thrilling than anything I have ever done before, and I do hope to pursue this activity more vigorously.'

In the early evening light, with the sun setting majestically on the horizon, Walter settled himself into a chair, and as he watched the ocean he thought about the day. He pondered Omai's change of mood but couldn't think of anything that he had said that could have been responsible.

Walter was well aware that all had not gone smoothly for Omai's homecoming. His immediate family had been overjoyed of course, but the rest of the Islanders had been far less welcoming than Walter had expected. There were undoubtedly some very significant undercurrents in the relationships amongst these people. Omai had not been treated with the respect that his position should have dictated, and Walter had noted some open hostility in the way he had been received. In fact, it had only been when Omai had shown his wealth in the precious red feathers that the Islander's lusted after, that he had been treated with proper respect. Walter knew that Omai had traded for those feathers in Tonga and in his world, they represented a fortune. Whatever Omai's commitments and responsibilities were, it was evident that he was on edge. Walter had been loath to broach the subject with his friend up till now, but perhaps the time had come to find a way to do so.

The sky was suddenly illuminated by a streak of lightning, underscored by the quiet rumble of thunder in the distance. Walter smiled for a moment. The Islanders, no doubt, would read this as some omen or another, possibly foreshadowing some misadventure or disaster for which the Gods needed to be appeased.

Tired from the unusual amount of physical exertion of his day, Walter decided to go to bed. He was filled with a sense of achievement and satisfaction that had eluded him for most of his life. It was puzzling that such a simple activity like gliding across waves could elicit such contentment, but then, on the other hand, he had challenged his deep-rooted fear of water and been successful. Walter had always felt a deep sense of shame at his weakness, and he thought that he had now lifted the burden of that character flaw. If nothing else, being forced on this journey had given him this opportunity to prove to himself that he was not a coward.

As Walter, still excited, settled into his bedding, he drifted into a fitful sleep. His vivid imagination took the day's success and added more detail to his mind's rambling visions in which he saw the waves breaking on the island shore where men, women and children were playing and surfing in and around the water. Suddenly, a monstrous wave reared up, broke and thundered towards them. The massive, foaming white water crashed up against the beach, tearing all the inhabitants away from their home. In the broiling sea, all he could make out were the thrashing bodies of the drowning Islanders. In the aftermath of the devastating wave, only a small child was left standing alone and crying at the edge of the denuded beach.

The horror of the dream woke Walter with a start. His heart was racing, and his breath heaved in and out of his body. Sitting up in his bed, with his skin drenched in sweat and his hair clinging to his face, he was acutely aware of his wet shirt sticking to his back, slowly cooling his skin.

It took him some time to calm himself and as his mind and body settled back to a more relaxed state, Walter chose to put such a disturbing dream about death and destruction out of his mind. Deliberately focusing on the captivating beauty of the women, and then narrowing his attention to the remarkable vivaciousness of Vaitea, Walter allowed himself to visualise her soft skin and bright smile and those luscious breasts. Settling back into his bed, he finally drifted off to sleep again, but this time to a much more pleasant set of dreams.

Chapter Twelve

*I*t turned out that Walter had little time to practice riding waves, or for Omai to teach him how to swim, as Omai was required to translate for the Captain, who had unwittingly become embroiled in the political machinations of the Tahitians. Apparently, a war with the island of Moorea was imminent, and the Tahitians expected the English to provide military aid and to support them in battle.

There had been many meetings with the chiefs over the last few days, but today Walter had found himself invited to be part of the English contingent, along with the Captain and some of the officers, and with Omai as translator. The discussion was heated, and the one of the principal chief's, To'ofa, was at the centre of the factions that appeared to Walter, to be pressing their case for the English to be involved. The Captain and Tu sat in silence listening, and to Walter it appeared that they looked increasingly frustrated.

To'ofa suddenly jumped to his feet and in rapid Tahitian addressed the assembly. "Tuté says he is our friend, but do not friends help each other in dark times, do they not fish together and surf in the good times? Tuté does none of these things, yet he has taken the name of Tu and Tu has taken the name of Tuté. This

English has come only to take what he needs and then to leave. He has no care for the lives of the people of O'Taheiti. Were he our friend, he would come and take Moorea with us to help us stop our enemies. With the English weapons, those on Moorea will not want to fight and will surrender quickly. Tuté's help would save many lives."

Omai translated To'ofa's speech for the Captain loudly enough for Walter and the others to hear, and while there were shouts of approval from the gathered chiefs, Tu was silent, deep in thought. Cook stood to respond, and he was apparently angered by the demands put on him. "Omai, tell them that I will not go to war against those who have not offended me. I will not send my ships to Moorea."

Omai translated, speaking rapidly and Walter wondered if the Tahitian was merely conveying meaning, but as To'ofa sneered, he knew that Omai had translated Cook's words quite literally.

"Here it is, from Tuté's own mouth." To'ofa paused dramatically. "He will not help his friends."

A large number of the assembled shouted angrily while the occasional Tahitian appeared to agree with Cook. Walter saw Bligh turn to the Captain and although he spoke very quietly, Walter was able to hear him implore Cook to reconsider. He argued that his refusal to even discuss this matter was out of keeping with the friendship between Tu and the English. "By their tradition, we have an alliance with him and his people."

Omai leant across to speak softly to Cook. "Captain, Bligh is right. We must help. My people are your allies."

But before Cook could answer, Tu rose to his feet. He looked at the English and in Tahitian addressed To'ofa. "I do not doubt Tuté's friendship. Perhaps he needs to see that we do not want him to do this for us, but that we do this thing together as allies and friends. We must, therefore, show him how prepared we are for this war."

On Tu's signal, the assembly rose and organised itself into a procession led by Tu and his retainers, with To'ofa, Cook and his officers following as they filed outside and headed for the shore. As they reached the waterline, Walter was stunned to find hundreds of canoes now assembled in the bay, all in different formations and obviously ready to be launched. On a signal from Tu and To'ofa, an enormous number of warriors emerged from the tree line and quickly formed themselves into crews for the variously sized canoes on the beach, while the procession itself broke up into smaller groups that boarded the larger canoes. Drums and conch horns sounded, and the beached canoes were launched into the bay to join the rest of the fleet.

Two large war canoes had remained on the beach, waiting for the Chiefs and the English. The warriors were waiting patiently for the royal party and their visitors, their paddles raised in the air. Tu turned and invited Cook to board his canoe and then in what was later described by Cook as a brazen political manoeuvre, To'ofa tried to steer the Captain to his canoe. Cook, however, was no stranger to political games, and he diplomatically disengaged himself from To'ofa and boarded Tu's canoe.

In the less formal context of the canoe, Cook knew enough Tahitian, and Tu enough English, for the two to have a good conversation that did not require Omai's skills as a translator, so Omai and Walter stayed behind. Once the flotilla had departed, Omai led Walter along the beach to a medium-sized canoe and asked him to join him. As they pushed off, his friend asked him if Tuté had spoken to him about the next stage of the voyage. Walter was surprised by this. It had only been the previous evening when the Captain had asked him to join himself and Dr Anderson for a private talk, and he was still thinking about the implications of that discussion.

The next stage of their voyage would have the ships sailing north into the far reaches of the Pacific up towards the Arctic Circle. Dr Anderson was very concerned that Walter's current reasonable state of health would deteriorate rapidly once he was back on board ship, and forced to subsist on sailing rations. And the dank, enclosed spaces of the crew's quarters would be no refuge from the cold as they went further north. It had been his assessment that Walter would most probably not survive the trip.

Turning his head so he could look at Omai he answered his question.

"Yes, he has. He feels I should stay here with you until he can return from the north. It will allow me to improve my overall condition and gather my strength for the return trip."

Omai was quiet for a moment, and when he began to speak, it was with gravity in his voice that took Walter back. "Listen well, my friend. No matter what we think, Walter, most of us can only make choices with what we know at the time."

Omai paused, looking across the water. "I think you know well what I mean. In my case, I felt that I needed to come back, allied to the English to liberate my home, Ra'iatea." He stopped again, a slight quiver in his voice. "Seeing how things have changed here, I have decided that I was wrong."

Walter was aware that the many shifting alliances amongst the different Islands had changed. This had been one of the reasons why Omai had not been welcomed back and was no longer seen to be of the elite class. His friend then went on to tell him about what he had learnt about the factions amongst the principal chiefs, and the potential danger that was evident in their constant vying for power. The council and To'ofa had today demonstrated the precariousness of their friendship with Cook. Then there was the problem of the Spanish, who had also visited the islands and had undermined the Tahitian's respect for the English.

Omai swallowed, and then continued in a solemn voice. "What I was looking for, I now know I will never find here. There is no opportunity here for me to liberate my home, and with the current level of distrust and anger amongst some of the ruling council, you may be in danger if you stay here. But I have a better idea. You enjoyed riding the waves, eh? And you have asked me to teach you, so I have decided that I will teach you to master the ocean. But you must promise me to also learn the legends and practices that make this more than simply an amusement." He paused. "In return, you will speak to Cook to keep me on board the ship as we, you and I, head north, where, along the way, we will land in Hawai'i."

"Hawai'i's? What is that?"

Omai smiled. "Hawai'i's is a place, not a what," he paused. "I do not think Tuté will turn the request down, as I know that he is looking for new lands and he will need to find food and water before heading further north. Along the way that he must travel are the islands of Hawai'i, a place where Tuté will find what he needs. There, Walter, and not here, is where we will find what each of us needs."

"So, you have been to this place?" Walter inquired.

"No, my friend. But I know it is there from the legends of my people."

"So, how do we find it? And who are the people that live there?"

"We will find these islands because we know where they are, and the people that live there are descendants of ours. We are of one people."

Walter did not find this reassuring. "So we are forsaking one precarious situation for another, possibly an even more precarious and unknown one?" Walter mused.

Omai smiled. "Well, you could certainly think of it that way."

"Let me ask you this. What do you hope to find there, Omai?"

"What I have not found here. Respect and a new life, free from the past." Omai paused for a moment. "Pretty women and better surf would also be enticing, eh?"

Walter laughed. Reflecting on what Omai had said, he thought about how his own world had changed. Forced from his own country, and dependent on Captain Cook and his officers, his circumstances were not too different from Omai's. Both men were looking for a life free from the pain of the past. When Cook had spoken to him about staying in Tahiti, Walter had agreed to it with the understanding that he would be doing so with his friend Omai as a companion, and Vaitea as an added attraction. Omai's revelations about the political situation and its inherent dangers changed everything.

Omai's plan to stay on board for another destination had just presented an intriguing, although possibly dangerous, alternative. Stay here where there were known dangers, or go elsewhere to possible unknown threats. Of course if this Hawaii place turned out to be dangerous they would then be forced to stay on board the Resolution, a possible death sentence for him. As he turned the idea over in his mind, Walter also wondered how he could influence the Captain to change his plans. Cook had been challenging and not particularly well disposed towards either Omai or Walter of late, and such a request would likely require more influence with Cook than he personally had at this time. They needed someone to argue the case on their behalf, especially the usefulness of finding new lands.

"It sounds like a reasonable proposition, that we stay together and go to this place Hawai'i, but I fear I may not be much use in persuading the Captain." He paused for an instant and then smiled. "But, I think Mr Bligh may be the one to put your proposition forward."

Pleased that each could see an advantage in their agreement, both men sat back quietly, watching the spectacle of a large fleet of canoes heading towards the beach at an impressive pace. A wave of sound suddenly rolled towards them, as drums and conch horns and chanting cut through the air.

They watched as the warriors landed and led a mock battle further up the beach, then, as quickly as they had beached, the warriors re-boarded their canoes and swiftly returned to the middle of the bay. There the fleet broke into two groups that practised naval manoeuvres and battle strategies at sea. Walter, watching this as an outsider, was impressed by the discipline and cohesiveness of the Tahitians, seeing clearly that they would be very dangerous opponents.

෮෪෮෪෮෪෮෪

Sitting on Tu's canoe with the chief watching the display of power and military prowess of the Tahitian's, Captain Cook was looking for a way he could diplomatically resist the demand that he provide support in their upcoming battle. His thoughts were interrupted by Tu asking him if he could see how much mana his people

possessed. And therein lay one of his problems. He could see just
how dangerous these Islanders could be.

Cook carefully pondered Tu's request before replying. "Tu, I do
not wish to offend you. You have my word on this. But there are
other things I need to consider. I have my orders from my King. I
also must try and keep my crew as safe as possible. You know, Tu,
we are on a scientific expedition and are not really equipped for war.
At the same time, I do value our friendship, and it pains me that I
may have to refuse your request for help."

Tu's response was what he had expected. He was polite, but it
was clear that he was disappointed and in his own words saddened
by Cook's refusal to aid someone who was his friend. It was clear
that Tu's expectations were based in the traditions of his people, but
there was also the issue of Tu's own prestige and power amongst the
Ari'i. Cook was well aware that To'ofa's challenge at the council
meeting was a serious matter for Tu. And if Tu's position changed
amongst the ever-shifting alliances of the chiefs, the position of
himself and his crew would be more tenuous. In fact, thinking about
the situation as it now stood, with the political climate becoming
more unsettled, his plan to leave Walter Beaumont behind may not
be wise.

Later that evening when he was back onboard the Resolution,
Cook was not particularly surprised that he was feeling out of sorts
and irritable as he sat down for dinner with his officers and passengers. He was not happy about the way that Bligh had challenged
him at the council meeting, and he was frustrated by the possibility
that he would have to change his plans. So when Bligh opened up
the conversation again, asking him to explain himself, he found
himself having great difficulty staying calm.

Young Beaumont's look of intense interest in his reply gave him
pause. It was worth the time to educate all of his men as well as his
passengers, about the broader considerations that had to be taken
into account. He gathered his thoughts then turned to Bligh, who
had been the one to initiate the discussion. "Mr Bligh, I want you to
consider this. Last time I was here the political situation was

completely different. I cannot afford to alienate any of the natives in this region as all of us are dependent on their goodwill."

During the ensuing discussion, Beaumont, having failed to understand the complexity of the shifting alliances that they need to deal with, reiterated Bligh's earlier assertion. That Tu's people were their allies. Cook took affront at this, as there was an inherent judgment of his ethics in this argument. He could feel his anger burning at such presumption from any of them, but especially a passenger who was there because his own judgment had been so abysmal as to kill a man.

As the argument about their responsibilities to their friends, as opposed to their obligations to pursue their stated mission, raged across the table, Beaumont brought up the issue of honour. Being young and foolish, he still believed that there was some a straightforward and easily understood path to decisions about what was the right thing to do. Finally, having had enough of the discussion, Cook decided to end it. "Mr Beaumont, I lead this expedition, and the lives of many, including yours, rest upon my very practical decisions."

With that, he looked around the table at his men and suggested that they get on with their dinner. He had made his decision based on sound reasoning, and as far as he was concerned, the subject was closed. Gratified that all of them, including Mr Beaumont, adhered to his orders for the debate to end, he turned his attention to his meal, only to find that he had no appetite and that his guts were as unsettled as his mind and temper.

Chapter Thirteen

*W*alter had been trying to formulate his approach to Bligh about Omai's desire to leave Tahiti with the ships when they headed north. His own predicament was not as problematic, as he now had excellent reasons to stay onboard the Resolution and continue on the voyage as initially planned. All of the officers and crew were now aware that the political climate of the islands has changed and there had been many discussions amongst the men about their increased sense of danger.

Omai's position was not as obviously precarious as his own. Although he was no longer considered to be part of the Ari'i, his family were comfortably settled and had a good life. If he gave up any idea of taking back the power and prestige his family had lost in the factional fighting of the last few years and aligned himself with one of the leading families, Omai could still have a good life. Walter was unsure how he was going to broach Omai's request to journey north with the English, but he still thought that Bligh could be more receptive initially than the Captain.

Now that the rain of the last few days had finally stopped Bligh was back on the island, having been on the Resolution supervising repairs until that morning. He was alone and didn't appear to have any call on his time at that moment, allowing Walter and Omai to approach him. Walter opened the conversation with some pleasantries and then spoke about his concerns about the proposal that he stay on Tahiti.

It was at this point that Bligh offered the information that he and the Captain had also discussed this in light of the political situation amongst the Islander's, and that they too had realised this may not be in Walter's best interests. Walter knew it was a stretch to use this as an opening to bring up Omai's case, but he went ahead anyway.

There was an expression of concern on Bligh's face as Walter spoke of Omai's dismay at the changes in his position, and his assessment that there was little for him in Tahiti. But this changed to a look of confusion when Walter informed Bligh that Omai wanted to re-join the Resolution. As Walter continued, telling him that Omai had information about islands to the north inhabited by people related to the Tahitian's, Bligh's face became unreadable.

"I'm not sure I follow you, Mr Beaumont. Now, if I understand you correctly, you wish me to support your petition to Captain Cook to have Omai continue aboard the Resolution, in exchange for information regarding a group of islands to the north called Hawai'i?"

Omai, having listened quietly now interjected and spoke to Bligh himself, informing the officer that he, along with all of the Islander's, had knowledge of all of the peoples who lived in the islands of the ocean that the English called the Pacific Ocean. "I can continue to be of great use, Mr Bligh. What I have not shared with you is that my knowledge includes navigating the ocean between here and further to the north."

Bligh looked at him speculatively and asked why he had not spoken of these skills previously. To Walter's mind, it was evident that no one on board the Resolution had considered their amusing guest to be anything other than a passenger being returned to his home. Now, as all of them were learning so much more about the Islanders, Omai's claim to skills hitherto undisclosed was not surprising. The Islanders had shown themselves to be quite crafty and secretive.

Omai just smiled and responded that there had been no need to do so before, but that he was now willing to trade his knowledge for safe passage on to Hawai'i where the English would be able to restock their ships. He then continued to talk about his situation in his own words, describing his feeling of no longer having a home here in Tahiti.

"As you well know, Mr Bligh, the situation here has changed, and this leads me to believe that neither Walter nor I am safe to stay here. My suggestion offers all of us certain opportunities. You will discover new lands and be able to provision the ships for the long voyage north, I will be able to find a more suitable home, and Walter will be safe with me."

Bligh responded thoughtfully. "Selfishly, I can see some advantages in this, but I do not understand your reasons to travel to those particular islands? Surely one of the other islands closer to Tahiti may suit your needs better."

Walter had found it difficult to stay out of the conversation, and he now eagerly jumped in. "Mr Bligh, do you remember seeing the islanders ride the waves the other morning?" He waited for a moment, and when Bligh did not respond, he continued. "Well, in any case, let me tell you, I have tried it, and I can assure you that it is the most exhilarating feeling I have ever experienced. This man, Mr Bligh, is a master of the art of riding waves, and he tells me that in these islands of Hawai'i, they have perfected this art even further. It is his deepest desire to venture forth and pit his skills against these Hawai'ians and learn from them as much as he can."

Bligh sighed. "Mr Omai, you're asking that Captain Cook provide you with passage to islands to the north, that is populated by people that you know about but with whom you have had no previous contact. How do you know where these Islands are and that you would be welcome there?"

"We have the stories and legends that tell us, Mr Bligh. Many generations ago some of my people voyaged to Hawai'i where they settled, finding a land much to their liking. Later some voyaged to the land you now call New Zealand, and at other times they returned to Tahiti. As you are aware, all our languages are similar and have only changed slightly as the generations passed. We are brothers, all of us."

Bligh acknowledged the truth of what Omai had said about the similarities amongst the South Sea Islanders, and their languages were only differentiated by small adaptions. But he continued to question why Omai would leave all that he knew to travel to another set of Islands so that he could learn more about riding waves. At this point, Walter wondered if he could influence Bligh by encouraging him to see just how extraordinary the experience of riding waves really was, but Bligh's response was to question his sanity.

"Have you lost your senses, man? Firstly, you could barely hide your disdain for this journey, and now you want me to help you persuade the Captain to take an excursion so that Omai can indulge his hedonistic desires somewhere else in the oceans." He paused, shaking his head. "And as for my personal exploration of this dangerous pursuit of riding waves? I think not, Sir! I have absolutely no intention in jeopardising my personal well-being in any such fashion." He drew in more air to continue. "And as for you, Sir, you have quite clearly gone native."

Bearing the brunt of Bligh's reaction, Walter had to acknowledge that he may not have chosen the best argument. In reflection, he had to admit that had someone suggested this to him a year or so ago, he too, would have questioned their state of mind. He sighed, "Mr Bligh, if that is the worst that can happen to me, then so be it!" He paused, knowing that he needed Bligh's support. "I beg of you, at least assist me with my request and I assure you that you won't regret it."

"Well, that remains to be seen, Mr Beaumont," Bligh said. "Perhaps there could be some merit to be found in this venture. After all, our brief is to explore new lands and being able to provision the ships along the journey is always an opportunity not to be taken lightly." Bligh stopped and looked out at the lagoon and then seeming to have made a decision he continued. "I will give you my word, as a mark of friendship to you both, and the slim possibility that this may be of use to us, that I will speak with the Captain about your request, irrespective of how insane parts if it appear to me."

Pleased with Bligh's assurance, Walter put his hand on the officer's shoulder. "That is all I can ask for. You have my heartfelt gratitude, Mr Bligh!"

Chapter Fourteen

*T*he dilemma about whether they should act as allies in the fight with the islanders of Moorea had been resolved, as the battle had been fought and won without the English, but it left a brewing antagonism between To'ofa and Tu. Since Cook had wanted to visit the island and he could now do so without compromising his position, Walter soon found himself standing at the rails of the Resolution admiring yet another paradise.

Like so many of these islands, there was a natural harbour created by the lagoon, its water the characteristic light blue hue, that shimmered like a sapphire in the sunshine. The gentle waves lapped at the shore of the land that rose up into a single emerald-green mountain peak with what looked like carefully folded formations of lush forested slopes.

Looking into the lagoon Walter tried to identify the variety of fish and rays casually floating below, occasionally spotting a reef shark and wondering if they found sailors palatable. He had seen the islanders feeding these animals, fearlessly entering the water with the beasts who eagerly would snatch fish from their hands. Here they lazily swam around, unperturbed by the events above.

Then, Walter's peaceful reflection was shattered as the Captain

stormed onto the deck, screaming for his officers. "I've had enough
of these damned thieving heathens! I want that goat returned to this
ship immediately. Mr Gore, Mr King and Mr Williamson damn it,
Sirs, where are you?"

From different parts of the ship, the three officers hurried to
Cook as he continued his relentless tirade. "I want a landing party
arranged immediately! I want that goat retrieved and the thief
apprehended." Cook stopped to catch his breath. "Mr Williamson,
take forty men and scour the island. Whatever huts and canoes you
find, burn them. Is that understood?"

Walter was appalled by Cook's ferocious temper. Not only by
the way that Cook appeared to have lost all control and any
semblance of proper behaviour, but his orders were out of propor-
tion with the seriousness of the so-called crime. Without thinking it
through Walter interjected and challenged the Captain only to
have him turn on him. "Mr Beaumont," Cook's voice bellowed at
him, "if you continue with this insolence in questioning my orders I
will have you slapped in irons, and you will continue the remainder
of your stay here in the confines of the brig! Do I make myself
clear?"

Shocked at Cook's outburst, Walter abandoned any attempts to
reason with the Captain. What surprised him was that from
amongst the officers it was Williamson of all people, who spoke up
and tried to challenge Cook, but he, too, was soundly intimidated
and threatened into backing down. As the officers organised a
landing party, Walter and Omai locked eyes and in unspoken agreement joined the men heading to the longboats.

As they neared the shore, he saw several large war canoes lined
up along the beach, and a little further inland a small group of
houses and gardens could be seen nestled in the shade of the
coconut palms. The moment the boat beached, Williamson jumped
out onto the sand, quickly followed by the Marines. The second
longboat with Gore and another group of Marines joined them,
and the expedition was swiftly organised.

One group was sent to destroy the canoes, while the rest of the
men were sent to search through the village for the goat and to find

the Islanders. They were to apprehend anyone they saw and bring them back to the officers for questioning.

The men fanned out as ordered and unleashed, they went about smashing and burning the canoes, dwellings and gardens. Walter, looking on, was outraged by the wanton destruction of the Islanders' belongings. He knew that interfering would simply end up with him being punished, but he felt that he had to do something. Turning to Omai, he was puzzled by his friend's calm acceptance of this destruction. Asking his friend why he was not outraged by what was occurring, Omai simply shrugged and told him that these were the people who were responsible for his own exile.

Walter hated feeling helpless. He tried to intervene by talking to Williamson, but all he did was set up another confrontation with the officer. Williamson forcefully rebutted Walter's attempts to get him to cease the carnage. Trying to push Walter away, he said between gritted teeth that his orders were clear. "Mr Beaumont! I have as little choice in this as you! Now get out of my way!"

Suddenly distracted by one of the Marines, who shouted something about 'natives', Williamson turned and hurried towards the edge of the village. The officer had taken only a few steps when Walter, infuriated that he wasn't being listened to, again demanded that Williamson call off his men.

As Williamson turned toward him, he pulled out his pistol and brought it up, aiming it directly at Walter's chest. It was this genuine threat to his life that finally forced him to realise that he had been out of line. He had pushed Williamson too far, and as he stared back at the officer, he felt a calm come over him. He had no idea if Williamson would pull the trigger, but he knew instinctively to stay still and quiet.

"Mr Williamson! Drop your weapon!"

Williamson stood motionless, his arm outstretched, his pistol now aimed at Gore who had placed himself between Williamson and Walter.

Gore spoke calmly but forcefully, "You will put your weapon away, Mr Williamson or I will place you under immediate arrest."

Williamson appeared to deflate, his arm slowly dropped, and his shoulders sagged. Looking totally frustrated, Williamson abruptly swung away from Gore. He shot Walter a look of pure hatred, then turned on his heels and ran up the beach to follow his men who were busily setting fire to everything they could find. Walter, suddenly short of breath, nodded to Gore. "Mr Gore, I owe you a debt. You have my thanks."

Gore did not immediately answer Walter. He was watching the men, his face an unreadable mask. When he did turn back, his expression was stony, and his eyes cold and disapproving. He held Walter's gaze for a moment before he spoke. "Mr Beaumont, whatever you may think about Mr Williamson, he is carrying out the Captain's orders."

Walter felt compelled to try to reason with the officers. The Captain's orders, fuelled by fury, were unconscionable. "Surely you don't condone..." He began only to be interrupted by Gore. "I strongly suggest that you refrain from interfering with an officer's duty, Mr Beaumont. I am well aware that you are finding this voyage challenging, but the Captain's orders will be obeyed irrespective of what you think. Is that understood?"

With that said, Mr Gore turned and went further up the beach to join his men leaving Walter to stare at his back, feeling defeated and quite exhausted from his confrontation with the two officers. Taking a breath, Walter realised that his chest felt constricted and that he was, in fact, feeling unsteady on his feet. He groped his way over to a log and sat down with it at his back for support. He had barely settled himself when he was wracked by a coughing fit which seemed to strip him of all of his remaining strength. Wiping his mouth on his white silk handkerchief, he found it covered with a bloodied stain. And then everything went black.

⁂

Omai later told Walter that they had returned with both the goat and the man that they had identified as the thief, only to find Walter unconscious on the beach. By then it had begun to rain, and visibility had become compromised, so it had taken quite a bit of planning and several trips to get everyone back to the Resolution. Apparently, after they had settled him back into his hammock, Mr Anderson had checked in on him and judged his condition not to be overly serious. Omai said that the surgeon had reported that it was typical of consumption and that he expected Walter to be recovered in a few days.

While Walter was semi-conscious and confined to his bed, the consequences of the Captain's anger was played out on deck. Walter was only vaguely aware of the noise that a small group of Tahitians were making up above him. It was much later that Omai and the crew told him about what had happened.

The Marines had captured an Islander, whom they thought was the culprit. The other Tahitian's had been deeply distressed to see him with his hands tied behind his back and had tried to intercede with the Captain. But the Captain had been unremitting in his insistence that the man is punished and would not accede to any of their attempts to argue for mercy. Omai told him that all Cook seemed to care about was that the goat had been returned and that the thief should be punished.

The punishment that the Captain ordered was extreme and brutal. He had demanded that the Islander have his head shaved and his ears cut off. Omai had been forced to translate this to the man and the attending Islanders, and he told Walter of the distress that this had caused. They had slashed their heads with shark's teeth and wailed in agony, but the thief himself had been brave and stoic, and not descended into an emotional state, but stood proud and strong in the face of his proposed disfigurement.

Then unexpectedly, the Captain had turned to Mr King and demanded that the crew member on watch at the time of the theft be given a dozen lashes. The crew understood that the officers had no choice but to follow orders, but Omai reported to Walter that he did not think that the officers agreed with the Captain. Never the less, they had proceeded to mete out said punishment as ordered.

The Islander, who had until now appeared calm, started to struggle as one marine tightly gripped his head while another, wielding a sharp razor, began to roughly but methodically, remove his hair. Omai described how, having completed the job, the marine had casually wiped the blade on his trouser leg and looked up at Mr King.

According to Omai, the second officer had appeared reluctant but had nodded to the crew member, and with a quick motion, the marine cut the man's right ear cleanly off. Before he could duplicate this with the Islander's second ear, Mr King had quietly interceded, telling the marine that this was enough. Omai had told Walter that both King and Gore had been murmuring before this, and it was his assessment that they did not want to continue with the punishment.

As soon as the Islander had been untied, he had jumped to his feet and, lunging through the group, he had dived overboard and disappeared into the lagoon.

It was now the crewman's turn, and Williamson had been in charge of his punishment. Omai was sure that he had enjoyed inflicting pain on the hapless sailor, describing how they had stripped him and tied him akimbo, with Williamson himself taking the Cat-o-nine-tails and using it with relish.

Omai had told Walter that after the sailor had received his punishment, the rest of the Islanders had left The Resolution. Omai believed that Williamson had a grudge against the sailor who had been singled out for punishment. The rest of the crew had been forced to witness this brutality, and Omai thought that they had been upset by it.

Over the next few weeks, as his illness ran its course, Walter was often visited by Omai and some of the crew he had made friends with, and they had kept him informed of the what was happening as he lay confined to his sickbed.

The Captain, who had been increasingly irritated by the political wrangling between Tu and To'ofa had been heard railing against the intolerable situation that was emerging in Tahiti. When Walter had asked Omai if the Captain's behaviour at Moorea had made the situation worse, Omai said that it appeared that diplomacy was failing, and he believed that it was the Captain's own inability to control his temper that was causing a lot of the problems.

Which was why only a few days after Walter had fallen ill, the ships had weighed anchor and left Tahiti to pursue the next stage of their mission.

As they headed north, the Captain's mood seemed to improve, but this did not last. He was often in his cabin, attended by Mr Anderson, which fuelled the rumour amongst the crew that he was ill. Walter had suspected that Cook was suffering from some ailment before they had reached Tahiti, and a couple of comments that Mr Anderson made while tending him confirmed this.

Now, as he spoke to the crew, it had become apparent to Walter that Cook's dark moods and unpredictable behaviour were alienating the men. They were wary of him, and he had been told that before they had left the islands, several of the crew had tried to desert the ship. The harsh punishments now being meted out for any infractions had eroded the crews' respect for their Captain.

Yet, according to Mr Bligh, who also had been a regular visitor to Walter on his sickbed, the Captain had shown his usual keen intellectual interest and been able to interact with the crew in a light-hearted way when they had found some small reef or atoll to explore. It seemed to Walter that whatever was ailing the Captain was changing the man he knew, and he found this saddened him.

It was fortunate that it was during one of the Captain's lighter moods that Bligh had approached him with Walter and Omai's proposition. It had been just before they had left Tahiti and were exploring a small uninhabited atoll. The Captain's love of exploration was his primary focus at that moment, and so the opportunity to discover new, inhabited islands to the north, excited his imagination, and after a long talk with Omai, the Islander's request to sail with the Resolution was granted.

Cook had already informed Walter that he would be better off remaining on board before they had departed Tahiti, so Omai had settled back into the routine of the ship while he, Walter, remained confined to his hammock. Walter had also become aware that Mr Anderson himself was now ill and the surgeon informed him that he, too, had consumption.

Walter and Omai continued their customary conversations

about the Islands during which it seemed to Walter that Omai was somewhat melancholy and the Islander admitted to missing the two Maori boys, who had decided to stay on in Tahiti in the care of his family. However, Omai insisted that he did not regret his decision, and that he was looking forward to the challenge he had set himself in the Islands of Hawai'i.

Both Bligh and Omai often talked about their new collaboration wherein Omai was showing Bligh how the Islanders navigated across the oceans. Bligh was fascinated by the way the Islander's read the currents, being able to detect a landmass before it appeared on the horizon by watching the wave patterns, and small changes in the currents. But he was most impressed by Omai's ability to read the stars and place the ship's position. And all without a compass or sextant.

As Walter's health improved, he started spending time on deck again, and he found that he enjoyed watching Bligh and Omai spend hours each day on the quarterdeck watching the ocean. The officer enthusing about his new respect for the Islander's skills, and Omai enjoying being able to demonstrate his knowledge, and be acknowledged for it.

Walter's days started to find a rhythm wherein he watched his friends and the crew while also working with Mr Webber. The two of them would spend hours pouring over their notes and drawings, and working on the catalogue of the flora and fauna of Tahiti, as they sailed towards the north of the Pacific Ocean.

A query, a question,
I put to you:
Where is the water of Kane?
At the eastern gate
Where the sun comes in at Haehae;
There is the water of Kane.

One question I ask of you:
Where flows the water of Kane?

Deep in the ground. In the gushing spring,
In the ducts of Kane and Loa,
A wellspring of water, to quaff,
A water of magic power -
The water of life!
Life! O give us this life!

(Ancient Hawai'ian Chant from Kauai)

Chapter Fifteen

"*D*ear Mother,
    We have been immersed in the realities of life at sea over the many weeks it has taken us to travel north from Tahiti. Just after leaving Huahine, we became aware that the two ships were completely infested by a plague of cockroaches. They are hideous creatures that crawl and scurry through everything, and Captain Cook was eventually forced to seek out somewhere to anchor so that the ships could be thoroughly fumigated. We found refuge on a tiny speck of land that has now been named Christmas Island due to the timing of our arrival. The crew amused themselves with catching and feasting on turtles, which turned out to be an abundant food source.

    With a much cleaner ship, we continued our journey north and on the 2nd of January 1778 the lookout had sighted land, and in the distance, I could hear waves breaking. As we came closer to the coastline the sight was as spectacular as any I have seen in the Society Islands. In parts, the steep cliffs are intersected with rocky beaches, and in other places, huge waterfalls cascade into the ocean. The swells that pound the shores are powerful, just as Omai predicted, and he confided in me that the legends say that riding the surf here is one of the truest tests of courage that any man can face and a time when he can indeed become one with the ocean.

    After my brief but exciting experience of riding waves in Tahiti, I very much doubt that I will ever master the much more powerful waves in these regions, although I confess that to have the opportunity to perhaps even witness such a spectacle would be thrilling enough.

Omai tells me that the people and language are similar to his, and it should not be difficult for him to assimilate as he hopes to make a life here. As for myself, I own to have some apprehension about the plan to leave me here on these islands. I have little choice as my constitution has been ravaged by illness, and the climate further north is unsuitable for my health, and the Captain has promised that he will return as quickly as possible so that I can rejoin the ship. However, I expect that I will have ample time to immerse myself in the experience and to study how these people, so isolated from the rest of the world live in what can only be called a tropical paradise."

Over the last few weeks as Walter's health improved he had started to really enjoy sitting on the quarterdeck, happily occupied with his notes and drawings, and his conversations with Mr Webber. He found being focused on a task he enjoyed gave him great satisfaction and he had managed to stay out of trouble by avoiding Williamson. He knew that his enmity with the man has put him into an awkward position with the Captain, so Walter had been very conscientious in his duties and stayed well away from Williamson since they had left Tahiti. Now as they approached their destination, Walter was relieved that, for his part, the third officer appeared to have been judiciously avoiding him as well.

It seemed to Walter that they had both come to understand that neither could afford to anger the Captain as they had before. Walter knew that he had overstepped the mark on several occasions by challenging the Captain, and he felt a certain amount of shame for his ingratitude. He had been thinking a great deal about his current situation as the year had come to a close. It was somewhat daunting to know that he had been close to not surviving this last year, and he pondered what the next one would have in store for him. Would he still be alive when the Captain returned to pick him up from these unknown islands he was about to be marooned on?

Although no longer prone to seasickness, consumption had

wasted Walter away, and he felt weaker and more vulnerable than ever before. In the early parts of their stay in Tahiti, Walter's recuperation had been aided by the clean water, and a nutritious diet, as well as the care given to him by the women of Omai's family. They had used a peculiar way of rubbing his body that felt like he was being pummelled. In the immediate aftermath, the treatment was exhausting, but a short time later, he would experience a powerful feeling of invigoration. He wondered if the women of this Island practised the same method of treating the body's ailments.

As the Resolution and the Discovery had made their way towards the Islands of Hawai'i, the supplies of fresh food that they had taken on board in Tahiti had begun to run out. Walter was well aware that whatever supplies the Captain would be able to barter for here on Hawai'i, would not last the whole journey north, and back again, which reinforced for Walter that he had little choice, no matter how apprehensive he was about being left behind on an uncharted Island. He knew that to stay on board would probably be his death sentence.

Watching Cook and William Bligh deep in conversation on the other side of the quarterdeck, Walter reflected on what he had learned about these men. He had come to admire their toughness and the keenness of their sense of adventure. Both men were remarkably talented, and the fact that they had been able to work with Omai's very different way of looking at the ocean was a testament to their intellect and acquired wisdom. However, Cook's mercurial temper was a blight on his otherwise impeccable reputation.

Now that they had reached their destination, Omai was excited, and he was quick to reassure Walter that he would be with him to help him. His enthusiasm was infectious, and Walter's own natural optimism, as well as his acceptance of the inevitable, kept his fear at bay. At least to some extent. The wind dropped for a moment, and in the ensuing calm, Walter could make out part of Cook and Bligh's conversation. "I see Omai made good on his promise, Sir."

Cook nodded thoughtfully. "So he has, Mr Bligh, so he has."

Neither spoke again but continued to stare out to the island. Then the Captain straightened up and squared his shoulders.

"By the way, Mr Bligh, muskets and pistols are to be loaded only with shot. We are not here to make enemies." He paused. "Call me when we make landfall." Bligh nodded. "Aye, aye, Sir."

As Cook disappeared below deck, Walter focused his attention on the green Island looming in front of him. From where he stood, it was clear that its coastline was diverse and ranged from rocky cliffs to sandy beaches, backed by green vegetation and forests rising up into the mountainous interior. From time to time, Walter thought he could make out small signs of habitation like the rising plume of smoke or a glimpse of huts. *What will I find there,* Walter mused.

Chapter Sixteen

*S*tanding on the edge of the cliff with the vast blue sea spreading out beneath them, Kanoa carefully scanned the horizon, curious about the strange objects steadily heading towards their Island. Koa, his apprentice, a tall, well-muscled man with a chiselled face, stood quietly beside him, equally absorbed by the objects in the distance.

Neither man spoke, their attention focused on the deep blue ocean. Kanoa was conscious of Koa's tension, but the young man kept it well in check, his face expressionless. *I have taught him well,* Kanoa thought proudly. Too much emotion led to bad decisions. He had known too many men who had lost their lives as a result of being carried away with undisciplined feelings.

As the objects continued to approach, Kanoa surmised that their lives, all of their lives, were about to change irrevocably. And yet along with his anticipation, he also felt a touch of sadness. Although Kanoa was not Kahuna Kaula, a seer, one who could prophesy the future, he had a finely tuned intuition that had, on numerous occasions, quite literally saved his life.

Some time ago he had a dream. In it, he saw a massive wave of white water wash ashore and destroy the land and everything on it.

At the time Kanoa thought nothing of it but could this be what the dream had foretold? As there was no immediate answer to his question, Kanoa knew he would have to wait patiently and see what unfolded.

A little earlier, Kanoa had sent a messenger to Waimea to alert everyone. Even though only two objects were approaching, he had suggested that they should be prepared for a fight. He felt confident that, should there be a need to defend themselves, they were more than capable of doing so.

The wind carried a cacophony of sound up to Kanoa and Koa. The rhythmic beating of drums and the drone of conch horns were all interspersed with the excited voices of the people.

From his elevated position, Kanoa watched as hundreds of canoes launched into the ocean to swiftly paddle and sail towards the two objects. Seeing them closer to shore, he was now sure that they were strange, large vessels. Single-hulled with several masts set with sails, they looked awkward and slow in the water. They may not be fast, Kanoa thought, but he could see that they were able to carry a lot of sail on their three masts.

In contrast, the large double-hulled canoes sprinted across the water. He smiled, confident the two foreign vessels would not outrace any of the canoes that he could build. He did admire, however, that they could carry many more men and goods in the hull.

"Come, Koa, let us go back."

Koa nodded and silently fell respectfully in behind Kanoa, who was his *Kahu*, his teacher, and the two men began making their way down to the beach.

By the time the canoes surrounded the two ships, it was clear that they, whoever they were, had come in peace. Now men, women and children of all ages were swimming around the ship, and the spectacle on the water continued to attract an ever-growing crowd of people.

Onboard the Resolution there was great excitement amongst the crew at seeing another Island and people similar to those of Tahiti. Most of them had prepared themselves for the long, tedious and arduous journey into the cold, and this proved to be a pleasant diversion from what was to come.

In the excitement officers, crew and Marines all rushed onto the deck. They crowded along the railings closest to shore, causing the ship to list dangerously. Gore quickly ordered them to stand back and to take turns, allowing only a small number at a time occupy the railing.

Walter, sitting at the highest point of the quarterdeck, watched as two huge and beautifully decorated canoes, bearing white standards, rapidly approached the anchored Resolution. The vessels were exquisitely built with contrasting timbers for different parts of the canoes, and the sails were of such workmanship that they resembled the ship's sailcloth. Across the deck stood several rows of powerfully built warriors, more heavily muscled than the Tahitians. But like the Tahitians, they were equally heavily tattooed.

Walter counted sixty paddlers in each canoe, while also carrying high-ranking officials dressed in red and yellow cloaks, holding staffs and fans of different descriptions.

The warriors quickly secured the vessels to the Resolution and two groups of Hawai'ians boarded with great ease and agility. Tension amongst the English sharply increased as armed Hawai'ian warriors clambered onto the ship. Standing in formation, the Marines instantly readied their muskets.

"Mr Phillips, have your men stand at ease!" Gore's voice rang across the deck.

"Aye, Aye, Sir!"

It seemed to Walter that despite Mr Phillips orders, the Marines appeared reluctant to obey.

"At ease, men!" This time the marines obeyed while the rest of the officers and crew arranged themselves around the ship as befitting such an occasion as welcoming a chief.

Walter regretted that he had to stay seated in his chair. He was just too weak to stand through the official welcome. It did, however, give him the opportunity to sketch the scene in front of him. Walter was thoroughly impressed with the whole pomp and ceremony the Islanders had brought to the ship. In that way, it was not dissimilar to any royal occasion in Britain.

Through Omai's translations, it unfolded that the Hawai'ians were led by three chiefs and priests, although it was not clear to Walter who was what. There was a man called Ki'ikiki, a weathered individual who looked like he was in his late fifties, and who appeared to have seniority in the group. Then there was a man called Ku'ohu, also in his fifty's by all appearances.

The most impressive was a man called Kanoa, a giant whose long, carefully oiled black hair was tied into a massive topknot. He stood alongside the warriors, belonging to their group but yet somehow apart. His stature and presence suggested that his role was independent but powerful. Walter sensed that this was a man of great influence amongst these people.

Like the others, Kanoa's body was carefully oiled and glistening in the sunlight. His heavily muscled left arm and lower body were intricately tattooed in geometric patterns and Walter was reminded of the Tahitian tattoos which were similar, but not the same.

Ki'ikiki, Ku'ohu and Kanoa were all dressed in yellow and red *malo*, the Hawai'ian equivalent of loincloths. Draped over their shoulders were long red and yellow feather cloaks that almost touched the deck. Except for Kanoa, who held his under his arm, the men wore crested helmets of the same colour and make,. Walter was taken aback by the similarity of the headgear to that of the ancient Greeks. It was as if the Ancients had relocated to the Islands of Hawai'i only to be rediscovered by them eons later.

The group of ten, armed warriors appeared to be vigilantly observing everything they could from their position behind their leaders. Their weapons were a curious mixture of spears, both long and short, tipped with shark's teeth, and clubs, that were made of dark wood, beautifully stained with some kind of oil.

Ki'ikiki began a rhythmic recital as he cautiously approached

Cook. Omai later told him that, although Cook believed it to be a prayer, it was, in fact, a greeting. Having completed the welcome, Ki'ikiki knelt before Cook and then rose to his feet again.

On a signal from Kanoa, a warrior carrying a woven basket filled with fresh fruit, vegetables and fish walked across the deck towards Cook. The man knelt and presented the basket to the Captain. Placing it at his feet, the warrior touched the deck with his forehead and then slowly moved back.

Cook smiled effusively and kept nodding in appreciation. He signalled Bligh, who handed him a package wrapped in a piece of black cloth. As he unwrapped the gift, he produced a beautiful, shiny, metal knife with a large blade. With grand ceremony, Cook presented the gift to Ki'ikiki, who could barely contain his pleasure at such a valuable item.

"Omai, please translate for me."

Cook cleared his throat, his signal that he was about to make a speech of some importance.

"Greetings from the great King George. We have come from a faraway land called Britain, and we have yet further to go. We would like to trade for food and water to provision our ships for our journey north. I also have a request. I have two men who wish to stay here in the Islands. Omai, who wishes to ride the waves of your Island and Mr Beaumont here, who is ill and unable to continue north. I ask for you to allow these men to stay on the island until our return."

Hearing Omai's translation, Ki'ikiki nodded.

"Aloha and welcome to the Island of Kauai. Whether these men can stay is for the Ali'i Nui and the council to decide. But you may come ashore tomorrow and get what supplies you need."

Pleased with their first encounter, Cook and Ki'ikiki stepped towards each other and, as was the custom here too, pressed their foreheads together and exchanged breath.

Walter smiled, breathing a sigh of relief. So far so good, he thought, as my life will depend on how well this proceeds.

Chapter Seventeen

*S*everal days later Walter watched three longboats being prepared to be lowered into the water. He knew that he looked pale and gaunt, and he leant wearily against the mast while his belongings were carefully stacked beside him. The sailors had wrapped Walter's possessions in oilcloth to protect them from the inevitable drenching they would get on the way through the surf and began to load the luggage into the boats.

Despite Walter's anticipation at landing, his mood was sombre. He knew that much depended on how he would cope with the transition to life here on the Island and the very thing that he needed, namely medical attention, would not be available.

As Walter watched all the activity on deck, Williamson barking orders caught his attention. "Come on, you lot, get a move on!"

Walter's curiosity was piqued when the officer, a sly look on his face, disappeared from sight for a brief time. When he appeared again, Walter could see that Williamson was now armed with his musket and pistol. He rejoined the crew and continued to organise the men as they prepared the boats.

Although Walter noted Williamson's brief absence and the fact that he had armed himself, he dismissed it as of no real importance as his attention was more focused on the sailors, who had neatly secured his luggage in the longboat and were now waiting for him to board.

As Walter took his place by the gangway, John Webber approached him. "I want to thank you for your work, Mr Beaumont. You have been a great help." Webber paused for a second, and when he continued to speak, he did so with a sombre tone. "Remember to exercise your talent here while you wait for us. I am looking forward to adding your work to our collections."

Walter smiled. "I'll do my best, Mr Webber, though I doubt that I'll ever be as prolific and diligent as you."

"Well, in any case, bonne chance et bonne santé!"

Walter bowed. "Merci, Monsieur Webber."

The two men shook hands. Webber coughed awkwardly as he looked around. Walter was wondering if Webber wanted to say anything else when the Illustrator turned abruptly and without another word walked away.

Walter had been unaware that Cook was waiting off to the side and when the artist was out of earshot, the Captain took the opportunity step in beside him. Walter sensed that Cook seemed to be as uncomfortable with the situation as Webber. Cook peered at Walter for a moment and cleared his throat. "I wish you God's speed, Mr Beaumont." Cook looked away and stared into the distance. He was silent for a while and then spoke with what Walter took to be an almost mournful tone, "You do understand, that I have had little choice in this matter."

This surprised Walter as the Captain was not usually prone to justifying himself, nor had he ever shown himself to be overly sentimental. "I do, Sir. In light of my health, I suspect this is as good as I can hope for."

Cook again cleared his throat and then squared his shoulders. Leaving Walter behind was obviously a burden to the man. "Spoken in good spirit, lad."

The Captain then did something Walter thought was entirely out of character. He patted Walter on the shoulder. It was a paternal gesture that came quite unexpectedly. "Take care, and let me assure you that we will see you soon enough."

Touched by Cook's uncharacteristic display of emotion, Walter's eyes welled up. He quickly wiped his eyes. "Thank you, Sir, and to and the crew I wish you God's speed."

Cook signalled a couple of sailors to help Walter into the long-boat, and, having seen to it that he was safely secured, he disappeared from Walter's sight.

The crew pushed the boat away from the ship, and as it made its way to shore, Walter turned to wave. There on the quarterdeck, he saw Captain Cook standing motionless. Then the Captain slowly lifted his hand and tipped his hat in a salute. I will miss the old grouch, Walter thought, knowing that for the most part, Cook had always meant well. Ah well, all going to plan, I'll see him soon enough.

Walter turned his attention to matters at hand, and as he sat in the bow of the longboat, he carefully watched the faces of the sailors as they rowed in a steady stroke towards the shore. As he was still uncomfortable in the small boat, he clung to the railings with a firm grip.

A sizeable swell from the northwest had hit the coast and, in the last few hours, it had in fact, gotten even bigger. Just like the waves, Walter's anxiety surged. Despite spending time in the crystal waters of the lagoons in Tahiti, where he got accustomed to the feeling of being submerged, his fear of drowning still haunted him. So the only thing he could do was to cling nervously to the gunnels of the boat. The only small comfort was that the faces of the crew assured Walter that he was not alone in his terror.

Earlier on the deck of The Resolution, Walter had listened to a passionate discussion amongst the men about whether they should wait a day to see if the surf would drop. More than a few of the crew had expressed that they were not keen to tackle the big swell. Yet, despite the treacherous conditions, they were desperate for freshwater, and landing on the beach presented the perfect opportunity to replenish other food supplies.

As the discussion swayed to and fro like the deck of the ship, the officers finally cut the debate short and ordered the crews to go ahead with the planned landing. The crews would drop Walter and Omai off and collect the much-needed supplies. The subsequent tension amongst the unhappy men created a testing atmosphere in itself, and small spats had erupted from time to time amongst the crew as the longboats were being loaded.

Like Walter, most of the sailors could not swim and they feared being thrown out of the boat into the surf where they knew that they could drown. The Marines faced their own challenges with their heavy uniforms and equipment. The weight of it all meant that they had little opportunity to stay afloat, let alone swim. Drowning was a genuine threat on any landing where the surf pounded the beach.

With Walter's back to the waves, his only gauge to what was happening was the changing faces of the sailors in his, and the boat next to them. As they got closer and closer to shore, most of their expressions had turned from concern to fear. In the shifting currents of the surf, the sweep of one of the other boats appeared to struggle to keep that vessel on an even keel, but he managed. Walter was impressed that despite the challenge of keeping the boats on course, the sweeps bellowed ample encouragement to their crews. "Put your backs into it, lads! We'll be fine!"

From time to time, they kept the pace by yelling, "Stroke! Stroke! Now steady, lads!"

Not once did the sweep of the boat look back behind him, working purely on instinct, and of having landed a longboat in all sorts of conditions, and what Walter assessed was his dogged determination that the size of these waves was not going to get the better of him.

On the beach, a massive crowd of Hawai'ians had assembled and were shouting and waving to the approaching boats. Watching the throng, Walter was not sure if they were trying to urge them on or to warn them. In any event, the trip to shore was proving more dangerous than anyone had suspected. As they came into the break zone, one of the boats pitched down the face of a wave, bouncing along just in front of the white water, perilously close to capsizing.

"Boat your oars!" The sweeps order thundered over their heads. Walter quickly gathered that the oars now proved to be more dangerous than useful. A few boat lengths from the beach, the waves crashed over the gunnels. The Marines were the first to be thrown in the water and just as they feared, most of them were restricted by their heavy clothing and gear. Clasping on to oars and some empty barrels they struggled to stay afloat. Eventually, Walter saw that the Marines had reached the shallows where they scrambled on to the sand. He was confident it was only fear and sheer determination that got them onto the beach. There, many collapsed from sheer exhaustion. Meanwhile, in the shore break, some of the Marines had to be rescued by the Hawai'ians, who deftly pulled them out of the water.

Swamped by another wave, their boat washed unceremoniously up onto the beach where it rested in the sand, rolling from side to side, spilling some of its load into the frothing water.

Meanwhile, the boat carrying Walter headed steadily towards the beach, and without turning around to see what was behind them, he knew that their turn had come to cross the stretch of surf between the edge of the reef and the beach.

The sweep yelled to the crew, "Put yar backs in it, lads or ya'll be drownin' like the rest o'them!"

Their strength boosted by the rush of adrenaline, the sailors, did their best to pick up speed just in time to avoid the lip of the wave crashing down onto them. Suddenly engulfed by the frothing white water, the boat surfed towards the shore, eventually sliding onto the sand. Relieved to have avoided being swamped and drowning in the surf, the crew hollered with the joy for their successful landing.

Walter, keen to get onto the beach, tried to get out of the boat as quickly as he could, but being so weak, he lost his footing and fell into the seething water. Suddenly finding himself submerged, he was conscious not to panic and then from somewhere above, Walter felt the grip of someone pulling him up, and with their help, Walter thrashed his way up toward the beach. Spluttering and spitting he heard Omai telling him to stop fighting and let him help him. Walter, having not realised that he has been strug-

gling against a rescuer, immediately relaxed and let his friend
help him.

Blinking madly, trying to clear his eyes of the wet sand that had
covered him from head to toe, Walter and Omai struggled up onto
the beach and away from the chaos of the floundering boats and
their crews.

Seeing the English battle in the shore break, the Hawai'ians had
rushed in to help them as best as they could. Men, women and children were equally interspersed in the surf assisting the English to
get themselves and their goods onto dry land. Walter and Omai
watched the last boat reach the shore break. It, too, was immediately swamped by a breaking wave.

Williamson, who Walter thought should never have been given
this duty, was agitated by the drenching he had received, and when
the Islanders tried to steady the boat, he stood up. In his hand was
his pistol. He yelled ferociously at the Hawai'ians. "Back away from
the boat, you black heathens! A pox on you all!"

One of the men naively tried to grab the weapon in
Williamson's hand and a deafening explosion cut through the air.
The man fell lifeless into the water and a dark, a red stain spread
through the foaming sea, turning it pink. The shock and confusion
as to what had just happened to the man had the Hawai'ians
instantly retreat. Two of the Islanders seized the lifeless body of
their companion and having picked him up, they ran up the beach
from where they swiftly disappeared into the forest.

The incident took place so quickly that most of the sailors struggled to comprehend what had happened. Some of them looked to
the officer for an explanation while Walter, still trying to catch his
own breath, was speechless and floundering in the sand.

Omai, closest to the tragedy, was utterly outraged by
Williamson's action. He jumped angrily into the shallows, and with
one swift motion, pulled Williamson out of the boat and onto the
sand. With a single punch aimed at Williamson's temple, Omai
knocked the baffled officer out cold. Then, scooping the unconscious man up, he dragged him up the beach and flung him unceremoniously onto the dry sand.

The Tahitian looked around expecting some form of retaliation from the crew, but none of the crew or the Marines showed any interest in taking a stand against him for attacking Williamson. In fact, none of them showed the least interest in helping the third officer at all.

Walter felt that most of them were more preoccupied with their own condition and with the possible repercussions of what had occurred. Some of the Marines positioned themselves to keep a close eye on the path leading into the forest from which any retaliatory strike could eventuate.

Slowly the chaotic scene on the beach became more orderly as the men managed to secure the boats and collect all of the bits and pieces that had been swept up onto the beach. The sailors and Marines then spent most of the afternoon establishing a makeshift camp on the beach, securing its perimeter with logs and bonfires and were now quietly sitting around, and preparing whatever food they had available.

Exhausted and subdued, the English sat and lay scattered around their belongings. As the sun set behind a group of grey thunderclouds, an uneasy calm had descended onto the beach. The lack of wind in the trees and palms added to the eerie mood where barely a conversation was to be heard.

Walter was aware that they were all fearful of the consequences of killing one of the natives. While they were still on the ship, several of the sailors who had earlier on traded with some of the Hawai'ians had spread the word that the natives in these parts were not averse to eating their enemies, a practice that they shared with the Tangata Whenua of New Zealand.

The sailors convinced that it was merely a matter of time before warriors would emerge from the forest and exact revenge for their fallen friend, reinforced the perimeter guard around the camp. But nothing could ease their tension. From time to time, strange sounds would emanate from the forest, causing everyone to immediately reach for whatever weapon they had available.

Williamson paced restlessly along the perimeter. He, too, was startled by every noise he heard. As if to reassure himself, he kept muttering that he was not going to die in this godforsaken place. Every now and then, he ordered the men to do something to fortify their position. Although the crew obeyed his orders silently, he was subtly ostracised from the group as a whole. The Marines, equally wary of being too close to Williamson, organised themselves into a separate group altogether.

Walter and Omai stretched themselves out on a bed of palm fronds a small distance away from the rest of the crew. They had used a natural outcrop of black, volcanic rock to create an excellent shelter from which they were well protected from the wind, and they had spread some of their clothes across the rock so that they could dry.

Lying back, Walter and Omai watched Williamson's pacing. I was right, Walter thought bitterly, Williamson had proved to be a danger to them.

"I can not believe that Williamson may have jeopardised every-thing!" Walter spat the words out, but Omai's only response was to encourage him to get some rest so that they could deal with what-ever eventuated. But Walter didn't want to be pacified. "Surely you must see that the man is a menace. We should let Cook know what he has done!"

Omai just looked at him and shook his head. "Get some sleep, Walter", was all he said before he rolled over and left Walter with his thoughts. Unable to sleep he pulled his journal out and using the light of the fire to see, Walter decided to write about the day.

Chapter Eighteen

*J*t had been a strange day, thought the Mo'i of Kauai
Kamakahelei, as she sat on the raised platform over-
looking the interior of the ha'lau, the Great Meeting Hall. The hall
was filled to capacity with her chiefs, Kahuna and warriors and the
crowd was a kaleidoscope of colour, with most of the nobility
dressed formally in the red and yellow of the Ali'i.

Kamakahelei was at ease in her ability to present herself as a
woman of wealth and power and was proud that, along with her
husband, Kaneoneo, she was able to rule their people with a level of
benevolence, unlike many other chiefs.

She was also pleased that their daughter Lelemahoalani was
here with them, sitting slightly to the side of her, attentively
observing the proceedings. Kamakahelei was deeply satisfied with
the woman her daughter had become. Not only tall and stunningly
beautiful with hair as black as a lava flow, but more importantly, she
was intelligent, and she took a keen interest in the governing of the
island. If the need arose, she had the talent to become an excep-
tional leader.

Next to Lelemahiolani stood Kumahana, her older brother, who was generally more concerned with sport and warfare than the affairs of state. He was finely-built and sported intricate tattoos around his arms and thighs, that he had acquired as a demonstration that despite his lack of size, he was as brave a warrior as any, and always ready to face battle and the pain it could bring.

When Kanoa told her of his sighting of the strange canoes, Kamakahelei understood immediately that life was about to change in a way no one could have anticipated. She then gave offerings to the gods, praying for good omens, and most of all, peace for her people.

As the 'awa ceremony opened the council meeting, she found herself distracted, and looking around the hall her attention was caught by the sight of Kanoa who also seemed to be in deep thought, staring at the ground in front of him. Her heart warmed, thankful to have such a man, not just as an advisor, but also as a friend. Yes, she thought, Kaneoneo and I are lucky indeed.

The interior of the ha'lau, their vast meeting hall, was lit by torches and fires that cast an intricate pattern of light and shadows across the people assembled. She looked across their faces and mused on whom she could trust, and who would try and leverage gain for their own sake from the arrival of the haole, these pale strangers.

Her gaze fell on Koa, Kanoa's apprentice. How ironic, that at the very moment that she wondered about loyalty that she should search out Koa. The boy was from a prominent noble family on Moloka'i and had come to Kauai to be apprenticed to Kanoa. She remembered him as a child. Taller and stronger than most of his peers, he had shown clear leadership, not so much by his physical attributes, but by his cunning and single-minded determination to win, and to succeed at whatever he did. Despite being very charismatic, Koa frequently chose to use force to secure an advantage just because he could. As is often the case with young men, this earned him respect and a growing group of followers.

Many rumours abounded around the young man. Some thought Koa's family practised sorcery and that the boy would one day show his hand through its use. Others held him in high esteem as his lineage led back to the Great Kahuna of Moloka'i, who had a tradition of deep learning and magic. It was well known amongst the Islanders that Kanoa himself had spent much of his own youth there, gathering the intricate knowledge and skills that made him so invaluable to Kamakahelei.

The Queen was deeply concerned that Kumahana, her own son, had been seduced by Koa's apparent charm and hidden cruelty, especially as the two had become virtually inseparable since their childhood. Together, they had forged an alliance that led many young warriors eager for the profits of battle, and the power and influence that any victory would bring. Even some of the older chiefs began to align themselves to Koa's group.

Kamakahelei continued to watch as one of the retainers passed a cup of 'awa to Kanoa, the Kahuna Kalai, her canoe carver. She felt that he was entitled to be acknowledged as more than a craftsman. He was an accomplished warrior and a skilled statesman, and Kamakahelei took every opportunity to remind him of his value to her. But Kanoa would point out to her that carving was his passion and the ocean his love, while the other things he did were out of necessity. She smiled as she reflected that he often reminded her that he preferred to be acknowledged for his passions and love, and not for what he was compelled to do. He was indeed wise, Kamakahelei thought.

Kanoa took the cup and drained it, casting the Mo' i a quizzical look as if to ask what she was thinking. Kamakahelei smiled, allowing her warmth to radiate out to him. It did not escape her that Koa was watching her closely, and so reluctantly she let her smile fade into one of serene neutrality.

As the 'awa ceremony came to a close, it signalled the opening of the proceedings. Ku'ohu stood up and proceeded to announce formally, "The God, Lono, has returned! The prophecy has been fulfilled."

A murmur ran through the ha'lau like a wave. Koa quietly shook his head. Although still Kanoa's apprentice, he was an accomplished warrior, and like the Kahuna, had trained in Lua, a secret martial art developed in the last few generations. When Koa spoke, he did so with the confidence of someone born to lead.

"With respect, Ku'ohu, we do not know for certain if Lono has returned."

In the ensuing silence, Kanoa chose to slowly rise to his feet. He was an excellent orator when the need arose and so could resort to all the skill and theatrics he needed to hold the council's attention. The Queen knew that he understood that this was a moment that was too important for him not to give it his best.

Kanoa stepped dramatically around the circle, coming to a standstill in front of Ku'ohu. He looked intently at the priest. What he was about to say would not make him popular with the Kahuna, but Kamakahelei was reassured by the fact that the two of them had been at odds before, and had always been able to resolve their issues and to continue to respect each other.

"They are not gods." Kanoa paused, his voice resonating within the hall. He wanted to give the council time to absorb the ,meaning of his words. "They want to trade food and water with us and have asked that we allow two of them to stay and live among us." He stopped and carefully looked around the hall. "That is not what gods do." Kanoa paused again, allowing the gathering to reflect on his observations. His voice then rose powerfully.

"They are men, and," he winked and added mischievously, "they smell like shit."

A howl of laughter erupted in ha'lau, breaking the tension that had been building up. Kamakahelei, too, couldn't help laughing. Kanoa had always displayed impeccable timing, she thought.

Ka'eo sat frowning, he was one of the few chiefs, not laughing. "But even if they are not gods, they have great mana. Look how their stick that throws fire killed Koa's cousin."

A frown appeared on Kanoa's forehead as he reflected carefully for a moment on Ka'eo's observation. The Queen knew that he was about to suggest a course of action that was quite uncharacteristic of him. "Yes, so perhaps we should kill them now before they bring more pain and sorrow!"

A look of surprise crossed Koa's face, which was quickly replaced by excitement. He bowed to the Mo' i. "Ali'i Nui, their floating island contains many things that could be of use to us, especially great stores of iron." He paused. "We should take this prize, Ali'i Nui, and then rid ourselves of these smelly strangers."

A loud murmur rippled through the assembly. Many chiefs nodded with approval. The goods they could gain would be of great use, especially the iron that they saw on the ships. This would give them the advantage they needed against the many Ali'i from the other islands who were preparing for war. And this bounty to have arrived at the very time when Kalaniopu'u from the big island of Hawai'i was trying to extend his control and influence across the rest of the island chain, should not be wasted.

Kanoa continued to walk around the circle. The Queen knew he was playing a dangerous game that could backfire on them both. Too many of the warriors were ready to fight, while those of the Ali'i who wanted to rule peacefully were being pushed into the background. Kanoa knew as well as she did, that what would change their minds would be that the perceived loss was outweighed by the potential gains.

"My ambitious apprentice may be right, we could gain much." He stopped and slowly looked around the circle, silently connecting with each and every one of the chiefs and Kahunas. "But at what cost?" His voice boomed through the ha'lau, hanging pregnant in the air.

Ki'ikiki nodded gravely. "If we give them what they ask for, they will leave, but if we harm them many more may come."

The discussion continued passionately for a time giving Kamakahelei a chance to reflect on the various opinions that emerged. Still, the debate essentially boiled down to either killing the strangers and appropriating the ships and their content, or to create a peaceful alliance with them.

Kamakahelei suddenly tapped her staff sharply on the mat-covered platform, a dull thud echoing through the hall. She had made up her mind, and the ha'lau descended respectfully into silence.

"My father once told me we can learn much from those not like us." Her voice echoed through the ha'lau. "This is such an opportunity." She kept her expression sober as she waited for Kanoa to speak. The two of them had played this game before.

"Ali'i Nui, let us be prudent. We have what we need, why want more?"

She smiled at her friend and advisor. "Your council has always been sound, Kanoa, but there is much at stake here. Chief Kalaniopu'u wages war from Hawai'i and the knowledge of the haole may be useful to us in defending ourselves should it come to that."

She paused for a moment and looked around the ha'lau. She knew that most of her people saw the sense in what she was proposing. The risk was worth it.

"My decision is that we meet these strangers in the morning and welcome them with aloha."

Kamakahelei was very satisfied with the meeting's progress. It had gone precisely the way she, Kaneoneo and Kanoa had planned it. The council felt consulted, they had averted bloodshed, and yet they still stood to gain from the arrival of the strangers. It was now time for Kanoa to bring up the request that not only the Tahitian be allowed to stay, but also one of the haole. Once he did so, she responded by demanding that he could remain if he obeyed the kapu.

The Mo'i looked around the circle of chiefs and priests. They all agreed just as she knew they would. This would be an opportunity to discover more about these strangers.

Kamakahelei looked outside of the circle, curious to see if the warriors were equally as united in this decision. Not surprised, she noted that there were a large number of them clearly dissatisfied with the outcome of the council meeting. The young men were eager to prove themselves in battle and increase their power and wealth, but they had not yet the mana to challenge her or the council. However, too much frustration and they could become dangerous. The line between peace and war grew steadily thinner and more difficult to navigate.

Saddened, she looked at Kanoa who was also keenly watchful of the warriors and could obviously see the looks of dissent in the group. She recognised that he too knew that their future would require strong leadership if they were to continue to avert a war. At least the arrival of the two vessels had proven a distraction from the tides of unrest amidst her people.

Chapter Nineteen

a rustle from the lush, green forest had woken Walter just in time to see a group of Hawai'ians cautiously appear on the edge of the beach. Instead of the weapons that he had been expecting, the Islander's were carrying baskets of food and gourds of water. After the previous day's events, the English were all on edge, and although there seemed to be no threat, the Marines were quick to grab their muskets as they hurriedly got to their feet.

Williamson was already up, having spent much of the night pacing along the shoreline. Pistol in hand he was shouting at the Marines to ready themselves for a confrontation. Not prepared to abide any more stupidity on the third officer's part, Walter was quick to intervene, growling at the man to stop being provocative.

While Walter judiciously placed himself in front of Williamson, Omai hurriedly stepped up to greet the Hawai'ians, apparently hoping that he could stave off any potential hostilities. Seeing the Tahitian, the warriors around the Kahuna appeared to relax a little and the big man, clothed in a beautiful girdle of kapa cloth and a red kapa cape clasped around the neck, stepped forward with his left fist clenched. Omai followed his example until the men's faces were only inches apart. Despite the tension amongst the English, the two men completed the ceremonial greeting of forehead touching and the exchanging of breath.

As the Tahitian and the Hawaiian stepped apart, the other natives placed the food and water they had brought on the ground and then retreated a few steps. "Ia Orana, Tahuna," said Omai in Tahitian. Walter, watching the greeting carefully saw that the leader of the group frown and then speak rapidly to Omai. Walter could not understand what was said, but he knew in his guts that it was about him. There had been no formal acceptance of his request to stay on the islands, and yet here he was on their land.

Omai answered the warrior and then turning to Walter told him that they were indeed questioning his presence. Omai said that he had told them that Walter was too ill to stay on board the ship and that the healer on the vessel had recommended that he spend time on land. Then turning back to the leader, whom he had named as Kanoa, Omai continued the negotiations for their acceptance as guests of the Hawai'ian's.

Walter watched Kanoa nod and point to the food and water, while Omai kept pointing to the English trade-goods. After further discussion, the two men appeared to agree on something.

Kanoa turned and spoke rapidly to the others then turned back to Omai and after a brief exchange between the two of them, Omai looked satisfied and smiled. He turned and slowly walked back to Walter. "Walter, remember this man from the ship?"

Walter nodded, thinking that it was not very easy to forget such an impressive-looking man. "He has come to take us to his council." Relieved that what could have turned into a confrontation had obviously been dealt with effectively, Walter smiled at the waiting Islanders. He was feeling a little weak this morning and wondered briefly if they could have something to eat before heading off, but thought better of it when he saw the look on Williamson's face.

The man was still agitated, and he was recklessly waving his pistol around like someone deranged, pointing it at the Islanders and apparently prepared to shoot someone if he had any provocation at all. The Marines were confused but had their muskets cocked and ready. Walter could clearly see that if Williamson gave the order, they would shoot at the Islanders.

Walter, already enraged by the idiocy of the man snapped at him with all of the authority that he could muster. "Stop! For pity's sake, they have given you no cause to be so antagonistic Mr Williamson! Put your gun down and let us act like the civilised men that we supposedly are."

Walter looked around at the Marines and seeing them waver, he continued speaking. "Mr Williamson, in a few hours you will leave this place. I, on the other hand, may well remain amongst these people. I am, quite literally, at their mercy. I ask you not to jeopardise my position further than you may already have with yesterday's shooting." He stopped for a moment and as Williamson did not respond, continued more forcefully. "Put your weapon down, Mr Williamson, and I promise you that Captain Cook will not hear of your actions yesterday."

Williamson still did not reply and continued to train the pistol on the group of Hawai'ians. Determined to resolve the matter one way or another, Walter now pulled his own weapon from his jacket and aimed it at the officer. "If you do not drop your gun, Sir," Walter continued, "I will take it upon myself to end your miserable life so that you can no longer inflict your temper upon others."

Williamson, wavering, hesitated for a moment longer and then broke into a sly grin. "As you wish, Mr Beaumont!"

The officer holstered his pistol, turned on his heels and without another word or look, walked over to the longboats.

Fatigued by the effort of dealing with Williamson, Walter's arm dropped to his side. He stood there for a second, then slowly and carefully replaced the small pistol back in the holster under his jacket.

The tension slowly eased, and as the Marines lowered their weapons, some of them gave Walter a look of approval, their expressions of relief telling him that they had been loath to get caught up in an unnecessary conflict.

As the sailors quickly collected the food and water that had been deposited on the beach by the natives, the Marines promptly dismantled the makeshift camp. It took them very little time to ready themselves for the return to the ship, and with a perfunctory farewell, they launched the longboats and headed out into the lagoon.

Walter was acutely aware that the tussle between himself and Williamson had shown his own people in a feeble light. Watching the leader of the group of Islanders, who was charged with taking them to what would be his home for the foreseeable future, Walter was sure he had seen a flicker of concern in the man's eyes before his face shut down and became unreadable.

Omai and several of the natives gathered his, and Walter's possessions, and following Kanoa, they moved into the cool shade of the forest. The morning sun broke through the canopy of branches and cast streams of light across sections of the path which was well worn and obviously maintained. Birdcalls rang out, and the wind blew gently through the branches of the trees, while there were rustlings from the ground cover off to the side of the path, indicating small animals hidden by the foliage.

The group walked in silence in a smooth rhythm that Walter would have enjoyed before his illness, but now he was finding it hard going. So, it's come to this, he pondered, suddenly feeling a wave of melancholy and grief for his lost health and strength wash over him. But rather than allowing himself to be dragged down into some dark, emotional abyss, he quickly decided that this would not do. Common sense alerted him to the fact that he risked being his own worst enemy in these unfamiliar surroundings. No, he thought, this was not the time to get too maudlin about either his health or his dubious future.

To keep himself distracted from these serious rumination's, he took his time to look around. Like Tahiti, the land was fertile and abundantly populated with birds, and although much of the vegetation was familiar it appeared subtly different from the plants he had seen elsewhere in the South Pacific. The air was an aromatic mixture of the ocean, with the earthiness of the uplands interspersed with the strong scent of flowers.

Despite the reality that he was rapidly tiring, Walter was

enjoying his surroundings until he heard Kanoa say something and the column of men suddenly stopped on the pathway. The big Islander made his way back to Omai, who was in front of Walter and spoke to him in a quiet but emphatic manner. Walter had no way of understanding what was said, but he felt a prickle of apprehension as he watched Omai's back tense, and his friend turned and spoke to him gravely. "Walter, whatever happens right now, do nothing, or this could be your last breath."

Two warriors had stepped up beside Walter and they now smartly and efficiently threw him to the ground. Before he could even begin to protest about his treatment, his hands were pulled up behind his back and quickly bound. Then, one of the warriors rolled him onto his side and slid his hand roughly around in between Walter's jacket and shirt, apparently searching for something. Having retrieved the pistol that Walter had carried in a holster under his arm, the colossal warrior held it up to his face, and for an instant scrutinised it, before placing it cautiously into a small pouch he had slung across his shoulder.

Walter was then to his mind, rather roughly brought back to his feet and planted firmly between the two warriors. Having taken Omai's warning to heart, he made no move that could be misinterpreted as being hostile. Being rash and impulsive at this point may well cost him his life, so he allowed himself to be guided along the path. However, it didn't take very long before his exhaustion, and the discomfort of having his arms behind his back started to show itself. Stumbling, he found himself being dragged along by his guards, and this is how he was ignominiously brought to their destination.

Walter found himself immediately at the centre of attention. His guards let go of him, and he swayed back and forth for a few seconds, trying to ignore the groping hands as best he could, but as the dizziness took over, he let himself collapse to the ground. Lying there, he tried to look around and make sense of the blurred images around him. Tired, sore and barely conscious, he saw only images of bare feet and legs of different shapes and sizes. As the sound of voices faded, he slowly lost consciousness.

Chapter Twenty

*K*amakahelei had called another council meeting after Kanoa had informed her that the Tahitian was a canoe-carver and navigator and deserved an honoured welcome. The Kahuna wanted the introduction of the Tahitian to have a ceremony befitting a guest from such a great distance, especially one from the place of their ancestors. 'He had come from Kahiki.' Kanoa thought. There were so many questions he wanted to ask the Tahitian.

While curious on the one hand, on the other Kanoa was still very concerned with what he had witnessed on the beach. He felt the need to inform the Mo' i as quickly as possible that he had observed the malihini's (strangers) willingness to use the stick that throws fire. The situation was now more complicated than it had first appeared, Kanoa thought.

"As you all know, the two malihini seek permission to stay. The fair-skinned one is unwell, and cannot continue with his voyage on the large wa'a." Kanoa paused. "The other man is a Kahuna Kalai Wa'a, a canoe builder and navigator who has come from Kahiki."

A wave of excited voices rose in the ha'lau. Kanoa gave the

assembly a little time to consider the news. He then raised his hand, and the voices died down.

"He wishes to learn to ride the big waves."

Murmurs of approval emanated from the seated chiefs and Kahuna. It had been many generations since anyone had come from or gone to Kahiki. Curiosity and wonder gripped the council members.

Ki'ikiki, always the serious one, expressed his concern about the pale stranger bringing illness to the village which Kanoa could see mirrored in the expressions of many of the council. Ki'ikiki also asked to hear from Koa about the acceptance of the haole, given it was his beloved cousin who had died during the conflict on the beach. "Koa, what have you to say on this matter?"

The young warrior had been sitting quietly but now got to his feet to address the assembly. "It has been a long time since we were voyagers and now here is a man from across the ocean, from Kahiki. We should welcome him to stay as a guest and allow him to ride the waves with us. It is our honour to have him here."

He stopped speaking for a moment and theatrically walked around the council. He paused briefly and then began to talk again, his voice brimming with anger. "But my cousin was killed by the haole's weapon that shoots fire.' He pointed dramatically at the entrance to the hall and the general direction of the hut where the haole was currently being held. "That man should have no place here."

Approving voices echoed from different parts of the hall while Koa paused again and continued walking around the circle. "But I have considered the Mo' i's words, and sense the truth of them." He paused dramatically. "We must learn from him."

Kanoa had been watching Koa with considerable interest. Since the arrival of the two strangers, the young warrior had been acting more secretively. He had watched Koa remove the weapon from the haole, but the young man had not given it to him, as Kanoa had first expected. This would have been the respectful thing to do. Yes, he thought, there is a good reason to be concerned.

Kamakahelei looked thoughtfully across to the Kahuna. He had told her about the incident on the beach and how he felt that the pale strangers could not be trusted, despite having the honour of bringing a Kahuna Kalai wa'a to their island. She decided, however, that she was determined to make the most of this encounter.

Kanoa looked up to see the Mo'i watching him. He lowered his head. "It is clearly your decision, great Mo'i."

Kamakahelei sat quietly contemplating the situation, apparently trying to sense the mood amongst her people. In the silence, Kanoa could feel the tension in the ha'lau rise. Finally, the Mo'i signalled two guards, to attend to her and after a brief moment to hear their instructions they quickly left the meeting hall, calling another two warriors to join them The ha'lau immediately erupted into noisy discussions amongst the council and Kanoa noted that the Mo'i watched them closely.

ċaċaċaċaċa

Walter had woken to find himself in a rude hut that Omai had informed him had been erected to house him. Omai had apparently been offered shelter in one of the guest huts, but he had remained by Walter' side, explaining to Walter that he had been unconscious for many hours. Encouraging him to drink some of the water and eat some fruit, Omai continued to fill Walter in on what has occurred since he had collapsed. Omai had not been able to gain access to Kanoa during that time, but there had been no open hostility displayed towards them so far.

They were talking when a small group of warriors stepped up to the hut and roughly dragged Walter to his feet. He swayed as the sudden movement caused him to feel dizzy, and Omai was quick to come to his aid, but the two warriors shifted themselves into position around him, apparently planning to drag him if he couldn't walk.

Walter shrugged the hands that held him off and took several gingerly steps forward. So far, so good, he thought, and he followed the warriors out of the hut into the bright light of the day. The Warriors stayed close but did not try to manhandle him again, and they directed both him and Omai to a building that Omai called the ha'lau.

He felt like an exhibit in a circus, as he entered the crowded meeting hall. Many craned their necks to stare at him while others turned away from him.. Flanked by the warriors, Walter was directed to face a platform where he could see several people, including a middle-aged woman, dressed in ceremonial feathers, seated above the rest of the council.

Following Omai's lead, he clenched his left fist and went down on his knees. From that position, he noticed a pillar of about four and a half feet in height in the middle of the empty space between him and the platform. Looking oddly out of place, he wondered what it was for, as he waited for whatever was to happen next.

He felt the keen gaze of the woman on the platform who was identified to him as Kamakahelei, the Queen. Embarrassed by the state of his clothing, Walter hoped that he would not be judged too harshly. It made sense to him that the Mo'i would weigh up all of the various factors involved, and that she would be making her decision about him based on what was best for her people.

Kamakahelei tapped her staff resoundingly on the ground. "We welcome the Kahuna Kalai wa'a, Omai. Rise."

As ordered, Omai got to his feet just in time to have a young man place a lei around his neck. He smiled at the Tahitian and then pressed his forehead to his. He returned, quietly, to his place beside the platform.

"As for the haole," the Mo'i continued, "the decision of this council is that he shall stay."

She looked intently at Walter and continued to speak much more slowly than she had previously. Perhaps she knew that he did understand a few words of Tahitian and might be able to understand her. However Omai continued to translate for her, so Walter was clear about the warning he was receiving.

"For now, Omai will be your Kahu and teach you the kapu. Obey the law and you will live."

This pronouncement was followed by another of the Council standing and coming up to stand before Omai and Walter. Naturally being careful to articulate his words carefully for Walter's sake, the man, Ki'ikiki pointed to the pillar and spoke.

"Understand this, haole. Observe the fate of someone who has broken the kapu."

Omai continued to translate. "They want you to know your fate should you break the law."

Walter was well aware that he was not greeted with the traditional exchange of breath, and he wondered whether it was because he was ill or because he was not welcome. He was curious and somewhat anxious about what they were planning to demonstrate to him to make the point about being law-abiding. Looking around, he saw the warriors shift their attention to the entrance to the ha'lau.

Ki'ikiki signalled a warrior at the back of the hall, who quickly disappeared outside. Seconds later, there was a sudden loud commotion cutting through the silence that had descended on the ha'lau. The turmoil outside reached a crescendo as the wails of several men, women and children cut through the air.

Two warriors dragged a young man through the entrance into the hall to the pillar in the middle of the floor. Shocked, Walter suddenly realised what it was for. The man was roughly forced to his knees, and his back was pulled up against the pole.

One of the warriors then produced a long chorded and looped rope, and now expertly threw it around the man's throat. Each one of the ends of the rope was then held by a warrior, and together pulling in opposite directions, they began to tighten it.

A sharp hiss of air escaped the young man as the rope cut off his air supply. He desperately fought for breath as the warriors slowly increased the tension on the rope. With every passing second, the thrashing of his body against the pole became more and more frantic.

As the air rattled through the man's constricted throat, and his eyes bulged from his head, he continued his pointless struggle for life. Slowly his efforts weakened to finally ceasing altogether. He sat there for a moment, a pitiful sight made even more dramatic with his tongue protruding from his mouth. Then, in an odd sort of a movement, his head fell onto his chest. Another twitch of his body, the final gurgling sound of the escaping air from his now lifeless body and then - silence.

For a moment, the body was precariously balanced on its knees, then the warriors released the rope and the man's corpse slowly toppled forward, slumping to the ground where it lay, its lifeless eyes staring at Walter.

To Walter, it appeared that all eyes were now on him. He sat there, mortified, staring transfixed at the lifeless body of the young man. He felt the bile rise sharply in his throat, bitter and acidic, burning its way up to his mouth. It took all his strength to maintain his composure and desperately fight back the urge to vomit.

Without a word, Kamakahelei and her family rose and proceeded to leave the ha'lau. A stream of people followed them out into the square.

Two warriors and a couple of young men stayed behind and waited alongside Omai and Walter. It was Omai who broke the silence. "Come, Walter, its time to leave." Having stood up, he bent down and helped Walter, who was struggling to get up, and then they too left the ha'lau.

Neither of them spoke as they were escorted back to the hut that had been provided for their shelter. Walter wondered how the young man had broken the law, and if his crime had been deserving of such punishment. Not for the first time he thought that he may have well put himself into a far more precarious position than if he had stayed on the Resolution.

Chapter Twenty-One

*O*utside the ha'lau, a frangipani-scented light breeze ruffled the feathers of the kahili., the two standards about eight feet tall with intricate feather arrangements at the top of the pole, and placed at the entrance, signified that nobility had been present for a meeting.

Small groups of people, consisting mostly of chiefs and their warriors, congregated in the square in front of the meeting hall, enjoying the balmy afternoon air. Most were engrossed in earnest discussions about the recent events that had taken place and how the pale stranger had reacted to the demonstration of the kapu.

Koa, surrounded by his group of warriors, was flanked by Kumahana, the Mo'i's son. The two men were known to be inseparable, and it was rumoured that Kumahana saw Koa as his superior rather than the other way around and that he would often defer to Koa before making a decision. The group were animatedly discussing the stranger's ships and their content when Kanoa approached them.

As the Kahuna walked up to them, the group of young men respectfully stood aside and greeted Kanoa warmly. He acknowledged them one by one and then turned to Koa. "Come, walk with me."

As the two men walked towards the village, Kanoa maintained a thoughtful silence, only breaking it when they reached the fern edge that marked the beginning of the lush, green forest.

"You did not say much in council, Koa."

The young warrior smiled wistfully." Have you not taught me to be brief with words but sound in action?"

Kanoa returned his apprentice's smile and diplomatic response. He did, however, wonder why Koa was trying to flatter him. Kanoa castigated himself for being too suspicious and cast the thought aside. He had spent too much time with intrigue, and he had become too suspicious.

He looked fondly at his apprentice, recalling with great affection the day he brought the boy to his kauhale many years ago. He is a man now, Kanoa reflected, and a warrior, fierce in battle. He had seen Ku, the god of war, emanate from his apprentice's face, letting all know that there was a man not to be trifled with.

"The great chief is right, Kahu, we can learn a great deal from the haole."

Kanoa nodded. "If not, then we can sacrifice him to Ku, securing our victory over the haole, when they return to collect their own."

Koa smiled and then stopped. It was obvious that he had immediately grasped that Kanoa had just led him to consider the seriousness of such an action. Leaving him to ponder that idea later, Kanoa changed the subject. He smiled broadly." Now, to more pleasant things." He put a fatherly arm around Koa's shoulder. "What of you and Lani?"

Kanoa had gathered a while ago that it was not easy for Koa to talk about this subject. Koa's courting of the Queen's daughter had been a challenge for him, but Kanoa was sure that Koa understood that Lelmahoalani was worth the effort. A marriage to the Mo' i's daughter was an essential part of both their aspirations and plans for Koa's future. Unfortunately, Koa was more comfortable in the company of warriors than the self-assured Lani.

. . .

"Lani is a stubborn woman, Kahu," Koa growled. "She makes me beg for her attention." He forced the last words out through gritted teeth. Then, looking a little embarrassed, he admitted that some of the other men laughed at him for being a love-struck fool. Smiling at the frustrated young warrior, Kanoa encouraged him to be patient and to persevere. He was rewarded with a welcome response.

"My skin is like the soles of your feet, Kahu."

Kanoa nodded to himself. Koa's use of that old axiom was an acknowledgement of his wisdom in the matter and that his apprentice was going to heed his counsel. He stretched himself out and warmly slapped his apprentice on the back.

"Well said, my Haumana, well said."

Chapter Twenty-Two

In honour of the arrival of the Tahitian, Kamakahelei had decided to organise a celebration, and she had given instructions for a pa'ina, a feast that she hoped would help to lift the mood of the village and give her people something to enjoy. She was very well aware that with the events of the past few days, and the execution of the young man in the ha'lau, death needed to be balanced out with the lighter side of life. Life and death, the queen thought to herself, are our constant companions, but how much life and how much death would these strangers bring?

Once the preparations for the festivities were on their way, The Queen decided this was the time to seek out her daughter Lani to tell her that they, along with the court and their guests would be returning to Kapa'a, the royal seat on the eastern side of the Island.

Kamakahelei had arranged for Omai to be escorted to the beach so that he could be taken back out to the stranger's ships to inform their leader of her decision to let the haole stay on the island. So she was happy when she was informed that the strangers had left their anchorage and were making for the open ocean. The speed with which they had departed would allay the fears of some of her warriors that the stranger's were seeking more than fresh supplies.

As Kamakahelei and Lani walked along the beach, bathed in the golden light of the afternoon sun, she knew that in that very moment the balance between life and death was being swayed by those ambitious enough and bold enough to seek out and conquer others. Kalaniopu'u had laid plans for an expansion of his influence and power that threatened her kingdom, just as he had done to others. But what to do, she thought. Were the strangers with their iron and weapons an answer, a possible solution to the threat from within?

Kamakahelei knew that she had no answer to this as yet, but she had decided that it would be useful to find out more about the strangers before they returned. Turning to her daughter, she informed her of her decision. "I want you to learn the haole's language. In turn, you will teach him to speak like us."

Lani replied with a cutting edge in her voice. "Let someone else do this." Taken aback by her daughter's retort,

Kamakahelei scrutinised Lani for a moment, and then rather than rebuke her, she decided to ignore her child's petulance and explain why she had chosen her for this task. "I am asking this of you because I can trust you." She paused, choosing her words carefully, needing Lani to understand why this was important. "Times are changing, and you need to learn that sometimes unpleasant things need to be done."

The Queen didn't allude to which aspect she was referring to as being 'unpleasant', but the Mo'i felt that Lani could make of it what she wanted. What she did emphasise, as they spoke further about her plans was that this was a task that was important and that she was entrusting it to Lani because she knew she was capable.

Lani listened carefully to her mother, "I am sorry. Of course, you can trust me to do whatever is necessary to assist you."

Kamakahelei was pleased that her daughter had accepted her responsibility as the daughter of the Mo'i. "I know you will do your best. Now we must reassure our people that all is as it should be."

And with that, the two women joined the court and the local villagers at the feast.

꒰ꙅ꒰ꙅ꒰ꙅ꒰

Sometime before sunrise, Walter and Omai were woken by a retainer and informed that they would be leaving Waimea to relocate to Kapa'a where they could be close to the Mo'i and her court so that they could all learn from each another.

As was the custom the court assembled at sunrise for the traditional morning prayers, and after the morning dew and mist had evaporated Walter and Omai, together with Kamakahelei's people gathered on the beach. A large fleet of large double-hulled canoes lined the shore. About fifty-five feet long and capable of accommodating up to sixty people, they were an impressive sight.

Walter carefully surveyed the vessels and marvelled at their impeccable workmanship. They were made of two types of wood which had been polished to a perfect sheen. Omai had told him that they used Koa wood for the hull and he could see that they had used timber of a lighter shade for the superstructure. The whole canoe was mostly held together by an ingenious system of sennet ties and joins, and the artist in Walter was captivated by the aesthetics of the vessels, as much as by their functionality.

Tearing his gaze away from the beauty of the canoes, Walter surveyed the mass of assembled people along the tree-lined path that led to the village. He and Omai had been informed that they, and the crews of paddlers and warriors that stood patiently by each vessel were waiting for the Mo'i's arrival. Walter estimated that there were approximately two to three thousand people between the village and the ocean.

The whole scene was reminiscent of royal processions at home, or anywhere in Europe. These people were not the savages that Williamson decried, but a prosperous people living in a complex society with all the potential that any civilisation could hold.

Two warriors now approached them to show them to one of the smaller vessels into which their belongings had already been loaded.

Walter was not only pleased, but relieved that the Hawai'ians had shown both consideration and respect for their property, given their experiences in Tahiti where pilfering had been such a problem. Here this was apparently not something he would need to be too concerned about. However, he decided that vigilance was still called for as they were at the very beginning of their time here and knew nothing of what was to come.

Rising above the bustle surrounding the fleet, the drone of conch shells announced the arrival of the royal procession as it headed to the beach. At the front of the long line of courtiers were the kahili bearers followed by the litter carrying Kamakahelei. Armed with spears, clubs and shark-teeth studded weapons the Mo'i's guard flanked her litter, while more of her elite guards brought up the rear. As the red and yellow coloured procession made its way, Walter watched the common people fall to the ground prostrating themselves the moment the litter carrying the Queen came into view. This gave the whole scene the feel of an undulating wave of humanity that finally came to a halt at the edge of the shore.

Having arrived at the largest canoe, Kamakahelei was carried onto the vessel where the litter on which she sat was secured onto the deck spanning the two hulls. The Kahuna and her guard took their places around her, and then to the echoing sounds of the conch, the vessel was pushed into the sea.

As the shells continued to drone, Walter and Omai were instructed to board their canoe. Once they were aboard, the rest of the crews and warriors took their assigned places and with a signal from one of the tallest men that Walter had ever seen, their vessels were pushed into the sea.

When all the canoes were off the beach, the paddlers brought the fleet into a formation similar to the procession. Walter was astonished at the speed and efficiency with which this occurred, and no sooner had they gained a certain velocity towards the open ocean when the sails were hoisted and driven by the power of the wind, the vessels literally leapt across the water.

Overnight the size of the waves had dropped, and although

Walter was apprehensive at being so close to the water in an open vessel, he was not as worried about the rolling surf as he had been landing at Waimea. Comforted by the Hawai'ians expertise in managing the canoes, Walter felt a sense of exhilaration in this unexpected sea voyage, and despite still being weak, he decided that he would enjoy the journey to where ever they were headed as best he could.

Rather than ploughing through the water, the canoes appeared to skip over the surface. Walter, dressed in his usual apparel, soon discovered that being half-naked would have been much more comfortable. Within a short period he had been entirely drenched with not a single dry stitch of clothing left on him, so, by the time they had rounded the bottom of the island, Walter had followed Omai's example and stripped down to his breeches, only leaving his cotton shirt on for protection against the sun.

As they travelled, Omai shared with Walter what he had gleaned so far from some to the locals about the Hawaiian's customs and laws. Walter was grateful for this as he knew that following the kapu was essential if he was not to get himself into trouble, and having witnessed the punishment for breaking the laws he was very keen to learn. Most notable were the restrictions placed upon contact with chiefs, which also applied to all people of known spiritual power. It was kapu to enter a chief's personal area, to come in contact with his hair or fingernail clippings, to look directly at him and to be in sight of him with a head higher than his. Wearing red and yellow feathers was kapu unless you were of the highest rank.

Walter listened carefully, but the more Omai explained, the more confused and worried he became. How would he ever survive this place? Fortunately, two crossed staffs, each with a white ball of feathers atop, often symbolised areas that are kapu, which to Walter's mind was one of the most helpful bits of information he could be given.

Omai had also discovered some useful information about the way the land was divided, with each area governed by a chief and apparently managed in a very similar manner as it was at home. The ahupua'a was a customary land division that was equivalent to a county in England, consisting of a portion of an island that went from the top of the local mountain to the shore, following the banks of a stream. These land divisions varied in size, depending on the economic means of the location, and were meant to support roughly equal numbers of people.

Walter was turning all of this over in his mind as the sun faded from the sky, and to the light of torches on each canoe, the fleet approached the sheltered landing of what he assumed was to be their new abode, Kapa'a in the Waialua ahupua'a, on the east side of Kauai.

Chapter Twenty-Three

*U*nder the starry sky of Kapa'a, Omai and Walter readied themselves for an uncomfortable night in a primitive dwelling on the outskirts of the village. As before, Omai had been offered a substantial hut befitting a Kahuna, however, thankfully the Tahitian had again made it abundantly clear that he would stay with his friend in the very rudimentary dwelling that had been given to Walter. In reality, it was not so much a dwelling, as it was a lean-to that had been enclosed on three sides. In front of the dwelling was a stone fireplace. The bare, dirt floor was covered with old and used mats that had been discarded by a previous owner and offered little protection from the damp earth.

Not too far away from their hut, an old man had been busy replacing the mats in his hale. Walter had watched as Omai had approached him to barter for them. On his return to their hut, Omai said he had been willing to trade a couple of iron nails for the mats but that the old man thought he was making fun of him. During the exchange, the old man had told him that the nails were treasures for the Ali'i and that he would have no use for them. But he also had no use for his old mats, so he had offered them to Omai as a gift.

As Omai displayed his gift, Walter was less than enthused by the used and thin quality of the mats, but Omai remained positive about the fact that they had received a gift. "They may not be new, but they will do for now in keeping the damp from our bodies."

Walter thought that Omai had been overly generous, offering two nails for them, and wondered if his friend had forgotten the lessons he had learnt from his attempt to buy status and standing in Tahiti. By the time they had left his home, much of what Omai had brought from England was gone. However, Omai was happy, and this time had not wasted his limited resources, so Walter thanked him for finding the mats, and the two of them started to set up their inferior accommodation as best as they could, including finding space for the luggage they had brought from the ship.

Despite having been relegated to the edge of the village, the Hawai'ians had made sure that all of Walter's possessions had been placed neatly by the hut. Unlike when he arrived on the Resolution where his luggage had been reduced to one sea-chest and his leather satchel of drawing material, it now included a sailcloth satchel that stored his curiosities from the journey to date as well as some kitchen utensils, a knife and a fork.

He was pleased to see that everything was intact and accounted for, but Omai cautioned him not to be too confident despite appearances, pointing out that these people were probably as capable of pilfering as the Tahitians and they still needed to exercise care. Walter mused how, on the one hand, the Islanders they had met previously were ready to take things from the English ships without a thought, yet at the same time leave all sorts of goods lying about that would never go astray. I wonder if I'll ever understand their rules around possessions, Walter thought, puzzled by the apparent inconsistencies of the of their laws.

When they had finished organising the hut and their goods into the cramped space, Omai prepared a simple evening meal of yams and a few pieces of meat on a stone fireplace just outside of the hut. Once they had eaten, tired from the day's events, they had settled down on their makeshift beds.

Walter was uncomfortable, and he rolled restlessly from side to side, wondering if Omai was as out of sorts with the bedding as he was. Morose, he stared into the dark. He was exhausted but unable to drift even into a fitful slumber, his mind continually recalling the horrific scene of the young warrior's strangulation. He tried to banish the images from his mind, but it was indelibly etched into his memory, and now in the quiet of the night, that memory seemed to dominate his thoughts, and the sight of the young man dying repeated itself endlessly from beginning to the grisly end.

Fed up with the constant stream of disturbing images, Walter finally managed to force his mind to focus on something more pleasant. Ironically, it was his experiences in Tahiti and his wave riding that had the desired effect of calming him down. He was curious to realise that not only was the memory soothing, but he soon found himself thinking of how pleasant it would be to re-experience it.

"Now that we are here, will you teach me to ride the waves?"

Walter waited for Omai to reply, but his friend was silent. He thought that Omai must have already fallen asleep, but then Walter heard him shifting on his matt. "In time, my friend." Omai paused, "But first we need to help you stay alive."

"Yes! I am not overly confident that I can either avoid offending people here, or succumb to this wretched illness of mine. The Kapu is complex and confusing, and as you know, I've never been good at sticking to the rules. But what of you, Omai? Is this place anything like what you expected?"

Again, Omai took his time to answer, and when he did, it was to tell Walter that he honestly did not know if they had made the right decision coming here. Like Walter, he had reeled from the harsh and cruel lesson the Hawai'ians had demonstrated to them at the council meeting. Omai was concerned that there could be a hidden agenda here that he had failed to grasp, and that he had brought Walter into peril. He was now aware that despite the similarities between Tahiti and Hawai'i, there were enough differences to make this place more alien than he had initially wanted to admit. Now, as he spoke quietly through the dark, he acknowledged that he did not have full knowledge of their customs and taboos. And this included those that controlled access to the waves and surfing.

They discussed their shared concerns for a time, and the more they spoke, the more Walter realised that Omai had lost his confidence since returning to Tahiti, where Omai had to acknowledge that his plan to recover Raiatea for his family was impossible. Walter and Omai agreed that the only thing they could do was to keep their eyes and ears open to anything that could provide a clue to their circumstances. They needed to learn to navigate the social customs and layers of etiquette to keep themselves safe. Since that included the rituals and protocols in regards to surfing, Walter and Omai would both have to be patient. It took Walter some more time to get to sleep, but having been able to speak to Omai about his fears left him feeling less alone and s little calmer.

Chapter Twenty-Four

*B*etween periods of short bursts of rain and the cycle of sun and darkness, days passed in a gentle rhythm. Omai, mostly concerned about Walter's health, had spent much of his time gathering what he needed to help Walter continue to recover. Following local custom, he set up sufficient stores of food to last them for a reasonable number of days, and he dug a small imu, an earth oven, which would enable him to provide them with regular basic meals.

The menu consisted mostly of bananas, yams, breadfruit and fish but much to Omai's delight his favourite meat, pork, was available. As good fortune would have it, he had been able to organise a steady supply of that meat to add to their larder.

Aside from pork, one of the Island staples was a taro paste called poi which was a favourite dish in these parts. Having prepared some following his neighbour's instructions, Omai handed Walter a small bowl. "Try it and see what you think."

He watched as Walter carefully inspected the purple mash at the bottom of the bowl, sniffing it, and obviously dubious about the contents. Walter dipped two fingers into the sticky smooth paste and moving his fingers cautiously to his mouth, he carefully placed his poi-covered digits onto his hesitant tongue. "Well?" inquired Omai.

Walter pulled a face. "It's bland," he offered and then suggested ruefully that it was possibly more useful as glue than food. Omai laughed goodheartedly at his friend's joke, knowing that bland or not, it was nourishing food that Walter needed.

Having done the best he could with the lean-to, Omai's ambition was to establish a more permanent and appealing home for the two of them. According to local protocol, he was required to approach the Mo' i for both a piece of land upon which they could build and permission to acquire the materials he would need to complete this work. He would also require the much-needed expertise of a Kahuna to assist with the selection of a building site, plus the construction and the blessing of the new dwelling.

When Omai had finally been allowed to speak to Kanoa about his plans, the big Hawai'ian had readily agreed that they needed a proper place to live. He had no objections to taking Omai's petition to the Queen, and the Kahuna had promised that he would get back to Omai with an answer as soon as the Queen had made a decision on the matter.

So he was not surprised when early one afternoon he was joined by Kanoa as he was examining some trees in the forest. "Omai, I have some news from the Mo' i."

Given that the Kahuna was smiling, Omai allowed himself to be optimistic. "Aué, I hope that the news you bring me is good, Kahuna?"

"The Mo' i suggested that since you may be here indefinitely, you should take the opportunity to build a kauhale."

Omai breathed a sigh of relief which was quickly replaced by a sense of excitement. The news was better than good. A kauhale was a group of houses, each dedicated to a specific purpose. A compound like that was indeed a generous offer from the Queen and would mark Omai's position in this community as being more than merely respectable. He was being honoured. It also meant that he could attract a beautiful girl to share his fortunes with him, although, he did feel that there was no urgency in that regard.

There were still many girls to pleasure before he wanted to rely on the company of one or two.

"Let me thank you, Kanoa. This is good news, indeed." Omai gripped the big man's arms in a sign of gratitude. "I hope that I can rely on you to guide me in respects to the necessary preparations."

Kanoa smiled in response to Omai's obvious delight and enthusiasm and reassured Omai that he would, of course, help him. As the two men walked back to the village, the Kahuna asked Omai if he had left his home by choice, or if he had been compelled to do so.

Surprised by the blunt question, Omai stopped and carefully reflected on how he would answer. He was keenly aware of the other man's position and influence. In the short time that they had been on the Island Omai had heard enough stories expounding the exploits of this man.

Officially Kanoa was a man of a lower class than the Ali'i, yet he appeared to have a more significant influence on the regent than many of the chiefs. Omai, an astute observer of politics and etiquette, had picked up this important, but subtle, discrepancy of order. But the question remained how the Kahuna had secured such a revered position.

Omai's pondering was calmly interrupted." Carefully weighing your answer suggests that you either have something to hide or that you are deciding on who and what I am."

Kanoa delivered his remark so matter of factly, that it had Omai stand in awe of this incredibly astute man. He had rarely seen such powers of perception. "I am here purely by choice, Kanoa." He reassured the Kahuna. "Kane called me to journey the oceans, and so I have travelled across the seas for many years and have seen many lands. I have met many different people and learned about many strange customs. When I returned to Kahiki, I found that the way things had changed there did not please me. I knew then that it was time to move on again."

The Hawai'ian nodded thoughtfully, then told Omai that he had longed to voyage across the oceans and that as it had been many generations since someone had left Hawai'i to voyage or indeed visit from afar. He was pleased it was someone who had travelled beyond the oceans that they knew.

Omai sensed that Kanoa was intensely interested in what he could tell him of his voyages, and for the first time since they had arrived, Omai felt this might be something of value to give in return for their being allowed to stay. As they continued making their way through the dense green forest, Omai noticed a tree he did not recognise and asked Kanoa what it was suitable for, thinking about the materials he would need for the kauhale. But Kanoa's answer set his mind off in a completely different direction as the Kahuna, having looked at the tree for a moment had informed him that it would make a good olo.

Kanoa's reference to the longboards used by the elite of the local people to ride the powerful swells, had Omai's heart skip a beat with anticipation. Since having arrived on Kauai, he had quickly figured out that the Hawai'ians had specialised in some forms of wave riding to very high a degree. Before he could learn these new ways of catching the waves, he needed to learn as much about the kapu as he could. He steadied his excitement with a deep breath. All in good time, he thought, first Walter and I need to get a decent place to live.

As they entered outskirts of the village, Kanoa informed Omai that he would like both him and Walter to meet with his apprentice Koa so that they could exchange a little more information about their language, and answer their questions about the political and social aspects of the Island.

Omai had no doubt that the meeting would be helpful for both him and Walter, but he also figured that Kanoa must have an agenda that had far more to do than learning about the English. He also had no doubt that to decline would be rude and possibly even an insult, so despite his misgivings, he agreed to meet with Koa the next day.

Returning to their hut, Omai found Walter sitting quietly working on his drawings. The Englishman looked a little pale but smiled brightly when he looked up. Omai was pleased he had something positive to share, and he excitedly told him the news about the kauhale and how they would build it.

⫷⫷⫷⫷⫷

At first light and to the unfamiliar sounds of the local birdlife, two men arrived to escort Walter and Omai to an area at the edge of the village. Several large mats had been spread under a huge tree that cast ample shade across the open space beneath it. Omai noted that a large gourd of water and a variety of fruit and small parcels of food had been placed on one of the corners of the matt.

Slightly to the side, on another matt, sat the Mo' i's daughter Lelemahoalani, who informed them that her mother had asked her to join Koa. It was evident to Omai that the large Hawai'ian was in charge. With the confidence of an aristocrat, he led the discussion while the princess listened carefully.

"Pelekané, let me explain. The islands are ruled by the Ali'i, chief of whom is the Ali'i Nui. Together with the Kahuna, we rule all that you see."

Omai translated this to Walter and explained that it was not that different from what he had seen in England where the King and the Church controlled the daily lives of their people.

Koa continued his explanation of life on the Island. "Then there are the people, the Maka'ainana, who work the land and fish, and below them are the kauwa, the slaves, you will know them by the mark on their forehead. Here in Kauai, all of us are all ruled by the Mo' i, our Queen."

The warrior paused for a moment to scrutinise Walter. "Tell me, Omai, what is this Pelekané's place amongst his people?"

Omai reflected on Koa's blunt question. Both Kanoa and Koa had been interested from the beginning in Walter's social status. "Koa wants to know what position you hold in England amongst your people," Omai explained to Walter.

"Then tell him that in my land I am Ali'i. In my land, we, too, have a King, and many Ali'i to rule over the common people, and our Kahuna are called priests."

Walter answered directly to Koa and Lani, who smiled at the way he used a few Hawai'ian words in his explanation. As Omai conveyed Walter's response to Koa, he watched the young warrior as he absorbed this information. After a short pause, Koa's piercing gaze carefully scrutinised Walter. Then his eyes narrowed, and he asked;

"What made him leave his land?"

That question had Omai realise that Koa had been carefully briefed by Kanoa. He looked up at Walter. "Koa wants to know why you left. What should I tell him?"

"The truth, my friend." Omai nodded. "He killed a man and had to leave to preserve his family's honour."

Koa nodded. "Then you are either very brave or foolish, haole."

He had barely finished speaking when Walter was suddenly wracked by a coughing fit. He pulled a handkerchief from his pocket and held it against his mouth. When he pulled it away, the white cloth was stained red. Koa and Lelmahoalani jumped up, a look of repulsion on their faces. The young warrior looked at Walter with some revulsion.

"You are still ill, haole!" Koa paused, drawing away from Walter. "You lack the breath of life. We do not need your illness here. You need to be cleansed. I will arrange it."

Walter looked confused as Koa and Lani hurriedly left them. "What did he say?"

"It was a play on words, Walter. He says that you lack the breath of life. As you know in the Islands, we greet each other with the honi, by pressing noses and inhaling at the same time. This is very important, as this represents the exchange of ha, the breath of life, and mana, spiritual power between two people. Your illness not only means that you cannot exchange the breath of life, but to Koa it means you have no mana, no power."

Chapter Twenty-Five

*A*s Koa had promised, he organised the Kahuna la'au, the
healer, to tend to Walter and under a darkening sky with
ominous clouds gathering, two men arrived to fetch Walter and
Omai from their hut. Walking between the two, with Omai close
behind them, Walter allowed the men to lead him through the rain
to a large hale on the other side of the village.

The Hawai'ians in the procession were all dressed in the white
kapa capes and draped with ti-leaves to protect them from the rain.
The ensuing downpour made the green of the leaves shine like
lacquered panels, while the water dripped off the capes as they all
slowly, and ceremoniously approached the hale.

As the small procession of men walked through the central part
of the settlement, there was an odd mixture between the stillness
and the splashing sounds of the rain in the ordinarily busy village.
Few villagers could be seen in the open. Those who ventured out on
witnessing the procession would disappear immediately into a
nearby hut. Even the animals, usually running about freely,
appeared to have vanished.

As they entered the interior of the large hut, Walter sucked in
the smoky air. He could smell sweet perfume intermingled with the

spicy aroma of wood and herbs, and he could see the glow of several small fires casting strange shadows. As his eyes took a little time to adjust, it was a few minutes before he saw that he was standing in what was mostly empty space.

The interior of the hale featured a platform the length of a person and around the walls sat many men also draped in white kappa capes. To Walter's mind, they appeared ready for some ceremony to begin. Along another wall sat several musicians, beating soft rhythms on varying sized drums, while nose flute players added a melodic feature to the drum beats.

With Omai's reassurance, Walter accepted a cup of what turned out to be ti juice, offered by one of the men who had escorted them to the hale. He had already learned that ti leaves had many uses, such as wrappings for offerings, for cool food storage, for food to be cooked in, as fishing lures on hukilau nets and as clothing, such as rain capes and sandals. But he was now informed that it was also used for medicine. The leaves had relaxing properties, which Walter was apparently about to discover, according to Omai who translated for him.

One of the men motioned him to lie down on the platform while another Kahuna began to chant. As Walter stretched comfortably out on the mats in the centre of the hut, the Hawai'ians began the ho'oponopono, a traditional healing ceremony aimed at dispelling sickness and evil spirits.

As the ceremony progressed, Walter watched as the Kahuna mixed various aromatic herbs, then several other men began to pummel his body in a regular pattern while another held his head and wrapped it in damp ti leaves. The procedure was different, yet similar to the one he had learnt to enjoy in Tahiti, and Walter surrendered himself to the mighty hands and arms of the men. Underscored by the rhythmic chanting, the hypnotic atmosphere seduced Walter into an ethereal experience that rivalled even the most profound opium-induced state he had yet experienced.

※※※※※※

Outside of the hale, nature chose to accompany the cleansing with an explosive thunderstorm, cutting the black of the night with thunder and lightning. In the surreal interplay between light and darkness, the shadowy figure of a tall man crept around the exterior of the hut, evidently searching for something. Every now and then he would stop and listen intently to the darkness and then carefully take a few more steps. Hearing the crack of a stick in the distance, he suddenly froze, waiting for a moment, and then continued his careful exploration of the outside of the hut.

Another flash of light suddenly illuminated the gnarled figure of an old woman silhouetted against the dark grey of the storm. In her hand, she held a large, carved stick that she thrust threateningly into the air towards the now frightened man. "Get away with you! Rascal!"

The booming voice belied the frail frame of the woman, and obviously shocked by the apparition, the terrified man fled, disappearing swiftly into the nearby forest and the night. The old crone chuckled mischievously but when the flashes of lightning again lit up the night, she, too, had disappeared. Oblivious to the commotion outside of the hale and amidst the steady beat of the drums and the drone of the chants, the ho'oponopono, continued its measured pace.

Chapter Twenty-Six

*A*lthough Walter needed a few days of rest before he felt the real benefits of the healing ceremony, he had to admit to Omai that whatever scepticism he had about the healing powers of the Kahuna before the experience, this had disappeared entirely. The combination of the massage and the regular ingestion of the herbal concoctions over the last few days had accelerated Walter's recovery, and he was pleased with his progress.

Thinking about what sort of medical intervention he might have experienced back in England, Walter came to the conclusion that it most probably would not have made him feel as good as he did in the fresh and dewy air of a new morning, fragrant with the scent of plumeria. It was Walter's first foray out of the village since the healing ceremony, and he was enjoying the casual walk towards the site of his and Omai's new home.

Along the way, he listened with quiet amusement to Omai's account about a rumour that had spread through the village. It appeared that the gods had taken an interest in Walter, the haole. One of the villager's had said that he had spoken to a girl, who had heard from a warrior, that the ho'oponopono had been protected by Pele, who had frightened away a spy from the other side of the island. Walter thought the story, demonstrated that there were a lot of similarities between the Islanders, and the villagers at home in England when it came to the supernatural. He also couldn't help but agree with Omai, that he did indeed need all the protection he could get.

Arriving at the site of their new home, Walter could see that Kanoa had been true to his word. He had arranged to have a suitable place for the compound located close by the Kahuna himself. Omai explained to Walter that they should feel very fortunate that the Mo' i had allowed them such an excellent plot, close to the ocean as befitting a canoe builder. Over the past few days, all the materials needed had been delivered and prepared for construction. Then yesterday, the hard toil of making the stone platforms for each building within the hale had begun.

A large number of slaves had been assigned to prepare the ground and the rocks for building, while others were making the wood poles, mats and grasses needed to complete the structures that would become his home. As Omai pointed all of this out to him, Walter reflected that Omai himself seemed to be more confident and settled than he had been. Looking around at the beginnings of the construction, Walter identified some differences between the Islanders approach to the task, and what he knew would have been how it would have been tackled at home in England. There were similarities as well, and he was fascinated by this, and keen to know more.

As Walter sat on a log to the side of the site watching the men work, with Omai at the centre of the action, he thought about what he had learnt about the customs to the Islanders. Omai had informed him that the Mo' i had decided that a pa'ina, a feast to welcome his Tahitian friend, was to be celebrated, and as the day progressed the village was being prepared for this event.

This would be much the same as the feast that had been organised when they first arrived, and like that pa'ina, it would be the men who would be responsible for the preparation of the food. This, of course, was not unique to Hawai'i. The men of all the other Islands he had visited had also been tasked with feeding the people, but Walter still found this amusing,

However, there was another custom that he found perplexing rather than entertaining, and that was the separation of the men and women at both meals, and in their sleeping arrangements. It was kapu for the sexes to mix while eating, which to Walter's mind was a great pity. To have a meal without the good graces and beauty of a pretty woman was to his mind a significant loss. But then again, Walter thought, not being able to sleep with the woman you loved was an even more substantial loss.

Walter was surprised how easily he had wiled away a couple of hours watching the men work and pondering the cultural aspects of his new life, but he was happy to leave the building site once Omai signalled that he was ready to head off back to their hut. As they walked into the central part of the village, Walter and Omai could see that areas around the edges of the vast village square had been prepared for the evenings' feast. Lauhala mats have been rolled out, and centrepieces made of ti leaves, ferns and native flowers have been laid the length of the many of the mats. In the imu, the ground ovens, meat, fish and vegetables were cooking slowly, waiting to be brought out at just the right time, and bowls filled with poi, and platters of cold meat were also being set out.

In the late afternoon, the two friends joined the others as the people began to gather around the square, and Walter noted that they assembled according to their station in life. The ordinary people would feast in a completely separate part of the square from the elite warriors and Ali'i Nui. When Walter quizzed Omai on what determined rank, Omai looked at him curiously and pointed out that, like in England, it was ancestry that defined your status and position. The further back that you could trace your ancestry, the greater your connection to the gods and therefore, the greater your mana, your power.

Having been accepted as Ali'i of Kauai, Walter sat with Omai who had been recognised as Ali'i of Tahiti, and they sat on the edge of the larger group of Ali'i. Walter had been feeling progressively better and stronger, and smelling the various aromas of the different types of food made his mouth water.

While chewing a piece of fruit, he took the further luxury of indulging himself in the beauty of the girls and women who had come together to dance. Their traditional dress was a kapa skirt that left their breasts exposed, which Walter found very appealing. The men, of course, wore the malo, a loincloth, which so far he had not emulated, although Omai had rid himself of English clothing very quickly upon settling on Kauai.

As he surveyed the assembled women in the dim light, he suddenly spotted a particularly striking young woman. Tall and slender, she stood several inches above her companions, while her dark eyes were set in a soft, but regal face. Her skin, most of it unashamedly exposed, had the colour of dark honey and, having been well oiled, glistened invitingly to any observer in her vicinity. Walter was particularly impressed by her lush, thick black hair, unequalled amongst the other women as it cascaded down to her mid-thigh.

Her body was exquisitely balanced between the symmetry of her breasts, whose nipples proudly reached out to him, and the cheeky line of her buttocks that led towards her luscious thighs. With each swaying motion, Walter silently prayed to the gods to reveal that special space between her legs where he could imagine losing himself forever.

Lost in his own lustful thoughts, Walter sighed. Then, suddenly, as she moved further into the light, he recognised that it was Lani, the Queen's daughter. He remembered her from that horrific council meeting, where she had stood beside the Mo'i on the royal platform, watching everything with great interest. And she had also been at the meeting with Koa the other day. Walter was suddenly brought back to reality by a sharp nudge of Omai's elbow to his ribs.

"I strongly suggest, Walter, that you stay away from her. Koa has a strong interest in the Queen's daughter. It would not do to upset that man."

Disappointed, Walter let out a deep sigh and reluctantly looked away. Omai was right, Walter thought, I should heed his advice and look elsewhere. "You're right, my friend." Walter tried to keep his reply as casual as possible, but his eyes kept being drawn back to her, as she alluringly swayed her hips to the rhythm of the dance. At some stage, inevitably, their eyes met, and Walter smiled. *'Lelema-hoalani'. What a lovely name.*

Walter practised the lilting tones silently, and at that very moment he thought that he had noticed her looking towards him again. He had always played a game that two glances meant the girl was interested in him and having tested his theory many times in the past, he had found it to be entirely accurate. Walter's heart jumped ever so slightly, but before he could take that thought any further, he was distracted by a young boy offering him a parcel of food wrapped in a banana leaf.

Absentmindedly, he was about to refuse when Omai chastised him, telling him he must eat. His friend was apparently keeping a close eye on him, and Walter's first reaction was to be a little irritated. Still, he quickly understood that this could be a matter of manners, and albeit with some reluctance, he reached across and took the food from the boy's outstretched hand.

Walter thought that he had enough to eat, but he unwrapped the green banana leaf, exposing a succulently roasted piece of meat. As the smell of it permeated his nostrils, he felt the sudden unexpected gnawing hunger and enthusiastically broke off a bit of the meat. Carefully biting into it, he started to chew the soft portion and was surprised by the unusual, but flavoursome, taste. He stopped for a moment, trying to identify the meat's origin. Well, it's not pork, he thought. Unable to determine for himself what sort of meat it was, he sought out Omai's opinion. "Mmm, this is delicious, but what is it?"

Omai, his own mouth full, and in the process of licking his fingers, pointed to a dog running about. "Never!" Walter's response apparently reflected his shock, as Omai burst out laughing, his dark eyes filled with tears at Walter's expense. Walter had seen dogs used for food in Tahiti, and on the other islands, but as far as he was aware, he had never had one served to him. Thinking about it, he decided that this was not really a problem for him, mainly as it was delicious, so he happily resumed eating from his leaf parcel, and went back to watching the dancers.

Walter's eyes quickly found Lani dancing amongst the other women and girls, but almost immediately to his great disappointment, the dance was over and she suddenly disappeared with the rest of the dancers. As he craned his neck to see if he could find her, Omai reminded him of his warning.

"It will do you no good to pursue this one, my friend. Look around, are there not many beautiful girls here?"

Walter had to admit that there was an abundance of beautiful and, no doubt, willing girls who may well be open to spending time with him, but he knew himself very well. Forbidden fruit had always been so much more exciting. Although the rest of the evening was filled with more dancing and music, to his great disappointment, he never got another glimpse of Lani that night.

Chapter Twenty-Seven

*T*ime passed, marked only by the cycle of day and night, and the rhythm of eating, sleeping and working to regain his health and strength. Walter had gotten into the habit of taking walks along the shore and swimming in the shallows of the lagoon. Following Omai's instructions, he practised moving through the top of the water and submerging his whole body, face included, challenging the old fear that had shamed him in the past.

Walter also spent much time observing the kauhale take shape. Watching the workmen, he sketched what he saw, conscious of trying to preserve the many scenes of the men's activities as well as village life, ever mindful of the limitations of his own resources of paper, pencils and quills.

He was fascinated by the organisation and craftsmanship that was exercised in the construction of the compound. Everything appeared to go smoothly with almost no conflicts, and what he mostly heard was the rapid chatter and laughter amongst the workers. Many of the villagers would wander by to check the progress and on one morning even the Mo' i unexpectedly arrived in a formal procession.

Walter was fascinated by her large litter and by the contingent of retainers and warriors surrounding her. As the procession came closer, the kahili carriers called out, announcing the visit of the Mo' i and everyone in sight, including Walter, dropped to the ground in obedience to the kapu.

Surveying the kauhale for a few moments, the Mo' i smiled and then waved her retainers on, obviously ready to leave the building site. As soon as her procession was out of sight, the workers immediately jumped to their feet and returned to their tasks as if there had never been any interruption at all.

And then, on a clear blue evening, Omai returned from the compound to announce excitedly that the final touches had been completed and that tomorrow would be the perfect time for the dedication ceremony for their new home. "Everyone will be here, Walter, so you must dress in your best clothes."

Not having looked at his best attire since it was packed on board the Resolution, Walter felt he should check that it was in a fit state for the celebrations, so he removed his clothes from the smaller travel bag and carefully laid them out.

Looking down at his coat and breaches, he smiled, remembering his vanity and a time when he would never be seen in anything but in his best attire. Now here he was, feeling like he needed to reacquaint himself with each and every garment, including his shoes.

Walter reached for his shirt and slipped it on, and as he pulled it down, he thought at first that it must have shrunk, as it appeared a little tight across the shoulders and chest. He dismissed the thought, reassured by reminding himself that it had been some time since he had worn a full suit of European clothing, and also that his clothes were as he had left them, untouched now for many weeks. But as he continued to try his clothes on, he soon realised that none of the clothes fitted the way they had before. All of them felt tighter and he felt more constricted by them.

Having no mirror, Walter looked around for Omai only to find that he also had put on his best European suit. At the sight of his friend Walter smiled to himself. Well, doesn't he cut the fine figure?

"Omai, take a look. Are my clothes tighter than before?" Walter turned around to allow Omai a closer inspection.

The Tahitian smiled. "I think, my friend, that the clothes are not smaller, but that you are bigger." He came up closer, tugging at various parts of Walter's suit trying to adjust it to a better fit and pointed out to Walter that he could see quite a few differences.

Walter knew that his skin had been tanned, but Omai said that his hair was lighter and some of it streaked almost white from the sun. "It makes your eyes look brighter, blue like the lagoon. But also, Pelekané, you look much healthier."

Omai grinned at him, and Walter realised that he had noted some changes but not paid too much heed to them. Despite his illness, he had been far more physically active since being on the island, and from the feel of his clothes, he had obviously gained in size, especially around his arms and chest. He tugged and pinched at his clothes to get the best possible fit without tearing the stitches. "Well, I may look healthier, but more importantly, I feel it." With a sense of satisfaction, Walter decided that as a finishing touch to his attire, he would wear his sword.

And so it was that the next day Walter and Omai stepped out from their rude little hut appearing as two gentlemen about town, ready to promenade around the high streets of London, except that they happened to be on a tropical Island surrounded by the people of a completely different civilisation.

With a cheeky twinkle in his eye, Walter turned to Omai. "Well, my friend, how do I look?"

Omai grinned at Walter, and quickly engaging in the game, bowed to him. "Sir, you are indeed a handsome fellow. No maiden can resist your charms."

Returning the gesture, Walter bowed deeply and with a sweep of his hat held in his right hand, replied. "Then let us not waste precious time and let the festivities begin."

Laughing heartily, the two figures then strode theatrically out towards their new home. Some of the Hawai'ians, seeing the two in their finest, appeared initially to be somewhat awed, but they quickly regained their infectious good humour and laughed with them. A few even mimicked their bow.

The news of the dedication had spread quickly, and in addition to the workers, a large crowd had gathered in the new compound. As Walter and Omai approached, the various voices and the cries from the very young children were hushed, as a small procession led by the Kahuna, Kalama, arrived. Kalama had been involved in the construction of the kauhale, and it was he who was now officiating at the dedication.

Now that they were all gathered, they entered the compound ceremoniously, and Kalama placed an offering of a white piece of kapa and a red fish in the doorway of the largest building. He then reached for the piko, a braid of thatch, hung from the doorway and slipped a block of wood under it. Then, with the ceremonial adze handed to him by an assistant, the Kahuna began to chant while cutting the braid to the rhythm of the words.

At the end of the Kalama's chant, Walter half expected a great cheer to end the complete silence that had engulfed the compound, but nothing happened, other than the procession moved to the next building where the same ritual was repeated amidst the same silence as before.

As each building was dedicated to the gods, it was then decorated with leis of flowers and braids, while some of the villagers and workers had brought gifts that were now placed inside the main hale. As the formality of the dedication ceremony came to a conclusion, Kalama led the group to the village square where another feast had been prepared.

As Walter sat, eating and drinking, trying to catch the voices of the Islanders, he reflected on the strange course his life had taken so far. Who would have thought that he, the well-bred, sophisticated English gentleman, would sit cross-legged on a grass matt in a brocade and silk suit at the reception feast for his new Hawai'ian home? Surely life could not get any stranger?

Chapter Twenty-Eight

*T*he next morning the village had taken on a semblance of order after the previous day's dedication and feast and Walter and Omai sat in front of their newly built sleeping hale. Removed of their finery of European clothes, Omai was again in a malo, while Walter was back into the linen shirt and buckskin breeches he had become so fond of. The two men were enjoying the morning's air and their new home when Lani confidently strode into the compound.

Walter was about to jump to his feet when Omai's hand on his arm stopped him. He was unsure of the proper protocol so he sat quietly and listened while she spoke to Omai. He managed to understand some of what she said, and he made a guess that she was here to teach him Hawai'ian. The gods must be smiling on me, Walter thought to himself, for I could not have wished for more. Omai confirmed this translating for him that Lani's mother had sent her to them to learn English and teach Walter Hawaiian.

Once he had finished translating for Walter, Omai nodded to the pretty young woman and motioned to her to sit beside them, but as Lani knelt down beside the two men, she looked at them and frowned. Lani leant over to Walter and sniffed the air around him.

Wrinkling her nose, she contorted her face and recoiled. "Aué, Kanoa was right, the haole stinks!"

Omai burst out laughing while Lani jumped to her feet.

"This is not funny." She chided Omai. "I will not teach him anything unless he has a bath and smells better."

With that outburst, Lani turned and disappeared into the village, leaving Walter trying to work out what just occurred. "Are you going to tell me what just happened?" he inquired impatiently when it appeared that Omai was just going to sit there and hold his sides laughing. Omai duly translated what Lani has said and then barely able to stop his fits of laughter, he added; "My friend she is right. I have neglected to teach you cleanliness."

Walter stopped for a moment and thought indignantly that he had not believed himself to be in the least bit unhygienic. "But I only bathed a week ago, and I swim most days, how could I smell that bad?"

Walter lifted his arm and smelt himself and had to admit that his shirt was somewhat grimy, but Omai simply laughed raucously and shook his head. "My time in England and on your ship has dulled my nose. We must have truly become much too close, my friend, for me not to smell you out." Omai stopped to catch his breath. "But I have just the remedy!"

When Walter pressed Omai for more information, the Tahitian refused to elaborate on what he had planned, however later that morning, Walter found himself up to his waist in the crystal-clear water of a freshwater pool, while Omai sat casually on a rock.

Several naked slave girls surrounded Walter and were vigorously scrubbing his back and chest. One of them occasionally went to wash below his waist, but despite the temptation, Walter vigilantly kept her hands from dipping to his nether regions. His sense of propriety did not allow for being vulnerable in such a manner. But on the other hand, the scene had a playful touch to it, and though he feigned the pitiful victim, he was enjoying the attention the girls bestowed in him.

Omai, sitting on the edge of the pool with a pile of Walter's clothes beside him, kept shouting instructions to the girls who were only too keen to oblige. While Walter exhorted the girls to be gentle. But not understanding him, the girls simply continued scouring his body.

"Omai, when do you think that I am sufficiently scrubbed?" He paused and winced as one of them finally overcame Walter's vigilance. He swiftly grabbed her roving hand and pulled it out of the water. "Surely they'll draw blood if they continue!"

Omai laughed and obviously decided that his friend was clean enough he clapped his hands and motioned girls to leave them and the pool. As they prepared to leave, Omai handed them Walter's clothes telling Walter that they needed as good a scrub as he had. Walter had to admit he was not keen to put his dirty clothes back on his now clean body. Omai provided Walter with kukui and coconut oil so that he could rub it over his body, and a malo to wear. Now standing in there in front of his friend Walter felt exposed and self-conscious. He couldn't help fiddling with the loincloth trying to ensure that it provided him with some dignity, while Omai, looked at him and nodded approvingly.

"This is much better, my friend." He stopped and cocked his head to the side. "Some of the girls may even find you slightly more attractive now."

Walter laughed at Omai's backhanded compliment while thinking that he was really only interested in one girl. Knowing that Lani would be joining them at their halo to begin his lessons in Hawai'ian, he felt a growing excitement and suddenly became aware that the malo was not going to be a particularly modest article of clothing, and would therefore not leave a great deal to anyone's imagination. Sighing, he decided to think of something a little less arousing.

Soon enough Walter and Omai found themselves sitting beside the lovely daughter of the Mo' i. Before Lani had arrived, Omai had reminded Walter how important it was that he know his place and that Lani was merely here to teach him Hawai'ian, and for Walter to teach her English, and nothing else.

Walter grudgingly accepted that not only was he not in a position to offer Lani the opulence he may have been able to, had they been in England, but here, his position was tenuous. The ever-present threat of disaster if he broke kapu could not be ignored. And, from a purely practical point, he did not feel suitably dressed as a noble in his white loincloth that hid virtually nothing.

In the back of his mind, Walter decided that the ignominious position he was in would not do and that at the earliest possible opportunity he would put his mental capacity to good use and find some solution to this dilemma. But in the meantime, Lani's polite, brilliant smile brought him back to reality.

"We can now get on with what my mother has asked of me."

Omai laughed as he translated what she had said, while Walter tried unsuccessfully to show as little skin as possible. And so began Walter's first formal lesson in the Hawai'ian language.

From that day on Walter's daily routine expanded to include bathing, which was something he quickly came to appreciate, even enjoy. The daily practice of completely immersing himself in the pool by the waterfall and washing with a sponge from the ocean, and the Hawai'ian version of soap, had him coming away from each experience both invigorated and refreshed.

And so it was that one morning, after his swim he had gone to the pool to bath and was standing waist-deep in the water, when he was startled by the sound of something behind him. He abruptly swung around and saw Lani step briskly into the clearing around the pool. "I can see that you have taken to bathing. That is a good thing." She spoke slowly, obviously giving him an opportunity to understand what she was saying. Lani paused, then smiled at him, and he noted that she looked a little flushed.

He smiled automatically in response, raising his hand in greeting but quickly dropped it to cover himself as he became conscious of how clear the water was. While he stood there feeling extremely self-conscious Lani continued:

"You are beginning to enjoy some of our customs." Walter nodded while Lani paused again. "Perhaps we can surf together sometime, Pelekané'?"

She didn't use his name but rather the Hawai'ian permutation of Pelekané', the Tahitian word for the English. Most of the islanders had come to simply refer to him in that way, and it looked like it was going to stick.

Initially, Walter didn't like the reference, but he had come to accept it. He even thought that it had an exotic tone to it, befitting someone who had travelled far and wide. Struggling to understand her, he just nodded and pointed to Lani and himself. "'Ae, 'oe, a'u, kaha! Yes, you, me surf."

Trying to remember the Hawai'ian words, he appeared to get his message through because Lani smiled and then quite casually waved and disappeared into the forest.

Naked, Walter remained in the waist-deep water, watching the spot where Lani had disappeared, half wishing for her to reappear. Moments passed, and until he languidly sighed and got out of the pool, realising that he had become a little chilled, with goosebumps marking his arms and legs. Smiling to himself he marvelled at how he had become more acclimatised to the temperatures in these parts. Only a few months ago he would have found the water and the air too warm.

But then, who knows, Walter thought, *it may be Lani that has given me goosebumps.*

Chapter Twenty-Nine

"*Dear Mother,*

    It has taken me some time to adapt to my circumstances here, including to their insistence that I bathe daily. Fortunately, I have now come to appreciate its virtues and feel most out of sorts if I have missed my daily ablutions.

The land here is rich and abundant with life of all kinds, especially in the seas. The people have come to farm the ocean's bounty in a way I have not seen anywhere else. They have built an intricate system of tidal rock pools wherein the fish are bred the way we breed cows and sheep.

Today, I was fortunate to witness two of the men ride the waves most expertly on significantly more sizeable swells than those ridden in Tahiti.

As soon as they had paddled to the smooth water beyond the surf, they lay at length on their boards and prepared for their return. They then rose to their feet and travelled with rapid velocity across the crystal face of the swell towards the shore. The grace with which they did this was remarkable.

I must tell you, Mother, that since leaving Tahiti, the desire to emulate the Islanders in their pursuit of mastering the waves has become quite the obsession with me and I am determined to completely overcome my fear of water."

Omai had spent a considerable amount of time with the Hawai'ians in recent days, leaving Walter to his own devices.

Although he was curious about Omai's absences, he did not press his friend overly into making any sort of confessions in regards to what he was doing.

As Omai had spent a lot of time making sure that Walter understood the kapu, he felt assured that he knew enough to avoid significant infringements of the law. At least he sincerely hoped that this was true and not just wishful thinking on his part, so he spent most of his time sketching and writing in his journal as a safety precaution.

From the onset of his lessons with Lani, Walter decided to compile a dictionary of Hawai'ian words. Slowly, over time, he had gathered quite a respectable work, including some phrases and sayings the Hawai'ians were particularly fond of. Walter had learnt that they had absolutely no written language and all relied on an oral tradition, that was complex and melodic, and that contained their rich and diverse history on all aspects of their lives.

The more he understood this, the more Walter developed a respect for the skills of the many Kahuna, who were the masters of the crafts and sciences of their civilisation. He pondered how readily he used the word 'science.' But how else could he describe the effective and efficient use of the land and the sea? These people cultivated fish similarly to how his own people cultivated sheep in England. Yes, Walter thought, the use of the word 'science' was, in his opinion, entirely justified.

Walter was more than keen to explore, and watch the Hawai'ians in their pursuits in and on the water, and to sketch as many of their pastimes as he could. Foremost, it gave him an opportunity to acquaint himself with the shore and gather his courage to venture further into the ocean here. Up to this point, he was still confining himself to the shallows, taking few risks that might find him out of his depth.

Walter had discovered a spot where a group of rocks provided a good vantage point to watch the surf, and as it was a lovely afternoon, he had made his way through the forest to the shore to take advantage of the view. Climbing onto the rock, he made himself as comfortable as possible on the volcanic ledge, and opening his bag, he extracted his journal and some charcoal.

As he looked out to sea, he saw Koa and Kanoa gliding elegantly across a beautiful, clean wave and he once again marvelled at the skill and grace these big men could muster, when executing the manoeuvres that helped them turn across the face of the waves.

Fascinated by Koa and Kanoa, Walter watched the two men repeat their performance time and time again and only occasionally saw one or the other fail in making the ride to shore. When one of them did tumble into the water, there was a light-hearted humour to the mishap, that appeared to do nothing to dampen the good spirits they obviously felt.

Despite the age difference between Kahuna and apprentice, Koa did not seem to have more stamina than the older man. Also, Walter observed, Kanoa was often in a better and steeper section of the rising swell, enabling him to get to his feet quicker than Koa and thus establish his dominance over the wave.

As the sun began its long descent into the sea, Walter watched the two men make their way to shore. Even from a distance, he could see them grinning. They paused on the edge of the sand, the long wooden boards nestled in the crook of their arms and resting against their shoulders, their dark skin blending with the shimmering hue of the wood, while the boards towered above them.

After a few moments the two men shouldered the heavy boards and began making their way up the beach towards the village. Seeing them come closer to where he was sitting, Walter decided to make his retreat into the forest. He did not feel comfortable being confronted by them without the security of having Omai with him to translate, and he did not want to inadvertently cause some offence that could bring dire consequences on both their heads.

※※※※※

Having walked up the beach Kanoa and Koa, stopped to catch their breath. Despite their fitness, the huge boards were quite a burden and exacted their toll. Placing them on the sand, they sat down facing the surf and the approaching sunset. They had both seen the Pelekané walking into the forest, so Kanoa was not surprised that Koa mentioned him, but he was surprised by the content of Koa's question.

"Will you teach the haole to ride waves, Kahu?"

Kanoa took his time to answer. He had not thought about doing so, but it was an intriguing idea. Yet, he also thought it was an odd question from his apprentice. What benefit would it be to teach this stranger anything of their knowledge and rituals? The Tahitian had already done some of that, at least of the things he knew of. No, he had not thought about the haole in that way at all.

Kanoa shrugged his shoulders. "I don't know. He is not strong, and he has little mana. What can one do with someone like that?"

Koa looked around as if to ensure they were out of earshot of others, and then lent close to Kanoa. "If he taught me to throw fire from his stick we would have great mana, Kahu, more than anyone on this island." Koa paused and then continued. "If we gave him what he wants, then he would be bound to return the gift."

Kanoa sat quietly for a moment absorbing Koa's words. His apprentice was right, but he was also impulsive and ambitious, and this was dangerous. He needed Koa to understand the ramifications of the way he was thinking, so he lowered his voice and responded in the deliberately serious tone that he always used when trying to impart a valuable lesson.

"I have known many ambitious men, Koa," he paused, leaning closer, "and most are dead. Do we really need the stick that shoots fire to have mana?"

Koa leapt to his feet, obviously frustrated by Kanoa's response, and spat out his reply. "Why do you want to discourage me? I will make a strong chief, and I will lead our people to greatness!"

Kanoa sighed. He had quietly hoped that Koa would react differently, with more wisdom. Patiently, he got up and gripped the younger man's shoulder." I know that you are strong, Koa, but your heart and soul must be true as well."

However, Koa rejected Kanoa's wisdom and appeared to see an insult where one was not meant. He shrugged Kanoa's hand off his shoulder, shouting; "You have no faith in me! Shall I be your apprentice forever?" And with that, Koa turned, picked up his board and without another word, stormed off to disappear into the forest.

Kanoa sighed. He looked out contemplating the surf, bathed in the vibrant yellow and orange of the sunset and then needing to reconnect with the force of life around him, he picked up his board and headed back into the water. Sliding onto his board, he paddled out a little, then hesitating for a moment he turned back towards the shore. Something had pulled his attention back to land, and as he scanned the edge of the forest, for a split second, he caught sight of what he thought was the figure of an old woman disappearing into the woods.

Could it be, he thought as his heart skipped a beat, *Pele*? He shook his head, smiling to himself. During his many adventures on different islands, he had never seen a god. No, it must just be one of the old women from the village, who was obscured by the distance.

Chapter Thirty

$\mathcal{W}$alter was pleased with his decision to disappear into the forest when he did. From there, he would feel secure from any potential form of inquisition by the two Hawai'ians. He had no desire to cross paths with Kanoa and Koa right now and satisfied that they had not seen and followed him, he headed further into the shady woods.

Koa's reaction to Walter's illness had left him feeling even more vulnerable beside the young warrior. The man was the epitome of the quintessential soldier who, in any culture, would have inspired loyalty in his men and instilled fear in those forced to face him.

But unlike Kanoa, whom Walter had seen dispense kindness, Koa showed no warmth, no empathy and certainly no sympathy. There was a cold, calculating edge to the man. Walter had heard that when Koa lost his temper, he had a tendency to explode with fury, and in that respect, Koa reminded Walter of Williamson. However, unlike Williamson, Koa was a man used to exercising power, and he used a certain calculated benevolence to obtain what he wanted. The question that plagued Walter was how could he ever expect to compete with a man such as this. He decided that as much as he wanted to bed Lani, it was not to be. He would just have to get used to that idea and be done with it.

Casually strolling along the tree-lined trail, he was suddenly startled by a croaky voice from behind him. He whirled around only to be confronted by an old, withered crone.

Small of stature, she was dressed in a brown kapa wrap-around that hid much of her withered frame. Brown ferns crowned her head and looked as if intense heat had locked them in time. Walter thought they must have been green once, but, by the look of them, that had been a very long time ago. Similarly, the matching fern bracelets and anklets had the same aged and withered appearance. Around her neck, she wore the sort of necklace he had seen the Ali'i wear as a sign of their nobility. Omai had explained to him that it consisted of bone and human hair. Yet despite her withered appearance, this old lady did not strike him as frail.

"Have pity on an old woman." She tottered a little closer to him, and he instinctively took a step back. "Come, you have young legs, carry me a while so that I can rest."

Walter was uncertain how to deal with this unexpected apparition. She spoke English, yet that could not be, he thought. He looked about, wondering if Omai would suddenly appear, declaring it a good joke. But there was no one, only he and the old woman facing each other in the dim light of the forest.

"There, always just thinking of yourself, eh?" The crone cocked her head and chuckled. "How bad this is; how sick I am; how my brother and father hate me and how they made my life miserable."

The words sharply penetrated the core of his being, resonating in his chest. How could she know these things, he thought. Could it be that Omai... Walter instantly dismissed the thought. But before he could get some sort of explanation organised in his mind, a solid beautifully carved stick had suddenly appeared in the old crone's small hand and came cracking down on his exposed shoulder. Lightening quick, she landed another blow before Walter could react.

"Stop it!" She shouted at him, her voice booming through the forest. "Now, pick me up and carry me, so my weary legs can rest awhile."

His shoulders stung from the blows, but for some reason he could not fathom, he did as he was told and bent forward. The old woman climbed nimbly onto his back, where she sat quite firmly, her thighs wrapped around his sides as if he were a horse. She tapped him lightly in the shoulder and Walter took that as a sign that she was ready to move on so he began to walk, and after a little while heard the crone muttering to herself. Try as he might, he could not make out what she was saying. Suddenly, she tapped him on the head with her staff.

Walter flinched. "Ouch! Don't do that!"

The old woman was undeterred. "Quiet! Here," she pointed to a spot on the ground, "put me down."

Walter bent forward, and the crone climbed off with the same agility she had used getting onto his back. Standing on the firm earth, the crone seemed to straighten up, belying her age and frail frame, and with her piercing eyes now fixed on his. Walter felt them drilling into his soul. For a moment, he thought he could see flashes of fire in the depth of them, and he instinctively drew back from her.

"Remember, pale one, when the rat is careless, the cat comes around."

Puzzled and confused, he shook his head. "You speak in riddles, old woman. What do you mean by that?"

She threw her arms up, and Walter thinking she was going to hit him again, flinched. But she spun him around to face the other direction and pushed him along the path with remarkable strength. Even if he wanted to, Walter realised, he would not have been able to stop her. "Aué, too many questions! Now, be off with you."

Stumbling forward, he turned to face her again, only to find himself standing alone on the deserted path, the trees swaying in the breeze.

Walter stood there for a minute staring at the empty space and absentmindedly went to scratch his head. Having begun to think that he was hallucinating, the pain from the bruise on his head forced him to accept that this encounter with the crone was not a figment of his imagination or of a troubled mind.

In a sudden burst of energy, Walter sprinted back to the village where he found Omai, who had apparently been searching for him. The Tahitian anxiously demanded to know where he had been, worry etched all over his face but Walter, still confused and perplexed by his experience, was a little short with his friend and snapped at him that he had been down at the beach.

Then taking a breath and calming himself, and realising he had been churlish with his friend, he quickly apologised and decided to tell Omai about what had happened in the forest. "You know, on the way back, I met this strange, old woman. She made me carry her, but," he paused again and leant forward towards Omai, "the most peculiar thing was that I am sure that she spoke to me in English."

Walter still half-expected Omai to declare the whole thing a setup, aimed to amuse himself at Walter's expense, but the Tahitian appeared instantly alert. "She actually spoke English to you? What did she say?"

"Something about a rat and a cat." Walter paused, thinking. "But I have no idea what she meant. Do you know who is she?"

Omai looked at Walter with an excited expression, and lowering his voice, he stunned Walter with his reply. "I have heard stories about this. If they are right, then the old woman is Pele, the goddess of fire. She came to test you." Omai looked admiringly at Walter. "You must have passed the test."

"What makes you think that?" Walter asked, reminding himself that Omai like all of the Islander's had very strong convictions about the presence of their gods. His own automatic denial of the supernatural manifesting itself to him as an old woman didn't change the fact that he had a bruise on his head and that the whole experience was a puzzle.

"Because she warned you about something."

Walter sucked in his breath, then grinned and slapped Omai on the shoulder. He laughed out loud. "Omai, my friend, that is super-stitious nonsense. I am sure that there is some sane, rational explanation."

Omai was visibly irritated by Walter's dismissive attitude towards him. Walter, in turn, felt guilty. He had been insensitive, and now

Omai had become withdrawn, and when Walter tried to make amends he simply advised him to speak with Kanoa about the incident, and what the old lady had said to him. As Walter couldn't just accept that he had been visited by the goddess of fire, the two men spoke no more about it, but he caught Omai watching him with a questioning look several times that evening.

After the encounter with the crone, life settled back into its usual pattern and Walter spent the next few weeks concentrating on his language lessons with Lani, finding great pleasure being in her company. Word had apparently got around the village of Walter's mysterious encounter, and some of the villagers would smile respectfully at him as he went about his business.

A little uncomfortable with the unexpected attention, Walter decided to check with Lani if she had taught an old woman any of the phrases she had learnt from him, but she just shook her head looking puzzled. She had apparently not heard the rumours, so he decided to abandon asking her any further questions, lest he upset her with his inquiry.

When he wasn't spending time with Lani, he continued to familiarise himself with the foreshores and the beaches around the village, as well as trying to understand the people's relationship to the sea and the surf.

Omai, on the other hand, was spending a lot of time with the Kahuna Kalai wa'a and Koa, discussing the craft of carving canoes. Walter only saw the Tahitian around mealtimes when the two would catch up on various pieces of news and gossip, including Omai's blossoming love life.

One morning Walter sat on the beach watching the men, women and children frolicking in the surf, busily sketching the scenes in the water. Almost everyone was riding a wooden board of some sort, and many were of differing lengths. Walter was so preoccupied with his work that he was utterly unaware of Koa's approach until his looming shadow suddenly alerted him to the warrior's presence.

"Pelekané! Come!"

The strict order left no room for argument, and Walter jumped to his feet. As he gathered his journal and pens, Koa was already walking in the direction of a large clearing to the north of the village. To Walter's surprise, he realised that Koa had been learning English, and had apparently made some considerable progress. It had never occurred to him that Lani may have other pupils.

As the two men crossed the clearing, Koa headed towards a large pile of rocks situated on the far side of the field. The warrior knelt down and removed a few stones to carefully extract a package wrapped in kapa from underneath one of the larger rocks.

Curious, Walter watched Koa unwrap the parcel, and much to his surprise, he removed Walter's pistol from the kapa cloth. The warrior carefully held the weapon up, and then motioned Walter to show him what to do.

The hairs on his neck stood up as Walter recognised that he could be in danger. He did not cherish the thought of refusing Koa a lesson in handling the gun, but on the other hand, he intuitively knew that this was dangerous and could get him into trouble.

Walter gingerly took the pistol from under Koa's watchful gaze and scrutinised it. The weapon was in good order, the kapa cloth keeping any corrosion at bay. Sniffing the barrel of the gun, Walter looked up at the Hawai'ian. "This has been fired," Walter said quietly but clearly so that Koa could understand his words.

The smell of gunpowder lingered in his nostrils, a telltale sign that the pistol had been recently discharged. Koa motioned to Walter to hand the weapon back, and at first, Walter hesitated. He had decided many weeks ago that should the gun resurface, he would resist any coercion to teach the Hawai'ians the use of it. But what choice did he have? Handing the pistol back to Koa Walter prevaricated.

"There is nothing to show you."

Koa took the gun back, clearly frustrated with Walter. He aimed into an empty space and pulled the trigger. To Walter's relief, there was no metallic click followed by the anticipated explosion. Koa shook the weapon angrily towards an imaginary target, obviously frustrated by the guns failure to function. Then grabbing Walter roughly by the shoulder, he turned him around and propelled him towards the path to the village.

Koa pushed Walter forward as the two of them entered Omai and Walter's kauhale. Koa stopped, and looking around, called out. "Omai, where are you?"

Omai emerged cautiously from one of the huts, in response to Koa's command and a young, naked woman stepped out from behind him. Her hair was dishevelled, and her face deeply flushed. Breathing heavily, the girl looked irritated at the untimely interruption, and despite the tension in the air, Walter had to smile. Omai was such a rogue, he thought.

"I am here, Koa." Omai, too, was trying to control the telltale signs of having been caught in the midst of passion.

"Tell the Pelekané to show me how to throw fire."

Omai turned to Walter. They had discussed the disappearance of the gun before, and Omai had advised Walter that withholding any information on how to use it would inevitably create problems for them. Now the time had come, he spoke calmly as he looked directly into Walter's eyes. "Think carefully, my friend. Koa is in a dangerous mood."

Having spent months trying to create as few problems as possible with the Hawai'ians, Walter's patience was stretched, and he decided that his own assessment of the situation should dictate his response. He turned to the Hawai'ian and pulling himself up as straight as he could he addressed Koa using his best Hawai'ian. "I can't. There is no more fire for the stick."

Koa looked at Walter in surprise. He had obviously not expected the Englishman to have such a good command of Hawai'ian, nor that he would stand up to him.

"Walter, this is no time to play games." Omai's cautionary words hung in the air for a moment.

Walter was emphatic. "There is no more fire in this stick." He shrugged his shoulders. "I can not teach you, Koa."

Koa looked suspiciously at the two men, his face contorted in anger, and suddenly, he roughly pushed past both men and entered the hut Omai had emerged from. Somewhat confused, Walter and

Omai stood in front of the hale, they could hear Koa rummaging through the interior. The noise suddenly stopped, and a minute later, Koa emerged holding the exquisitely crafted gun case belonging to Walter. He held the case dramatically into the air, ensuring that they could see it.

"What is this, Pelekané?" He shook the box at Walter. "Perhaps this is what you need to make the stick throw fire." Angry, Koa pushed the case roughly into Walter's chest. "Do not treat me like a fool."

In the course of the terse discussion, a group of villagers and warriors had gathered, curious about what was taking place. In the momentary, hushed silence, Omai and Walter looked at each other, neither daring to say or do anything, but Walter knew he was the one to resolve this and there could be only one course of action. He saw no way other than to comply.

"As you wish, Koa. But there is a limit to how much fire I can make."

Obviously pleased at Walter's capitulation, Koa nodded emphatically and used the pistol to point back to the field. "There you will teach me, Pelekané. In that field."

Koa's eagerness to get the demonstration underway had him almost run towards the field, whereas Walter followed slowly into the open space, the villagers behind him.

"Here! This will do." Koa said as he planted himself to one side and passed the pistol over to Walter.

Under Koa's careful scrutiny, Walter opened the gun case and took out the shot and powder and slowly loaded the pistol. Once he was ready, he looked at Koa who just waved him on, his keen eyes watching every move Walter made. Spying a fallen coconut on the ground some twenty or thirty paces away, Walter decided this was as good a target as any.

Checking that all of the observers were behind him, Walter stood up straight and squared himself against the target, raised the weapon, took aim and squeezed the trigger. The explosion from the discharged weapon reverberated across the field, and the coconut exploded a second later.

While the villagers had put their hands across their ears, trying to muffle the noise from the gun, Koa's face only showed excitement, and he imperiously reached for the weapon. Despite his reluctance, Walter knew he had no choice but to surrender the gun.

As he started to hand it over, careful that the barrel pointed away, not only from himself but also the Islanders who had followed them to the field, Walter was surprised to see Kanoa unexpectedly step from the thick bushes that ran along the edge of the clearing. With just a few long strides, he stood beside Walter and, with an outstretched hand, demanded the weapon. Turning to his apprentice, Kanoa spoke with unquestionable authority. "Koa, I will take the weapon."

Rage flashed across Koa's face. "But the haole was showing me how to master the fire in the stick, Kahu!"

"There is no need to learn this now. At the right time, we can all learn from the haole," was Kanoa's sharp reply.

Uncertain of feeling relieved or not, Walter watched the Kahuna take charge of the volatile situation. He couldn't help but admire the man's calm demeanour. Koa, obviously torn between his desire for the pistol and his obedience to his master reluctantly backed down. He was apparently unwilling to challenge Kanoa further, and stood to the side and watched his master as he headed back to the village without another word.

Then barely containing his rage, Koa glared first at Walter and then at Omai. His eyes flashing with malevolence the warrior suddenly turned and ran off. Walter felt a cold shiver run down his back, and a foreboding sense of dread came to life. He knew that he had made an enemy of Koa, and at some point, that would come to a head.

Walter turned to Omai who was looking at the spot where Koa had disappeared. Then the two men looked at each other, knowing that they were given only a temporary reprieve. Somewhere and somehow, Koa would exact revenge.

Chapter Thirty-One

eaumont Manor, England, 1779.

Lord Beaumont watched his eldest son with distaste. Jonathan pulled a clay pipe from the pocket of his coat and proceeded to load it with tobacco. The fact that Jonathan had taken up the disgusting habit of smoking a clay pipe was terrible enough, but to do so here in the Library and reception rooms was completely unacceptable. Despite his disapproval so far he hadn't reprimanded Jonathan, even though the stench of that awful weed had come to overpower the rich smell of old books, parchment and paper in this part of the house. It had invidiously crept into all the fabrics and permeated the atmosphere that left little room for more pleasant aromas.

His feelings for Jonathan perplexed him as they seemed to swing like a pendulum between approval and disapproval. On the one hand, Jonathan had proven himself to be an excellent businessman, industriously expanding the family fortunes, and taking his place in the halls of trade and power. But on the other hand, he had a minimal appreciation for subtlety and nuance and often used his wealth and social position to intimidate and control others.

Jonathan drew back on the pipe while spinning a globe of the world around with his fingertips. The clicking sound that this made irritated Lord Beaumont even more as he thought about his fractured relationships with his sons and, of course, his wife. And these very uncomfortable realities had now intruded into his ordered world in the form of a letter from the Admiralty. A letter that contained deeply troubling news.

Jonathan, always cunningly astute, had been watching him closely, and Lord Beaumont realised that his son must have seen some hint of his distress in his expression, because looking back up from the letter, he found Jonathan's piercing gaze directed at him. "Bad news, Father?"

He was about to reply when his wife Eleanor swept into the Library. Her entrance put Lord Beaumont immediately on edge and he marvelled, not for the first time at her impeccable timing. George must have told her of the letter from the Admiralty, he thought as he watched her stalk towards him, her beautiful face stiff with repressed emotion. "Well, what is it?" The edge in her voice gave away her anxiety.

Alexander Beaumont was well aware that since Walter had left, Eleanor had always kept a lookout for news, and he also knew that she had solicited a friend in the Admiralty to keep her well abreast of any word from the expedition. To date, however, as far as Lord Beaumont knew, she had not heard anything. Looking at her now as she stood waiting for an answer, his first impulse was to make light of the news he had just received. But before he could even open his mouth, she demanded that he tell her the truth.

She snapped at him, her gaze sweeping the room and landing on Jonathan before focusing back on him. "Do not treat me as a child! God knows that both of you have tested me more than I care to say." Her eyes watched him like a hawk, waiting to pounce if he should try to placate her in even the smallest manner.

"As you wish." He glanced down at the letter he was holding, knowing there was no way of softening it anyway. "We have word from the Admiralty that Walter's health was too poor for him to remain on the ship, and Cook was forced to leave him on a newly discovered Island in the Northern Pacific".

Lord Beaumont watched the shock of this news write itself on her face. He hesitated. It was going to be his fault, no matter what the truth of it was, and he was not looking forward to telling her the rest of the news. But he knew he must.

Clearing his throat, he continued; "Regrettably, Captain Cook was then viciously murdered by the savages on another island. Consequently, John Gore has taken command of the Resolution, and for some inexplicable reason is returning to England without Walter."

Jonathan, who up to that moment had stayed quiet, now broke the silence. "Ah, the perils of a sea voyage."

Lord Beaumont looked at his son, seeing the inappropriate smirk that accompanied his insensitive comment. Still, before he could respond, Eleanor turned on Jonathan, and her reaction was swift and telling. Tears welled up in her eyes as she looked at their eldest and firmly reprimanded him for his callousness in the face of the dangerous situation his brother was now placed in.

Lord Beaumont, who was in no mood for any more drama, stepped in smartly. "Yes, indeed." He glared at Jonathan. "Some suggestions as to what we could do would be of more use at this time, Jonathan, truly."

"Perhaps a memorial service to the dear departed souls could be arranged." Jonathan offered. This callous, offhand response was obviously too much for Lady Beaumont. She slapped Jonathan sharply across the face. "Your sarcasm at a time like this is completely uncalled for." She snapped, her eyes filled with tears and her mouth thin with rage.

His mother's distressed reaction finally seemed to get through to Jonathan who, looking chastened, dropped his head and apologised to them both. Lord Beaumont briefly wondered how his two boys could be so different and have so little sympathy for each other. But at least Jonathan had stopped being flippant, and the tension in the room dropped slightly.

Eleanor had warned him the day Walter had come home with the news of the shooting, that she wouldn't forgive him if Walter were harmed. Alexander Beaumont regretted deeply his decision not to fund the trip to Europe, but it was no good getting distracted by this now. What to do? That was the question.

An idea started to take shape in his mind. "So, what we do know is that Walter is on an Island, and we have to assume that Cook would not have left him there if he didn't think he would be able to manage." He leant back in his chair. "An agent to act on our behalf may be an option, or, I may need to go myself."

"Father, what are you talking about?"

Lord Beaumont paused and looked at his wife, who coldly stared back at him, then turned to his son. "Jonathan, there have been numerous occasions since your brother's departure, where I have had cause to reflect on my behaviour. Not only towards your brother, but similarly towards your mother, and I have found myself wanting." He sighed deeply. "I have no intention of facing my maker without at least some attempt to redeem myself."

Lord Beaumont silently stared at the letter lying on his desk, and he felt his resolve harden. "I intend to bring Walter home... to where he belongs."

The response Lord Beaumont got from his son was unexpected. "Father, this is nonsense! The idea of you searching the ends of the earth for Walter is utter madness. Your health has been problematic for months now, and several times you have had to leave important functions because of the pains in your chest. A trip like this could kill you." Jonathan was emphatic. "I will not have it."

Surprisingly, his wife added her voice to this pronouncement, telling him he was a fool to think that this was the solution. But what alternative did he have? An agent would not have the same enthusiasm for the task, and despite what Eleanor thought, he did love Walter, and he was not prepared to leave him to rot on some godforsaken island.

Lord Beaumont's musings were interrupted by Jonathan, his

voice thoughtful as he spoke. "If I may be so presumptuous, Father, neither you nor an agent are an appropriate choice for such an endeavour." Jonathan paused for a long time. "Let me do this, Father. If fortune continues to favour me the way it has, then I may turn this into a profitable opportunity, in addition to returning Walter to the bosom of the family."

Lord Beaumont, a little suspicious of Jonathan's motives, looked at his wife who nodded in agreement as she wiped the tears from her eyes. Having her support for the plan was one thing but trusting Walter's safety to his brother was another. Looking back at Jonathan he used a stern voice to make his point. "Search your conscience, my boy. You are to do this with the right intentions. Walter is to be your first priority."

"I know, Father." Jonathan replied in a conciliatory tone.

Sitting back in his huge chair, Alexander Beaumont braced himself against the burden of decisions as he drew a deep breath, trying to ease the pain in his chest. Watching his wife walk over to the bay window and lean against it, he was keenly aware that over the years since Walter's departure she had aged. The long hours of worry greying her hair and rounding her shoulders and making them lose their resolute demeanour. His decision made he spoke.

"We will await the return of the Resolution with Cook's charts because we will need them to find Walter. This will give us time to prepare."

He watched as his wife turned back to face both him and Jonathan. She gave them both a long hard look, then just said; "We shall see."

Her icy observation left Lord Beaumont nervously pondering his decision. Jonathan was right, however, and as the pain in his chest slowly eased, he knew that he was not the man for the job, no matter how determined he was.

As his wife walked through the library door, it closed with a sharp snap as the lock caught the latch. The sound echoed through the room, and as its last remnants faded, Lord Beaumont looked earnestly at Jonathan. "You know that Walter may be dead."

His chilling observation hung ominously in the air. "That may well be the case, Father, but for Mother's sake, we must at least try and determine his fate."

Lord Beaumont nodded, watching Jonathan resume his previous spinning of the globe. However, this time he did so slowly, and then abruptly stopped it with his index finger pointed at the centre of the Northern Pacific Ocean.

Chapter Thirty-Two

It was a grey, rainy day and as Kanoa waited for an audience with the Mo' i, water dripped persistently from the thatched roof of the royal residence, plopping rhythmically into puddles running along the edge of the dwelling. Kanoa, feeling uneasy about Koa's desire for the Pelekané's fire stick, had decided that it would be safest under the control of the Queen, and to that end, he had made his way to her hale.

As Kanoa was welcomed into the presence of the Mo' i and her husband Kaneoneo, he found himself alone with the royal couple. Their personal guards the only other people in the massive hall. They were far enough away not to be privy of any conversation between them, which suited Kanoa as it wouldn't do to have this discussion spread through the Court.

Kamakahelei motioned to Kanoa that he could stand before her, a privilege that she bestowed on him due to their long friendship. Kanoa was well aware that amongst the common people there had always been rumours that Kanoa had special privileges and it had given Kanoa the enviable status that he was somehow exempt from the kapu, but few dared voice that opinion openly.

Standing before them, the gun case in his hands, Kanoa raised his hand in a casual greeting. "Ali'i Nui, I bring you the stick that shoots fire. It belongs to the Pelekané, but it is greatly desired by others. I am concerned that it could become a dangerous problem in the hands of those who seek power, and so I wish you to have it for safekeeping."

"We have no wish to possess this thing. It is a tool of magic and belongs to the realm of priests." Kanoa was stunned by the vehemence of her reply. The Queen paused for a moment and then continued more calmly. "I agree with you that this is a potentially dangerous weapon, but it is for you and the other Kahuna to find a way to make it safe."

There was no argument that he could make against her pronouncement and so Kanoa nodded his head and accepted her decision. He would have to find another way to keep this weapon away from Koa and any other impulsive young warriors who thought it would give them mana.

Before Kanoa could take his leave, Kamakahelei suggested he stay, a deep frown on her forehead. "It is good you are here, my friend. We have just received grave news that Kalaniopu'u's warriors killed Tuté, the leader of the Pelekané's people before the other haole sailed away in their canoe."

Kanoa considered the news for a moment and instantly realised that Tuté's death would change many plans, including his. Kalaniopu'u was an ambitious man, but like Koa, prone to being impulsive. However, Kanoa did not think he was rash enough to jeopardise his ambition to conquer all the islands.

Kanoa wondered what had transpired on Hawai'i that led to the death of the strangers' leader. No matter how he looked at this event, he could see no good in it.

Another consideration was the fate of the haole that they had left behind here. Walter was no longer a temporary visitor who would have, in due course, left them. Tuté's death meant that the haole was here to stay.

Since the arrival of the Tahitian and the pale stranger, Kanoa had watched the pale one from afar, and despite his strangeness, Kanoa had come to like what he saw. He had spoken often enough with Omai who relished in telling stories of his exploits in this far away land called England. In amongst the tales of intrigue, Omai had tried to give him a picture of Walter as a man lost even in his own land, eventually having to flee his own home.

Despite Kanoa's curiosity, he had chosen to continue to keep his distance from the pale one. He had been undecided about the best way to manage this stranger, but now that Walter had no choice but to stay here, all of them would have to come to terms with his presence and what that meant. The man himself, being abandoned in a foreign land, would need time to get used to this turn of events.

He looked up to find the Mo' i watching him as he contemplated this news. There were many possible consequences of this attack on Tuté by Kalaniopu'u, but the look on Kamakahelei's face told Kanoa that she was not ready to speak of this at this time. Instead, she kept the focus on Walter.

"We need to tell him what has happened, Kanoa." She said as she motioned to one of the guards who quickly left the hall. "Lani tells me he is a good apprentice and is learning our language well." She smiled broadly. "She says that he smells much better now, too."

Kanoa agreed that this was something that had indeed changed, and then, being dismissed, he left still carrying the gun case he had hoped to give into the keeping of the Mo' i.

꽈꽈꽈꽈꽈

Walter had been re-organising some of his papers and trying to catalogue his drawings when one of the Queen's elite guards had arrived at the kauhale. As Omai was out somewhere, he had no choice but to accompany the guard on his own, and he was feeling some trepidation as he was escorted to the royal compound.

Remembering his manners and keenly aware of the kapu around any interactions with royalty, Walter quickly prostrated himself before the Queen. He waited for her to motion him to his feet and watching her from the corner of his eye, he realised that she was contemplating what to say to him. This increased his concerns even more, but he could never have guessed that he had been called to her to be told that Captain Cook was dead.

The Mo'i had informed him that there had been a skirmish on the island of Hawai'i, and the great chief and some of his men had been regrettably killed. More to the point, her scouts had looked for the two ships, and from what they could see and the reports from other sources, it was clear that they had left the waters of Hawai'i. Her scouts had reported that the ships had sailed well and truly beyond any reasonable reach of Kauai.

It took a minute for the news of Cook's death to sink in. Walter was deeply shocked. This meant he now had no way of returning home. A chaotic jumble of thoughts and feelings confused him for a moment, but one idea crystallised in his mind. He was, in no uncertain terms, stuck in this place, and that was not his original intention. Fear and anger warred within him as he recognised that he had been abandoned.

He had no idea whether the expedition had continued with more exploration or left the islands and headed home. It could take years for the Resolution to get back to England. That would be years before the charts of this part of the Pacific would be available for another expedition to be launched, even if there was a will to do so. And it could be years before any other European vessel would again stray into these waters.

As his mind raced through the myriad of consequences, Walter was barely able to control his emotions. Abandoned in the middle of nowhere! Why? Taking deep breaths to calm himself, Walter started to reason out what may have occurred. They must have had reasonable cause to sail away without him. It would not have been an easy decision for any of the officers to make, and that it would have been made based on the ships circumstances and the needs of the entire crews.

Sighing deeply, Walter looked up at the Queen and her husband. He was aware that they were studying him, trying to judge the impact the news had on him. Yet, in their eyes, he saw some compassion. In that moment, he felt that they understood his turmoil and pain and he bowed before speaking, partly to clear his head, and partly to hide his tears. Walter desperately felt the need to be alone.

"I appreciate you passing this terrible news on to me, great Mo' i. In light of it, I hope that you will favourably consider an extension of my stay here in your realm."

Kamakahelei nodded warmly and smiled at Walter. "Pelekané, you are welcome to stay for as long as you wish. You have our word on this."

Walter bowed. "Mahalo nui, great Mo' i."

Walter left the ha'lau only to wander aimlessly about the village. In the darker recesses of his mind, a little flicker of thought sprang alight. He knew what could calm him. It had been a long time since he thought about the opium. With a renewed spring in his step, Walter headed back to his hut, where he quickly rifled through his bag. There, right at the bottom of it, was what he was looking for. Snatching the pouch from the bag, Walter left his hut and headed down to the freshwater pool that had become such a place of comfort and contemplation for him. His only thought now was to calm the emotional tempest raging in his mind.

His pace quickened, and he almost ran the last stretch of the path. Reaching the pond, Walter sat down on a rock beside the water. He looked at the pouch in his hand. The well-worn leather had lost its sheen. Walter was about to open it when he stopped. Why did he suddenly feel reluctant to reach for its contents? His fist closed around the pouch. Distracted, he stared into the water, trying to decide what to do.

Amidst the rhythmic splashing of the waterfall, he calmed down. As he began to reflect on his life here on the island, it occurred to him that he was not as disturbed by being stranded here as he had first thought. So why had he felt so distressed? Was it about never seeing those he loved again? True, in his heart, he needed to come to terms with the fact that he may never see his mother or Edward again. But his father? There was too much pain in that relationship to yearn for it. And Jonathan? Walter felt no loss in that regard.

As he continued to sit by the pool, lost in time and place, he was startled to hear Omai walk up and sit down beside him. Walter examined his friend from the corner of his eye. "It seems you were right. It appears your gods have a very different life in store for me." Walter said softly.

Omai's smile was gentle as he put his hand on Walter's arm. "I am pleased that you are here to stay, my friend." Omai paused. "Now, maybe you and I will come to ride those mountains together."

The two friends sat together for a while, contemplating the reflections on the surface of the water, while the spray from the waterfall drifted as a gentle mist across to the forest. Occasionally the light broke through the droplets, refracting into small rainbows.

Omai broke the silence." Do you want me to stay, Walter?"

Walter shook his head. "No. I'll be fine. I just need some time to get used to the fact that I may never see my home again."

Omai nodded and then pointed to the pouch. He slapped Walter on the shoulder as he got up to leave. "I trust you'll do what is right, eh."

As Omai disappeared, Walter opened the pouch. He paused for a second then resolutely tipped its contents into his hand, letting the little black pills roll around in his palm. There, he thought, was the means to that elusive state of numbed calm, his own inner Elysium. For so long, he had used this method of dealing with the emotional turmoil of his life, but now contemplating the remnants of his past sitting snugly in his palm, that seemed a lifetime ago.

Ever so slowly, Walter tilted his hand. The pills rolled out along his fingers and dropped into the water. One by one, he watched them descend into the crystal clear depths of the pool, and as they disappeared, he felt a sense of serenity permeate him. Walter had forgotten that this feeling even existed, but now he knew that in giving up the last of the pills, whatever ties that had bound him to his past, were now broken.

Relieved, Walter smiled to himself as he sat there for a moment longer. Then he slowly got up and stood motionless by the edge of the pool, looking across the water, weighing the pouch in his hand, and then with one swift gesture, Walter threw it across the pond.

As the pouch arched gracefully through the air, it splashed into the water. Walter watched it slowly disappear into the depths of the pool, and then turned and casually walked back to his kauhale.

Chapter Thirty-Three

*K*anoa and Kaneoneo had spent the day enjoying the warm waters together, spending many hours in the steady rhythm of paddling out to sea and then catching waves back to shore and repeating this over and over again, stopping only occasionally for fresh water and some food. The ocean had been generous, and they had been able to surf one of their favourite breaks uninterrupted, helped by the fact that Kaneoneo had declared the break to be kapu, forbidden to all, other than himself and other Ali'i.

Now, at the end of the day, Kanoa and Kaneoneo were back at the Kahuna's kauhale, standing in the boathouse where they were carefully oiling the long boards. There was an air of easy familiarity between the two childhood friends, and they were chatting casually about the events of the day, when the Ali'i Nui suddenly changed the subject.

"Lani tells me the haole is keen to surf. He wishes to learn, but Omai has yet to teach him."

Kanoa nodded. "Omai does this out of respect for me. He feels that it is my decision whether the haole surfs here or not." Kanoa paused thoughtfully. "The Pelekané is a strange one, Kaneoneo.

Always there, always watching. It is as if he is searching for something." He looked up at his friend. "And now he has no way to return to his home."

Kaneoneo stopped and, from a wooden bowl poured more oil onto his board. Then, with a white kapa cloth, began to evenly distribute the liquid across the length of the wood, leaving a dark sheen where it had been worked into the grain. He would stop from time to time, leaning over and putting his face close to the deck of the board to see that the oil had been evenly distributed.

"True. But now we shall see what manner of man he really is."

Kaneoneo continued to spread more oil across the board and then, vigorously, rub it into the wood.

"Now," he stopped to admire his work, running his hand along the smooth surface of the board, and casually asked, "what of Koa?"

Kanoa felt a sudden heaviness hearing his apprentice's name, but he knew that Kaneoneo wanted to listen to what he thought about the young man's recent actions.

"I know Koa is difficult and has become less willing to take my advice." He stopped and looked at his chief. "But I still think he will become a wise chief. Just give him time, my friend."

Kaneoneo frowned. "Perhaps. But the eel is a fish that moves skyward."

The chief was fond of sayings, and Kanoa abruptly stopped what he is doing. "Are you trying to tell me that Koa will let nothing stand in his way?"

"You have always had a soft spot for Koa, ever since he was a child. You see things in him that many others struggle to find."

Kanoa looked at his friend and saw that he was watching him closely. Kaneoneo nodded gently toward him as he continued. "Look clearly at his actions, my friend. I often wonder what Koa really wants, my daughter or Kauai or even more than that?"

Kanoa, reluctantly, had to accept that Koa's actions were not necessarily those of a man who was content to see things unfold for themselves. Koa's past clearly suggested that he would try and bend people and circumstances to his will without the necessary consideration for repercussions. The incident of the stick that shoots fire demonstrated that quite well. When Kanoa had described the circumstance to Kamakahelei, she had expressed concerns in regards to Koa's lack of respect for his Kahu and had enquired of Kanoa why he would let such an action go unpunished. He had accepted the Queen's concerns but asked her to trust his judgement on the matter. As always, Kamakahelei stood by him, trusting his intuition.

⸮⸂⸂⸂⸂

At the same time that Kanoa and Kaneoneo were busy oiling their boards, Koa and Lani were strolling casually along a path in the forest. The lush vegetation offered a shady, retreat from the heat of the open areas around the village and the air was scented wth the perfume of an abundance of flowers.

Koa watched, as from time to time Lani would stop to pick a blossom, inhale its scent and then discard it, caught up by the beauty around them and not, as the excited young warrior wanted, paying very much attention to him. Finally he broached the subject that he had brought her here to discuss.

"Lani, when you and I are together, as husband and wife, we will build a new kingdom. One bigger than Kauai."

Lani frowned , "How do you know that we will be man and wife?"

Koa looked at her tying to keep the scowl of his face, unsure if she was joking or serious. She was supposed to greet his plans with the same enthusiasm as he had delivered them. Stopping, he grabbed her arm and turned her to face him, angry that she continued to show reluctance to agree to their marriage. She struggled and tried to pull away from him. "One day, Lani, I will be Mo'i of all the islands, and I want you to be by my side as my wife."

Furious, she hissed at him. "And how will you do that, Koa? With what army? You dare speak like this, while my mother still lives!" She tilted her head to the side, challenging him. Koa refused to be deterred by her taunts, and he pulled her closer to him. "I will find a way, Lani! And sooner than you think."

She managed to wrench her arm free from his grip and ran off into the forest. Koa was infuriated, and watching her disappear into the dimming light of the day, he lashed out with his short spear, mutilating a bush and scattering the leaves around his feet, growling in frustration before he too sprinted back to the village.

Later that night, in his dimly lit hut, Koa and Kumahana shared an evening meal. As was usually the case, the Queen's son was listening intently to Koa, who busily outlined his ambitious plans of conquest.

"Kumahana, you and I are brothers, bound together forever by oath. The haole have found us, and more of them will come, as will Kalaniopu'u. Now is the time for us to take action."

Koa had deliberately reminded Kumahana of their loyalty oath. It reassured him to know that the Mo'i's son would do whatever he wanted. They had agreed many years ago when they were children that Kumahana had no desire to be the Ali'i Nui and that the two would share the burden of leadership. It was an agreement no one knew of, and Kumahana never questioned it, even as he grew up to be an accomplished warrior.

Koa knew that his friend loved him and was happy to be at his side, so leaning forward and putting his hand on Kumahana's arm, he spoke quietly for only his friend's ears to hear. "I will share something with you. A Kahuna on Oahu has foreseen that a great warrior will unite all the islands under one Mo'i." He paused and when he spoke again it was with a deep conviction. "That Mo'i, my brother, will be me."

Kumahana looked at Koa in surprise. "On Hawai'i, many say that it is Kamehameha the prophecy speaks of."

Koa snorted with disapproval and then grinned. "It is the victorious that interpret prophecies, my brother."

"But what if we fail?" Kumahana asked.

"Then may I be devoured by Pele."

Chapter Thirty-Four

*O*ver recent times the people of Kapa'a had been working on the construction of a new hei'au, or temple. Walter had learnt from Omai that here, as in Tahiti, there were many temples of various sizes across the islands, dedicated to the many different gods of the Hawai'ians. Some hei'au were simple stone altars, while others were large stone temple structures sitting on an elevated position, surrounded by massive stonewalls up to eight feet high. Inside the walls were tall, carved tikis of the gods, and places for the offerings and temple goods.

As the construction was nearing completion, Walter had found himself a sheltered position from where he could watch, and sketch the Hawai'ians working on the walls of the temple. Large groups of slaves and workers toiled under the careful supervision of the Kahuna and the Ali'i who were directing different aspects of the construction.

Working on his sketch of the building site, Walter noticed Koa up on the framework for the scaffolding. Given Koa's status he thought it a bit peculiar that the young warrior would be working on the site, especially at the task of adjusting the ties, but thinking nothing more of it he went back to his drawing. When he looked back up again at the scaffolding Koa had disappeared.

With the sketch finished, Walter decided to pack up and head down to the building site where he saw Omai, Kanoa and Kalama inspecting various aspects of the construction. They were preoccupied with examining the huge stone platform that was still surrounded by the towering scaffold. It was a massive wall, only one side of which had been completed, with the other side still only half finished. The scaffolding provided support, as well as guiding the line of the stonework.

As Walter strolled towards Omai and Kanoa, he suddenly heard a grinding noise. He was horrified to see that part of the framework was giving way under the weight of the stone. Slowly tons of rock began to shift and collapse towards Kanoa and Omai. Shouts and screams from the workers rang out above the noise of the grinding stone.

Realising that both Omai and Kanoa were in imminent danger, Walter dropped his journal and bag. In a burst of speed, Walter lunged towards Kanoa, propelling the Kahuna out of harm's way. As he and Kanoa went down into the dust, he caught a glimpse of Omai jumping clear of the tumbling stone blocks and bamboo. Walter felt an immediate sense of relief that Omai had also avoided death.

Amidst the chaos, Koa suddenly appeared, followed by several warriors. The men raced towards them. Walter, still on the ground entangled with Kanoa, felt wrenched up by the arm and literally thrown away from the Kahuna. Before Walter could react, he was being shoved and forced onto his knees by Koa.

Confused and terrified that his situation had something to do with the kapu, Walter froze. In the commotion, he could hear Omai protesting loudly to Koa, who snarled back at the Tahitian. It took no time at all for Kanoa's formidable voice to boom out demanding that both Omai and Koa be quiet.

Walter raised his head to see what was going on. Kanoa was slowly getting to his feet, his arm injured and bleeding. One of his attendants attempted to help him and examine his injury, but

Kanoa angrily brushed him aside. Instead, he called Kalama to his side. They spoke quietly for a moment and then went over to the collapsed scaffolding. Both men started to carefully inspect the sennet ties and ropes that were scattered amongst the debris.

With all eyes on Kanoa, he suddenly squatted and picking up one of the ties he called Kalama over.

"What do you think?" The Kahuna said as he showed the end of the rope to Kalama. Walter couldn't see what they were looking at, but he could see the reaction on the faces of everyone around them. Kalama raised his arm and silence descend onto the worksite. "This rope has been cut. This was no accident!" The news that the rope had been deliberately cut caused a muted stir amongst the assembled workers.

Walter was still trying to come to terms with this information when Kanoa approached him. The big man extended his good arm to Walter. "You have saved my life, haole." Kanoa drew a deep breath. "For that, I owe you." Since the warriors were still hovering over Walter, Kanoa waved them off. "Let him up."

Slowly Walter got to his feet. He looked around and noticed that amidst the commotion, Koa had disappeared. He was confused by the young warrior's odd behaviour, but before he could think about it further, he was distracted by Kanoa's mighty hand on his shoulder. The Kahuna spoke with great power the assembled mass of humanity. "Whoever has done this treacherous thing, shall live in fear, for he knows I will find him."

As Kanoa's warning thundered across the building site, the Kahuna left no-one in doubt that he would keep his word.

The incident had attracted more and more people who were now crowding around them, apprehension and confusion written on their faces. Walter, still anxious despite his release from the watchful gaze of the warriors, was relieved when Omai joined him as they waited for the Kahuna to decide what he wanted to do. After a quick word with Kalama, Kanoa asked Omai and Walter to accompany him back to the village. Surrounded by a guard of warriors the small group set off in silence.

Although eager to discuss the situation, Walter kept quiet. He knew that the Kahuna was evaluating every aspect of what had taken place. Then, without warning, Kanoa stopped and looked intently at Walter. "Can you recall what the old woman said to you, Pelekané?"

Walter was surprised at the unexpected question. He hesitated. What had Omai told Kanoa? Despite Omai's explanation, Walter could make no sense of his strange encounter with the crone and had simply tucked the experience away. As he reflected on it, he sensed the Kahuna's impatience.

Walter cleared his throat and relayed the words as exactly as he could remember them. To him, the story of the rat and the cat was vague if not meaningless, but he continued out of respect. He immediately realised that the Kahuna hung on every word of Walter's account. He added as an afterthought, "Although none of it makes any sense to me, Kanoa, Omai firmly believers that the old woman was warning me.".

Kanoa walked silently alongside the Englishman, studiously keeping his eyes fixed on the rocky path in front of him. When he looked up again, his voice was almost a whisper. "No, my friend, she was warning all of us."

After the midday meal, Walter decided that he needed to wash off the dirt and dust from the mornings' events, and the lure of some time to himself at the quiet pool in the forest was irresistible. He had a few deep grazes on his arms and legs where the sharp gravel of the building site had torn at his skin. Just walking to the pool had a positive effect on his heightened emotions and he felt a great deal calmer as he scrubbed himself down, carefully avoiding the grazes.

He rinsed off by dunking himself under the water, but despite the pleasurable sensation of the cool water over his face he didn't linger, and quickly surfaced. Walter was far more comfortable in the water now, but there was still an element of anxiety about having his head submerged. He could feel his hair clinging to the middle of his back so he bundled it into a thick ponytail and wrung the water out. It occurred to him that his hair had grown substantially since he had been on the island.

Having rubbed himself dry, Walter was reaching for his malo when Lani suddenly appeared at the edge of the clearing and called out to him "Aloha, Pelekané."

Walter was taken aback by the girl's sudden appearance. Still not entirely at ease with being nude in front of others, Walter quickly covered himself. Trying to preserve some sense of decorum, he responded as nonchalantly as he could in his best Hawai'ian.

"Aloha, Lelemahoalani."

He was confused when Lani didn't respond or immediately launch into a conversation, which was her usual approach to their interactions, and he felt himself become alert, as if anticipating something terrible. Her expression was difficult to read, and she remained silent at her eyes ran over the length of him. Then Lani cocked her head to the side as if contemplating a piece of art, trying to decide if she liked it. In his previous life, Walter knew what he would have assumed by her perusal of his half-naked form, but here, and with Lani, he dared not make any inopportune move. So he just smiled warmly at her and waited.

Walter's heart almost skipped a beat as she smiled invitingly at him. Since his Hawai'ian had improved, they had spent less time together, and he had missed her company. It wasn't just that she was beautiful, she was also intelligent and quick-witted, with a sharp sense of humour. Feeling like he should say something he made a silly quip about lady's knocking before entering a man's private chambers. Even as the words left his mouth, he was irritated at his own awkwardness.

Fortunately, although obviously puzzled by what he had said, Lani didn't seem to be bothered or offended and continued to smile at him. Finally, she told him why she had come to seek him out. Lani had heard about the incident at the building site and wanted to thank him for his bravery in saving Kanoa. She also wanted to check that he was not injured and did not require assistance with healing.

Walter, keen to play down any perceived heroics, simply replied that anyone would have done the same thing and he just happened to be the one there today. This answer seemed to appeal to Lani, and her smile widened and Walter thought he could see tenderness in her eyes as she looked at him, which he had not seen there previously.

Lani, her expression soft and sweet, stepped close enough to him that Walter could smell her fragrance, a mixture of coconut oil, frangipani and a touch of musk. He drew in a deep breath. Walter found the combination of an intoxicatingly heady and arousing mix. He had to stop himself from reaching out and merely pulling her to his chest, and it left a longing ache in his body.

"You have a humble heart, Pelekané." Her voice had dropped to almost a whisper as she reached out and took his hand. As she squeezed his hand and told him how she appreciated this aspect of him, Walter closed his eyes and immersed himself in her fragrance and touch. His heart had already been racing, but now it jumped, thudding against his chest, and he felt a hot rush of lust almost wholly overwhelm him.

Walter felt her let go, and then heard a quick rustle of leaves, and opening his eyes he found that she had disappeared back into the forest. Sighing deeply, Walter wondered how long he could stand this self-imposed abstinence, but being totally honest with himself, he knew he wanted no-one else. And she was not for him.

༄༅༈༅༈༅

The oil lamps cast flickering shadows across the interior of Kanoa's hut and the air carried the aroma of roasted meat and steamed vegetables. Kanoa, feeling he wanted something to take his mind off the day's events, had decided that there was no better way to do this than to share a meal with a trusted friend like Kaneoneo. Right now he needed to be with someone whom he could trust implicitly as deep down, Kanoa was still reeling from the realisation that there had been a deliberate attempt on his life.

As a result, he was not particularly hungry, but he couldn't help appreciate that nothing seemed to disturb his friend's appetite. Kaneoneo reached across to a small bowl of poi, a favourite dish of his. He carefully and delicately dipped his fingers into the bowl and scooped some of the purplish paste out, bringing it to his mouth. The chief noisily sucked the poi from his fingers and smacked his lips together.

Reaching for another portion, he looked up at Kanoa. "I heard of the accident at the hei'au, Kanoa. I am relieved that you are safe."

Kanoa was not keen to discuss the incident as he wanted time to think about the events of the day through but the word 'accident' bothered him. "It was no accident, Kaneoneo. The ties on the scaffold had been cut enough to take a while to break, which just so happened to be when Omai, the haole and I were in the path of the rock fall."

Kaneoneo frowned. "Do you think someone wanted to kill the haole, or the Tahitian Omai? I wouldn't have thought anyone would see the Pelekane as a threat."

Kanoa thought about it for a minute. "No, I don't think it was either Walter or Omai who was the target. Walter has no importance, and Omai has become well-liked for his skill as a carver. Neither of them is involved in the politics of the village."

"But who would want you dead? You are a much-honoured man. Everyone loves you." Kaneoneo replied, his voice expressing his apparent disbelief.

Kanoa had been thinking about a previous conversation of theirs, and some unpleasant insights were starting to make sense. "I think your earlier warning was true enough, my friend."

Kaneoneo looked at him, and a hint of sadness filled his eyes as he acknowledged that they had to contemplate such a betrayal. "What will you do, my friend?"

Kanoa shrugged his shoulders and smiled conspiratorially. "You know me," he said, shrugging his shoulders, "though the sea is deep and rough, the coral rock remains standing."

Chapter Thirty-Five

*T*he following day, Walter was woken up by the busy and noisy activity of the villager's and so slipping into his buckskins, he stuck his head outside to see what the commotion was all about. He was surprised to hear that the Mo' i had decided that the village should celebrate his bravery in saving Kanoa from death under the debris of the collapsed stone wall. When Walter asked Omai about this apparent habit of spontaneous feasting, the Tahitian said that Kamakahelei used these gatherings as a way to reward the community, and demonstrate her commitment to them.

Walter, who understood only too well the political benefits a good party could have, still could not stifle his reservations about being heralded a hero. Still, when he questioned Omai further, he found that his friend approved of the Mo'i's generosity. More importantly, he told Walter that the Mo' Kanoa and I had insisted that Walter is treated as the honoured guest and that all of the chiefs had agreed.

And so as the sun slowly set over the horizon, the torches were lit, and people began to assemble in the vast square. Walter, only slightly more at ease at being the centre of attention, had been collected from his hale by a small group of warriors who had escorted him to the raised platform where he now sat amidst the Ali'i and Kahuna. He remained flanked by that small group of warriors, apparently as a mark of honour and respect, although he held a suspicion that it was possibly more for protection than honour.

Perhaps it was both, Walter thought. Walter had asked Omai what he thought, but the Tahitian appeared to have been in to be two minds about the idea as if he was reluctant to accept that either of them needed protection.

A conch droned, announcing the traditional formalities. Walter already knew that any feast in the Polynesian Islands began with the customary 'awa ceremony, and he was well aware of the mouth-numbing properties of the beverage. He had tried it in Tonga and in Tahiti, but always rejected it in favour of a stiff drink of rum as he struggled with the taste of it. Under these circumstances however, Walter knew that he could not refuse the honour of partaking in the peppery, sandy concoction. Omai had assured him that the Hawai'ians tended to drink the 'awa quickly. It was bad manners to let it linger in the mouth too long and once downed, it was customary to have a small bite of food to cleanse the palate.

Walter keenly watched as the opening ceremony moved onto the ritual prayers and offerings to the gods and ancestors known as aumakua. All this was accompanied by numerous chants and the hula, the traditional dance performed by both men and women. As was the case in Tonga and Tahiti, the chants and hula were performed with exacting precision and theatrics and left Walter feeling a strong admiration for the people and their ritual and art forms.

Many of the Islanders had visited Walter's kauhale during the afternoon and presented Walter with an assortment of gifts, which he had found touching and at the same time, embarrassing. However, being keenly aware that he should follow proper protocol, he had dutifully accepted these gifts, and carefully placed them in his hale. From amongst those gifts, he had chosen a beautiful kapa cloak and a fern headdress to wear at the feast as a sign of honouring his hosts.

Now sitting amongst the other guests, he found that he could not find a comfortable place on his brow for the headdress, and the colourful flower leis that were strung around his neck, their scent wafting up his nostrils, itched and made him sneeze. When Walter turned his head, they also tickled his chin, causing him to scratch from time to time. He was surprised at how heavy they felt. Amidst all of natures finery enveloping him, he was hot and uncomfortable. To make matters worse, the more he tried to look dignified for the occasion, the less he actually felt it. It was ironic, he thought, that even here in this paradise, getting dressed up meant being uncomfortable.

Walter was suddenly distracted from his discomfort by Kanoa, who had gotten to his feet and walked towards the platform upon which Kamakahelei, Kaneoneo and the royal family sat.

Having been preoccupied, Walter had missed what an imposing figure Kanoa cut in his festive best. The Kahuna was dressed in a red and yellow feather helmet and cloak, and in his left hand, he carried a beautiful feather fan while in the other he held an exquisitely carved staff, called a ko'oko'o. His voice, filled with power, was pitched so that all could hear him as he addressed the gathering.

"Ali'i Nui, I stand before you a humbled man. When the haole came to our island, I was not pleased to welcome him. But our wise Mo' i said we should learn from those not like us." He paused, clearly weighing his words carefully and to add to the dramatic effect of his oratory. "I have done so. Not only has the haole saved my life, but I have also learned that one can wish for something too much, and fail to see the obvious."

Again the Kahuna stopped, dropping his head dramatically. Then, in a striking gesture of raising himself to his full height, he threw his arms up. "The Pelekané wishes to learn to surf. If he has the courage, then he shall have what he wants."

For a moment, there was a hushed silence as everyone looked at Walter, who was trying to digest the Kahuna's words. Suddenly a huge cheer erupted from the crowd which to Walter's mind, seemed to take a long time to die down. Finally as the noise faded, Walter glanced around. Feeling somewhat embarrassed, he caught a glimpse of Koa who was seated on the other side of the square with Kumahana and a group of warriors. Although Koa's face was barely visible, Walter could see that his expression was like a stone carving, his muscles taut and set. There, too, was a stillness about Koa's posture that seemed to Walter to betray a level of tension and alertness.

Kanoa stood there listening to the accolades from the villagers, showing himself a to be a master of gauging the mood of a crowd, then he slowly turned to look at Koa. As master and apprentice locked eyes for a moment, Kanoa continued.

"I now stand before you, to say that the Pelekané will be my apprentice. He will learn our ways and live freely amongst us." As Kanoa finished speaking, he signalled for Walter to join him. Confused and wary, Walter slowly got to his feet. Another cheer erupted from the assembly as he stepped off the dais and slowly crossed towards the standing figure of Kanoa taking his place next to the Kahuna, whose powerful voice rang out again.

"E kala mai `oe ia'u a me e komo mai. Forgive me and welcome, my apprentice."

Bending slightly down to Walter, Kanoa leant forward and much to Walter's surprise, the Kahuna pressed his forehead to Walter's in the traditional greeting. The gesture triggered a roar of drums and conch shells resounded through the moonlit night, the sound carrying above the excited cheers of the crowd.

Kanoa took him by the arm and led him ceremoniously to his own dais where warriors respectfully made room for the two men to sit down. Walter sensed that Kanoa was thoroughly enjoying the moment. He, on the other hand, felt apprehensive, and looking around at the crowd of smiling faces, he spotted the frozen figure of Koa.

Suddenly, a craggy shape at the edge of the square caught Walter's attention. He immediately recognised the old woman of the forest and turned to the Kahuna. "Kanoa, quick." He thrust his arm out. "The old woman, she is over there!"

"Where?" Kanoa asked. Walter, still pointing towards where she had been, turned back only to realise that she was gone. Disappointed, he shook his head. "She was there a minute ago." He was puzzled by the way she could so quickly disappear, and he found himself scanning the crowd trying to reassure himself that he didn't just see things. Turning back to Kahuna, he found him studying the edge of the forest with an expression of intense curiosity and thoughtfulness. This suggested to Walter that Kanoa had taken his assertion about the old woman seriously.

Chapter Thirty-Six

$\mathcal{K}$anoa's announcement to the festive crowd that Walter was now his apprentice had done little to change Walter's daily routine. What it had done was make him even more vigilant than ever with regards to Koa. Walter was sure the young, ambitious warrior would seek retribution of some kind at some time.

Omai had tried to reassure him that now that he was under the auspices of the great Kahuna, Koa would not dare anything so blatantly obvious, but this did little to comfort Walter. Then on a grey, wet morning without any prior discussion or warning, Kanoa arrived at the kauhale. Walter and Omai had just stepped out from their sleeping hut when they found the Kahuna with a big bag slung across one shoulder, and three large stone adzes balanced on the other shoulder. Kanoa smiled at them. "So, Pelekané, you want to ride waves with us? If that is so then, I will need to make you a board. And for that, I need to find the right tree, and you will help me."

For a moment, Walter was speechless. He quickly gathered his composure." This is a great honour, Kanoa." He stammered, "Mahalo."

"Yes, it is, Pelekané," quipped Kanoa. He winked at the befuddled Englishman, "But one that well deserved. Come, gather what you need for the day and follow me."

They collected food, which they wrapped in ti leaves and kapa, some gourds of water and a few other items as quickly as they could, so has not to keep the Kahuna waiting. As they headed out of the village and into the forest, the local people greeted them with great respect, some even falling on their knees in recognition of Kanoa's status and power.

Kanoa set the pace, and the three of them walked in silence through the dark canopy of the forest. The path rose to a steep incline, and as they climbed steadily up the hillside, the sun started to penetrate through the gloom, and Walter could see glimpses of blue sky as the clouds retreated.

By the time they reached a grove of tall trees, Walter was drenched in sweat and straining to breathe, but the beauty of the trees awed him, taking his mind off his aching chest. Each tree was more impressive than the next.

Walter watched Kanoa stroll thoughtfully between the tall timbers, carefully examining each tree by running his hand along its trunk. Sometimes the Kahuna would stop and press his ear against a particular tree and tap the trunk in a way that Walter found intriguing. Still, despite his curiosity, he kept silent instinctively knowing not to intrude on the process.

Kanoa pointed to two robust trees. "See these? They will be perfect for the boards. We will cut the trees and split them into planks to be carried down to the village, where I will carve the boards. Then I will dedicate them to the ocean, and you will learn to surf. But first, we must ask the gods for permission and give thanks for their gifts."

By now, Walter knew that many aspects of Hawai'ian life were accompanied by a ceremony to the Gods. He watched Kanoa face the trees and from the bag, pulled out the necessary offerings of a piece of pork, a dead chicken and some taro.

"O Kupulupulu! Here is the pig. Here is the chicken. Here is the food. O Kupulupulu! O Kulana wao! O Ku-ohia laka! O Ku waha ilo! Here is food for the gods."

As Kanoa's powerful voice echoed into the forest, Omai joined the chant. At the end of which Kanoa placed the promised gifts at the base of each tree. Then, with the stone adzes, and in complete silence as required by tradition, they proceeded to chop the two trees down.

It took some time before the first colossal tree creaked loudly and then tip towards the ground to crash noisily to the forest floor. Once the second tree had been felled and also lay on the ground, Kanoa showed Walter how to clear the branches off the enormous trunks, leaving just the bare log. Working together, it took very little time for the logs to be prepared for the next stage.

Carefully using wooden wedges, they then began to split each tree, ending up with the planks from which Kanoa would shape several boards. Satisfied with the result of their work, the men stacked the timbers on top of each other, and with great effort, the three of them lifted the wood onto their shoulders and began making their way back to the village and Kanoa's kauhale.

Walter almost collapsed under the weight of the timber, most of his strength already used up in the work they had done so far, but he was determined to carry his share of the burden. As they walked down the mountain, Kanoa began to speak. "Come, let me tell you the importance of what we are doing and how it is done."

Kanoa explained to Walter that there was great mana in riding the waves, and that to do so correctly required the right board which requires finding the right tree, cutting it down, preparing the wood, treating it, and finally dedicating it to the ocean. All of which called for a great deal of patience and skill that took years to master.

And so during the next few weeks, Walter watched the Kahuna spend days carefully scraping, chipping and cutting the planks to obtain the desired shape, depth, width and length that he felt was appropriate for a board Walter was going to surf on. Then using coral and sharkskin sanders, he smoothed and polished the wood by hand to the slickness, that apparently, promised Walter the best balance in traction, speed and manoeuvrability.

Finally, Kanoa had one of the young men from the village go out and collect kukui nuts which he burned to soot, and then mixing it with an extract of ti leaves, he turned the mixture into a dark stain that he liberally applied to the length and breadth of the whole board.

As Kanoa spread it out across the wood, Walter saw the fine grain emerge in a beautiful, shining pattern that reminded him of some of the most elegant furniture in his home in England.

Walter was keen to take his new possession immediately into the ocean, but Kanoa and Omai were quick to remind him that first, he needed to be able to swim proficiently in deep water. Apparently, Walter's amateurish morning swims in the shallows were a matter of much amusement amongst the villagers, and Kanoa informed Walter that he was determined to rise to the challenge of teaching Walter to swim.

It was only later that evening that Omai informed him that Kaneoneo had been teasing the Kahuna that it would require divine intervention from Kane to get the Pelekané to stand let alone ride a board. Wagers had been placed amongst the Ali'i, and as it turned out, Kanoa was not the favourite. More than ever Walter was resolved to do his very best. He had strived long and hard never to be the butt of anyone's jokes again. So he was determined that this would certainly not be the case in what quite possibly was to be his permanent home.

In the early morning light of the next day, Walter, Kanoa and Omai stood in the shallows of a nearby beach preparing Walter for his first challenge in his journey to ride the waves. The Kahuna explained to his two charges that he wanted to focus his attention over the next few days on putting the final touches to their new boards, and he wanted Omai to help him with this.

Walter, on the other hand, was to concentrate on gaining more confidence in the water. To do this, he suggested that Walter start to go further out into the surf so that he was just out of his depth and practice floating.

Watching Kanoa and Omai disappear up the beach and out of sight, Walter was relieved to be left to his own devices for a while.

He tentatively surveyed the small surf and decided that he could manage. He carefully immersed himself the water, gingerly moving further into the waves than he would typically have done. Slowly and steadily, Walter dunked himself delicately in and out of the water, self-conscious and anxious about calling attention to himself, but at the same time aware that he must look like he was practising a strange sort of dance

His peaceful dip was suddenly interrupted when he was startled by a noise from the bushes. He spun around to carefully scrutinise the shore; however, he saw nothing even after careful surveillance of the edge of the forest, so he allowed himself to relax again, and taking Kanoa at his word, he lifted his feet from the sandy bottom to float on his back. He had been practising this in the freshwater pool, but despite feeling more buoyant in the saltwater, the movement of the waves made him more than a little nervous.

He was concentrating on staying calm and letting the water support his weight when he found himself unexpectedly tossed over from beneath and as he snapped open his eyes, desperately seeking the sandy bottom with his toes, while his arms flailed about in panic, he found himself surrounded by a handful of naked girls. They splashed frivolously around him, laughing as their breasts bounced provocatively around on their chests, seemingly with a life of their own, and their eyes flashed with mischief.

Bewildered by their sudden arrival, Walter tried not to stare at their nubile figures, but as they came closer, he was riveted by the way the water had given their skin a delightful sheen. The girls giggled as they started to rub themselves against him and pulled him by the arms in an attempt to drag him from the water. Embarrassed by his growing erection, he tried to disengage himself, resisting valiantly, determined to maintain some dignity and control.

Realising that their hapless quarry was determined to evade dry land and inevitable exposure, the girls, still giggling, were back on the beach as quickly as they had appeared in the water. They stood there, in all their naked glory, the sun refracting the pearls of water, creating the illusion of sparkling jewellery through their hair and on their skin. Walter blinked, while the girls continued to try and coax him out of the water with lewd and blatantly suggestive movements of their hips.

Walter's plaintive cries for them to desist fell on deaf ears, and the girls persisted in their lascivious displays, leaving nothing to the imagination. Determined to stand his ground, Walter covered his eyes, hoping that they would see that he was not going to participate, even though he was sorely tempted.

Suddenly, there was an abrupt silence. Surprised, and curious, Walter spread his fingers to peer between them. There, on the beach, the girls had stopped their antics and were huddled in a conference. He could hear them discussing whether he was playing hard to get or if he was genuinely trying to resist their advances.

As one of them looked across to Walter, she noticed his attempt to peek at them and she screeched excitedly, pointing towards him. Apparently thinking that Walter may, after all, come to the party and play, they started to run back into the water, when one of the girls suddenly bent down and retrieved Walter's only piece of clothing, his malo. Taking the opportunity to tease him further and prolong the game, she held it high in the air, mischievously waving it about like a flag.

"Pelekané, if this is what you want, you will have to come and get it from me. But in return, you will need to show me what mana you have!" The girls laughed out loud, their delight in the game enhanced when one of the others called out. "I have heard that he stands like a rock in the sea.

"Yes, come, Pelekané, let the rock rise from the sea."

Walter smiled at the cheeky metaphor but already self-conscious enough, he decided that the safest place by far was to stay in the surf. What a dilemma, he thought. In England, he would have had no hesitation to follow his natural inclinations to ravish these pretty, willing girls, yet here he was, reticent and self-conscious.

After his short and delightful liaison with Vaitea in Tahiti, Walter decided that his days of simple lustful romps were at an end. Much as he had enjoyed that brief encounter, he now found himself wanting something more meaningful. After all, the very cause of him being here stuck on an island in the Pacific Ocean was a lustful and hedonistic lifestyle, that had led to his ill-considered and irresponsible behaviour.

When he told Omai of his decision to practice abstinence, the Tahitian thought this was an utterly foolish idea not to be emulated in any way, and especially not to be promoted to others. He made Walter promise that he would keep such ridiculous notions to himself, and not spread them amongst the women on the island. In fact, Omai informed him that he believed that Walter had finally succumbed to the usual conflict the English had about anything sexual.

Walter, however, was not to be dissuaded and had explained to Omai that the next woman he would bed would become his wife for life, just as he should have done in England, and it was with that in mind that he continued to resist the girls' advances. His best bet, he decided, was to stay in the water waiting for Kanoa and Omai to return.

Then amidst all the laughing and general commotion, Lani slipped out from behind the bushes. Walter had no idea how long she had been watching the bawdy spectacle. Mesmerised, he watched as Lani walked down to the edge of the gentle lapping surf. As she stood there with her hands on her hips, she was a commanding figure of earthy, feminine authority, a smile hovering around her beautiful mouth.

The moment she had stepped out of the forest, the other girls instantly dropped to the ground, prostrate to pay the Queen's daughter due respect. Lani turned and signalled them to stand, saying in an amused voice.

"Don't tease him! Can't you see he is uncomfortable." She winked at them. "Leave him to me."

The girls laughed while another pouted. "But you have Koa to play with."

Getting agitated, Walter moved back into slightly deeper water, hoping for some escape route. But before Lani could reply, Kanoa and Omai arrived back at the beach. It did not take them long to realise what had been happening. They roared with laughter while Walter, standing in chest-deep water, was waiting for the girls to

leave so he could retrieve his malo with some semblance of propriety. Good-naturedly, Kanoa chased the girls, including Lani, away
and all of them ran giggling back up the path and off into the
forest.

Once out of sight, Walter emerged from the surf and quickly
tied the malo around his waist. "Thank you for your swift assistance,
gentlemen." Walter's sarcastic remark simply amused Kanoa and
Omai further.

As he tried to adjust the malo, Kanoa pointed at the bulging
loincloth. "It appears to me that we returned to early, my friend."

Omai laughed at the Hawai'ian's suggestion. The Kahuna
continued good-naturedly. "Isn't it about time that you found a girl?
Look at Omai here, he is like a bird flitting from flower to flower,
always busy." Kanoa slapped the Tahitian loudly on the back.

"I'm not sure that would be such a good idea, Kanoa," Walter
replied earnestly. "When I do that, it generally ends in trouble."

"Well, it can not be good for you to not have the company of a
fine girl." Kanoa looked around. "But enough of this. I think its
time to head home for now. We have other work to do."

On the way back to the village, Kanoa, who'd been absorbed in
thought, looked Walter up and down. "The girls tell me that you
swim like a rock."

Walter, smiled at the comparison, a little relieved that the
Kahuna was not referring to another type of rock. "You could say
that, but where I come from, there is little need to swim like a fish."

Kanoa nodded, then the slight smile on his face suddenly disappeared, creating a more sombre demeanour. "Riding waves can be
deadly to the unskilled, or those who do not respect the ocean." He
paused and looked straight at Walter. "And so you will need to learn
to swim like a fish."

Walter was excited, but also apprehensive, and he could feel his
body tense up as he thought about what this meant. Having obviously seen Walter's reaction, Kanoa reached over, and placing a big
hand on his shoulder spoke with to him in an encouraging tone.
"Take heart, haumana, to ride the massive waves, Omai, too, will
have to train hard."

Omai nodded, but despite his expression reflecting the seriousness that the discussion warranted, his words were filled with
humour, as he agreed with the Kahuna. "It is true, Walter, for now, I
am no more than a lowly sea slug clinging to the bottom of the sea."

Kanoa amicably slapped Walter on the back. "So, get some food
and a good sleep tonight because you have much work to do."

Distracted by the fun of teasing Walter, the three friends had
failed to notice that they had been shadowed by a lone figure in the
forest. As the men entered the village, a tall warrior stepped out
from the bushes behind them.

Chapter Thirty-Seven

*T*he next day with the first rays of light illuminating the top of the forest, Kanoa, Walter and Omai headed to the beach. In spite of the early hour, many of the children were already playing, swimming and surfing. Seeing the three men, they excitedly ran over to greet them and Walter wondered if they anticipated that 'the Pelekane' would provide some unique entertainment. However, Kanoa, his mind obviously on the task at hand, seemed to be in no mood for any further distractions and shooed the children away.

"Today, Pelekané, you will learn to swim like a fish."

Encouraging Walter to follow, Kanoa and Omai quickly swam out beyond the breakers. To the cheers of the children, who had reappeared to watch the unusual spectacle of seeing an adult learn to swim, Walter made his way into waist-deep water. Then inch by inch, he moved forward, mustering all of his courage to let the water envelop his body. He only stopped when he was standing on the very tips of his toes.

Walter drew in a deep breath. Mustering all of his courage, he launched himself into the deep. Using his arms to propel himself over the waves, Walter lost his concentration, and as the foaming water engulfed him and pushed him under the wave, he forgot to hold his breath and found himself struggling to regain the surface.

Just as the feeling of panic started to overwhelm him, he felt a hand grasp his arm, and he found himself hauled to the surface. Coughing and spluttering, Walter's fear was transformed into embarrassment when he realised that he had been rescued by one of the young boys.

With powerful strokes, Kanoa swam across to Walter. "So, what were you waiting for?"

"I... I couldn't reach the surface!" Walter gasped.

Kanoa looked at the breathless Englishman and wondered out loud if he was perhaps expecting a little too much of Walter and he softened his tone. "Well, then we really need to start you from the very basics. Now, I have seen you float on your back, and that is a good start, so show me how you do that."

Patiently, Kanoa and Omai helped Walter change his position from floating on his back to shifting over to his front. He was competent to do this in still water however he found it to be far more challenging in the waves. After some time, Walter began to master this and at the same time control his breathing without going under and choking. Eventually, he succeeded in gently gliding across the surface of the water for a short distance. The two Islanders spent most of the day working with Walter to improve his confidence to the point where he was able to increase the power of his strokes and pull himself through the water. Walter realised that the problem was that he remained fearful of the water lapping across his face and that this was unavoidable out here in the waves. Kanoa's patience with him made Walter more determined. He couldn't abide the idea that he would fail, even if it killed him.

By the end to the afternoon, Walter was totally exhausted with aching shoulders and his throat raw from all the saltwater he had swallowed. As the sun disappeared into the ocean, the Kahuna finally called it a day and the three of them started back to the village. Bone weary and sunburnt, Walter was immensely grateful and relieved when Kanoa announced he had other responsibilities the next day and Walter could rest.

Despite his aching body and painful skin Walter slept soundly that night, however just before drifting off, he resolved to protect himself from the stinging rays of the sun in future. And so the next morning Walter ventured out sporting a green woven sun shade fashioned by Omai and covered up in a long-sleeved shirt.

Over the months Walter's interest in recording the sights and scenes of Hawai'ian life had remained a constant in his life on the island. Despite plans to the contrary, his excursions into the hinterland always seemed to lead him ultimately back to the beach. His ever-present journal and sketchbook, now made of kappa as he had long since run out of paper, were a particular drawcard for the younger children, and they would come to watch him draw.

Walter enjoyed their company, and together they would set out to explore and to find suitable places for him to work. It was their company that helped Walter master more and more of the Hawaiian language while also learning about the goings-on in the village.

Having been given the day off from swimming lessons, Walter and his entourage of children were walking along the edge of the water, when he steered them towards an outcrop of rocks where he could sit and watch the Islanders surf. Unlike the day before when the surf had been small, in fact almost non-existent, this day saw a solid chest-high swell running onto the beach. As he set himself up to draw the scene, he noted that more and more of the villagers were arriving, having obviously abandoned the morning's chores in favour of a good time.

Most of the people stood up to ride the waves on boards of various sizes, but a few were lying down on much shorter boards, and several young boys appeared to be merely content to surf the dumping waves at the edge of the sand.

Walter thought this was an especially dangerous endeavour as the wave would pitch steeply and break violently onto the wet sand taking the surfer with it and unceremoniously dumping the rider into a churning mixture of water, sand and whatever other debris was at the edge, including other bathers. As the wave would recede, the person would emerge covered in sand and usually hollering with joy at the ignominious end of their ride . At the same time, the others around them would immediately try to imitate or better the previous performance.

Walter's primary interest was the riders on the long boards catching the larger waves further out to sea. While he was paying extra attention, he realised that one skilled rider, in particular, was Lani. Although she was on a shorter board than most of the men, she rode with the same skill and agility Walter had seen the men display.

Mesmerised by her grace and beauty, Walter completely forgot about his sketching and was simply riveted by her glistening, naked figure silhouetted against the blue of the wave and sky.

This time as Lani raced towards the shore on one of the waves, she must have spotted Walter sitting on the rocky outcrop, and to Walter's delight, she smiled and waved to him. Instead of turning back to the ocean, she brought the board onto the sand through the shore break, elegantly stepping off the beautifully shaped plank onto the beach. Leaving it on the sand, she walked over to Walter, and as she neared, the kids melted away, giving their princess the expected deference custom demanded.

Entirely absorbed by her nakedness, Walter became aware of growing tension in his groin. Embarrassed, he tried to focus on anything but her alluring figure. But try as he might, he could not hide his excitement as he watched her naked form approach.

"What are you doing, Pelekané?" Lani asked innocently.

Walter tried to focus on the page in front of him. He cleared his throat, painfully aware of the on-going strain in his groin. He could not help wondering why he was so self-conscious here where nudity was so commonplace.

"I'm drawing," Walter held up his sketchbook, "see?"

He turned the journal around so that Lani would focus on the page and not his crutch, but she kept looking at him rather than at the page he had presented to her to scrutinise. "Show me more!" Her eyes were fixed on his face, and Walter blushed deeply. Lani smiled, slipped in beside him on the rock and dropped her gaze to the paper in front of her.

Walter soaked in the scent of a mixture of saltwater and kukui oil that wafted toward him and looked directly at her face to distract himself from the way she leaned closely against his body. Seeing her eyes widen as she looked at his drawings, he saw that she was impressed.

"These are very clever, Pelekané. Lani said as she looked up at him. "It is just like real life!" Her eyebrows drew together as if assessing a precious artwork and as she looked back at the work and then up at him again, he sensed that the intensity of her gaze was evidence that she was seeing him in a different light. "They are very beautiful." She said quietly.

"It gives me great joy to draw the life I see around me. Here!" Walter said as he turned the page revealing a picture of the island shore. Lani looked at it, and then reached over and turned the page obviously wanting to see more.

"Who is this?" Lani asked. Walter looked down at the face of his mother. He was suddenly struck by a pang of sadness and longing for her. He sighed. "That, Lelemahoalani, is my mother, Eleanor Beaumont."

Lani cocked her head to the side, her wet, jet-black hair cascading down the length of her body, like a dark curtain shading her. Her hand reached out and touched his leg gently. "You must miss her."

She was right, Walter thought, I do miss her. He had come to realise that what he wanted and longed for most was pure affection and tenderness. It was that need that had prompted his choice not to indulge himself amongst all the nudity and open sexuality of the Islands. Walter's throat tightened with sadness, and he swallowed hard. "Yes, I do. Very much."

Lani gently placed her hands upon his, the warmth of them touching more than merely his skin. For a brief moment, they sat together. Walter wished for time to just stand still, preserving this moment forever as Lani's face softened into a warm, tender smile.

Then, out of the blue, Lani gave him a playful push, jumped up and ran back to where her board lay in the sand. Turning she waved to him before picking it up, with what Walter thought was deceptive ease, Then she threw the board back into the ocean, launched herself onto it and paddled back out to the line-up.

For Walter, left sitting there, the ache in his body for her touch stayed with him as he watched her for a few more waves before deciding to head home.

꞉ꙮ꞉ꙮ꞉ꙮ꞉ꙮ

The next few weeks had Walter swimming as much as Kanoa and Omai could keep him in the water. It always took place before an enthusiastic crowd who would never hesitate to make interesting suggestions on how the Pelekané could improve his skills.

Much to everyone's surprise and he suspected Kanoa's relief, Walter began to show significant improvement in his ability to swim both in the river, where he had to swim upstream for strength and endurance, as well as in the surf, where he began to familiarise himself with the fickle moods of the ocean.

Walter had to admit that he too was pleased with his progress, and he wondered when Kanoa would allow him to take his new board to the sea. When he approached him about it one morning at the beach, Kanoa said, "You are now able to swim and the time has come to learn to surf without a board. To do that you must swim as hard as you can into the wave. Let me show you."

Kanoa and Omai quickly swam into a few waves closer to the shore and surfed them into the beach. Walter watched what they did carefully and then waded out to where the waves were starting to break in the hope that he could duplicate their manoeuvres. Waiting patiently for a moment until the next swell came towards him, he tried to launch himself into a wave. He pushed his feet into the sand on the bottom and then threw himself forward into the unbroken wave, but it merely passed over him and ran its own course, riderless.

After a few more failed attempts, Walter finally succeeded in successfully launching into a wave by swimming hard into the swell. To his utter surprise, he could feel the surge of the wave take hold of his body, pulling it forward. He forced his head above the water

and could see the shore rush towards him. Close to the beach, the
wave accelerated, and Walter was sucked over onto the sand with
sufficient momentum to force the air out of his lungs. Despite the
less than elegant finale, Walter rolled onto the beach, shouting with
the excitement of having caught his first wave in Hawai'i.

That evening, just before the sun set below the horizon, Walter
sat in front of the hale. He felt proud of himself for having challenged his fear of the water sufficiently to begin feeling confident,
and that sooner, rather than later, he would ride a board on a wave.

Chapter Thirty-Eight

"*Dear Mother,*

How proud you would be. I have learnt a great deal since arriving on these islands. I have become sufficiently skilled in their tongue to be able to converse with the natives quite freely, and at length, which has made my enforced stay here much more comfortable and pleasant.

More importantly, however, I have managed to overcome my fear of the water and have become a more competent swimmer. Finally, my training with the boards begins, and the impending challenge of riding the ocean surges makes me feel more alive than ever.

Although I struggled initially with the physical challenges Kanoa and Omai set for me, I have made sufficient progress with coping in the water and with the waves. My ability to swim, compared to the Islanders, still remains in its infancy but Kanoa, my patient teacher, has assured me that I am an apt pupil. When my physical skills fail me, my courage and determination will carry me forward to success.

I cannot describe how thrilled I was to feel the surge of power that embraced me when I successfully launched myself into an ocean swell and the exhilaration of riding a shortboard, barely the length of a small child, across the face of a wave.

When not in the water, Kanoa has also taken the time to teach me how to recognise and understand the patterns and the flow of the currents and how to judge where there are dangers in the water due to the many rip tides and obstacles below the surface. My progress, such as it is, has not come without a price and I had had to contend with my fair share of injuries, not too dissimilar to when I was a child learning to ride a horse., only now I don't have you to comfort me in my pain.

Though I do miss your tender care in my needy times, I have met a girl here that set my heart racing in a way it has never before. Unfortunately, as she is the Queen's daughter, Omai has warned me to abandon my desire for her and to look for love elsewhere. The law of this land has strict rules of conduct and to break them, invites the most serious of consequences. In the past, this would have stimulated my determination, but now, hopefully, a little wiser, I intend to respect the hospitality of these people and not cause offence."

Kanoa, always true to his word, had finished two boards, an Olo for Omai and an Alaia for Walter. Omai's olo was about fourteen feet long and weighed around 80 pounds, a serious weight to carry even for a very fit Polynesian. The Alaia was a much shorter and smaller board with a square tail. Relieved that his board was smaller but curious as to why, Walter asked the Kahuna to explain the differences. Kanoa had smiled, "You have much to learn, Pelekané. The size of your board will not only make it easier to carry but more importantly the smaller board is easier to manoeuvre in the surf."

Kanoa, together with Omai had instructed him on how to care for his precious gift, and now back at his hale, Walter was carefully oiling his board and preparing it to be wrapped in kapa when, outside of the canoe hut, he heard a soft and seductive voice. "Would you like me to help?"

Lani's question was utterly lost on Walter, who stood mesmerised by the vision of her. Lani stood in the frame of the door wearing a narrow kapa wrap around her waist. It was tied on the side, drawing Walter's view to her long, shapely leg while her hair spilled down the front of her body, hiding her breasts. To Walter, she was a sensuous silhouette, lit from the back, giving her an ethereal appearance and captivated, Walter could barely answer her.

"Uhm, well no, I mean, yes." Stumbling over his words, he silently chided himself for being a blundering idiot.

Lani smiled coyly and stepped into the hale. Together they wrapped Walter's new board in the long, soft sheet of kapa. Tying it up with the sennet rope, Walter then hoisted the Alaia shoulder high and carefully lifted it into the ceiling rafters beside Omai's board.

As he stood there, straining under the heavy board, Lani reached out and seductively ran her fingers down the corded muscles of his back, sending a shiver down his spine. Trying to ignore her, Walter slid the board into the rafters and stepping away from Lani, he carefully rubbed some of the residue oil from his hands into his arms before reaching for a clean cloth to wipe his hands clean. It was only when Walter had finished that he looked at Lani, his mind scrambling to formulate an intelligent question, any question actually. Before he could say anything, Lani gently pressed her fingers to his lips.

"Shh. Come, take a walk with me."

Lani took Walter's hand and led him out of the hut and down a lane towards the forest. He followed uneasily wondering if he was misreading the invitation, tugging at her side, trying to get her to slow down.

"Lani, I'm not sure that this a good idea."

"Why not?" She sounded a little hurt, and the last thing Walter wanted to do was to upset her for not showing more enthusiasm for whatever she had in mind. But he suspected that what she had in mind was dangerous and much as he might want it, he also did not want any trouble.

"I don't want to cross Koa."

"Koa?' Lani sounded surprised then after a brief moment of thought, she dismissed his concerns. "He is always bent on trouble. Just ignore him."

"But..." Lani placed her hand over Walter's mouth. Turning, she pulled him down the path to the lovely clearing surrounding the freshwater pool that Walter often frequented. Laughing, she slipped out of the kapa wrap and now completely naked with her shapely rear seductively beckoning to Walter, she jumped into the pool.

Unable to resist any further, Walter abandoned reason and made the only decision he could, and removing his own clothing he hurriedly followed Lani into the pool. In a couple of strokes, he had reached her and pulled her into his arms. Lani seemed to melt into his body, but when Walter automatically tried to kiss her on the mouth, she pulled away, looking uncertain.

"This how we kiss where I come from," Walter whispered into her ear. Lani looked at him for a moment and then tentatively surrendered her mouth to his. She seemed to like this new form of intimacy, and she passionately took charge of their union, her hands skilfully stirring him in a way that Walter had longed for. The movement of her body against his ignited his desire further, and he felt transported into his long-held fantasy.

Suddenly reason intruded, swamping Walter as if an imaginary bucket of ice had been dumped on his head. What was he doing? He dragged himself from Lani's embrace, and quickly lifted himself out of the pool. Lani followed him onto the edge of the pool, her expression puzzled. She looked up into his face, her eyes wide with surprise. "Why do you stop? Have I done something wrong?"

"No!" Walter said, in what he recognised immediately was in a far too abrupt tone. He didn't know where to begin. He was afraid and confused. He tried to explain. 'You are the Queen's daughter. In my country you are a Princess, and, well, we do not simply make love to the Queen's daughter."

Walter knew that he was not making sense, but he had no idea what he should say to this woman that he wanted so much, but knew he shouldn't treat her as a simple conquest. He had never wanted to hurt Lani, but now he was fearful that he was doing just that. Walter felt more awkward than he had for many years, and nothing at all like the experienced seducer he had always thought himself to be.

"Well, that is silly." Lani shook her head. "Here, we make love when, and with whom we want."

Walter didn't know how to answer that. He didn't know how to tell her that he wanted so much more with her than a casual liaison. In the uncomfortable silence that ensued, Walter watched Lani's expression changed from confusion to anger. Before he could even begin to formulate a response Lani grabbed her skirt and without looking back, ran down the path and back into the forest.

Desperate to fix the mess he had made, Walter's immediate thought was to pursue Lani, but he stopped as he realised that not only had she disappeared, but the moment had been lost. Sitting down heavily on one to the rocks that surrounded the pool, he tried to tell himself that it was probably for the best, but deep in his being, Walter knew that he had lost something precious that he might never find again.

Chapter Thirty-Nine

*I*kaika walked along the path towards the temple complex deep in thought. He had some misgivings about his alliance with Koa, and he needed to speak with him so that he could decide what would serve him best in the future. He knew that now was the time for him to make his decision, as Koa had demanded that all of his comrades make it clear whether they would give him their allegiance.

Ikaika had always trusted Koa's judgment and had been one of his most ardent supporters ever since they were young boys but to choose Koa would mean going against his own family. They would not approve of him aligning with Koa because Koa was proposing to challenge the Mo'i and his family has been aligned with Kamakahelei from the beginning of her reign.

Koa was intent on becoming the new Mo' i, and he was gathering his supporters close to him. Ikaika had thought long and hard about Koa's ambitions and the consequences of his choosing to go against his own family, but he had been persuaded by Koa's arguments. Like Kumahana, Kamakahelei's son, who was a close friend and supporter of Koa, Ikaika wanted to be his own man and make his own choice.

Koa was convinced that the haole posed a significant threat. And he, like many of his comrades agreed with Koa that the arrival of these strangers on the islands would herald monumental changes to their lives. He also agreed with Koa that the Mo' i did not appreciate this and was therefore not to be trusted to deal effectively with that threat. On the other hand, to go against the authority of the Mo' i and her powerful supporters and to fail, would ruin his own chance to win power and glory.

There were two problems that he could see. One was how Koa was going to deal with the challenge of Lani's growing interest in the Pelekané. There had been much discussion amongst the warriors about this being a test of Koa's resolve to obtain power.

But in Ikaika's mind, it was Kanoa's public declaration to take the Pelekané as an apprentice, that was the most significant issue. He knew it worked against Koa's demand for the warriors to align with him. Kanoa was a powerful kahuna and if the legends are true, not one to make an enemy of. Those who did ended up as a pile of bones or fish food, and this was not something Ikaika wanted to see in his future. Yet Koa had enough mana to openly challenge Kanoa. That meant something. More importantly, Kanoa had not stood against Koa. Yes, the situation was much more convoluted than any of them had anticipated, and any decision needed to be carefully weighed.

Coming up to one of the smaller temples in a clearing near the top of a rise, Ikaika was relieved to find Koa alone as it gave him the opportunity he had been hoping for to raise his concerns. After greeting his comrade, he got straight to the point. "Kanoa continues to prepare the haole for surfing." He paused, waiting for Koa to react then added, "This kanaka shows courage and determination."

Koa did not respond, his face a stoic mask, much like the wooden tiki at the entrance to Ku's temple. Watching closely for any hint of what Koa was thinking, Ikaika then surrendered his most crucial piece of information. "Last night Lani went to the Pelekané's hale."

Much to his surprise, Koa still did not react. "You are not angry?" Ikaika's probing question finally got a response from Koa.

"No, the haole is already a ghost."

Ikaika nodded slowly. He clearly understood both the meaning and the implication of Koa's matter of fact statement. "That may not be wise, Koa. People say that Pele speaks to him."

"Then let Pele try and protect him!"

Ikaika was shocked by Koa's openly bold words. No one dared to challenge Pele unless they were prepared for the fire that rained from the sky. But Koa showed no fear as he calmly warned Ikaika that he should be careful not to succumb to tales for old people and children.

Ikaika thought carefully about this. It made sense to him. Why would Pele care for a stranger? He liked Koa's confidence, and his preparedness to deal permanently with the threat of the Pelekané.

Ikaika knew now what his decision would be. Koa had provided him with the answers he was seeking, and Ikaika was convinced that what he wanted was to be aligned with a warrior with such powerful mana.

As if he had recognised Ikaika's commitment to him, Koa smiled approvingly and slapped him on the back. "You have done well, Ikaika to come and tell me what the haole does, and who he sees." He leant closer. "When the time comes, I will reward your loyalty well."

Pleased with the offer, Ikaika nodded. He trusted Koa, not only as a good warrior but also as a leader who was true to his word. Koa smiled in acknowledgment of Ikaika's acceptance of their pact. "Go now and speak to no one of this, my friend."

He nodded, now more convinced than ever that he was making the right choice. Reassured Ikaika took his leave, each man heading in different directions, quietly blending into the darkness of the forest.

⚜⚜⚜⚜⚜

Neither Ikaika nor Koa had the slightest idea that their short encounter was being watched. As the two men departed, Kanoa quietly moved through the trees, and once they were out of sight, he stepped out onto the path.

The conversation Kanoa had overheard between the two young warriors left him with the indisputable fact that he could not put his concerns to rest anymore. But for now, Kanoa decided that the best course of action was to keep Walter out of the way, busy and surrounded by those well disposed towards him.

As Kanoa made his way back to the village, he pondered how he could undermine Koa's influence over the warriors who had taken a stand against Walter. After dismissing several ideas, he came up with a plan that he thought may work. So on his return to the village, he went to see Omai and consulted with him about the proposed venture, and organised him to ensure Walter's attendance. If all went well, it would leave its mark on the Pelekané, but it would also give haole more standing amongst the warriors.

A few days later, just before sunrise, Kanoa beached a sizeable double-hulled canoe in a quiet corner of a cove, and he and his most trusted warriors disembarked and began to prepare the boat for a day on the ocean.

Looking up along the beach expectantly, Kanoa saw Omai and Walter walking along the shore towards them, and he couldn't help smiling when he saw the curious and slightly puzzled look on Walter's face.

"Aloha, Pelekané."

Kanoa waved in greeting, knowing that the haole had no idea what was in store for him this day. He almost burst out laughing as the two men joined them. Walter wrinkled his nose when he caught a whiff of the basket. It contained large chunks of raw meat and fish that had been in the sun far too long.

Kanoa was obviously not the only one amused. The small group of warriors snickered conspiratorially, while Kanoa worked hard to maintain a neutral expression. He just carried on with coiling the rope before throwing it into one of the hulls. Before anyone could spoil his fun, Kanoa turned to Walter.

"Today, I have a surprise for you, my friend."

Watching Walter assess the ropes, baskets, bait and hooks, Kanoa was not surprised when the haole guessed that they were going fishing. Unknown to Walter, this was a serious understatement. While the warriors burst out laughing, Kanoa just slapped the puzzled Walter on the back and confirmed that yes, they were going fishing, but this time they were fishing for courage.

There was another howl of laughter from the warriors and Kanoa could see that Walter was irritated about being the brunt of their joke, but he just responded by asking Kanoa what he wanted him to do.

"For now just get in the canoe, Pelekané. When we need you to do something, we'll let you know soon enough."

And so they all climbed onto the canoe's superstructure, while several of the warriors pushed the catamaran into the deeper water before jumping aboard. On a signal from Kanoa, they raised their paddles and then collectively dipped them into the light, blue water and in no time at all, they were heading out to sea.

As they crossed the reef and headed out beyond the breakers, the men prepared the triangular sail that had been sitting neatly folded on the deck. As it unfurled, it trapped the wind, and the boat surged forward.

¿à¿à¿à¿à¿à

Walter decided that he would just wait for instructions and sitting quietly in the safety of the hull he silently watched the crew perform their various duties. At the same time, Kanoa continuously scanned the surface of the ocean. Suddenly, he shouted. "Mano! Shark!"

That single word galvanised the crew into a well rehearsed set of actions generating a wave of excitement that washed over everyone on the canoe including Walter, who was suddenly infected by the rush of adrenaline. He was on a hunt for a shark! Looking over at Omai, he saw that he was pointing out over the bow, so lifting himself up and holding on tightly to a rope that was strung along the side of the hull he peered out over the water.

Unlike the smaller reef sharks he had seen from time to time in Tahiti, this was a colossal beast. Walter, his eyes riveted on the massive dorsal fin, suddenly understood Kanoa's quip. Fishing for this beast would require a lot of courage.

Kanoa snapped out orders in rapid succession as one of the men tied the bait basket to a long line and attached it to the mast. Still hanging on to the container, the man then scrambled to the front of the canoe where he quickly let it slip into the water. There it stayed, dangling just below the surface trailing a greasy slick.

At the same time as the bait trailed its odour through the water, enticing the shark towards it, Kanoa handed Omai a long line, one end of which was tied into a noose. Having taken the line and checked the noose at the end of it, Omai clambered to the foremost position of the canoe and placing himself vicariously between the hulls of the vessel. Walter watched the Tahitian eagerly scan the water for any signs of the beast.

As Walter watched all the frantic but well-co-ordinated activity, he suddenly realised what was about to happen. It all had to do with the method of the hunt. Walter looked across at Kanoa, whose face sported a broad grin, while his dark eyes flashed with a maniacal intensity, fuelled by the passion of the chase. When Omai cast a glance back, Walter saw a similar look on the Tahitian's face. His friend continued to cling precariously between the two hulls but appeared oblivious to the risk. At that moment, Walter concluded that there could be only one explanation. These men had lost their minds. "Stop! You men are deranged!"

Kanoa threw his head back and roared with laughter. "Only if you were the bait, my friend."

Right then, Walter caught sight of the shadow of the colossal fish racing towards the canoe. Having caught the scent of the bait, it now accelerated towards the basket suspended between the hulls. As the shadow changed into the streaking, deadly missile, Omai leant forward, suspending the noose just above the water.

From below the canoe, the enormous, dark-grey shadow of the

tiger shark raced towards the basket of bait. Just as the shark was about to close its gaping jaws around it, Kanoa pulled hard on the line attached to the basket, pulling the bait from the water, just out of reach of the enormous shark's snapping jaw. In what seemed to Walter a moment frozen in time, Omai casually slipped the noose over the massive head of the animal.

The shark, sensing the restriction of the noose, tried to descend to the safety of the deep. The front of the canoe dipped for a moment, but the secured line forced the animal to stay near the surface, while Omai kept the basket in front of the shark's snout. In its futile pursuit of the bait, the shark only served to tow the canoe along at greater speed.

"Aué!" The roar of success erupted from the crew, and Omai virtually leapt with joy at lassoing the shark. As they raced across the water, every now and then the massive beast broke the surface, displaying its gaping jaw and rows of razor-sharp teeth in its attempt to reach the bait.

Walter, having regained some composure, was well and truly mesmerised by the colossal shark travelling between the hulls of the canoe. He inched forward, trying to get a closer look at the beast. As he tried to make sure that he was still securely holding on, he shifted his weight just as the catamaran lurched across a wave. Walter's foot slipped off the edge of the deck, and he fell between the hulls.

Walter's leg brushed against the rough, sandpaper-like skin of the shark. Convinced he was about to die he instinctively reached up just as a powerful hand gripped his. One of the warriors swiftly pulled Walter back onboard.

Stunned by his close encounter with the monster, Walter lay on the hull for a moment. His arms ached, and his heart still raced at the thought of having almost become fish bait.

"Take more care, Pelekané," said the warrior leaning over him. "The Gods may not always favour you."

Speechless after his potentially fatal encounter with the shark, Walter could only nod, and it took some time for him to recover from the fright.

As he sat up, he saw Omai reach down and slip the noose from around the shark. In an instant, the beast disappeared into the depths.

Omai reached for the bait basket and again threw it out between the hulls. "Now it is your turn, Pelekané!" Kanoa called out to the cheers of the warriors.

Walter was suddenly bathed in cold sweat. It dawned on him that what he just witnessed was merely a demonstration of what he was expected to do. It was he who was expected to fish for courage. For an instant, it seemed that the only sound he could hear was the rushing of the water against the hulls. Or was that the blood rushing through his body?

Walter looked around. He was surrounded by the expectant faces of Kanoa, Omai, and the warriors. At that moment, Walter surrendered to the only course of action he could take to earn the respect of these men. His mind cleared, and calm replaced the nervous energy that up to that moment had been coursing through his body. He leapt up and grabbed the noose, and looked across the water to where suddenly a large fin broke the surface. It was as big or bigger than the one before.

"Mano!" Walter cried out.

As before, everyone jumped into action. Like Omai, Walter positioned himself on the front edge of the deck, each foot braced against a hull while he wrapped an arm around one of the stays. He kept his weight in his knees to act as springs absorbing the up and down motion of the canoe as it cut through the waves.

The basket of rotten fish dangled in front of him, trailing an oily slick and when Walter looked down he saw the huge dark shape of the beast shoot towards the bait. Tempted to look back to see what Kanoa was doing, Walter resisted. He knew that the Kahuna knew what he was doing. The basket shot up into the air seconds before the massive jaws of the shark snapped shut. As quickly as the shark had surfaced, it disappeared again.

Walter knew to wait. The shark would not let the tempting basket of fish escape so easily. It would be back. Sure enough, the shark had circled back and launched another assault on the basket. This time Walter was ready. As the beast matched its speed and trajectory to that of the tasty bait, Kanoa drew the basket up towards the surface. The shark must have seen this as an opportunity to lunge forward, and its head went straight into Walter's noose.

Walter let go of the rope just in time to let the sennet rope run out as the shark dove down. A massive cheer erupted as Water jumped back on deck. The men quickly secured the rope, and the captive shark became their ocean-going beast of burden.

"Now you know how to fish for courage, Pelekané!" Kanoa called out to him. "This is a lesson you must never forget. Whether you are hunting sharks or surfing."

Walter realised that he understood the lesson that Kanoa had taught him. It was his decision whether or not he would let fear control him.

In all the excitement of the hunt, Walter suddenly realised that the sun was now at its zenith and the beast was still towing them. Soon enough, however, it was clear that the fish was tiring, and finally, the Hawai'ians reversed the catamaran, dragging it backwards which, Omai explained, would cause the shark to drown. Walter thought this was curious, wondering how a fish could drown but he did not argue, deciding that after what he had just witnessed, and more importantly what he had succeeded in doing, these men knew what they were talking about.

Having secured the dead shark to the canoe and being done with their sport, Kanoa ordered them to return home. The sun was dipping into the ocean as they paddled up to the beach where they were greeted with cheers and chants from a large crowd. As was frequently the case, someone had composed a poem to mark the occasion and amidst the man's recital, the warriors beached the canoe and dragged the massive shark onto the beach. Exhausted, Walter jumped off the canoe.

⸙⸙⸙⸙⸙

In the early morning with the dew still on the ground, Walter sat in front of his hut and on a pile of matts in front of him, lay his open satchel. He had his kapa paper, pencils,, and charcoal lying all around him and on his lap lay his journal, his hand flying across the page, capturing the extraordinary experience of the tiger shark hunt. With so much to put on paper, Walter was utterly engrossed in his work and oblivious to the world around him so when Kanoa knelt beside him, he jumped, startled by the inter-ruption.

"Kanoa! You gave me a fright." Walter took a deep breath and settled back down. Kanoa looked at the materials around Walter, and the sketch of the canoe on the beach being loaded with goods. Obviously intrigued, Kanoa looked admiringly at the sketch and then at Walter.

"You must teach me how to do that someday, Pelekané." But before Walter could answer, he opened his fist, "But here, I have something for you."

In the palm of his large hand lay a necklace made of black strands of hair, at the end of which hung a large shark's tooth. Walter suspected that it must be from the beast they captured yesterday.

Kanoa placed his hand on Walter's shoulder. "You have shown courage, Pelekané, and I believe that your true nature, to be a man of the sea, is emerging. That means that you need protection and," Kanoa tapped on the shark's tooth now resting on Walter's chest, "this tooth will give it to you. Always wear it when you go into the sea."

Without another word, the Kahuna got up and walked away. Walter watched Kanoa head towards the upland, and as the man disappeared in the distance, Walter realised that he felt a kinship with this man who, only a short while ago, had him as a potential sacrifice to a god that traded a life for a life. He could not help but ponder that in the short space of time that Kanoa had accepted him as an apprentice, he had spent more time with the man than he ever had with his own father.

As his hand closed around the shark's tooth, tears began to well up and roll down his cheeks. He tried to fight them back, but eventually, he just surrendered to them and allowed himself to give in to his sobs of loneliness and regret, but mostly gratitude.

Slowly the pain in his chest eased, and the tears stopped. Walter was suddenly aware of a dull ache in his hand. As he slowly released his grip of the tooth, he watched drops of blood slowly drip from the cut, splashing onto the white paper in front of him. *An unconscious offering, Walter thought, but to whom?*

Chapter Forty

*I*n the time that Walter had been living amongst the people of Hawai'i, he had come to appreciate their relationship with nature. Everything was seen as alive and as possessing a spirit, so it came as no surprise when Omai told him to prepare for a dedication ceremony for their new boards to be held at sunrise the next day, down by the ocean shore.

Keen for the opportunity to ride the surf on his own board, Walter woke that morning with a great sense of anticipation and excitement and eagerly jumped out of bed and called out, "Come, Omai, my friend, there is no time for dawdling today."

It didn't take much to persuade the Tahitian to get up. He also had been enthusiastically awaiting the dedication of the boards, and was more than ready. Together they lifted Omai's olo and Walter's Alaia from the rafters of the canoe house and brought them outside. Kanoa had looked them over the day before, his critical eye looking for any imperfections that may mar his workmanship and finding none, he had let Walter and Omai know where to meet him that morning.

Walking down to the beach, Walter and Omai met the Kahuna leading a small procession carrying baskets filled with flowers, ti leaves and other offerings. Once they had arrived at the beach, Kanoa ordered the boards to be laid on the ground, and Walter having placed his down next to Omai's, was struck by how impressive the two long dark boards looked lying there in the pale sand.

Kanoa bowed towards the sea, then threw a wreath of flowers onto the surface of the water and began a chant that slowly rose in volume to finally close with the droning sounds of the conch shells being blown by the men standing beside him. Another Kahuna approached Walter and Omai and splashed them liberally with water from a ti leaf.

Amidst the formality, Walter looked through the crowd to see if he could get a glimpse of Lani. Their last meeting had left him feeling deeply concerned about having hurt her, and he could only hope to have a chance to redeem himself. But, much to his disappointment, she was nowhere to be seen.

With the ceremony complete, the three men tightened their malo's and together with a number of the Ali'i, took their boards and paddled out to catch some of the small waves rolling towards the shore. Unfortunately, that day the waves would not rise to the call of the people, and after a few hours, the swell disappeared utterly. As they all made their way back to the village, Kanoa reassured him that there where many days of surfing ahead and not to be too disappointed.

Walter woke to the rooster's crow long before Omai and thinking that today the surf may be small enough for him to tackle it without the supervision of either Omai or Kanoa, he decided to go to the beach on his own. Remembering Kanoa's unambiguous instruction, Walter picked up his shark tooth necklace, smiled, and slipped it over his head before heading out to the canoe hut to collect his Alaia from the beams in the ceiling. Shouldering the heavy board, Walter set off towards the beach, completely unaware that Kanoa was watching him.

The lack of sizeable surf meant that the beach was deserted. Thankful for the solitude, Walter dropped the board on the water, slid his body into position and began paddling out through to the break. Despite the lack of size in the swell, he found it difficult to reach the outer bank of the surf. It was as if the surf had decided against his ambitious plan. No matter how much he tried, the rolling swell kept pushing Walter back towards the beach.

But Walter was determined, and he persisted, and after a few more setbacks, he managed to get beyond the breakers. Sitting up on the board, for a few precarious seconds, Walter struggled to find his balance, teetering from side to side. Once more, his tenacity proved useful, and he finally was able to relax into a more balanced posture. Just like being on a horse, Walter thought.

Having caught his breath, Walter began to pay attention to the surf. A few small waves were rolling towards him, but Walter waited patiently trying to remember all that he had learnt so far about selecting the right wave. Finally, he decided on a particular wave that he thought would serve his purpose and with great enthusiasm, Walter laid down on the board and started paddling hard towards the shore. What he had not done was to pay attention to his position on the Alaia. In an instant, Walter was violently propelled into the water as the nose of the board speared towards the bottom. Then, as the force of the wave tilted the tail of the board into a sudden sharp angle, Walter was unceremoniously driven into the deep. There he quickly encountered another unexpected hazard, the sandy bottom.

Surfacing, with sand filling most of his orifices, he spluttered and spat as much of the gritty filling out of his mouth as he could and then proceeded to clear his nose and ears. That, unfortunately for Walter, meant that his craft had made its own way to the beach and he was now forced to struggle to the shore to retrieve it.

Half swimming, half wading, Walter was eventually able to repossess his board and begin the same trials and tribulations as before, with the subtle difference that his persistence began to show some returns as he gradually started to improve.

After several more wipeouts, Walter eventually managed to precariously belly board a wave all the way to the sand. Excited, he continued to repeat the exercise a few more times, again with varying degrees of success. However, he finally decided that he had done enough for the day as he was exhausted, but he was also jubilant and looking forward to Kanoa's approval at his progress.

Back on the beach, he struggled with the heavy board, his arms aching from the continuous paddling of the morning. As he dragged the Alaia up the beach and laid it down on the sand, he was suddenly startled by a noise. Turning in the direction of the disturbance, Walter was confronted by the looming figure of a warrior whose face was entirely obscured by a gourd helmet. Armed with a club, the warrior lunged at him. Walter barely had time to bring his arms up in defence. But the man appeared to have no intention of hitting him because instead of belting Walter with the club, he wrapped his arms around his body, pinning Walter's arms to his sides and then began dragging him back to the water.

It became quickly apparent that the man intended to drown him. With a rush of adrenaline that gave Walter renewed strength, and determined not to meet such an ignominious end, he used every ounce of his willpower and strength and, struggled fiercely with the warrior. The Hawai'ian must have been caught off guard by Walter's strength as he hesitated for a moment which allowed Walter to fight back.

Another wave of adrenaline rushed through Walter. With almost superhuman strength, he managed to untangle himself from the warrior's vice-like grip and with all his might, he rammed his elbow into the warrior's chest. The man groaned and struggled to catch his breath, and doubled over staggering backwards, he inadvertently gave Walter enough time to sprint up the beach towards the forest and make his escape.

Still struggling for breath, the Hawai'ian was slow to pursue him, but he found his wind soon enough. The warrior sprinted up the beach, swiftly catching up to Walter, who had reached the edge of the forest.

Walter knew he needed a weapon anything to give him an advantage against the heavily muscled man and looking around, he saw a fallen branch on the ground. He scooped it up, and in one smooth, single motion, turned and delivered a stunning blow to the warrior's head. The man's momentum and the blow from the branch felled Walter's attacker, and he collapsed unconscious to the ground. Without waiting to see if the man was dead or alive, Walter sprinted into the forest and back towards the village.

Over the past few days, Kanoa had received word that groups of warriors allied to Koa, had made their way to the eastern side of the island. They had gone to great lengths to stay hidden, suggesting to the Kahuna that they were up to no good. It was the reason why Kanoa was watching Walter when he headed off to the beach that morning. The Kahuna had decided Walter needed protection, a task he now relegated to a couple of his own loyal comrades.

As Walter made his way out of the village, Kanoa quietly turned to the two warriors who stood behind him. "I do not like the Pelekané to be on his own. We all know what can happen to the unaware. See to it that no harm befalls him. Now, go and report back to me when he has safely returned to his kauhale."

Kanoa watched the two warriors as they quickly followed Walter down the path and he wondered if he would need to set guards here in the village as well. The thought of having to do so saddened him, but Koa's ambitions were forcing his hand.

It was nearing the middle of the day when one of the warriors returned to give his report to Kanoa. They had done as he had requested and stayed out of sight, and watched the Pelekané heading out for a surf. Luckily the swell was small, and they did not need to interfere with his fun. But the danger had come from else-where in the form of a warrior from the north of the island.

The speed with which the attack on Walter had unfolded, had taken Kanoa's warriors by surprise. They had watched from their hiding spot in the dense undergrowth. His men described what had happened in great detail and with a certain amount of relish. Kanoa was surprised to hear admiration for the haole in their voices. It appeared that the Pelekané defended himself skilfully and with great determination.

Kanoa was pleased that once Walter had beaten the man

unconscious, he had left the beach. "This is when we were able to take the helmet off the attacker and identify him." The warrior stopped for a moment, "But, Kanoa, the Pelekané has some mana. He is not as helpless as we thought."

I should have known, Kanoa thought. The Pelekané showed that he had courage on many occasions, the last time catching the shark. But this proves that he can fight.

Kanoa pressed the man for more details. Once he had heard all he had to say, Kanoa thanked his comrade and asked him to continue to keep an eye out for any other men from the other side of the island who may be lurking around the village. Pondering on what the best course of action would be, Kanoa headed off to the Royal compound to see the Mo' i and discuss what had happened.

And so it was late that same evening that he met with Koa to try to resolve the unfolding conflict between them. In the half-light of his hale, Kanoa silently watched the surly figure of Koa sitting in front of him. The young man was silent, obviously waiting for his master to make the first move. Kanoa knew that Koa was involved in the attack on Walter and that his apprentice was very aware that what he had done was kapu. Harming the Pelekané was breaking the law and Kanoa had every right to kill Koa for this.

Was Koa hoping that Kanoa's fondness for him would stay his hand? They had been like father and son since he had found Koa after a battle on Moloka'i. Koa had been a little lost infant, crawling along the edge of a battlefield searching for his mother and father. Kanoa had seen the boy and had been unwilling to let the child be killed, and then and there, he had decided that he would bring the child back to Kauai and rear him as his own.

Taking the initiative, Kanoa spoke in a solemn voice. "I'm told that one of your warriors attacked the Pelekané."

Koa's response was to insist that Walter and his kind would be the Islanders' destruction. Kanoa couldn't help but notice that Koa showed no remorse. Deep inside Kanoa was seething with rage at his apprentice's betrayal, but outwardly he kept his calm. "I am not certain of that."

Kanoa could see that he had taken Koa by surprise and so he

continued quietly, still hoping to foster a change in Koa's attitude. "Perhaps your own actions are more dangerous, Koa."

But Koa simply stared sullenly back at his master. What have I done, Kanoa thought. He shows me no loyalty and is only interested in his own ambitions. How could I have been so blind? Kaneoneo was right. My flaw is that I have only seen what I wanted to see.

"Koa, remember this well." Kanoa's tried a gentler tone, more fatherly, as he warned Koa. "The canoe is not swamped by the billows of the ocean, but rather by the billows from within."

Koa gave nothing back. He merely sat there, picking on a frayed corner of the matt he was sitting on. He was not prepared to meet Kanoa even halfway. The Kahuna had desperately hoped that the young warrior would see reason. All he wanted was an acknowledgement that Koa had made some bad decisions and an apology. I would forgive him, Kanoa thought as he looked into the dark, brooding face. But his apprentice quietly sat there, waiting.

Kanoa sighed, his chest aching with the recognition that he had lost his only family. A wave of anger replaced his pain, and he scowled at Koa, flicking his hand dismissively at the warrior, indicating that the audience was ended.

As Koa jumped up and hastily left the hale, Kanoa was forced to acknowledge that he would need to deal with this situation more effectively or risk the peace.

Before meeting with Koa, Kanoa had met with Kamakahelei and Kaneoneo to discuss the precarious situation between the different factions on the island and their possible consequences. Kamakahelei had made it clear that she wanted to avoid an all-out confrontation and hopefully head off a civil war.

They had all agreed that a plan was needed under the circumstances to diffuse the volatile situation. As a result, Kanoa had sent a messenger to Oahu with a cryptic message embedded in a cordial greeting to his friend Kahahana, the high chief of Oahu who would understand and make preparations.

Chapter Forty-One

*O*ver the next few weeks, Walter was careful to stay close to his friends, and although he spent a good part of each day surfing, he did so when there were other people around. He was determined to improve his balance on the Alaia and to become proficient at riding waves despite the swell being mostly small and lacking in power. His main ambition was to get strong and skilled enough to ride the Olo, the board of Master surfers.

Walter had been out for a late afternoon session when he noticed that groups of Islanders, both men and women, were coming out of the forest and crowding around the shoreline.

They were all intently watching the sunset and talking animatedly amongst themselves, and seeing that Omai was with them, he asked him what was making everyone so excited. Omai was just as enthusiastic as everyone else, and he clapped Walter on the back and told him that the swell was changing, and this meant that the next day would be a perfect day for surfing. "You'll see, we will have a great day, my friend."

The next morning Walter woke to the drone of conch shells reverberating through the morning mist and as he and Omai stepped out of their hut and looked out into the square, they could see many of the villagers eagerly heading off towards the beach. Omai was grinning at him, joy etched on his features and Walter realised that along with his friend, he, too, was infected by the excitement emanating from the crowd.

Walter searched for, and quickly spotted Kanoa, carrying his long olo. The Kahuna called out to them. "My prayers have been answered! Come, we are blessed with good surf today!"

Neither of them needed any persuading to join the rest of the village, and they quickly collected their boards and followed the others down to the ocean. When they reached the beach, Walter was surprised to find that it had been decorated with Tikis and stone markers. Many of the villagers were already out in the line-up while on the edge, priests were blessing the ocean and placing offerings on the water.

Reaching the shore break, they joined Kanoa and stopped to take some time to survey the surf, which Walter guessed was mostly for his benefit. In the last few hours, the swell had gradually increased in size, and Walter watched the waves with a growing sense of apprehension.

This swell was significantly bigger than what he had been practising in, and he was unsure about his ability to manage it. Seeming to sense his disquiet, Kanoa put a reassuring hand on his shoulder. "We have a saying here, when you want to do something, don't wait, get to it as soon as possible."

Walter was about to answer the Kahuna when Koa, Kumahana and another warrior walked over to them. Koa regarded Walter with a look of disgust, and when he spoke, he did so loudly enough for many islanders close by to hear him. "Haole, your pale carcass is not welcome here!"

The insult to Kanoa was unmistakable, but before the older man could react and deal with it, Omai snarled in Koa's face. "So, what do you intend on doing about it!?"

Apparently infuriated by the Tahitian's boldness, Kumahana struck out at Omai. The blow however never reached its intended target, as with lightning-fast reflexes, Kanoa intercepted the strike, firmly gripping the young man's arm.

Kumahana's face contorted with pain as Kanoa's hold tightened around his forearm. Ignoring the Queen's son, the Kahuna looked menacingly into Koa's eyes. "To hear, is life, to turn a deaf ear is death."

Walter understood the precarious nature of the situation. As the six men faced off, the tension etched into their faces, he mentally prepared himself for that energy to explode into violence. Then Koa snorted in disgust and signalled his men to back off, suddenly turning sharply and angrily stomping off, his comrades following him closely, leaving Kanoa, Omai and Walter looking at each other in shocked silence. Then, with a shake of his head, Omai turned back to the surf and following his lead, Walter tore his eyes from Koa's retreating back to find Kanoa and Omai grinning like schoolboys, and slapping each other on the back, they launched themselves into the surf with Walter right behind them.

As the first wall of white water pounded him, Walter suddenly realised that he might have been better off in a fight, rather than trying to deal with this much bigger swell. He struggled with his board, which unexpectedly seemed to now have a life of its own. Like an unbroken horse, it bucked his every attempt to control it. He tried to push it through the white water but was dragged continuously back to the beach, and gradually he felt his strength start to drain out of him.

Walter ruefully watched as Kanoa and Omai, on the other hand, made it effortlessly out to the line-up. Standing in the shallow water, frustrated by his failure to get beyond the break, he watched Kanoa take off and trim his board along the clean face of the wave aiming his ride so that he arrived at Walter's side. As the Kahuna gracefully stepped off his Olo, he grinned at Walter.

"You should have paid more attention when I explained the riptides to you. Come, follow me! I will take you through the break. "

Chastened, Walter accepted the jibe and smiled ruefully at the Kahuna. This time he launched himself back into the water following in the wake of Kanoa who paddled forcefully out into the channel. Without a great deal of trouble, the two quickly reached the line-up, and Omai threw a mocking salute in Walter's direction. "So, I see you've finally decided to join us."

Walter was not going to take the bait. "You can tease me all you like." He paused for a second, his face contorting into a worried frown. "But the real challenge now that I'm out here is to catch one of these monsters."

Kanoa looked at Walter with a thoughtful expression and then advised him to start with the smaller waves and then gradually, as he felt more confident, try to catch the bigger ones. Walter watched as both the other men took off, each catching a wave and disappearing towards the beach. Then sizing up one of the approaching waves, he told himself to be brave. Yes! This one is his!

This is it, Walter, you can do this! He muttered to himself under his breath as he lay flat on the board and began to paddle. Looking behind him just as the wave pitched up Walter paddled harder, however this caused a subtle shift in the position of his body and his weight, now slightly out of centre, meant that he did not have quite the control over the board he should have had. Undeterred, Walter leapt to his feet amidst the whistling and encouragement shouted to him by the other surfers. But unable to trim the board effectively, he shot down the face of the wave in a straight line. In seconds the white water completely engulfed him.

Below the surface, Walter was a tumbled about like a piece of driftwood. He struggled to the surface gasping for air and watched his board making its own way back to the shore. Dismayed, he realised he would have to swim through the frothing and seething water back to the beach to retrieve it. But Walter hesitated just a bit too long, and the next wave broke on top of him, burying him underneath tons of churning sea. This time, as Walter surfaced, he immediately struck out, and with stronger strokes, managed to swim towards the shore and his abandoned Alaia.

All his practice in the water was now starting to pay off, as he covered the distance to the beach using the waves to help propel him towards his board. He immediately made his way back out to sea and finally reached the rest of the surfers sitting casually in the

ocean waiting for the next set. Despite Walter's wipeout, they all
cheered and praised his courage and determination.

"It's a powerful feeling, isn't it?" The Kahuna smiled. "Now, next
time, Pelekané, do not look behind you. Keep your mind on where
you are going and not where you have been."

Walter smiled sheepishly at the Kahuna and decided that it was
worthwhile to take some time and recoup his energy and sit the next
few sets out. He used the time to watch the Hawai'ians take off on
variously sized waves, observing carefully the technique they used
for positioning themselves to get the best ride.

After a while, Walter turned his attention back to scanning the
horizon where he saw a massive wave build-up. Fear rose in the pit
of his guts. Walter was about to paddle further out to sea where he
knew he would be safe from the crashing wave, but Kanoa's voice
stopped him. The Kahuna had returned from his last ride and was
sitting close by and had obviously guessed Walter's intention.

"Walter, listen to me." Walter nodded. "Just being out here today
is a credit to you. Therefore this one is just for you, as a reward, but
you must harness the fear in you."

Kanoa turned and shouted to the others. "Let the haole surf
alone on this wave. Do not challenge him!"

The Islander's cheered loudly, urging Walter into the wave. He
turned and watched as the swell rise towards him. The surging wave
sent his heart racing. For a second, Walter was sure that all he
wanted was to escape this harbinger of impending doom.

"Oh, my God!" Walter cried out.

But Kanoa's words had reenforced Walter's determination. After
all, wasn't this what he had set out to do? Walter knew that he
wanted to master this skill. Taking a deep breath, he paddled into
the wave. This time, Walter focussed on everything he had been
taught. He effortlessly leapt to his feet and positioned himself. With
this weight in his knees, Walter could feel the board and the power
of the water beneath him.

Sliding the board across the wave, Walter sped along its face
with the lip crashing behind him. It was ecstasy! The rush permeated right through his body, replacing the fear he had felt only

moments earlier. He rushed towards the beach, and when he was close enough, Walter jumped off the board. The momentum carried him a few steps along the beach only to trip over and fall into the sand. But nothing could stop the elation he felt.

His chest heaving, Walter could hear the cheers of the crowd. He looked around to see the smiles of approval on the faces of the onlookers. As Walter got to his feet, he heard Kanoa calling him. "Pelekané," "Today you have excelled yourself! You really are a true spirit in the making, and you have become a man of the sea! This is truly something to celebrate."

Still trying to catch his breath, Walter took his time to answer. "To do what I have just done, my friend is celebration enough."

By now, Omai had joined them, and he looked at Kanoa with a sly grin. "Not bad for one who swims like a rock, eh?" They all laughed at Omai's joke then headed off to enjoy the rest of the morning in the waves.

All of the following day Walter was filled with enthusiasm, the exhilaration of his success riding waves sweeping over him every time he let his mind drift. He was happily in the midst of one of these reveries when Kanoa's arrival at the hale, dressed in a magnificent red and yellow feather cloak interrupted him. Looking majestic and imposing, the Kahuna was wearing a helmet made of the same materials, and as Walter and Omai greeted him, it occurred to Walter that Kanoa looked a little like an ancient Greek general.

Kanoa got straight to the point of his visit, asking them both to accompany him as he had organised something essential for them to see. So having grabbed some fruit and a gourd of water they had both set off following Kanoa out of the village.

The Kahuna led them up the coast in a direction Walter had not travelled before, and it was several hours later that they finally reached the top of a hill from which they could see, stretching out below them, a vast natural amphitheatre. Awed by the magnificent view, Walter looked out into the bay and saw a small fleet of ten canoes, each carrying about ten men.

Kanoa led them to a spot that enabled them to see the whole area and Walter realised that there were men on the beach as well.

"Now pay attention! You will see some of our best warriors fight. They are truly worthy of the people of Kauai." Having said that Kanoa signalled the men below.

Immediately the sound of numerous conch shells began to drone through the air, and the fleet of canoes headed swiftly towards the beach, where a large group of warriors were assembled. War chants rose into the air as the fleet neared the shore. As the canoes hit the sand, the warriors charged the land-based group and a mock hand to hand battle ensued. Suddenly, on a signal from a conch, the fighting stopped.

A tremendous roar rose up towards Kanoa, Walter and Omai, and they could clearly hear them call out:

"Great Kauai, Isle of warriors and land of men ever on the defence."

The demonstration over, Kanoa guided both Omai and Walter down the valley to where the Kahuna was greeted warmly by the men. Walter had been greatly impressed by the expertise and skill of the warriors, and when he told Kanoa of his admiration for these men, Kanoa said to him that they had used a particular style of fighting called Lua.

"They are trained in skills reserved only for the chiefs and some of the priests. True masters are able to kill an enemy with one blow to the head."

Then Kanoa's voice became more emphatic. "You are to speak to no one of what you have seen!" Walter was puzzled but agreed, wondering why Kanoa had brought him here.

He wasn't kept in the dark for long as Kanoa slapped him on the back. "Good, then we can include you in the training."

Surprised, Walter was pushed into a group of warriors, most of whom welcomed him, however, he could sense that there were a few who were not enthusiastic about having him join in their training. But no one said anything directly, all of them apparently too highly disciplined to challenge anything the Kahuna dictated.

Kanoa proceeded to organise the warriors to demonstrate some of the techniques of this particular style of fighting, and he showed Walter and Omai some of the punches and blocks. They, along with the warriors, continued to train for the rest of the day with only short breaks, and it was late afternoon before Kanoa called an end to the session.

As he guided them back to the village Kanoa confided that Walter and Omai would continue their training under his tutelage, so that if ever the day came that they required these skills, they would be well prepared. Walter had already guessed that the Kahuna was trying to ensure that both he and Omai had the skills to defend themselves, and he had no doubt who he needed to be wary of. Koa!

Chapter Forty-Two

*W*alter's sense of elation stayed with him for days and left him feeling ecstatic. He had, as he had promised himself, ridden with the masters of the ocean swells and held his own. Besides, the training in Lua had given Walter an increasing feeling of physical competence, and he liked the sense that both his body and mind were working well together. His health could only benefit from this conditioning after the ravages caused by his illness.

Word of Walter's surfing had spread quickly across the island, and when Kamakahelei heard of it, she and her husband, Kaneoneo, called for a massive feast to celebrate the Pelekané's achievement. Poems and stories were already being composed to commemorate his success.

On the evening of the feast, the crowd, fuelled by the potent 'awa, was in high spirits and the poems and oratory delighted everyone. One of the Kahuna had composed a chant in Walter's honour and, during the recital, Walter bowed politely to the composer. He then watched the hula that also told the story of this stranger from a faraway land who, stranded in Kauai, had learnt the ways of the kanaka maoli, the people.

When the hula finished, Kanoa, holding a massive fan in his

hand, stepped theatrically into the square, a bright grin spread across his face. "Tonight, we play Kilu."

The crowd cheered loudly, obviously anticipating more fun, and Walter quickly leant over to Omai. "Omai, what is kilu?"

The Tahitian smiled. "Ah, this is a game that you will enjoy greatly, my friend. Just wait and see."

"No, Omai," Walter was emphatic. "No surprises tonight."

"All right, all right! Kilu is a game of love in which a player on one side tosses a coconut shell at an object placed in front of another player on the other side. A hit wins a honi, a kiss." He grinned. "It's better than chess."

Walter breathed a sigh of relief. Was that what all the fuss was about? But it dawned on him that merely kissing, at least the Hawai'ian version of it, would not elicit such excitement in this group. There must be more to this, he thought.

As Kanoa swaggered around the square, Walter realised that the Kahuna was looking to choose a player. "Where is the bird with the curved beak that will suckle the Lehua flower?"

Fanning himself theatrically, Kanoa continued to walk amongst the seated men. He stopped in front of a very young warrior whom Walter had seen earlier in the surf, and to the cheers from the people, Kanoa tapped him on the crown of his head with the fan.

"Here is the bird!"

The young man grinned sheepishly and got up to sit on the matt. As Kanoa walked amongst the group of girls, he cocked his head and smiled. "And where is the beautiful Lehua flower?"

He turned and tapped one of the surprised girls on her forehead.

"Here she is."

The girl's face broke into a broad smile. She got up and placed her hands seductively on her hips. She then rotated them most suggestively, and Walter instantly understood what the real purpose of the game was.

To the cheers of the crowd, the girl took her place on the mats opposite to that of the young man. The two players now sat there with a distance of about ten feet between them and each had a short wooden pillar placed in front of them.

Kanoa held the kilu. It was half of a coconut shell, which he handed to the young man as the playing piece.

The crowd fell silent as the young warrior took careful aim and tossed the kilu at the wooden obelisk in front of the girl. That hushed silence was suddenly pierced with a disappointed moan as the kilu missed the wood.

Omai lent across to Walter. "That is unfortunate, my friend because now they will have to leave the game." And true enough the crestfallen pair left their places on the mats making way for the next two players.

Walter, who in his excitement, had continued to indulge in the 'awa, had mellowed to the point where his speech was a little slurred. He managed a slightly silly grin, but when he slowly looked up, he saw Lani amongst the group of girls, looking straight at him, smiling.

A burst of adrenaline sobered him up, and he quickly looked around to see if anyone was watching him. Reassured that he was unnoticed, Walter looked back. He smiled and waved at Lani. At that moment, Kanoa blocked his view, and the Kahuna tapped Walter on the head with the fan.

"A new bird has come to the islands never seen before. Let him seek the Lehua flower."

A roar erupted from the gathering, punctuated by rounds of clapping. It took Walter a few seconds to realise that he had been picked to play the game. He later admitted to Omai that he had overindulged in the awa, which that night had been much stronger than Walter was used to, hence his thinking was a little slower than usual.

Without another moment's hesitation, Kanoa walked directly over to Lani and tapped her head. She responded by giggling with delight. She, too, got to her feet and gyrated her hips in the same manner as the previous girl, convincing Walter that these girls had played the game on many other occasions.

"Here she is! The noblest of the flowers of Kauai."

Rising excitedly to his feet, Walter could feel the tension and heat in his loins. It spread through his body like fire. He had not felt such intensity since losing his virginity to Emma, and then during the ensuing weeks of passion that had eventually led to her dismissal. Yet even that painful memory was unable to quench the ardour he felt at that very moment.

Walter, reminding himself of where he was, strolled over to the matt, and after seating himself, he took the offered kilu from Kanoa. He bowed his head slightly to the Kahuna, and then he looked across to where Lani sat behind the wooden pillar, her smile radiating the most open invitation to him.

Gathering his wits, he hoped to do better than the previous contender. Walter slowly took aim and then, at what he prayed fervently was the right moment, released the shell towards the wooden pillar. In what seemed an eternity, the piece sailed through the air, then, with a sudden audible click, it connected with the wooden obelisk in front of Lani.

The crowd cheered and quickly went silent as she took aim at Walter's pillar of wood with her kilu. He held his breath and with every fibre in his body willed the shell towards him. A loud clack confirmed that his wish had come true.

Another cheer erupted as Walter and Lani got to their feet and walked towards each other. As she stepped up to him, Walter felt his heartbeat racing, not unlike when he dropped into the massive wave. Lani's scent suddenly brought him back into the moment. She stepped up to him, offered her face and waited for him to reciprocate.

Walter took Lani by her shoulders and pressed his forehead to hers, their noses barely touching. Walter closed his eyes, but he could hear her breath drawing in as if to take all of him into her being. Following Lani's example, the sweet smell of her permeated Walter's nose, elevating his desire to another level. Opening their eyes, Walter and Lani lingered. Both were aware that there was now a new bond between them.

Their moment of bliss was not to last long, as off to the side, the dark, brooding figure of Koa, now made itself known. Surrounded by many warriors, Koa openly voiced his disapproval at Walter and Lani having been picked to play the game. Then having disturbed the enjoyment of the game, Koa and his comrades pushed their way out of the gathering.

Kanoa quickly ushered Walter back to Omai's side. "Do not worry. Just go back to your place. All will be well, I assure you."

Lani squeezed Walter's hand and returned to where she and the group of girls were sitting. But Walter, disappointed by the way their game had been interrupted, found it hard to settle down and enjoy the festivities. As the game continued, he found solace in the awa while his need to be alone overrode his common sense. The moment Omai's attention was diverted elsewhere, he slipped out of the crowd and headed along the forest path.

Lost in thought, Walter had made his way to the waterfall where the noise of the cascading water made a reassuring sound that settled his nerves and helped him relax. Sitting against a tree trunk, Walter made himself comfortable. As the effects of the copious amounts of 'awa he had consumed took its toll, he tried to ponder the day's events.

Walter must have fallen asleep because the next thing he knew, he was being woken by a tickling sensation on the soles of his feet, and then along the length of his body. He sat bolt upright only to find Lani, holding a palm leaf that she ran mischievously along his side. She sat down beside him, letting go of the leaf, and then play-fully dropped her head into his lap, her face turned upward, looking at him expectantly. "Shall we finish what we began, Pelekané?"

"I can no longer find a single reason not to."

Lani laughed, and they kissed passionately. As they embraced, Walter ran his hand down the length of her, his searching hand about to explore the inside of her thigh when he heard a sudden rustle of leaves in the undergrowth. Startled, Lani sat up while Walter, placing his finger on her mouth, scanned the darkness surrounding them. There was another rustle, and in the dark, he saw what he thought was a shadowy figure disappearing into the bush.

"It's nothing." Walter tried to reassure both himself and Lani.

Wanting to believe that the noise must have been some sort of animal they settled back, making themselves comfortable on the moss beneath the trees. They had only relaxed for a few moments when the night was shattered by angry shouts from hostile warriors breaking through the thicket surrounding the pool.

In the dark, hands reached out, trying to grab hold of the two lovers, attempting to tear them apart. In an instant, Walter was up and trying to fight the intruders off although he sensed that this would be futile given the number of his opponents. But before he could finish that gloomy assessment of their situation, another group of warriors broke into the clearing, forcefully confronting their attackers.

In the chaos, Walter swept Lani up and together they started to run towards the darkness of the thick forest when a familiar voice boomed over the sound of the waterfall. "Pelekané, this way, quick!"

Recognising the voice of Kanoa, the two lovers turned and rushed towards him. Reaching the Kahuna, Walter could make out Omai amongst several other warriors and nodding to each other, they took off through the forest while Kanoa's warriors protected the rear.

Pacing his steps with Lani's, the two were running side by side, when Walter heard the hiss of spears cutting through the air. One of them barely missed him, burying itself menacingly in a tree just in front of him.

As they broke through the bushes onto the beach, Walter felt Omai push him towards a large catamaran packed with supplies and ready to go to sea. Several other canoes were beached close by in a similar state of readiness.

As the group rushed onto the beach, the warriors were beginning to push the vessels into the water. Walter stopped dead beside the canoe Omai had steered him to while Lani, without any hesitation clambered onto its deck.

"I'll be damned if I am going to run away." Walter turned to face Kanoa. "Let me fight Koa, one on one!"

With one swift movement, Kanoa simply picked a very surprised

Walter up and threw him onto the deck of the canoe. "I do not have
time for this, Pelekané! Just do what I tell you."

Walter shook his head, violently. "What about Lani. She can't
just leave!"

From the bow of the canoe, Lani called back. "I've made my
decision. I am going where ever you go!" Lani's words struck Walter
like lightning, his mind reeling with thoughts. She is abandoning
everything for me, he thought.

Love rushed through him, him, but he couldn't help to exclaim,
"But this is insane!"

"I won't change my mind." Lani's reply came just as Kanoa
handed a paddle to Walter. "Here, put to use what I have taught you
and dip it into the water!"

With that, the men in the canoes began to paddle as hard as
they could towards the open sea. Beyond the reef, they set the sails,
and the canoe surged forward. Looking back, Walter saw Koa, and
a number of his men had crashed through the bushes to the beach
and Koa screaming his frustration into the air. Impulsively the
enraged warrior threw a spear in the direction of the last canoe, but
it fell uselessly into the sea, far short of its mark. Walter knew that
for the time being they had gotten away, but there was no doubt in
his mind that Koa would follow.

Chapter Forty-Three

K anoa sat quietly in the aft of the canoe. His attention focused on steering the vessel towards the distant horizon where the faintest whisper of light heralded the rising sun. Occasionally he looked over to Walter and Omai, who were crouched beside him. Lani had taken her place at the bow of the hull and was resting, wrapped in a plain kapa shawl to ward off the chill from the ocean breeze.

Over the last few weeks and after many meetings with Kaneoneo and Kamakahelei, Kanoa had come to the conclusion that at some point, it was best if Walter left Kauai. None of them wanted to see the Pelekané harmed, and they knew that ultimately it was merely a matter of time before Walter's demise was achieved in some way or another.

They also knew that Koa was not going to stop challenging the established order under Kamakahelei. The young warrior continued to gather supporters and steadily build an army loyal to him. When questioned by the older chiefs, Koa would always claim that his men were training to defend the Island, because he believed that they needed to be vigilant of outsiders like the Pelekané, and naturally of Kalaniopu'u, the great chief from the Big Island.

Kahuna's thoughts were interrupted by Walter, who, of course, was not privy to any of the political undercurrents that were swirling around him. "Can you please tell me now why we are leaving the island?"

Deciding it was time to be open with the Pelekané, Kanoa answered.

"Koa has been looking for any excuse to challenge the Ali'i and the council. He is ambitious, and he has many supporters who also feel that we are better off without you, or your kind. He is using this in an attempt to split the council. As you know the Mo'i is not convinced that we should reject contact with your people, but she has made the decision that war on Kauai is to be avoided if at all possible. Getting you off the Island will hopefully be the start to calming things down between Koa and the council."

Kanoa leant across to adjust the steering oar. He was surprised to hear Omai chide Walter. "You also did not do what I asked, which was to find someone else to pay attention to."

Kanoa interrupted the Tahitian. "I doubt that it would have made any difference. Koa has set his mind on killing the Pelekané. He just needed the right excuse."

Hearing the men discussing their situation, Lani clambered back to the stern of the boat and snuggled into Walter, reinforcing in Kanoa's mind that he had been right about the bond between the two of them.

"That was not entirely his fault, was it?" Lani grinned at Omai and looked at Kanoa. "And you, Kahuna, how was it that you chose us to play kilu?"

"Well, some might think that the 'awa did cloud my judgment slightly. However, after the most recent challenges from Koa to the council, the Mo' i and I decided it was time to force Koa out into the open. After all, it would have come to this sooner or later, and Koa will not be deterred from using you as an excuse to start a war."

Walter nudged Omai. "I know I didn't listen to you, my friend, but if you must know I'm not sorry."

Kanoa drew himself up, settling into a more comfortable position on the stern of the canoe and wrapped his arm around the oar.

As they sat in silence for a moment, then Walter asked him where they were going.

Nodding in the direction of the horizon, Kanoa told them that he was taking them to Oahu and that he hoped that the matter of Koa's ambitions and his anger about Lani and Walter would be resolved by the Ali'i Nui while they were away. He was not surprised that Omai recognised their destination immediately, and excitedly told Walter that this was the island where waves are like mountains and heroes were made.

Kanoa smiled at Omai's poetic musings but reminded them that they would perhaps need more training for these mountains. Then, remembering that he had something for Walter, he reached down int the wooden chest near his feet and retrieved a tightly wrapped package. "Here, Pelekané, I brought this for you."

Kanoa watched as Walter carefully unwrapped the package to reveal his journal and his pencil case. Obviously touched by Kanoa's thoughtfulness, Walter looked up at him. "Kanoa! Mahalo, my friend! I am indeed grateful."

As the catamaran covered the distance, an air of optimism settled over those on board. Silently they sailed on towards the east, the only sound the creaking of the canoe and the lapping of the bow waves as it cut through the water. Every now and then Kanoa, quietly, looked aft to where several sails on the horizon were just visible, saying nothing to the others about his suspicion that they were being followed.

Many hours later Kanoa saw the shores of Oahu rise faintly in the distance. On the horizon, several canoes were heading towards them. It was to be expected that the warriors of Oahu would want to determine who they were.

Once they were assured that they were not a war party, they joined them, and together all of the canoe's sailed down the coast of the island. From time to time, conch shells would drone out across the water, signalling runners on the island to herald the arrival of visitors.

Kanoa watched the Pelekané as the coastline slid by them, and was amused when Walter observed that the most southern mountain that they could see looked like the face of a tuna. "You are almost right, Walter, but it's not the face but the brow of the tuna. We call it Laeahi."

As they arrived at their destination and beached the canoes, they were welcomed by a procession of Ali'i, Kahuna and warriors. As a small group of commoners took charge of the vessels and their contents, while Kanoa and the others were taken inland to the council of chiefs.

In the vast ha'lau a large solid looking man who was the ruling chief of Oahu and Molokai, Kahahana, sat surrounded by his council and guards. Making sure that Walter and Omai were properly placed for protocol, Kanoa paid his respects and greeted the Ali'i Nui in the traditional manner, before he petitioned the high chief for permission for himself, Lani, Omai from Kahiki and Walter from Pelekané, to stay on Oahu

Hearing Kanoa's request, a small group of chiefs in the council became agitated and before he could continue Kahahana interrupted him. "Kanoa, you know well that you are famed across the islands, and while I am the Ali'i Nui, you are always welcome here on Oahu. As for the strangers, I have heard of this Pelekané. Some say that he brings sickness and war."

Before Kanoa could reassure Kahahana, there was a commotion at the entrance of the ha'lau and Koa and his warriors, surrounded by Kahahana's guard, burst into the council. Without the traditional courtesies, Koa called out amidst the agitated voices of the chiefs.

"Hear me, Ali'i Nui, hear me, wise ones of Oahu. It is true. This haole has come to take our lands, our food, and our women. To make matters worse, he killed my cousin." Koa paused. "He is here because his people said he was too sick to travel. Look at him. Does he look sick to you? The haole cannot be trusted, and they must be thrown back into the ocean where they came from!"

Ka'opulupulu, Kahahana's Kahuna nui, obviously angered by Koa's lack of manners and etiquette immediately confronted him.

"And who are you to address the council in this way and to challenge the great Ali'i Nui of Oahu and Moloka'i?"

Kanoa chose to cut Koa off and not allow him to answer immediately. The timing here was critical. "Ali'i nui, Koa does not speak
the truth. This one," pointing at Walter, "defended us from the haole
who killed Koa's cousin."

Koa shook his head. "It does not matter which of the haole
killed my cousin. They will kill us all if we do not stop them."

Before Kanoa could reply, Kahahana pounded his large staff on
the ground frowning as he glared at those who had disrupted the
meeting. The council immediately quietened down, and all eyes
focused on the chief.

"The people of Oahu and Moloka'i and I have no quarrel with
the Pelekané.

It is my decision to allow him to stay. He is allowed to move
freely, without danger to himself or those with him." Kahahana
then looked directly at Koa and his warriors. "Anyone who harms
him shall be put to death. If you agree to this, you too may stay."

Kanoa was greatly relieved that they had all been put under a
kapu, and looking at the others saw that his feelings were shared,
but he saw that Koa was enraged, and the young warrior lashed out
angrily. "See how even the great Kahahana is blinded by the haole.
If we continue this way, we will become weak and end up slaves to
the white man. Think about my words and you will see the truth in
them."

Then, accompanied by his entourage, Koa stormed out of the
great hall. As he left, Kahahana signalled for Kanoa to move closer
to his side.

"I have had many messengers from Kauai in the last few weeks,
and so I knew about the tensions amongst some of your warriors.
Your Mo'i does not want this situation to escalate, and in this, we are
in agreement. Therefore the Ali'i Nui have given instructions that all
of you, including Koa, will be treated with aloha in the hope that
this situation will resolve without bloodshed.

Kanoa thanked Kahahana for his welcome and after the appropriate assurances that he and his companions would abide by the
decisions of the Ali'i Nui, they were led to a kauhale, that had been
allocated to them. As they entered the comfortable and well-main-

tained huts, they found that their possessions had already been transferred from the canoes, and Kanoa finally allowed himself to relax his guard. But only temporarily.

⚜⚜⚜⚜⚜

That night a huge crowd filled Kahahana's kauhale, a great compound surrounding a huge square able to house many people and guests. The smell of kukui nut oil and the light from the numerous torches permeated the dark of the night, illuminating the gathering.

On one end of the village square, Kahahana and his retainers were seated on a raised platform covered with large mats. Two guards stood beside the Ali'i Nui, while slightly off to the side Kanoa, Walter, Omai and their warriors, had a similar seating arrangement.

As customary, the Kahuna recited the opening prayers to begin the pa'ina, and after a welcome speech, there were many hula dances, displays from the warriors, and stories told while food and drink were consumed at a steady pace.

The feast highlighted the fact that Kanoa was highly renowned across the islands. Poems reciting his achievements and prowess as a canoe-builder, navigator, surfer and warrior, kept Walter fascinated. At one stage, he leant across to the Kahuna who had maintained a humble posture throughout the recitals.

"I had no idea that you were such a legend, Kanoa."

Kanoa shook his head. "You must not believe everything you hear, Pelekané. The people like a good story, and so the tale gets grander the more it is told."

Walter smiled but did not contradict his friend and teacher. He had learnt quickly that the Hawai'ians had an oral tradition, and that they took great pride in the accuracy of their accounts. As he sat back and searched the crowd for a glimpse of Lani, his attention was caught by Kahahana leaning towards him, his face alight with curiosity. "Pelekané, tell me about your life across the seas, and why you have chosen to come here to stay."

Being careful to address the Ali'i Nui formally, Walter answered that an unfortunate incident had forced him to leave his homeland and that he now felt significant shame at his irresponsible actions. He then went on to explain why he wanted to stay here in the islands and so he spoke of his travels and his friendship with Omai, and then what he had learnt in Tahiti.

"I saw men riding the swells of the ocean, something I had never seen before and had never imagined was possible. Since then, I have discovered a love for the sea, and a respect for life I did not have before." He stopped and looked across the hall where he had just spotted Lani sitting with the women. "And I think I have also found the love of my life."

Kahahana simply smiled while Walter sat quietly for an instant. He reached for his journals and opened it. Trying to keep it safe he had refused to leave it behind in the hale and had kept it with him. "But let me show you where I come from."

After waiting for an acknowledgment that he could move to be closer to the high chief, Walter got up to approach Kahahana. He carried his journal in a way that showed that it concealed no threat. Despite this, the guards kept a close eye on him, their spears dropped so that the points were only inches from him.

Impatiently, Kahahana waved them aside, and Walter moved closer and sat beside the chief. He opened his journal, the drawings spilling from it over his knees. He quickly sorted through his sketches, finding those that he had done of his home and family and showed them to Kahahana. The chief looked at them closely, commenting that the images of a land and people so different from his own were fascinating. Then looking back up at Walter, he nodded thoughtfully.

"You interest me Pelekané. These images that you make are very skilfully done."

Walter, gratified by the compliment, thanked him. "Mahalo, Ali'i Nui. I try my best."

Kahahana smiled. "You are as humble as Kanoa, Pelekané, a rare gift amongst some of us."

Walter suddenly had an idea. He reached for a blank piece of paper and a pencil and quickly sketched Kahahana. Within a few minutes, he completed a sketch of the chief. He held it up, and Kahahana took it from Walter's hand, excitedly holding it up so all the others could see it. Those close enough to catch a glimpse murmured their approval, and descriptions of the drawing began to ripple through the gathering.

"A gift to you, Ali'i Nui," Walter said, hoping that this small act of diplomacy would help to smooth the way for all of them in this new environment. As the chief looked at his own image, Walter pulled out a sketch of waves breaking on the beach near their village on Kauai. The chief looked at it carefully. Recognising the land-marks, he exclaimed, "Aué, I have been there!"

Walter nodded. "I have been told that the waves here in Oahu are worthy of legends."

The chief grinned, his eyes alight with enthusiasm. "They are, Pelekané." He paused and looked at Kanoa who nodded. "I have heard that you have learnt to surf while you have been on Kauai."

When Walter acknowledged that he had done his best to learn, but that he was still a novice, Kahahana smiled broadly and winked at him. "That is a good thing because tomorrow we shall all ride the waves together at a place called Ke-Kai-o-Malama!"

Walter had a sense that this offer was not as spontaneous as it may have appeared to the casual on-looker. He wondered if Kanoa had a hand in this, but he said nothing other than to thank the chief. "You do me a great honour, Ali'i Nui."

Walter returned to sit with Kanoa and Omai who were clearly enjoying themselves,. He searched the crowd for Lani and seeing her across the square, he managed to catch her eye. As was custom-ary, she was staying in the women's hut and was now seated with the other high ranking women.

As the evening was coming to an end, the women looked like they were preparing to leave the pa'ina, but Lani managed to dash across to Walter's side for a brief moment and reassured him that she was well cared for, and looking forward to having fun surfing in the morning.

"I will not see you tonight, then?" Walter knew he sounded a little forlorn, but Lani just smiled and gently stroked his cheek. "That sort of fun will have to wait, my love." And then she was gone, joining the other women and disappearing into the dark of the night.

Walter and his comrades also retired to their quarters, but the excitement of landing on Oahu, and having entirely no idea what to expect from the next day, left Walter feeling restless. He found it difficult to get to sleep, and then, when he eventually drifted off, his dreams of waves and the ocean were so vivid that he woke to the sound of the conch shells signalling the morning, feeling quite weary.

Dragging himself up, he found that Omai and Kanoa were already busily eating a breakfast of fish and taro. When they saw him emerging from the sleeping hut, they offered him a consider-able portion nestled in the middle of a banana leaf. Looking at it, Walter shook his head. "No, thank you, I'm not sure that gorging myself on mountains of food is going to help my nerves this morning."

"Fine. I'll have it." Omai said as he quickly took the leaf and began to eagerly devour its contents. Kanoa just laughed. "You'll make yourself sick, you crazy Tahitian." Then turning to Walter, he told him he needed to have something to eat even if it was just a small piece of fish. Knowing his friend was right, Walter accepted a morsel of fish and some coconut juice, and wandered over to look up at the cloudless sky.

Breakfast finished, Walter took a calabash and poured some water over his head and pronounced himself as ready as he would ever be. The three of them set off for the beach, with their guard leading the way and when they arrived, it was to join a considerable crowd already there. The area was decorated with banners, tikis and standards signifying the commencement of a royal occasion and they were told that the beach had a kapu placed on it, so the crowd consisted only of the nobility of Honolulu.

Hauled up on the sand were several large, royal canoes with many olos laid across their beams. Kahahana, it turned out, was a keen and accomplished surfer who, now surrounded by his guards and retainers, looked ready and eager to get out in the water.

While Kanoa, Omai and Walter were standing beside the group of nobles, Lani and some of the other women were led further up the beach to where they got into another canoe and paddled out to sea. Kanoa, obviously infected by Kahahana's enthusiasm, slapped Walter on the back. "Today, you will see something new, my friend. It is called lele wa'a."

Walter, feeling anxious about the day, found himself answering somewhat petulantly. "So, I have to contend with another challenge?"

"All of life is a challenge... to which we either rise or fall. "Kanoa's piercing gaze locked onto Walter, and then after a moment, his face softened. "Be happy, we have good weather, nice swell and good health. What more can you ask for?"

Feeling embarrassed by his childishness, Walter agreed." You are right, Kahu! There is no need for anything else."

He was pleased to see Kanoa smiling at him warmly, gratified that the Kahuna was so forgiving when suddenly their attention was caught by Kahahana walking towards them. In step with him was a tall, good-looking, young man who moved with the natural grace of an accomplished athlete. His red and yellow feather cloak was casually thrown across his shoulders and tied on the front, contrasting his dark, shiny skin, while on his head he wore a helmet also made of the same red and yellow feathers.

"Pelekané, I want you to meet a young friend of mine. He is a great warrior and an even better wave rider. Today, he has come to Oahu to test his skills in our waters."

Walter bowed while still trying to scrutinise the young warrior. The man had an engaging smile and piercing black eyes that suggested a keen intellect and humour. "Aloha. My name is Walter Beaumont, but everyone here calls me Pelekané, after the place I come from."

The young warrior's pearly smile gleamed at Walter. "Yes, I have heard of you. I am Kamehameha from the Island of Hawai'i. Later

I would like to hear more about this place you come from, but for now, let's enjoy the waves."

The young warrior looked around for a moment as if trying to find someone in the crowd, and then bidding them farewell he headed off towards one of the canoes. Very quickly after that they were all led to their places in a canoe and taken out to sea with the rest of the fleet, and as they neared the edge of the reef, Walter could see a vast crowd had assembled in canoes and on surfboards.

Looking around, Walter saw something that he had not seen on Kauai. Several men appeared to be standing on the water while propelling themselves forward with a long paddle. On closer inspection, he could see that the surfers were standing on longboards, skilfully balancing themselves in what he thought would be a precarious platform.

Kahahana's canoe had reached the break, just at the right time. A new set of waves was building upon the horizon and the paddlers skilfully swung the canoe around and began to paddle powerfully towards the shore. As the canoe matched its speed to the wave, Kahahana, deftly positioned himself between the main hull and the outrigger. He then lifted a huge board into position and held it parallel to the water.

Waiting for the right moment, Kahahana leapt onto the wave with deceptive agility for a man his size and age. Landing on his feet on top of the board, Kahahana expertly trimmed the Olo and raced across the face of the big swell.

Walter, awed by this novel approach to getting onto a wave, snapped to attention when he heard Kanoa's voice. "Pelekané! It's your turn!"

Unlike Kahahana, Walter chose to push his board into the water beside the canoe. As he jumped onto it, he was almost winded by the impact of the Olo on his chest. He had no time, however, to worry too much about his welfare or the fact that this was the first time he was surfing a board that size. A wave loomed up behind him already starting to curl and ready to break, the white water rushing towards him, so he took advantage of that section of the wave to launch into the swell. Walter managed to get to his feet in a fluid

motion, carefully trimming the board to head across the face of the
wave towards the shore.

In the background, he thought he could hear shouts of encouragement and cheers from the trailing canoes. About to hit the
beach, Walter jumped onto the sand and came to a running stop.
Flushed with adrenaline, Walter caught sight of Lani who was
running towards him, and he excitedly swept her into his arms and
turning, he looked about for Kanoa and Omai, but he was unable
to locate them in the crowd surrounding him. Putting Lani down
and pulling her close within his arms, Walter looked back out to
sea, still exhilarated from his own success at surfing this unique
wave. His gaze spied Kamehameha and pointing him out to Lani,
Walter was awed by the sight of the big warrior gliding across the
face of an incredibly impressive wave with great style and
elegance.

The two of them kept watching as the consummate surfer
stepped masterfully off his board onto the beach a short distance
away. Kamehameha nodded to Walter, but he was quickly
surrounded by his warriors, and without drawing further attention
to himself, the young warrior quietly left the beach.

That night during another feast Walter, Kanoa and Omai were
watching the hula dancers and laughing and joking with one
another about their feats of surfing, and the fishing that they would
undertake, while they were staying here on Oahu. Then amidst the
light-hearted banter, Walter noticed Kanoa stiffen and sit up, his
expression darkened, and when Walter followed the Kahuna's eyes
across the square, he, in turn, became instantly alert. Koa and his
warriors had entered the hall, but this time with the proper level of
respect.

They proceeded towards Kahahana, who sat elevated on a platform. Koa and his warriors stopped to bend down, their right fist on
the ground. The group from Kauai now formally paid their respects
to the ruler of Oahu. Koa spoke quietly at first, but soon his voice
boomed over the gathering of chiefs. "Ali'i Nui, the haole has
demonstrated today that he is indeed capable of wave riding. In this,
he has shown a desire to learn our ways. I say, let him demonstrate

more of his skills. I challenge him to a contest of three tests. One of speed, one of courage and one of strength."

With a sinking feeling, Walter recognised the trap Koa was setting. He lent over to Kanoa and whispered, "What shall I do?"

"Nothing!" Kanoa's voice was ice-cold. "I will accept Koa's challenge on your behalf. This, after all, is my fight."

Kanoa stood up to face the gathering. "I am the one who will accept Koa's challenge."

Koa looked surprised when he saw Kanoa get to his feet, and Walter thought it was probably out of habit that he reverted to the familiar salute between the two of them. "Why do you wish to compete with me, Kahu?"

"You know why, Koa." The Kahuna's voice almost broke with emotion. "Once I would have done the same for you."

Kanoa's expression gave nothing away, but Walter knew that the betrayal of his apprentice had hurt the Kahuna deeply. Now as they waited for him to choose the manner of the competition, Walter wondered, not for the first time, if any of this would have occurred if he had stayed on the Resolution.

Kanoa's voice boomed across the square for all to hear." I choose the running race, the boxing match and wave riding."

Kahahana held his arm up. "Kanoa, as you have chosen the competition, so Koa will choose the prize."

There was dead silence in the court as all eyes fell upon Koa. Walter wanted to protest, but Omai's hand landed on his shoulder a warning not to interfere with the age-old tradition.

"So be it then." Koa paused, allowing the tension in the square to build. "I choose the stick that throws fire, as my prize." He stopped speaking to look defiantly at Kanoa. "And should I lose, Kanoa can do with me as he chooses."

Kahahana, looking puzzled turned to Kanoa, who explained that Koa wanted for his prize, a dangerous weapon which belonged to the haole. Nodding his head, the high chief then asked Kanoa if he agreed to Koa's terms. Again Walter wanted to voice a protest, but Omai's firm grip on his shoulder stopped him. When Kanoa nodded, the court erupted in cheers and claps.

Satisfied with the outcome, Koa and his warriors once more paid their respects to the chief and his court and quietly retreated into the night. While Koa's warriors headed to different huts around the royal compound, Koa headed off by himself, taking care not to be seen, and made his way to the outskirts of the township close to the shore. Stepping through the entrance to a modest hut, he greeted his friend Kumahana.

Koa had decided that it was better for the queen's son not to be seen openly associating with him, either by Kahahana or the Ali'i Nui of his court. He had urged his friend to stay secluded as part of their strategy, so Kumahana had remained in the hut provided for them and prepared a simple meal. As they both began to help themselves to a variety of vegetables and some poi, Koa looked enquiringly at his friend. "Are the warriors ready?"

"They are. Just as you've commanded."

Koa smiled, pleased with the news. "Good. Soon it will all be over. Once we have conquered Oahu, we will return to Kauai as heroes. Then they will truly be in awe of the great Koa, Ali'i Nui of Oahu, Molokai and Kauai, and soon to be Mo' i of all the Islands."

Chapter Forty-Four

*O*ver the year or so that Walter had lived on Kauai, he had been impressed by the efficiency of the Islanders, and their ability to organise all sorts of events in a very short time frame. On waking the next morning, he found that it was no different here on Oahu with the competition between Kanoa and Koa. In an incredibly short space of time, everything had been set up for the first part of the competition, the running race, and a huge crowd was gathering on the beach. Kahahana, his court and commoners alike, were all congregating to witness the upcoming spectacle.

As the crowd settled in, Kahahana summoned the two combatants to step up to him, and Koa appeared from amongst his warriors wearing a simple, white loincloth. His dark-skinned body was smooth and oiled, making the chorded muscles of his legs and abdomen stand out, giving him an imposing appearance, while the tattoos around his thighs seemed to pulse with energy.

As Kanoa joined Koa, his massive chest and legs also glistening with oil, Walter watched from the sidelines. He heard the Islanders placing their bets, balancing the older man's experience against the younger one's energy. Walter knew that he wouldn't have had a chance, but even for the Kahuna, this contest was going to be a hard challenge.

Ka'opulupulu, Kahahana's Kahuna nui, called for silence, and then once the crowd's full attention was on their Ali'i Nui, Kahahana spoke.

"As agreed, the goal is to be the fastest runner, the best boxer, and the best wave rider. Two out of three wins."

A roar erupted from the crowd. Conch shells and drums rang through the air, and the competitors were led to the starting line. Kahahana explained that Kanoa and Koa were to run to the marker up on the cliff from where they were then to run back to the starting point on the beach. A distance of approximately two miles.

As the two men lined up, Kanoa appeared the epitome of calm, his face impassive as the crowd saluted him as the expected champion. Koa, on the other hand, displayed his arrogance by claiming that he had already won. Some in the crowd scoffed, while others warned the young man not to underestimate Kanoa.

When Kahahana raised his hand, Walter saw that the chief held a piece of white kapa cloth and immediately a hush fell over the crowd. Without any other warning, the chief's hand dropped. A thunderous roar erupted, and the race to the cliff began.

Kanoa and Koa sprinted down the beach, the sand bursting in small explosions beneath their feet and after a few hundred feet, the two men had settled into a rhythm of swinging arms and pumping legs. The course of the race was designed so that the spectators could view the entire event from where they stood gathered on the beach.

As the terrain began to elevate, Walter could see Kanoa pushing for the lead and creeping ahead of Koa, who responded by immediately stepping up his pace. Slowly he gained on the Kahuna eventually inching ahead of him. The track appeared to narrow, and he could see the two runners slow down slightly, but they remained too close for him to tell who was in front.

Reaching the marker at the edge of the cliff, both men turned to begin their run back down to the beach towards the finishing line. Now in the final stretch of the race, each of the men alternated in taking the lead. Then the two runners approached a critical section along the cliff, close to the crumbling edge and Walter watched in horror as Koa suddenly pushed into Kanoa, taking him by surprise. Kanoa stumbled, and the crowd gasped with shock, but the Kahuna was nimble, and instantly regained his balance.

Walter, like the rest of the spectators, watched in hushed silence as Koa continued to use his tactic of crowding Kanoa on the narrow track. Lithely, Kanoa stayed just out of range, but Walter could tell that Koa's tactic was draining the Kahuna's reserves as he had dropped behind his former apprentice.

As the runners reached the beach and headed towards the finishing marker, the excited crowd started shouting enthusiastically at them, encouraging the men to greater efforts. Walter, too, joined the crowd calling out to Kanoa. Head to head, the runners closed in on the marker, when Koa, in a final burst of effort and speed, accelerated to a sprint, covering the last fifty feet in a Herculean effort.

As Koa threw himself across the finishing line, there was no doubt as to who had won the race, and, without looking to Kahahana, Koa jumped to his feet shouting his victory to the crowd, who responded by roaring enthusiastically. Kanoa, his energy spent, dropped to his knees in the sand. His huge chest heaving as he, strained to catch his breath.

The official pronouncement of Koa as the winner of the first of the competitions had the crowd busily turning to the critical task of collecting their winnings while Walter and Omai rushed to Kanoa'a side. Walter reached down and helped Kanoa to his feet, but he shrugged him off and straightened up, easing the tension out of his muscles

"I'm fine, Pelekané. I am not yet a lame dog." Walter winced at the bitterness in Kanoa's voice.

Kanoa took a few steps and again stretched his body and his legs to ease the cramping muscles in his calves. Without looking back, Kanoa left the arena and headed off towards the kauhale. Walter, reluctant to simply desert his friend, fell silently in beside Kanoa.

As the sun rose the next day, Walter and Omai walked down to the beach where the villagers had prepared the vast grounds for the boxing match. People had already gathered, forming a large circle around the boxing ring, and as with the day before, there was much discussion about who was likely to win, with bets being placed equally on each of them.

As Kahahana, along with his guest Kamehameha, approached the arena with their retinue, the crowd parted respectfully to let them pass, then quietened down while their high chief settled himself on a platform that had been erected to give the Ali'i Nui a good view of the coming fight.

Spurred on by the previous days win, Koa jumped into the centre of the circle with an even greater arrogance and immediately began to taunt Kanoa and Walter, and all who supported them.

"This haole has come to our islands to cause mischief, and to take our women. And now he has persuaded Kanoa to fight for him." Koa paused for a moment as he strutted around the ring. "The Pelekané has no courage to stand up to me. So I will have to fight Kanoa, once my teacher who loved me like a son. But now we are sworn enemies all because of this gutless stranger. It is with a heavy heart that I fight Kanoa but he gave me no choice, and he will soon wish that he had never seen the haole. Defeating him will show you not only what a great warrior I am, but also that the gods are with me."

As Koa's supporters applauded him, he waited dramatically, obviously revelling in the theatre of the moment, before he continued. "Know that I will stop the haole and anyone else like him who threatens our lands. And all of you will be glad to have me as your chief!"

Koa fell silent. The crowd's attention was now on Kanoa who was expected to respond in kind to Koa's boasting. The crowd waited. Time passed, and the tension mounted, but Kanoa did not respond. With each passing moment, the crowd grew more restless, and murmurs rose from here and there. As if a great thunder exploded over the crowd, Kanoa's voice boomed out instantly silencing everyone.

"I wai no'u. Give me blood, haumana."

Hearing nothing but the ancient war cry, the crowd roared.

Walter, wanting to understand what was happening turned to Omai, who explained in a hushed voice that Kanoa did not need to boast or belittle Koa. He did not need to stoop to such a tactic. With that war cry, Kanoa had effectively let the crowd know that the match would be fierce and possibly to the death.

Walter, his apprehension about the outcome of the match tempered by his faith in Kanoa, watched as Kahahana stood up to signal the start of the bout, but before the High Chief could drop the white kapa cloth, Koa lunged at Kanoa.

A roar of disgust from the spectators filled the air and muted the sound of fist meeting flesh, as Kanoa nimbly blocked the first of a series of blows aimed at his face and body.

Koa was quick, and a blow caught Kanoa on the side of his face. He reeled back from the vicious punch, a trickle of blood slowly oozing from the cut Koa had inflicted. Without any hesitation, Koa pushed his advantage through another series of punches, but this time Kanoa blocked them all then retaliated with a series of strikes to Koa's face.

The younger man fell back, looking surprised by the speed and ferocity of Kanoa's attack. Brushing away the blood dripping from his nose with the back of his hand, he taunted the Kahuna.

"No matter what, Kanoa, I will win."

"Do your worst Koa. You failed to kill me once, and you will not succeed now."

Kanoa's words enraged Koa, and he rushed the Kahuna, but Kanoa nimbly stepped aside. Again he delivered another sharp left and right combination to Koa's head. Koa rolled with the punches to lessen the impact, but a mighty blow landed on his chest, lifting him off his feet. Falling backwards, Koa landed hard on the ground but instantly jumped back to his feet.

Breathing hard, the two men circled each other, each looking for an opening in the other man's defence.

Suddenly Koa stepped towards Kanoa and delivered two powerful blows. Kanoa blocked, then countered them with a devastating combination of punches that left Koa collapsing to the ground. He lay there, disoriented and bleeding from several nasty looking cuts, but despite his now swollen and bruised face, the younger man rallied, leaping to his feet, his eyes flashing with fury.

He rushed at Kanoa while at the same time reaching behind his back. In a blur Koa slashed out at Kanoa with a wooden knife, curved and studded with gleaming white shark teeth. The weapon glinted menacingly in the sunlight.

A wet, red streak opened up on Kanoa's chest. A gasp erupted from the crowd. The warriors, surprised by the appearance of the weapon, moved in to stop the fight, but a signal from Kahahana pulled them up. "The snuffing out of the light is up to Kahiki."

Walter couldn't believe that the High Chief would allow such cheating and he was appalled at the sight of the wound on Kanoa's chest, but the Kahuna himself remained calm, his face a mask as he spoke to his apprentice in a dignified voice. What Walter was unaware of at the time, was that Kanoa had anticipated Koa's treachery.

" So, this is how you have decided to reveal your true self."

His chest heaving and brandishing the wicked-looking knife, Koa closed in once again, but Kanoa skilfully avoided the shark's teeth and landed another series of violent blows to Koa's face and head. The younger man, stunned by the strikes, struggled to stay on his feet and swayed for a moment before he lunged again towards Kanoa with the knife. The spectators gasped, some calling out, "Enough!". But Koa missed his mark and staggered forward almost losing his balance.

Kanoa, with perfect timing, paused for a second as Koa teetered over to one side, and then in a brilliantly calculated move, he threw another punch that cracked sharply on the side of Koa's head. This time Koa crumpled unconscious to the ground.

Kanoa stepped back and carefully lifted his arms in a sign of victory, his face suddenly distorted from the pain of the ugly gash on his chest.

He looked over the crowd." It is finished."

Kanoa had barely finished the words when the sky suddenly darkened. The crowd fell silent. A clap of thunder exploded over the gathering, and rain poured down. The spectators roared with approval as Kahahana formally declared Kanoa, the winner of the bout.

"As of today, each warrior has won a bout so tomorrow will decide the final victor!"

Standing in the pouring rain, Kanoa's knees buckled. The crowd, seeing the Kahuna struggle to stay on his feet, cleared a path for Walter and Omai to assist their injured friend back to the hale. Lani rushed over to them to inspect the wound on Kanoa's chest then told them she would summon the healer and meet them at the hut.

Walter was deeply concerned as he watched the blood run down the Kahuna's chest, and once they reached their hale, he and Omai helped Kanoa to the sleeping mats and eased him down. "Kahu, you must rest."

The big man winced but uttered no sound as he lay back. Omai fetched a calabash of water and, with a cloth, began to wipe the blood from Kanoa's chest, gently cleaning the wound just as Lani arrived with the healer.

The healer was a small, wizened man, who bowed respectfully as he shuffled across to Kanoa. Kneeling down beside the injured man he slipped the large bag he had brought onto the ground beside him and peered closely at the wound before removing several small wooden bowls containing ointments and oils, as well as cloth for bandages.

"It is deep, this cut," was all he said as he took over from Omai and finished cleaning the wound. They all remained silent as he worked, bringing the edges of the gash closer together and applying a sticky looking ointment. The healer then looked at the Kahuna with deep concern. "You know that you cannot surf tomorrow, Kanoa."

The big man winced as the healer applied another layer of cream, but Walter, watching, wasn't sure if that was from the pain of the healer's salve or because of what it meant not to surf.

"I will take your place, Kanoa," Walter called out. "After all, Koa did challenge me, and it is only right that I try and finish this."

As he heard himself say these words, Walter wondered what in

God's name had possessed him. He was no match for anyone in the water, let alone when their fate rested on his abilities.

Kanoa nodded his head. "Thank you, my friend, but we can discuss this in the morning."

The Kahuna closed his eyes to end the discussion, and to allow the healer to do his work. After some time, the little wizened man gathered his belongings.

"I have done as much as I can. The rest lies with the gods."

Chapter Forty-Five

*W*ord of the final contest had spread across the eastern part of Oahu, and overnight people had arrived from far away to witness the final match, the surfing contest, between Koa and Kanoa. As much as Kanoa had a reputation as a skilled warrior, his status as an accomplished surfer was even more significant.

But as Kanoa and Koa arrived in the contest area, it was evident that both were severely battered and bruised from the previous day's boxing match. Both of their faces were covered in cuts and bruises, and Koa's left eye was swollen shut. Koa's knife had left a deep gash across Kanoa's chest that was hidden beneath a heavy kapa bandage, through which seeped a narrow trail of blood.

Kanoa slowly lifted his hand to signal that he wished to address the assembled crowd and a huge cheer rose up from the multitude of people.

"As you can see, Koa's cowardly cheating has left me at a disadvantage."

Koa grimaced while Kanoa waited for the people to quieten down.

"So with Kahahana's permission, I have decided that the Pelekané will complete the contest on my behalf."

Shouts of protest rose into the air. Walter knew that many of the islanders would have placed significant bets on the Kahuna and that they would now felt that they would be robbed of their opportunity to win. Hearing the objections, Kahahana raised his staff, and the dissenting voices dropped.

"I will agree with Kanoa's request. He has nominated his champion, and therefore it will be done."

However, as more calls of disapproval rose up from the crowd, Kahahana was forced to again raise his arms to silence them. Koa smiled at this, apparently assuming that his victory was now assured, which also appeared to be the thinking of many of the spectators who were now placing hefty bets on him, in the conviction that he would naturally win the contest's outcome.

Walter, on the other hand, stayed quiet. He did not want to admit it openly, but he felt that he had little chance of winning the surfing contest. Not only did Koa's skill and experience naturally far outweighed his, but Walter now knew that the warrior was not against using dirty tricks to his advantage.

They had talked about this earlier before leaving the hut when Kanoa had informed him that he had requested that Kahahana not interfere if Koa cheated in the boxing match. Walter understood politics, and that was what this was all about. The people of Oahu and their Ali'i nui now knew that Koa could not be trusted.

Despite Walter's misgivings, Kanoa thought quite differently about Walter's substitution for him in the surfing contest.

'All you need to do, Pelekané, is to catch one wave and cross the marker first. It will be about luck as much as it will be about skill. You have worked hard to gain your skills in the ocean and I could not have wished for a better apprentice. Many things can happen on a wave, even for one as experienced as Koa.'

Kanoa's words had reassured Walter slightly, but as he looked across at his opponent, he found Koa sneering at him. He watched Koa slowly run his fingers across his throat, leaving Walter with no doubt about his fate should he lose. Koa's message was all too clear.

Walter felt a tap on his shoulder. "Relax, ignore him," Kanoa reassured him. "Remember all the things that I have taught you, in and out of the water. Focus your fear, and let your mind and body become one."

"Kanoa, are you sure of this? Koa is more than likely to win this and then what?"

"You are right, Walter, this is a serious gamble, but remember, if you succeed then your life will be very different here. You will have truly earned your place amongst our people. You will have support and protection against those that wish you harm."

Kanoa paused and looked intently into Walter's eyes as if to delve into his soul. "I would not have agreed to this if I did not think you could, with a little luck, do this."

As Walter tried to digest Kanoa's words, Lani pushed her way through the crowd. She rushed up to Walter and pressed her forehead and nose to his. A subtle murmur rose up among the Hawai'ians.

Lani spoke quietly as she looked deeply into his eyes. "Ride well, Walter. I'll be waiting on the beach for you."

Walter was all too aware that Lani, also, would be at risk should he lose. He grasped her hand and placed it on his chest. "Mahalo, my love, but perhaps you should get to some place of safety as far away from here as you can."

But Lani shook her head. "I have faith in you, Walter, and I have prayed to Kane, who will protect you and guide you."

Before Walter could say anything more, Kahahana's voice rang out. "The betting is now finished, and it is time for the contestants to ready themselves for the surf. The first to pass the pua wins."

Two Olos, of equal length, were waiting for the contenders on the beach and as the sound of the conch shell signalled the start of the contest, Koa and Walter quickly reached for the heavy surfboards. Racing into the water, Walter and Koa launched themselves into the sea. The long paddle out to the break had begun.

Once out on the edge of the reef, the two surfers positioned themselves carefully away from each other. Peering out to sea, Walter scanned the horizon and realised that every now and then a bigger set of waves would break far out to sea, sending walls of white water towards the shore. He knew this contest would be short. One wave would determine the winner. In contrast to his own nervousness, Koa, despite his injuries, seemed entirely at ease.

Then, the first signs of an incoming set formed on the horizon. As the waves built up before them, Koa paddled aggressively towards Walter in a blatant attempt to intimidate him. "Haole, your troubles will be over very soon,' Koa sneered, "then you and your friends will be dead, and Lani will finally be mine."

Despite Walter's dire circumstances, he managed to look at his enemy and retort," Always the optimist, eh, Koa."

He knew that his advantage came from Koa underestimating him. Walter turned away and paddled into the steeper section of the wave but let the wave pass under him, banking on the fact that the second wave was usually bigger.

As Walter had anticipated, the second wave seemed to loom over him. Both men swung their boards around, and each began to paddle for the best position on that take-off, but being on the inside of Koa, gave Walter an advantage. Walter leveraged the steeper section of the wave to maximise the speed for both the take-off and to slide the longboard across the clean face of the swell. Unless Koa resorted this early to some treacherous strategy, Walter felt he had a chance.

Walter's heart began to race as he paddled hard. A little voice in his head shouted "Now!" and he jumped to his feet, and took the drop down the face of the wave. He looked to the side to see Koa place himself only a short distance away along the face of the wave and in an instant Koa, too was on his feet, sliding the heavy board across and ahead of Walter.

As they hurtled towards the shore, Koa kept crowding him, trying to edge him across into the white water. Walter knew Koa was trying to force him to make a mistake and wipe out, but he focused all of his effort on making his board slide away from Koa while managing to maintain his balance.

Walter was skilled enough now after many months of practice to bring the board up higher in the wave, where he could make the most of its speed to accelerate over the top of Koa, and away from the white water, and that is precisely what he did.

As they rode towards the beach almost neck and neck with each other and with the marker getting closer, Koa tried one more time to push Walter into making a mistake. Knowing he needed to avoid the warrior, Walter brought the board higher up in the face of the wave again. This manoeuvre accelerated the speed of his board and allowed Walter to shoot past the Hawai'ian, and as he shot past the marker, he heard Koa's angry bellow of frustration.

Pure unadulterated joy rushed through Walter's body. I've done it! His mind seemingly bursting with the taste of his victory.

Seeing Walter's narrow win, the multitude on the beach erupted in an absolute frenzy of excitement, while the gamblers cheered and complained respectively about the outcome.

Walter, surprised and elated by his victory suspected that this may not be the end of his troubles with the young warrior. None the less, he hopped off his board and ran through the shallows to the beach where Lani rushed into his arms. Omai overjoyed threw his arms around both, and in seconds the three were engulfed by the elated crowd.

Chapter Forty-Six

While the Islanders of Oahu were gathered to watch the surfing contest, a fleet of war canoes crewed by warriors from Kauai had been cutting through the ocean on a steady and threatening path towards Oahu. Each powerful paddle stroke brought the fleet closer to the unsuspecting Islanders on the beach, its relentless approach taking the canoes to a landing north of the contest area, and out of sight of the gathered crowd.

The warriors looked grim and determined. Wearing helmets and battle mats, there was no doubt what they had come for, and as they quietly paddled through the break in the reef to the deserted beach, there was only one person watching to see them arrive just up the coast from Waikiki.

The warriors quickly disembarked and silently disappeared into the surrounding forest to be met by Kumahana who had remained hidden since he and Koa, and the advance party had arrived three days ago. Now, meeting the rest of Koa's warriors as arranged, he led them close to the competition arena where secreting themselves behind the tree line they quietly encircled the area to wait in ambush.

Koa and Kumahana's assessment was that with the elite of

Oahu's nobility assembled and engrossed in the contest, their warriors would be caught completely off guard. They knew that the battle plan was risky, but Koa felt that with surprise on their side, they would be able to quickly gain the upper hand in the fight to win the day.

While Kumahana and the warriors waited for Koa to join them, the Mo'i of Kauai's son felt his excitement building, filling his chest with anticipation. Kumahana had chosen Koa over his mother many years ago. He had indeed come to believe that Koa had a much better vision for the islands than she did.

The two men had talked about Koa's ambition to grab the reigns of power out of the hands of Kamakahelei for many years, and now, untroubled by any feelings of loyalty to his mother, Kumahana knew they were getting close to doing so. They both knew the risks and Kumahana was positive that they had prepared for this moment with all the care necessary. Had they not been sacrificing slaves to Ku to secure good omens for the upcoming battle? Most importantly, they had gathered a large cohort of loyal warriors and built an army. If they succeeded with this hit and run tactic, they would eliminate Kahahana and Kanoa at the same time. They could then use the situation to force an alliance with the other factions on both islands, and in the ensuing leadership vacuum, Kamakahelei would have to deal with Koa as a powerful war chief and not merely as Kanoa's apprentice.

A quiet rustle amongst the trees announced Koa's arrival. Without a word, he quickly dressed in his battle mat and helmet and reached for a shark-tooth club that lay amidst a host of other weapons. Kumahana watched his friend as he weighed the club carefully in his hand, feeling the balance and weight of the weapon, and obviously satisfied that it would serve his purpose, Koa looked around. He nodded to Kumahana, who nodded back to affirm that all was prepared and that he and the warriors were ready, and then he lifted a large conch to his lips. As Koa surveyed the warriors Kumahana, convinced that everything was in place, took a deep breath and at the same time as Koa released a chilling war cry, he blew hard into the conch. The roar had barely died down when

Kumahana dropped the conch and reached for his spear. He had positioned himself so that with only a few steps he would be in direct line of sight of the chief, and so within seconds of the call to battle he had hurled his spear towards Kahahana.

An instant later, a spear cut through the air and pierced the chest of one of Kahahana's bodyguard's. Without a sound, the man toppled to the ground. The crowd already startled by the war cry, erupted in a chaotic scramble for cover, as missiles of all sorts flew through the air, followed by the furious onslaught of the hordes of Koa's men wielding spears, wooden shark teeth knives and clubs.

The battle for Oahu had begun.

ଽ▲ଽ▲ଽ▲ଽ▲ଽ▲

Within seconds of hearing the frightening sound emanating from the far side of the arena, warriors broke from the surrounding forests and began to cut down the spectators. Walter was shocked as blood-curdling screams from the dying men, women and children rose in the air. In an instant, the war cries of Kahahana's warriors rolled across what was now a battlefield and in the ensuing chaos, the people of Oahu looked to arm themselves with whatever they could. However, the speed and velocity of Koa's forces cost many lives.

It was the sight of Koa swinging a massive club at a helpless old man that spurred Walter to action. Amidst the confusion and mayhem, he held onto Lani and frantically reeled around, searching for Kanoa and Omai. He spotted them amongst the royal guard where he could see that Kahahana's warriors had organised a defensive wall around the Ali'i Nui.

Walter, desperate to get Lani to safety, pointed towards the fleeing mothers and children and started to drag her with him as he turned to follow them. "Stay close to me!" He shouted so she would hear him over the noise of the battle, but Lani baulked, and let go of his hand. "I'm not leaving. I will fight with you, and we will die together if we have to!"

Before Walter could comprehend this strange idea that a woman was going to fight with him, Lani had grabbed a spear out of the ground and, like any of the young men, entered the battle to protect the Ali'i Nui.

Kanoa's bellowing baritone cut across the cacophony of screams and shouts. "Omai, Pelekané! Today is what I trained you for!"

Walter, following Lani's lead, grabbed an abandoned club off the ground and fought his way towards Kahahana, forever grateful that he had trained with Kanoa and his warriors.

On reaching the platform, he found himself standing beside Kamehameha, who was holding several spears in one hand while using a single spear in his other hand to deflect any flying missiles directed at Kahahana. When Kamehameha saw Walter, he tossed him a spear.

"Here, Pelekané, do what you can!" In the melee Kamehameha continued to parry spears, plucking them from the air as they hurtled towards him and then throwing them back to the warriors of Kauai.

More spears came flying through the air towards them, but the two men were able to knock them aside. Fighting side by side, Walter marvelled at Kamehameha's skills as an accomplished fighter, but also as a man who exhibited a lust for battle that Walter had not seen before. The Hawai'ian prince had donned a fierce, ferocious expression that mimicked the mask of the god of war, Ku. Gone was the warm, kind face of the young man Walter had met days earlier. Eyes flashing and powerful arms swinging, Kamehameha felled one assailant after another. Soon the big Hawai'ian had them both standing amongst the dead and dying while the blood of their enemies dripped down their arms and chest.

A short break in the onslaught enabled Kahahana to rally his warriors and direct them to intercept a large group of enemy fighters, while runners broke away, heading off in different directions with the task of gathering everybody able to defend their island home. Some of the runners headed inland to call for reinforcements, while others raced to the water's edge to look for the Kauai warriors' canoes.

As the battle raged, Kamehameha rallied his own men, and Omai, Kanoa and Lani joined Walter and the royal guard. The Ali'i Nui was pressed by the constant onslaught of Koa's men. They struggled to maintain any sense of formation. Spears, as well as stones released from slingshots, were flying through the air, and it was only good fortune that none of the terrible missiles found their targets.

From time to time conch shells droned above the screams and cries of the battlefield but eventually as reinforcements arrived, lines of warriors, men and women armed with clubs and spears, pushed towards the beach intent on forcing the invaders back into the sea.

Walter watched as Kanoa suddenly turned. As he followed the Kahuna's line of sight, he saw Koa, his arm drawn back and about to release a spear. Some primal instinct told Walter that it was aimed at Kamehameha. Then, ever so quickly, that Walter almost couldn't comprehend it, he saw Kanoa expertly snatching the spear out of the air in mid-flight and then turn to step in between the two men. Master and apprentice were now face to face.

"Come, Kanoa, let's settle this once and for all. You will stand between me and what's mine no more!"

"And you have caused the sea to rise for the last time."

Koa reached under his battle mat, a sly look on his face as his hand emerged holding Walter's pistol. He aimed the weapon at Kanoa, but before Koa could pull the trigger, Kanoa threw himself at his adversary and a fierce struggle for the weapon erupted, during which the gun fell onto the ground as the two men continued to wrestle, rolling around on the blood-soaked ground, each man struggling to get the upper hand. Walter watched as Kanoa, having already inflicted several significant wounds to Koa's upper body finally managed to pin Koa to the ground with his leg, and raising a war club high above his head he looked down on his apprentice.

Koa knew his defeat, and death was imminent. With the last of his pride, Koa called out, "Kahu, honour me with a swift death!"

"Which is more than you deserve!" Kanoa screamed into Koa's face.

With a groan that turned into a bestial growl, Kanoa brought the weapon down on Koa's head with all his might. The head of the club struck Koa's skull with such force that his face exploded in a cloud of red and white. For an instant, Kanoa appeared frozen, but the demands of the fighting around him forced him back into action. Leaping away from Koa's shattered body, Kanoa rejoined the fray with the ferocity of the berserker.

Walter too was immediately pulled back to the battle, finding himself in the precarious position of being attacked by several of the enemy warriors he managed to keep them at bay, but realised quickly that without help he was doomed. As he swung his club in a defensive arc, he saw Kanoa, Omai and Lani fighting a path towards him, each of them targeting one of his attackers so that they could get to his side

Back to back, and with the help of a handful of Kamehameha's men, Walter and his friends continued to fight, but Walter could feel his energy-draining, and then, out of the corner of his eye, he saw Kahahana's reinforcements surge into the battle and cut their way through the enemy. Inch by inch, Koa's warriors, were being pushed back towards the beach their ranks decimated by the determined defenders. As they reached the sandy stretch, the Kauai warriors tried to rally behind Kumahana for a last-ditch assault, pushing hard against Kahahana's men in an attempt to break them up into small groups.

Walter realised that Lani, who had been fighting as bravely as any man, was visibly tiring, her lithe frame finding it harder and harder to keep the monotonous rhythm of slash, parry and stab going. Over the last few minutes, she had been drawn further away from his side, and Walter could see that Kumahana and Ikaika were intent on isolating her out of the group. Kanoa, pinned between a number of the enemy must have also noticed the assault on Lani and Walter heard him call out. "Omai! Get Lani away from the battle!"

"I will. But keep an eye out for the Pelekané!" Omai yelled back as he dispatched another warrior and quickly forced his way to her side. Desperate to join the Tahitian to protect Lani, Walter felt a sudden rush of power, and he brought his war club down across the shoulder of his attacker, hearing the bones crunch as the man collapsed to the ground.

Leaving him to his pain, Walter scooped up a spear and ran towards Omai just as his friend landed a mighty blow on Ikaika's head, killing him instantly.

As the young warrior collapsed onto the ground, the Tahitian reached out and pulled Lani towards him, but another tall, heavily-built warrior rushed at them swinging his club, managing to separate them once again. Then, with Omai, distracted and locked in battle with one of his warriors, Kumahana dashed in to take advantage of the opportunity to get close to his sister and make a grab for her. She struggled, unable to tear herself out of her brother's brutal grip as Kumahana pulled her away towards a gap in the melee.

Walter followed assuming that Kumahana was going to take Lani with him to the beach, but instead, somehow avoiding Lani's punches, he caught her hair and wrapped it around his hand,. He jerked her head back and forced her to the ground. She screamed in pain and fury as Kumahana raised his war club triumphantly in the air. He paused when he saw Walter running towards them, his expression was cruel, and obviously savouring the moment Kumahana let a cold grin spread across his face.

"Pelekané, watch me reunite Lani with Koa!"

Walter was stunned. "You would kill your own sister?"

Walter stopped, immobilised by fear, not daring to move lest Kumahana did his worst. He felt a gnawing ache of dread spreading through the pit of his guts.

"My oath to Koa is stronger than blood!" Kumahana bellowed. Glaring at Walter in triumph, he didn't see Lani's free hand desperately searching the ground for a weapon. Her fingers suddenly found the shaft of a discarded spear, and in a split second, she managed to wrap her hand around the spear, and with one mighty thrust, she rammed it forcefully into her brother's chest beneath his ribs and up into his heart.

· · ·

A look of surprise spread across Kumahana's face. He dropped the club while he let Lani's hair slip through his other hand, a puzzled look replacing the grin of only a moment ago. He stumbled back, and as his hand wrapped around the shaft of the spear, he slowly toppled to the ground.

Some of Kahahana's warriors rushed to Lani's side, immediately surrounding her protectively, and as one of them helped her up Walter saw her eyes widen with fear and gasping for breath, she called out "Walter. Omai needs help."

Walter spun around to see Omai locked in hand-to-hand combat with one of the remaining warriors from Kauai. Evenly matched, the two men fought ferociously. Each man's weapon clashed with the other's in a rhythmic thrust and parry, neither getting a definite advantage.

Determined to lend Omai assistance, Walter started forward but found his path blocked by the chaos of bodies and fighters. Aided by some of Kahahana's men, they fought their way towards Omai, but before he could reach him, he saw his friend suddenly lurch forward and fall to the ground where he rolled onto his back.

Kanoa, also seeing Omai collapse, rushed towards him, and launching himself at the Tahitian's attacker, he felled him with a savage blow to the head, crushing the side of the warrior's skull.

As Omai lay on the ground, more of Kahahana's warriors fought to form a wall around the small group surrounding the Tahitian. The wall of men and women allowed Walter to kneel by his mortally wounded friend. Frantically he tried to stem the flow of blood from the wound in Omai's belly.

Desperate, Walter looked around him. As he looked down at his wounded friend again, Omai weakly squeezed his hand. "Is Lani safe?"

Tears streaming down Walter's face. He struggled to focus on his friend. "She is, thanks to you." He paused, choking. "Omai, remember, you promised that we would ride mountains together."

Omai tried to smile, but could only manage to grimace. He

whispered, "We will, my friend. Remember, I will always be with you."

Choking with grief, Walter's voice gave out. All he could do was to hold onto Omai's hand and cradle it against his chest. As the sounds of battle receded, Lani joined him, and Omai rallied to call out for Kanoa. The kahuna knelt by the Tahitian's side and leaning forward, he gently asked the Tahitian, "Do you have a burden for me?"

The customary words to the dying had Lani sob loudly and begin to tear at her hair in the harsh realisation that Omai would not survive.

"Promise to take care of Pelekané and Lani for me."

"Mahalo, my brother." Kanoa bowed his head for a minute for Omai's request. He looked at the Tahitian. "Now prepare yourself for the red trail to Kane."

Omai's face suddenly contorted with pain and then a tired smile relaxed his features and he sighed, and with his final breath, his head dropped onto Walter's lap, his lifeless, empty eyes staring into the sky. As Walter looked down at Omai, he let his tears fall freely. He wept unashamedly for the friend who had given him so much and helped him on his journey to becoming a man.

Having lost their leaders, the warriors from Kauai were now in full retreat, while Kahahana's warriors pushed their advantage and began to mercilessly slaughter the remaining enemy at the edge of the surf, turning the sea pink with the blood of the fallen men.

As the exhausted men and women of Oahu surveyed the carnage, the air was filled with the groans of the wounded, and everyone's attention turned to helping those who still lived.

꒰ꑇ꒱ꑇ꒰ꑇ꒱

Many lives had been lost to one man's treacherous ambitious and in the following days' the angry discussions amongst the Ali'i added to the grief and pain of the survivors. The council sent messengers to Kamakahelei, telling her of the death of her son in his cowardly attack on the peaceful gathering on Waikiki. However, it was only through Kanoa's intervention that Kahahana did not launch a retaliatory strike against Kauai, the chief accepting that Koa had acted against his mother, the Mo'i as well as against Oahu.

Walter and Lani tried to deal with their own grief at losing Omai, by spending time with the other bereaved, and at the many ceremonies where the fallen were honoured. Then once the burial ceremonies came to a close, Kahahana announced that a pa'ina celebrating their victory was to be held.

Several days later, Kanoa, Lani and Walter met with Kahahana and his council to talk about the ramifications of Koa's attack. Lani spoke of her grief that her brother had betrayed their mother the Mo'i, and then aided Koa in his attempt to wrest power from the legitimate rulers of both Oahu and Kauai. Her very reason for leaving her people had been to try and avoid violence and division, but Koa had his own plans.

Kanoa, had extracted the truth of those plans from one of his surviving warriors, and so they all knew that the attack on Oahu would have come, irrespective of the arrival of Lani, Walter and Kanoa on the island. This reassured Walter, who had felt that his pursuit of Lani may have caused all of the pain and destruction that had befallen these people.

On the day of the feast, all of the survivors and many people from the outlying villages gathered to hear the Kahuna tell the story of the courage and bravery of the men and women of Oahu, and their victory over treachery, with chants and the poems honouring all those who died defending the village.

Walter, Kanoa and Lani were brought before Kahahana and his court, with Kamehameha and his entourage, and as Walter knelt before the Ali'i Nui, Kahahana's powerful voice boomed out over the gathering.

"Pelekané, together, we have faced a formidable and treacherous enemy in Koa, and I owe you and Kamehameha my life. Kanoa has trained you well. You and Lani are always welcome on Oahu to ride the waves and join us in our feasts. You, my friend, have truly earned that right."

Kahahana paused for a moment, looking around at the assembly. "I say, now, before all, Aloha to you. You are now Ali'i, for you have truly shown the courage and strength deserving of that position. You are no longer haole." He looked at the small group before him. "And now it is time for you to have a proper name. From here on in you shall be known to us as Kekoa, the brave one."

Walter felt tears well up. Touched, Lani came to kneel beside him. He looked up at the chief. "I am truly honoured, Ali'i Nui, and I thank you with all my heart for your welcome of me into your realm."

Kahahana smiled down at him, then turning to Lani he beckoned to her to stand before him. "Lani, heir and daughter of Kamakahelei, Mo'i of Kauai. Your bravery is a credit to your family. To all here, I want to declare that we do not hold you or your Mo'i responsible for the actions of Koa and Kumahana, and we acknowledge the deep friendship between our peoples."

Lani sank to her knees and thanked Kahahana for his hospitality and formally declared her friendship as the future Mo'i of Kauai to the people of Oahu. Then signalling to some of his retainers, Kahahana proceeded to present Walter, Kanoa and Lani with feather cloaks, weapons and other beautiful gifts and informed them that he had put aside land and slaves for them to use as there own when they were on Oahu.

Chapter Forty-Seven

*W*alter was well aware that the reason why Kahahana had been happy to invite him to spend time on Oahu, was that he wanted to learn both the language and the customs of the Pelekané. The wily chief knew it was merely a matter of time before ships from Europe would return, and he was hopeful that they would be prepared to trade with them. The threat of war with Kalaniopu'u was stronger than ever, and Kahahana also saw the opportunity to obtain weapons that would be decisive in any confrontation.

After much discussion, Walter, Lani and Kanoa had decided to stay on Oahu for a time. Messengers had been sent back to Kauai to let the Mo' i know of the deaths of Koa and Kumahana and to reassure her that Lani was safe. On their return, they had brought news that Kamakahelei supported the plan for Kanoa and Lani to act in a capacity that Walter thought of as diplomats to the court of Kahahana.

All three of them deeply missed their Tahitian friend and they, like most of the Islanders, needed to heal from that awful battle, each contending with their own demons. Walter had set Omai's now weathered surfboard as a marker at the place where he fell, often visiting to leave offerings at its base as a tribute, as was the custom amongst the Islanders. Over the next few weeks, Walter would often sit beside the board, thinking about Omai and he had noticed Lani down on the shoreline, searching the sea.

"What are you looking for?" Walter asked her one day after watching her spend a long time scanning the ocean.

"Omai." Lani's voice was filled with the pain when she said their friend's name.

She offered no other explanation and continued with her search. Puzzled, Walter called on Kanoa for an explanation.

"She believes that Omai will keep his promise and return as an aumakua, a guardian spirit. It is he who brought you to her, and she is certain that he will look after you, as your ancestors are too far away to do so."

Walter, missed Omai, not just as a friend but also as someone who had spent time in England and had some knowledge and understanding of Walter's own home, but he was also very grateful that Kanoa had stayed with him, and he cherished their growing friendship.

He was even more grateful that Lani had placed her heart and trust in his hands and soon after they were officially welcomed into the community, Walter had asked Lani to be his wife. She accepted without any hesitation, and so a wedding was arranged with the usual efficiency with which all Hawaiian celebrations were organised.

On a beautiful evening, amidst the assembled nobles and people of Oahu, Walter and Lani were married in the natural cathedral of a magnificent sunset, as they stood below the ancient volcano called Laeahi. Lit by a brilliant rainbow arching over them, Walter placed a ring his mother had given him, on Lani's finger as a symbol of their union. It was one of the few things he still owned that had come with him from England.

Settling into their life on Oahu, both Walter and Lani spent a great deal of time with the Council, and with the retainers that Kahahana wanted to learn the Pelekané's language and customs. Even with his now fluent Hawaiian, Walter needed Lani to help him to find the right words to describe the differences between European and Hawaiian ways of seeing the world.

Then the pattern of their days shifted, as a few months later, they began to oversee the expansion of their kauhale, adding new huts, and planting more gardens. There was a good reason for this. Much to Walter's great joy, he and Lani were now expecting their first child and later that year, Lani gave birth to a beautiful baby boy. From the very first, the child relished any time in the water, and since he would often scream loudly when either Walter or Lani tried to take him away from the beach, they had decided to call him Kaimana, meaning the power of the ocean.

As the end of their second year on Oahu approached amidst the celebrations of the Makahiki, a full moon illuminated the beach. The ocean was lit by hundreds of bonfires burning on the sand so that from a distance, they sparkled like a velvet blanket dusted with diamonds. Amidst this magical backdrop, men and women paddled a quarter-mile offshore to ride the glistening swells, guided only by the moon and the fires on the beach.

Dripping wet, Walter and Kanoa emerged from the surf, the reflection of the bonfires forming patterns across their bodies. Walter laid his olo on the sand, and as he straightened up, Kanoa gripped his shoulder firmly, a beaming smile on his face. Even in the semi-dark, the Kahuna looked as if he would burst with excitement. "What is it?" Walter asked, curious.

"The big swells will be here in the next day or so, Kekoa."

"So soon?"

Kanoa laughed. "Still frightened, my friend? You have shown to all of us that you needn't shy away from the challenge of the sea."

Kanoa's simple question tapped into the peculiar mixture of apprehension and anticipation in the pit of his stomach that had plagued Walter despite his growing competence in the ocean. He had often wondered if he would ever lose that feeling, especially as it was tinged by his sense of loss and sadness that Omai would never ride the mountains of the sea he had so dreamed of doing.

Walter knew that Kanoa, too, missed their friend and understood how he felt. Their own friendship had been strengthened by time and forged by combat, and as a result, Walter and Kanoa had become inseparable, swimming, surfing and fishing together. At times Lani had teased Walter suggesting that he preferred the Kahuna's attention to hers, but Walter knew she was proud of him for adapting to, and adopting the ways of Hawai'i. Especially at having become an accomplished waterman.

"It is the time, Kekoa," Kanoa spoke with a tone of reverence. He paused to look quizzically at Walter. "Do you feel ready for the challenge, haumana?"

"As ready as I can be, Kahu."

Walter knew that Koa's betrayal of Kanoa had been a source of great grief for his friend. He had seen him struggling with the guilt that he had somehow failed his apprentice. Now that he had his own child, Walter appreciated Kanoa's pain at the loss of Koa. It was not just the loss of an apprentice, it had been the loss of a son.

Chapter Forty-Eight

$\mathcal{W}$alter and Lani were busy in their gardens, supervising the workers as they extended one of the vegetable patches when the arrival of a runner interrupted them. As the young man ran up to the group, he came to a halt in front of Walter and dropped to his knees, panting.

"Lord Kekoa, you must come quickly. A ship has arrived from Pelekané."

Walter was immediately aware of Lani's look of apprehension. When she asked softly "What will you do?" Walter heard the concern in her voice. Both had understood that they would not remain undisturbed forever on their island, but neither had they discussed this eventuality. It was as if the subject was taboo despite the inevitability that the Europeans would return. Walter had not wanted to think too much about it, and so he had no idea what he would do now that a ship had actually arrived.

Reeling from the news, it took him a few minutes to compose himself. A ship from England? Walter tried to comprehend all the possible permutations of this seemingly simple piece of news. I should not be this surprised Walter thought, after all, that was one of the reasons he had been teaching Kahahana English.

Walter suddenly realised he had been staring at Lani, as she patiently waited for him to answer her. "I will go and see who they are and what they want, but I want you to stay here until I get back."

Taking her hand, he raised it to his mouth. "Do not fret. All will be well. You'll see." And then, when he kissed her palm, he smiled at her as reassuringly as he could.

Looking around, he saw Kanoa leaving his own kauhale, a questioning look on his face. Once Walter had told him what had happened, he gave orders to one of the retainers to gather some of his warriors, and within a very short time, they set out for the beach.

As they came down out of the hills, they were immediately confronted by the plume of smoke billowing skyward from the vessel anchored offshore. Walter hoped that the worst had not already happened and that there would be room for diplomacy, and tried to reassure himself that unless provoked, Kahahana would not have instigated any hostilities towards the ship. After all, that would have gone against the Mo' i's plans entirely.

Yet as they arrived on the beach, the thousand or so warriors assembled there told a very different story. The unmistakable evidence of a fierce skirmish littered the beach, all too reminiscent of the battle with Koa, and it was clear that blood had well and truly been shed.

Shocked, Walter turned to one of the warriors. "Palani, what happened here?"

The young man was quick to respond. "The Pelekané arrived asking for news of you, but when a group of us boarded the ship, they took us, hostage, to trade us for you." He drew breath and looked carefully at Walter, trying to gauge his reaction. When Walter said nothing, he continued. "We managed to escape to the beach, by setting fire to the ship, but the Pelekané followed us, and a fierce battle broke out."

The news reminded Walter of the story amongst the Hawaiian's that Cook similarly precipitated his own demise, and wondered when the English would ever learn from such mistakes.

"Stay close to me, Palani." Walter ordered. He wanted to keep the young man by his side as he evidently knew first hand precisely what had transpired. "Yes, Kekoa."

Reaching the shoreline, Walter, Kanoa and their warriors made their way through the crowd. As the men parted to let Walter and his group through, he saw many Europeans lying dead in the sand. He stopped to scrutinise the bodies around him, and an over-whelming sadness rushed through him. What could have caused this? He wondered.

Kanoa came up to him, and he felt his friend's hand gently touch his shoulder. "These men aren't Marines, Kanoa." Walter said as he looked across the bay realising that the ship wasn't a Naval vessel.

Looking back at the injured, huddled together alongside their fallen companions, he could see that some were barely clinging to life, felled by horrific injuries from the shark's teeth weapons, and with the distinct head injuries inflicted by the war clubs favoured by the Hawai'ians, Walter knew that many would not survive.

The less injured were trying to care for the critically injured, using whatever means they had to stem the flow of blood or to pack the wounds as best as they could. The whimpering and groaning of the Englishmen cut through Walter like a sharp blade, and he tried to clear his mind of the intruding images of Omai dying in a place not far from where he was now. He laboured to control his breathing to ease the constriction in his chest.

Regaining control, he continued to look around, and he saw amongst the English, a man dressed in what would have been elegant and expensive clothing, except for now they were torn to shreds. The man's right arm was injured, covered in congealed blood from a long gash. Suddenly, as if struck by lightning, Walter spun about to face Kanoa.

"It's my brother, Jonathan!" Walter hissed at the surprised Kahuna.

"Your brother, Kekoa? No wonder you look like you've seen a ghost."

"Not a ghost, my friend, but my past."

Kanoa nodded. Walter knew that his friend understood the

dilemma he faced. They had often spoken about the conflict between himself and his brother.

Struggling in disbelief at Jonathan's sudden appearance, Walter shifted about restlessly, keeping his face averted while he tried to calm himself down and think the situation through. Hearing his brother's voice raised in protest, Walter turned to see Jonathan struggling to get to his knees. The warrior standing guard immediately pushed him back into the sand. Obviously frustrated by the ignominious treatment and the dire predicament he was in, Jonathan exclaimed loudly." For god's sake, will someone listen to me!"

Another warrior raised a war-club, threatening to hit Jonathan. Who's only response was to cower and plead, "No, please, please have mercy!"

Knowing that he had to intervene, Walter signalled the fighters to step back. He, in turn, walked over so he could look down at his brother. Without a thought, he said the first thing that came to his mind.

"Beaumont's do not beg for mercy, Jonathan!"

The words hung disturbingly between the two men. They were their father's words, used to admonish them as they grew up. Walter watched Jonathan's head snap up. An expression of disbelief crossed his face.

Walter understood what his brother was seeing. No longer the fashionable fop, he was now taller, broader, tanned and muscled from several years of physical training and surfing. He could have laughed at the confusion on Jonathan's face if it were not for the seriousness of the situation.

"Walter?" Jonathan said in a tentative, croaky voice.

"Yes, Jonathan, it's me. Walter paused, wondering what to do.

The situation between the Islanders and the crew of the ship was delicate. He needed time to think, but Jonathan started babbling at him.

"Thank God, Walter, I have found you! But what has happened to you? Why have you gone, native?"

Walter did not reply immediately. Kahahana would not be

pleased with this. His plans for the opportunity to trade, and maybe even forge an alliance with the English could be ruined by the enmity created by his brother's actions. Either of those options would be much more complicated now after the death of some of Kahahana's own people and the loss of life amongst the crew of the ship. Walter remembered well Kanoa's attempts at dissuading Kahahana from invading Kauai after the attack by Koa and Kumahana. It had not been easy. The Ali'i Nui was not a forgiving man, and he had only reluctantly agreed not to retaliate.

Feeling somewhat overwhelmed by the potential disaster of this encounter, Walter snapped at his brother, telling him that they would speak later. Not unexpectedly, this did not suit Jonathan, who tried to jump up, only to be instantly felled by a blow of the guard's fist to the back of his head. The Englishman collapsed to the ground while Walter glared at the warrior, who shrugged his shoulders apologetically. Walter looked down at his unconscious brother. Jonathan had come back into his life like a phantom from the past, and he felt torn between wanting to welcome him, and wishing that he had never come here and put everything that Walter loved at risk. Then, of course, there were all the old wounds from the conflicts between them. Walter had to acknowledge that there was a part of him that liked the reversal in their circumstances. Unlike their positions at home, here he was the one with the power to cause Jonathan pain, and to make him afraid.

Walter stopped, not liking where he was going with his wild thoughts of revenge. Surely, he had seen enough of what hatred could do. Had he and Kanoa not talked about the need to rise above such things as ambition, hate, and power for power's sake?

Just as Walter was starting to formulate a plan, a group of Kahahana's personal guard arrived on the beach with instructions to take the prisoners to a secure pen. When Walter informed them that his brother was one of the Englishmen, he was assured that they had been told to ensure that the prisoners were provided with food and water and protected from retribution by the families of the dead warriors.

Walter turned to Palani and asked him to take him to the

survivors of the battle, and over the next few hours, Walter managed to piece together more details of the conflict between the Islanders and the English.

The warriors confirmed that it had been Jonathan who had ordered the sailors to take the warriors who had boarded the ship as hostages, to force the Hawai'ians to trade them for Walter, or news of Walter.

But they had taken a chief, and his warriors, men who were not prepared to accept being treated with such disrespect, and they had fought their way off the ship. When the Hawai'ians, amidst gunfire, and closely followed by longboats full of sailors, arrived on the beach, they had been joined by a large contingent of warriors. Completely unprepared to face a formidable force of skilled warriors, the English quickly sustained heavy losses and were forced to surrender.

Returning to the village, Walter sought an audience with Kaha-hana and told him what he knew. As he had feared the chief was furious at the insult to his people, but he was also determined to find a way to make the arrival of the Pelekané open up the opportunities for trade and alliances that he had been hoping for. After some discussion, Walter was given permission to continue to investigate what his brother wanted and then report back to Kahahana and his council.

Chapter Forty-Nine

*I*n the dimly lit ha'lau, Walter sat back on the raised dais covered in mats. Lani and Kanoa flanked him, while armed warriors lined the walls of the hall. He had deliberately dressed in a regal yellow and red cloak, helmet and malo. Large feather-tipped Kahili, the royal standards that honoured Lani framed the outer edges of the dais.

Walter looked around at his retinue. He wanted to make sure that there was no doubt about who was in charge. As one by one of the Hawaiians settled into their places around the walls, Walter was satisfied that he and Lani had created an elaborate royal theatre to impress any European. Then nodding to his chief warrior, he pounded his massive koa-wood staff on the ground to alert the guards that he was ready to receive the prisoner. Two guards disappeared through the doorway, and after a short time, there was a barely audible commotion just outside the door, and a moment later, the guards returned with an indignant Jonathan. Although he was not bound, the way the guards half carried, half dragged him, left Jonathan with little independent movement.

At the edge of a row of stones, the guards stopped, and Walter watched as they forced Jonathan to his knees with his head down, pleased that his brother had decided to remain silent. Imagining what his brother must be thinking of the spectacle in front of him, Walter smiled wryly at Jonathan as he strained to lift his head to get a better look at the stage before one of the guards quickly pushed his head down toward the ground.

Signalling the guards to step back from the prostrate man in front of him, Walter spoke in a deliberately calm and authoritative voice.

"So, Jonathan, what shall we do here?".

Jonathan, obviously angry at being treated as a prisoner, lifted his head and glared at Walter.

"Is the way you are going to treat your brother, Walter? Like a criminal?"

"Jonathan, it is your actions that have resulted in this treatment of you. In fact, you are lucky to be alive. Another chief would have killed you for what you did on the ship, and then on the beach." Walter paused. "So, for now, it is necessary, and until we have established what to do Jonathan, you will remain under, how shall I put it... my protection. After all, your behaviour was an act of war. And let me be clear with you, any breach of the law on this Island is punishable by death."

Looking shocked, Jonathan chose not to reply.

Kanoa leant towards Walter. "Think carefully on how you will treat your brother, Kekoa."

Walter looked at the Kahuna and frowned. "What do you mean?"

"Did you not tell me how it pained you to be mistreated by this man? Do you wish to continue the past, or forge a new future?"

Walter pondered Kanoa's words and decided that his friend was right. He had allowed himself to use the situation to be revengeful and unnecessarily harsh with Jonathan. "Thank you, Kahu. As always, you see the truth."

Walter turned back to Jonathan. "You need to understand that your actions have jeopardised my position here. I can only protect you and the ship's crew if you agree to abide by the laws here. Is that understood?"

Walter watched his brother closely. Hints of various emotions crossed Jonathan's face as the man tried to fathom the situation. What lingered was Jonathan's puzzled expression.

"Walter, I must confess that I assumed that your circumstances here were quite different and that you would welcome a chance to return home. Looking around, I can see that this does not appear to be the case. So my question to you is where to from here?"

Walter got up and stepped down from the platform and placed his hands on his brother's shoulders. "First, let's put the past behind us, Jonathan."

Walter pulled Jonathan gently to his feet. The two men looked at each other for a moment, and then Walter embraced Jonathan. For all of the conflict and rivalry throughout their childhood, Walter knew that they were still family, and he wanted very much to prove to both Jonathan and himself that he held no grudges.

Clearly touched by Walter and Jonathan's reunion, the warriors began pounding their spears on the ground and amidst the resonating sound, one of them began to loudly recite an epic poem honouring the memory of a cherished brother. As the man's voice climbed above the slowly diminishing sound of the pounding spears, Kanoa and Lani joined the two men, and with the formalities completed, they ushered Jonathan and Walter out of the ha'lau into the bright sunshine.

Over the next few days, Walter unveiled to Jonathan the life he had created on Oahu. He would take Jonathan on long walks around the kauhale's surrounding land, and while Kahahana expressed reservations in meeting with the English after the battle, he had given Walter the freedom to host them as guests, as long as they did not venture too far from the compound without guards. This was not a problem as most of the sailors and soldiers on the Island were still recovering from their injuries, and Jonathan, on Walter's request, had sent a messenger to the ship explaining the situation and ordering them to stay anchored, and under no circumstances to disembark.

One morning walking through the compound, which was, as usual, a hive of activity, Walter and Jonathan were chatting casually when Jonathan made an observation. "I am impressed, Walter. You have really excelled here in convincing them to keep you alive in a manner befitting a Beaumont."

Walter found himself irritated at Jonathan's implication that he had manipulated his position, and he quickly pointed out to his brother that he had not only earned the privileges that he now had, but that it was the generosity and help of the people he now called friends and family, that had made his life here possible.

And that was the opening that Jonathan had apparently been waiting for. "Walter, let me be blunt. When will you be ready to come home with me?" In the past few days, the two had spoken about many things, but both had avoided getting to the heart of Jonathan's reason for being there. Walter now knew that the news of Captain Cook's death had deeply shaken the Admiralty and that his family's concern for his well being led to this attempt to discover his fate, but Walter had avoided being drawn into anything further by Jonathan.

Walter stopped and looked at his brother. "What gives you the impression that I am prepared to leave?"

"I... I naturally assumed that you would be only too eager to trade this for your return to England to live out your destiny." Jonathan replied tentatively.

"Jonathan, your destiny is in England. You were born to it. I have chosen my destiny. It is here. I have a wife and a son who would not thrive in the cold of England, let alone find acceptance amongst our peers. And on top of that, Lani is the heir to the throne of Kauai, and she is expected to return to her home so that she and Kaimana can take their place amongst their own people. She is not free to join me if I return to England." Walter shook his head emphatically. "No, there is nothing I yearn to return to, Jonathan. Except for Mother... and Edward."

Jonathan looked down to the ground, a frown on his face. "I didn't know how to tell you Walter, Edward is missing in the colonies. His regiment was ambushed by the rebels and their Indian allies, and they were wiped out, but Edward's body was never recovered. He is, "Jonathan drew a deep breath, "presumed dead."

Walter was stunned. He tried to digest this news and realised that despite his fears for his friend, he had never really believed that Edward would fall victim to the war. He felt a wave of grief wash over him, and a terrible fear at the thought of yet another loss of a dear friend.

Jonathan fell silent showing some unexpected sensitivity and giving Walter some time to recover from the shock, and they continued their walk in silence for a while. When Jonathan did speak again, it was to quietly tell Walter that their mother missed him a great deal and that she would find it difficult to understand why Walter didn't want to return home.

Walter stopped and turned to look at his brother. He had thought about this a lot since Jonathan had arrived, literally on his doorstep, and he knew in his heart that his life was here with Lani and Kaimana.

"Look, Jonathan, you have found me, and I am safe and well. You can tell Mother that I have chosen my own destiny, and that for the first time in my life, I am truly happy. She will understand."

Walter watched Jonathan closely, knowing that his brother did not fully appreciate why he had chosen this life, so remote from England, and he knew his brother well. Jonathan would not readily accept that he had failed in his goal to take Walter home. But right now, Walter just wanted time to grieve for Edward, and when his brother tried to continue the conversation, he shut it down firmly.

"Enough, Jonathan! In a few days, your ship will be repaired. You have enough crew left to sail her safely to the nearest harbour, where you can pick up more men for your journey home." Walter stopped and looked out to sea. "Jonathan, the news of Edward has been most distressing, and right now, I want some time to myself. We can talk later."

Jonathan agreed, but Walter could hear the reluctance in his brother's voice. Not surprising really, Walter thought, given that Jonathan always sought to get his own way by sheer force of his will.

As Walter went to leave Jonathan with his shipmates, his brother again pressed him. "We need to talk this through. Mother and

Father expected you to come home if you were still alive. What am I to tell them? That you prefer to live like a native on an island?!"

Walter was sad and emotional, but he took a deep breath, and instead of reacting angrily, he merely told Jonathan they would discuss it later. Then knowing that he wanted to be alone, he headed to the beach to watch the waves and give himself time to deal with the loss of his childhood friend.

Over the next few days as the repairs to Jonathan's ship were completed and provisions of fresh food and water loaded, the two brothers spent many hours together. At first, Jonathan continued to try to persuade Walter to return home, telling him about his burgeoning business and the plans that he and their father had put in place to increase the families wealth. He promised Walter a role in this new mercantile empire and insisted that their parents would embrace Lani and Kaimana, but as Walter continued to resist, Jonathan appeared to finally accept Walter's decision that his life was here in Hawaii.

Walter had organised a farewell for Jonathan and his men, and so when the day of departure arrived, he and his family and household were all on the beach with the gifts that he had prepared for Jonathan, and his parents, ready to be loaded onto the longboats. It was then that Walter realised that Jonathan had not given up trying to persuade him to return to England.

"So, Walter, are you certain that there is nothing I can say that will influence you to change your mind?"

"Nothing at all, Jonathan. Give my love to Mother, and tell Father that he has nothing to fear from his maker. I have well and truly forgiven him for the past."

Jonathan reacted angrily, his face red. "Stop being unreasonable, Walter!" Jonathan lowered his voice glancing nervously at Palani, who was obviously getting agitated, his war club a prominent reminder of the danger the Englishmen still faced. "Father will not like this at all, nor will Mother. You must come home, I beseech you." He paused briefly. "You can always return if you wish."

Walter placed his hands calmly on Jonathan's shoulders, using the pressure of his grip as a warning to Jonathan that he was crossing into dangerous grounds.

"You have done what you can, Jonathan. Now go, leave me be."

Apparently infuriated by Walter's obstinate refusal to see reason, Jonathan abruptly turned away and took a few steps towards the longboat, then he suddenly stopped and turned, his sword in his hand. In a flash, Jonathan had its tip at Walter's throat.

Walter immediately raised his hand to stall any retaliation from his warriors, having seen Palani from the corner of his eye raise his war club in readiness.

"Walter, you have left me no choice. I will take you back to England, willingly or not."

Walter stood still looking at his brother when, on cue, an overwhelming number of warriors appeared along the edge of the forest lining the beach. Earlier, anticipating that Jonathan may resort to some form of coercion if he could not rely on his persuasive abilities, Walter had instructed his warriors and sought the aid of his allies, to make a show of power, but they knew they were not resort to violence unless absolutely necessary.

The soldiers and the boat crew were startled and readied their weapons.

"Jonathan, you have already made this mistake once. There are some things you just cannot obtain by force. Please, go home and live out the destiny you were born to and leave me to mine."

Jonathan looked torn and uncertain. He shook his head as if to clear his thoughts. "So, this is how it ends, Walter?"

"Only if this is the way that you want it to end," Walter replied. His words hung in the air for a moment, while Jonathan hesitated. He surveyed the intimidating warriors. Suddenly Jonathan's face crumpled, and he dropped his sword only to burst into tears. He reached across and embraced Walter.

When Jonathan finally let Walter go, he stepped back, his face full of remorse. "Forgive me, Walter, for everything. I had no right to do any of this to you." He put his hand on Walter's shoulder. Jonathan's hand lingered for a moment, then slowly withdrew it. "You've become a better man than me."

"I forgive you, Jonathan. We are brothers, and I want you to go with my blessing, knowing that the enmities of the past no longer need to define either of us."

As Jonathan nodded with relief, Walter motioned to one of his retainers. The man handed him a wrapped package and an ornately carved staff.

"Jonathan, I want you to take this staff and remember me by it. May it bring you strength and wisdom." He passed the staff over to his brother. "And here is my journal. I want you to take it with you, and give it to Mother upon your return. You will be helping me keep at least part of my promise."

Walter passed the package across, and Jonathan took it carefully into his hands. Far from being the small journal it started as, it was now a large and somewhat bulky volume of work, containing an impressive record of Walter's life in the Hawai'ian Islands. "You have my word, Walter."

"Then now that you have accepted that I will be here on Oahu with your sister in law and nephew, there is no reason why the family business interests cannot bring you back to these shores. The Mo' i, our king, needs some time to settle the anger that still exists amongst his people over the death of his warriors at your hands, but in the future, the opportunity for trade remains a possibility. There is no reason why we cannot see each other again."

Then, turning to Lani, who had been watching the brothers under the protection of Kanoa, Walter gestured for her and Kaimana to join him. Walter knew that despite all of his faults, his brother had been quick to embrace his nephew, whose dark curly hair, was contrasted by his father's piercing blue eyes.

Walter bent down and spoke lovingly to the boy. "Kaimana, it is time to say goodbye to your Uncle."

"Aloha, Uncle."

Jonathan bent down and kissed Kaimana on the cheek and fondly ruffled his hair. "Goodbye, my boy."

He then turned to Walter. "Well then, goodbye, Walter. Stay well and perhaps we will see each other again, sometime soon." Jonathan paused as a smile spread across his face." I am taking this opportunity to explore new avenues for the family business, and as you have so rightly pointed out, I now know where you live."

Walter laughed. "You are always welcome in my home Jonathan. I wish you the very best, and should we see each other again then be it with love."

Jonathan hesitated for a moment. He looked at them with tears in his eyes. "I came looking for my brother, and I have found a family. I do hope that there will be a chance for us to meet again."

Lani stepped up to him, pulling him close and Jonathan kissed her on the cheek, and then with a nod to Walter, he turned and boarded the boat with the crew as they shoved off.

Watching the skiff and the longboats as they headed out to the ship, Walter could see that Jonathan was turned towards the shore, and raising his hand in farewell, he hoped that his brother would come to understand why he wanted to stay on Oahu. As the melancholic drone of conch shells rose into the air, he saw Jonathan raise his hat in a final gesture of farewell.

Looking down at Lani, who with Kaimana in her arms leant into him, he affectionately placed his arm around her and the boy and pulled them close. Then together with their household, they watched the ship as it weighed anchor and sailed out of the bay.

Chapter Fifty

*W*alter couldn't sleep despite lying comfortably next to Lani, a rare pleasure in these islands where men and women slept apart. His mind was filled with thoughts he could not put aside. They had come with Kahahana's court to the northern part of the island where the winter swells rolled towards the shore, and where only the bravest amongst them dared to venture into the ocean to surf the mountainous peaks.

As he stared into the dark, he could hear the newly arriving swell pound the shore, reverberating through the bedrock like an earthquake. The sound and the vibration conjured up images in his mind of rising swells that towered towards the sky and then tumbled and broke into an avalanche of white water that would rush towards the rocky shore. Walter slid his hand from underneath the covers and let it rest gently on the ground where he could feel the subtle vibration from each breaking wave.

Since Jonathan's departure for England, he had not anticipated that he would ever compose a letter to his mother again, but now in the dark of the night, he found it comforting to think of what he would convey to her.

"Dear Mother,

Watching Jonathan leave closed a chapter in my heart that freed me to focus on my future here in the Islands.

Hours from now, I face the challenge of riding the giant waves. The Mountains of the seas that my dear friend Omai left his homeland to ride. Hearing the waves pound, the shoreline has my heart bursting out of my chest in anticipation of what lies ahead. Kanoa says that what these waves can do to a man is far crueller than what Koa's treachery could have forced upon me.

Should something happen to me, rest assured that Lani and Kaimana will not want for anything, for they have family and position here in their own homeland. Most importantly, remember that I have lived, for whatever time I have had, in a way that has left me fulfilled as nothing else could have."

Gently, he took Lani's hand into his. She was fast asleep, so she barely stirred. As she nuzzled comfortably into his chest Walter deeply inhaled the scent of her, and as always, it seemed to calm his nerves, and he slowly drifted off to sleep.

At sunrise the next morning, Walter was waiting at the edge of the surf, watching the priests in their ritual of mixing the water, and blessing the surfers. Hundreds of people chanted in unison, calling the swells from the deep ocean, and with each repetition of the chant, the voices became progressively more urgent and forceful.

As the rituals followed their prescribed course, a large group of Ali'i, led by Kahahana and Kamehameha were waiting patiently at the edge of the water for the massive shore break to subside, so they could paddle out into the surf. Then, choosing the right moment, they all leapt into the sea, their powerful muscles propelling them swiftly across the surface of the ocean.

Taking his eyes off the group heading out to the break, Walter focused on the men and women already out the back and saw one of the surfers catch a wave right into the beach, successfully passing the pua, the marker showing the endpoint of the ride. As the man closed in on the shore, he was greeted with shouts of approval from the crowd, and waving graciously in acknowledgement, a broad smile visible on his face he turned around and then quickly headed back out to sea.

On the beach, Walter watched the ever-increasing size of the waves with some apprehension while his friend Kanoa excitedly paced up and down, grinning from ear to ear. Turning away from the spectacle he saw Lani walking up the beach towards them, Kaimana perched on her shoulders, his little body bouncing up and down and his face lit with excitement. Walter had been honest with Lani about his unease, and his fear that he was far too inexperienced for this contest, and as she reached his side, he could see that she was worried. He tried to give her a reassuring smile, but he was sure that it must have looked more like an anxious grimace.

"Lani, wish me luck." Walter rubbed his arms anxiously, trying to loosen his tense muscles.

Lani kissed him and smiled. "Be true to your name, and all will be well."

Walter smiled, bent over, and kissed his son's head. The little boy instinctively reached over and dug his hands into his father's long, blond hair, which he had tied up into a topknot. Carefully and patiently, he untangled Kaimana's small but persistent hand and held it for a moment, before looking back at Lani. "I will do my best."

Then taking a last look at the face of his wife and son, Walter joined Kanoa, and dragging the long olo boards to the edge of the water, they launched themselves into the heaving ocean.

Avoiding the pounding white water, the two men deftly manoeuvred their boards into the channel. It was a long paddle out to the swell, and so when they arrived, they sat up to catch their breath and regain their strength, as the others already lined up behind the break greeted them enthusiastically. The banter will soon start, Walter thought. It always did.

Walter sat quietly on his long, masterfully carved olo, staring out to sea, letting the sound of the others chatting around him fade into the background. It occurred to Walter that he was never quite clear where something began and where it ended. Where had this journey really started? And, more importantly, where would it end? How, for instance, had he found himself in these islands, let alone, right now, in the ocean waiting for his turn to catch an enormous wave to shore, on a piece of wood? Had someone suggested this to him a few years ago, he would have doubled over with laughter. Yet here he was, a fish out of water. But then again had that not been how he had felt at home? Amused by his own contradictory circumstances, he suddenly realised that no, he was no longer a fish out of water, he had become a fish in the sea.

The sheer beauty of his surroundings awed him. He could never get enough of the ocean here, nor the land for that matter. As he waited for the next set of waves, he again examined his board, an exquisitely shaped plank of wiliwili, a wood almost as light as balsa. Kanoa had done an excellent job with the unusual wood, and Walter felt a sense of gratitude well up in him. He had come to love the Kahuna like a father.

The call for the surf to rise higher and higher floated across the ocean, resonating in the depth of his being, filling him with both excitement and fear. As if the surf needed to be any bigger than it was today. More massive than anything he'd ever ridden before, he felt a real sense of trepidation as he watched each set of waves thunder towards the shore.

Tuning in to the buzz of the conversation going on around him, he could feel the excitement that had charged the atmosphere, and he listened as the Hawai'ians boasted about their surfing prowess. They were egging each other on and making light of the size of the swell. All of them knew the potential harm that could result from what they were doing. Death was one possibility, and at best, it would prove to be quick and relatively painless. At its worst, it would result in a severe injury causing the sufferer to linger for weeks or months before succumbing to his injuries. Despite that, or perhaps because of it, they kept challenging each other to ride bigger and bigger waves.

Walter looked across at Kamehameha, who sat quietly nearby. He, like Walter, appeared to have chosen not to engage in any boastful banter and they smiled at each other, just as the energy in the group changed prompting Walter to refocus his attention back out to sea, where he could see a set of towering waves building up and heading towards the excited group. Kanoa, the only Kahuna surfing, that day raised his voice so that it was heard by all the surfers.

"Today, we ride these mountains of the sea, but tomorrow, only the gods will ride them!"

Walter knew that Kanoa's ritual observation heralded an even bigger swell over the next day or so, where only superhuman strength could master these elements. Steeling himself for what was to come, Walter's determination to find the courage to challenge the ocean had him focusing inward, and so while the banter resumed, he turned his attention back to the horizon.,

Kanoa paddled up to him. "Kekoa," the man's deep, resonant voice brought Walter back into the present, "just take your time, and don't rush into the wave."

Walter fought back the rising fear that wanted to turn into a panic, knowing that if he couldn't do so, it would be to his peril.

"Be the warrior, my friend!" Kanoa's voice was firm and forceful, but reassuring. "These are the waves that Omai came here to surf. So let us honour him here and now."

Walter knew that this is what he wanted to do. He wanted to surf these mountains for Omai as much as for himself, and lifting his head high and straightening his back, he looked at Kanoa and nodded in agreement.

"I am ready, let's go."

Kanoa grinned at him, then swung his board around and took off on a wave, and as he dropped down its steep face, he disappeared from Walter's sight.

Walter chose to take the next wave rather than wait any longer. His training and experience had taught him that the sooner he took off on a wave, the better, as it settled his fear. From the very instant he saw the rising swell, he moved into a well-rehearsed piece of choreography, and shifting his weight back on the olo, he quickly swung his board towards the shore. Lying down, he dipped his arms deep into the water, using all of his power to pull through his stroke and push the big board across the water.

Accompanied by the cheers of the other surfers, and with single-minded determination, he began to paddle into the wave for the

take-off. For the first few strokes, the olo seemed to be taking forever
to gain any forward momentum, so Walter dug deeper into the
water, paddling harder and harder. His efforts were quickly
rewarded, and the board began to glide with increasing speed across
the surface, and in seconds the velocity of the board matched that
of the wave.

Walter knew that timing was everything in surfing. Good judgment meant the difference between an exhilarating ride towards the
shore, where he would be greeted by an enthusiastic crowd or, alter-
natively, a crushing wipe-out under tons of churning water pushing
him into the depths of the sea and holding him there, his lungs
burning with the need for air.

As the angle of the face of the wave began to increase it lifted
him up, and in a split second, Walter leapt to his feet and began the
precarious descent down the face of the wave. In that instant,
nothing else existed in Walter's mind. He had a single purpose, to
make the wave. The reward of many hours of practice was that his
body had learnt what it needed to do, without any conscious
thought.

Continuing down the face of the wave, every fibre in Walter's
body was alert and ready for the crucial turn at the bottom. There,
the forces of nature would drive him to the critical section of the
wave, away from the danger of the crashing lip and the ensuing
thundering, frothing white water trying to envelop him. Walter
suddenly realised that the waves had been breaking faster than he
had thought. Before he could turn the board to the right, the enormous lip of the wave came thundering down on top of him.

Disappearing into the depth of the ocean, he was tossed and
tumbled in the white froth like a small rag doll. Unable to escape the
increasing pressure of tons of water, he was driven down into the
depths of the sea. There was a piercing pain in his ears, but as he
swallowed, he managed to equalise the pressure, and the relief was
instant.

Walter's mind, screaming for oxygen, had only one desire, to
fight to the surface so that he could breathe again. From hard-won
experience, he knew all too well that to surrender to that desire now

was to invite disaster. To try and fight the ocean meant that his body would burn the precious air in his lungs faster than necessary, cutting the time he had underwater to a dangerously slim margin. Unless he was close to the surface, he definitely risked drowning.

He felt like he had been underwater forever, but the wave continued to drive him deeper and deeper towards the treacherous bottom of the sea. As his body was ceaselessly tumbled about, Kanoa's calm and steady voice penetrated his surging panic. "Kekoa, relax, preserve your strength. If you don't fight the ocean, she will take care of you, and you will live."

Conditioned by his mentor's instructions, Walter let go, surrendering to the warm ocean, and letting it do with him what it would. His mind having quietened made the experience feel almost surreal, in fact, it now felt comforting and opening his eyes, Walter could suddenly make out columns of clear water reaching towards the surface. He kicked into one them, and, within seconds, he broke the green-blue surface, his grateful lungs drawing in life-giving air. 'Made it!'

As he looked around, he noticed that the Hawai'ians were scanning the ocean, their faces marred by concern. He waved to them, signalling that he was all right. They casually waved back, but their expressions didn't change, and he heard them shout back at him.

He was still trying to catch his breath to prepare for the long swim in after his board which luckily had ended up in the riptide, so while he was swimming in towards the shore, it was floating back out to sea. With powerful strokes, Walter covered the distance between himself and the olo, battling with the movement of the water and the currents, that pulled him in different directions, but he was resolute and managed to cut efficiently through the water.

Back on the board, he sat on it, trying to catch his breath and regain some of his composure, and having recovered somewhat he started to paddle back out, only to realise that in the time he had been preoccupied with retrieving the olo, the surf had been getting bigger and bigger. Fewer were making the drop on the waves successfully, and a number of the boards lay shattered on the rocky shore.

Waves up to twenty-five feet now thundered into the bay. Yet Kanoa, Kahahana, Kamehameha and a handful of others continued to surf the massive waves. To cope with the large sets, they moved further and further out to sea and appeared like small specks on the ocean.

As Walter rested again in the channel, Kahahana and Kamehameha successfully took off on successive waves, surfing as close to the beach as they could, then paddling to the shore to the roaring cheers of the onlookers.

Kanoa and Walter were now amongst the few remaining surfers in the water. On the horizon, ominous storm clouds were crowding the sky, and from time to time, lightning flashed, followed by claps of thunder. The two friends looked at each other, knowing only too well what the ominous weather meant. They had reached their limits of skill and endurance.

"I think this is the moment of truth, Kanoa."

Kanoa nodded gravely. "I know."

Walter drew a deep breath. "I want you to know that whatever happens today, I owe you a great debt of gratitude."

"The debt has been well repaid, Kekoa." Kanoa smiled. "You are more than my apprentice, you are like a son to me." He stopped for a moment. "Whatever happens now, I want you to know that you have become a great man. Never forget that."

Without another word, Kanoa spun his board around and paddled into the next massive wave, while Walter frantically paddled up the mounting, steep face of the monster. Clearing the crest, he was immediately confronted with another set in the distance.

Kanoa took off on the massive wave, and as he took the drop, the rail of the board caught so that Kanoa and his board sprawled across the smooth but massive face of the wave, only to be sucked into the thundering falls of the crashing lip, disappearing into the cascading water.

Focusing his gaze to scan the surf and see how Kanoa had fared, Walter was unable to find any sign of the Kahuna. Concerned, he paddled closer towards the shore, bringing him dangerously close to the impact zone when suddenly, Kanoa broke the surface. He floated there on his back for an instant, obviously trying to catch his breath before waving his arm, however, Walter could see that his other arm was dangling uselessly by his side.

Walter swiftly paddled towards him as behind him another enormous wave built up. "No, Kekoa!" Kanoa's voice was almost drowned out by a tremendous clap of thunder, followed by the sharp crack of lightning slashing the deep, grey sky. Sheets of rain began to fall, cutting the visibility to only a short distance.

At that moment, the massive wave pitched up and collapsed down, rolling like an avalanche towards the shore. First, Walter, and then Kanoa, disappeared beneath the turbulent white water. Moments passed, when Walter suddenly resurfaced and, mustering all his strength, swam to reach the Kahuna.

In the churning, watery chaos, the two men were now being pushed into the 'bone yard', that deadly place, where the white water impacts on the razor-sharp volcanic rocks. But despite the apparent danger, Walter never hesitated and bravely forced his way towards his injured friend.

On the shore, the crowd was silent. They have seen Kanoa disappear under the churning power of the waves and watched helplessly as first the Kahuna, and then Walter had gone under again. In the poor visibility, Kahahana and Kamehameha had difficulty making out what was taking place, but they knew that the two men in the ocean were in dire peril and they ordered their warriors to immediately go to their assistance. Without hesitation, several of the men instantly launched themselves into the ocean.

Meanwhile, Walter had reached Kanoa and had pulled him close, just in time to shield his friend from the deadly rocks. Another avalanche of white water reached them, pushing them under and pounding them against the rocks. Once more the two struggled to the surface, Walter trying to protect Kanoa as much as he could but now he was severely injured as well, and as the two of them clung to each other Walter could feel his strength ebbing away as both of them were persistently battered, their blood spreading through the foaming sea.

Weakening, Walter looked up to see that other surfers had

reached them and he was relieved to see Kanoa being pulled onto a board. Before the same could be done for him, however, another surge pulled him down into the depths of the water. In the churning sea, Walter lost his bearings, and as he swam towards what he thought was the surface, he violently struck the bottom, sending searing pain through his head.

A moment of calm enveloped Walter, wherein the old woman's face suddenly manifested in his mind. Her image stayed for a moment, swirling like smoke, and then it faded out. As he tried to make sense out of the vision, he searched the water for the signs that would lead him to safety, and he saw his shark-tooth necklace rising in front of his face as if it was guiding him towards the surface. Instinctively, Walter followed its direction, and he pushed up into the frantic hands grappling to get a hold of him.

One of the rescuers dove into the frothing ocean and came up beside him, and with his help, Walter was able to get into a position that made it possible for the others to grab him and pull him onto a board. As they arrived in the shallows, men wadded out from the beach to meet them, and Walter and Kanoa were carried to the shore.

Walter was aware that they had reached safety, and he tried to gather his senses. A healer was looking at his wounds, and he saw the look of concern on the man's face as he looked at Kahahana, who was close by.

Through a veil of blood seeping into his eyes, Walter saw several women already tending to Kanoa who was lying near him, and he had started to relax a bit when Lani reached his side. Stifling sobs, she dropped to her knees to cradle him in her arms, tears streaming down her face.

"Lani?" Walter's voice croaked, barely audible.

"Quiet, my love, I am here." She carefully brushed the bloody hair from his forehead, where he knew there was a deep gash that leaked more blood down his face, mingling with the saltwater and rain.

Walter waved his arm around. "Kanoa?"

The Kahuna called out to him. "I'm here, Kekoa. Thanks to you."

Walter smiled weakly, closing his eyes.

"That is good."

Satisfied that Kanoa was safe, Walter's remaining desire was to surrender to the fatigue spreading through his body, drawing him into a black pit of seductive oblivion. But Lani, gently tapping his face, forced him to focus on her.

"My love," Walter struggled to speak, "stay with me." His hand reached for hers, and she squeezed him tenderly. Bending over him she softly touched her forehead and nose to his and whispered. "Forever and always."

Then he felt her kiss his lips and vaguely heard her organising a stretcher, and he slipped into unconsciousness, the pain of being moved overwhelming him as he was lifted from the ground.

The next time that Walter was aware of anything, it was to find himself in his own kauhale, lying comfortably on his own matts with Kaimana poking him and telling him to wake up. Turning his head to look around, he was suddenly assailed by a burning pain across his forehead, but as he tried to lift his hand to his wound, he realised that his arm was aching as well.

Lani's voice caught his attention, then other voices, and as he focused his eyes, he saw that there were several people around him. He wanted to speak, to ask Lani about Kanoa, but he found himself slipping back into sleep, conscious of a little hand stroking his face.

Over the next few days, he was conscious of small periods of wakefulness and of being tended to by the healer and Lani, and although they had reassured him that Kanoa was safe and healing well, Walter didn't truly relax until the day he heard the big man's voice at the door of his kauhale.

It had taken months for all of his injuries to heal and many more for him to rebuild his strength. There had been many poems told of that day, the day he had ridden the Mountains of the Sea. Lani proudly told him that when they had brought him back from the beach that day the crowd had honoured him as a hero with the ritual chant 'Aia ho'i, ke kanaka no kaulu lanai". But all of those who had challenged themselves in those waves were hero's in Walter's mind. He was just glad he had survived it.

Now standing on the north shore, he and Kanoa were watching the waves rolling in towards them. 'Will you ride the mountains again, Kekoa?' Walter looked at the Kahuna and smiled. "I have a few months before the really huge waves arrive to ready myself, but yes I think I will." Kanoa grinned back at him. "Then we need to practice, eh?" And they both burst out laughing.

Walter looked back and waved to Lani, who stood up on the beach with Kaimana. She had to hold onto the young boy, who was straining against her, obviously wanting to join his father. But struggle as he might, Lani would not let him go.

Walter lowered his board to the ground, stretched himself out and then lifted the olo up and laid it onto the water. He nimbly jumped onto the board and confidently, without any hesitation, paddled out to the perfectly formed waves, closely followed by Kanoa. They climbed the ever steeper faces of the waves until they reached the take-off zone, joining the other Hawaiians who were taking advantage of the swell.

In the crisp sunshine, Walter swung the olo towards the shore and paddled into a colossal swell. In slow motion, the graceful and athletic figure got to his feet and dropped down the smooth face of the wave and disappeared from sight in the deep trough, only to reappear a moment later, having trimmed the board into the perfect glide.

Epilogue

$\mathcal{T}$housands of miles away, across the globe, it was a typical grey, cold English night, the rain pouring steadily down and drenching Plymouth as Jonathan's ship finally settled at its mooring by the dock. It had been, beyond a doubt a long journey back, he thought as he looked across the bleak, grey harbour, its surface broken by the falling rain. He was eager to get home to the Manor, and had arranged for a coach to drive him through the night.

After leaving the Sandwich Islands, Jonathan and the remaining crew had been forced to endure a slow journey as their ship limped back to Batavia, where the vessel could be refitted and resupplied for the journey back to England. He had been able to send a letter home via a merchant ship to let his parents know Walter was alive, but it had taken another six weeks before his ship had been able to leave Sumatra and make its way slowly back home.

Now, back in the cold climate of the Northern hemisphere, a weathered Jonathan walked down the gangplank lit by torches, to the waiting coach. Under one arm he had a large package, Walter's journal, and in the other, the staff Walter had given him. Since that day on the beach of Oahu, when his brother had given it to him, it had rarely left his hand, and he now twirled it expertly around his fingers, a trick that had taken quite some time to learn. He stepped into the coach, and as he settled into the leather seat, the coachman secured several large trunks and bags on top, readying the coach to leave.

Early the next morning as the coach rolled through the majestic gates and then proceeded up the winding road to the great house, Jonathan found himself grateful that the Manor was brightly lit up in the dark of the pre-dawn, welcoming a weary traveller. Looking out the window, he could see George run down the stairs ready to attend him the moment the carriage stopped, and he took a deep breath, feeling enormously relieved to be home.

Jonathan greeted George as the servant opened the carriage door and helped him step down onto the drive, then looked up to see his parents and several other members of his family hurrying down the stairs to greet him, and he found himself caught in a massive embrace with his father. Jonathan held onto him for a long time, then as the two men finally let go, he turned to his mother and kissed her on the cheek before hugging her.

Retrieving Walter's journal from the seat of the carriage, he turned back and handed it to her as his brother had requested. Lady Beaumont looked at it for a moment, and then with tears in her eyes she smiled clutching it to her chest as if it was Walter himself who had returned to her.

About the Author

Born in Vienna, Austria, a landlocked country, Gunter's family migrated to Australia in the early seventies when he was twelve years old. They settled on the Northern Beaches of Sydney, an epicentre of surfing and surfing greats. He immediately acclimatised to the outdoor lifestyle and forged a deep relationship with the ocean that focused on surfing.

Through surfing he developed an abiding passion and respect for the culture and history of the South Pacific. This eventually extended to other seafaring cultures.

His interest in what makes us human, led Gunter to study philosophy, psychology whilst pursuing a continuing passion for history and archaeology.

Professionally, Gunter trained as a psychologist and has now three decades of experience in psychotherapy, coaching, and training in organisations.

Furthermore he has extensive experience in the design and delivery of health education programs of promotion and rehabilitation services. In the early 80s he was involved in both drug and alcohol education services and, at the onset of the HIV/AIDS challenge, was involved in education support of health professionals in relationship to the issue.

As a result of his working addiction is it became very involved in post-dramatic stress disorder as is dealing with the number comes misleading consulting on this issue in organisations and private hospitals looking to provide individual programs for sufferers of the disorder it into you should treat people suffering from the consequences of trauma on regular basis.

Through his work in his private practice on the Northern Beaches of Sydney, Gunter became more and more conscious of the decline in men's mental health and more broadly, their struggle to adapt to the changes in gender and cultural norms around themselves and women. He began to critically analyse what was going on with men in society. He is now considered a specialist in men's mental health and works almost exclusively with men.

In partnership with his wife, Lorin, a mental health specialist and feminist philosopher in her own right, he launched a project called *Making Good Men Great*. It's aim is to help men understand the destructiveness of patriarchy on themselves and society and to begin being involved in evolving a new way of being men. Through a curriculum, men's groups and education Gunter is helping men to forge healthier relationships with themselves and others.

In the background Gunter had a burning ember to pursue human concepts and ideas within the nature of storytelling. At an influential meeting in Los Angeles with Phil Goldfarb, encouraged Gunter to begin to devote time and efforts in telling human stories in fiction. This led to his debut novel *Mountains of the Sea*. It combines his love of history, the ocean and surfing into a compelling piece of fiction.

Now married for over thirty years Gunter is a loving husband to his partner, Lorin, and a devoted father to a daughter and son, and grandfather of three, two boys and a girl. He loves spending time with them and the rest of his family. He is also an avid traveller.

Gunter Swoboda is an emerging author of historical biographies. This is Gunter's fourth book.

facebook.com/goodmengreat

twitter.com/gswoboda

instagram.com/gswoboda

Also By Winterwolf Press

LAURA C. CANTU

Betwixters: Once Upon A Time

Ole Grum's Tales: One Barmy Beetle

RUSS THOMPSON

The Loop Breaker: A Beacon and the Darkness

AUBRIE NIXON

The Age of Endings Book 1: Secret of Souls

The Age of Endings: Requiem of Sorrow

CHRISTINE CONTINI

Death: Awakening to Life: Seeds Planted

The One Light Series: Standing in a Dead Man's Body: A True Story of Crossing Over

CPSIA information can be obtained
at www.ICGtesting.com
Printed in the USA
BVHW070304040521
606354BV00001B/18

9 781947 782099